DEBBIE MACOMBER

Finally You

Previously published as *No Competition* and *All Things Considered*

mira

ISBN-13: 978-0-7783-3155-1

Finally You

Copyright © 2021 by Harlequin Books S.A.

No Competition
First published in 1987. This edition published in 2021.
Copyright © 1987 by Debbie Macomber

All Things Considered
First published in 1987. This edition published in 2021.
Copyright © 1987 by Debbie Macomber

This edition published by arrangement with Harlequin Books S.A.

For questions and comments about the quality of this book, please contact us at CustomerService@Harlequin.com.

Mira
22 Adelaide St. West, 40th Floor
Toronto, Ontario M5H 4E3, Canada
www.Harlequin.com

Printed in Lithuania

Recycling programs for this product may not exist in your area.

Also available from Debbie Macomber and MIRA

Blossom Street

The Shop on Blossom Street
A Good Yarn
Susannah's Garden
Back on Blossom Street
Twenty Wishes
Summer on Blossom Street
Hannah's List
"The Twenty-First Wish"
    (in *The Knitting Diaries*)
A Turn in the Road

Cedar Cove

16 Lighthouse Road
204 Rosewood Lane
311 Pelican Court
44 Cranberry Point
50 Harbor Street
6 Rainier Drive
74 Seaside Avenue
8 Sandpiper Way
92 Pacific Boulevard
1022 Evergreen Place
Christmas in Cedar Cove
    (*5-B Poppy Lane* and
    A Cedar Cove Christmas)
1105 Yakima Street
1225 Christmas Tree Lane

The Dakota Series

Dakota Born
Dakota Home
Always Dakota
Buffalo Valley

The Manning Family

The Manning Sisters
    (*The Cowboy's Lady* and
    The Sheriff Takes a Wife)

The Manning Brides
    (*Marriage of Inconvenience* and
    Stand-In Wife)
The Manning Grooms
    (*Bride on the Loose* and
    Same Time, Next Year)

Christmas Books

A Gift to Last
On a Snowy Night
Home for the Holidays
Glad Tidings
Christmas Wishes
Small Town Christmas
When Christmas Comes
    (now retitled *Trading
    Christmas*)
There's Something About Christmas
Christmas Letters
The Perfect Christmas
Choir of Angels
    (*Shirley, Goodness and Mercy,
    Those Christmas Angels* and
    Where Angels Go)
Call Me Mrs. Miracle

Heart of Texas

Texas Skies
    (*Lonesome Cowboy* and
    Texas Two-Step)
Texas Nights
    (*Caroline's Child* and
    Dr. Texas)
Texas Home
    (*Nell's Cowboy* and
    Lone Star Baby)
Promise, Texas
Return to Promise

Midnight Sons

Alaska Skies
  (*Brides for Brothers* and
  The Marriage Risk)
Alaska Nights
  (*Daddy's Little Helper* and
  Because of the Baby)
Alaska Home
  (*Falling for Him,*
  Ending in Marriage and
  Midnight Sons and Daughters)

This Matter of Marriage
Montana
Thursdays at Eight
Between Friends
Changing Habits
Married in Seattle
  (*First Comes Marriage* and
  Wanted: Perfect Partner)
Right Next Door
  (*Father's Day* and
  The Courtship of Carol Sommars)
Wyoming Brides
  (*Denim and Diamonds* and
  The Wyoming Kid)
Fairy Tale Weddings
  (*Cindy and the Prince* and
  Some Kind of Wonderful)
The Man You'll Marry
  (*The First Man You Meet* and
  The Man You'll Marry)
Orchard Valley Grooms
  (*Valerie* and *Stephanie*)
Orchard Valley Brides
  (*Norah* and *Lone Star Lovin'*)
The Sooner the Better
An Engagement in Seattle
  (*Groom Wanted* and
  Bride Wanted)
Out of the Rain
  (*Marriage Wanted* and
  Laughter in the Rain)
Learning to Love
  (*Sugar and Spice* and
  Love by Degree)

You…Again
  (*Baby Blessed* and
  Yesterday Once More)
The Unexpected Husband
  (*Jury of His Peers* and
  Any Sunday)
Three Brides, No Groom
Love in Plain Sight
  (*Love 'n' Marriage* and
  Almost an Angel)
I Left My Heart
  (*A Friend or Two* and
  No Competition)
Marriage Between Friends
  (*White Lace and Promises* and
  Friends—And Then Some)
A Man's Heart
  (*The Way to a Man's Heart* and
  Hasty Wedding)
North to Alaska
  (*That Wintry Feeling* and
  Borrowed Dreams)
On a Clear Day
  (*Starlight* and
  Promise Me Forever)
To Love and Protect
  (*Shadow Chasing* and
  For All My Tomorrows)
Home in Seattle
  (*The Playboy and the Widow*
  and *Fallen Angel*)
Together Again
  (*The Trouble with Caasi* and
  Reflections of Yesterday)
The Reluctant Groom
  (*All Things Considered* and
  Almost Paradise)
A Real Prince
  (*The Bachelor Prince* and
  Yesterday's Hero)
Private Paradise
  (in *That Summer Place*)

Debbie Macomber's
  Cedar Cove Cookbook
Debbie Macomber's
  Christmas Cookbook

CONTENTS

NO COMPETITION 9

ALL THINGS CONSIDERED 181

NO COMPETITION

One

Carrie Lockett carefully backed the fifteen-year-old minivan up to the rear entrance of Dove's Gallery. Shifting into Park, she hopped out the side door and raised the hatchback of the van to take out the large canvas. She didn't like what she was doing, but the portrait of Camille grinning at her every time she entered her work room was driving her up the wall. All right, she openly admitted it: she was insecure. But who wouldn't be, with a twin sister who looked like Camille?

"Darn you, Camille," she muttered disparagingly, though she knew she had nothing to blame but her own insecurities.

As an artist, Carrie had yearned to paint her fine-boned, fine-featured sister. Camille was lovely in a delicate, symmetrical way that had brought her admirers in droves. No one could look at Camille without being arrested by her beauty.

Awkwardly balancing the canvas with one hand, Carrie pounded on the rear door of the gallery.

Elizabeth Brandon opened it for her. The older woman's

astute gaze narrowed on the dilapidated minivan. "Darling, are you still driving that...thing?"

It was Elizabeth's opinion that a woman of talent shouldn't be seen in anything so mundane. If it were up to her friend, Carrie would be seated behind the wheel of a Ferrari. Carrie had no objections to that, but the middle-aged vehicle was all she could afford. "It's the only car I have."

"I hope you realize that if that 'thing' was a horse, they'd shoot it."

Carrie managed to smother a laugh. "I suppose. Now, do you want to lecture me about my car or look at this portrait?"

Already Elizabeth's keen eyes were examining the painting. "Darling," she breathed out slowly, "she's exquisite."

"I know," Carrie grumbled. No one would ever guess that the stunning woman in the portrait was the artist's twin. Camille's dark hair shone with a luster of the richest sable. Carrie's own mousy reddish-blond hair looked as though Mother Nature couldn't decide what color it should be. Even worse, Carrie had been cursed with a sprinkling of freckles across her nose that stood out like shiny new pennies the minute she hit sunlight. Camille's complexion had been peaches and cream from the time she was a toddler.

"Look at those eyes," Elizabeth continued, her hand supporting her chin. "Such a lovely shade of blue."

Carrie lowered her own greenish-gray eyes. Camille's eyes resembled the heavens, and Carrie's looked like dirty swamp water.

"She's intriguing."

Camille was that, all right.

"But I sense a bit of a hellion under all that beauty."

Elizabeth had always been a perceptive woman. One didn't become the proprietor of San Francisco's most elite art gallery without a certain amount of insight.

"Is she anyone I know, darling?"

The way Elizabeth called everyone "darling" continually amused Carrie. She struggled to hold back a smile. "No, I don't think you would."

"She owes you money?"

"No."

Elizabeth's astute eyes looked directly into Carrie's as a gradual grin formed, bracketing the older woman's mouth. "You've outdone yourself this time. She's fascinating."

"Will it sell?" The question was posed to change the subject. At the moment, Carrie was more concerned with doing away with the irritating portrait than any financial reward.

"I think so."

"Quickly?"

"Someone's coming in this afternoon who might be interested. He's bought several of your other pieces."

Carrie sat on the corner of the large oak desk while Elizabeth directed a young employee to hang the portrait out front.

"This 'someone' who's coming in this afternoon... Is it anyone I know?"

"I don't believe so. Have you heard of Shane Reynolds?"

Carrie wrinkled her nose. The name was oddly familiar, but she couldn't remember where she'd heard it. "Yes, I think I have."

"He's the architect who designed the new Firstbank building."

"Of course. Didn't he just win a plaque or something for that?" She idly rolled a pencil between her fingers, trying to put a face with the name. None came. If his picture had been in the paper, she had missed it.

"Oh, darling, you amaze me. Shane was presented the Frank Lloyd Wright annual award. It's the most prestigious honor given to an architect."

"Then he must be good."

"He's single." The statement was accompanied by two perfectly shaped brows arching suggestively.

Carrie shrugged. "So?"

"So let me introduce you."

"Now?" Shock echoed in Carrie's voice. "No way, Elizabeth. Look at me." She pushed back the headband that held her curly hair at bay and rubbed her hand down her jeans-clad thigh. "I'm a mess."

"Hurry home and pretty yourself up."

"He hasn't got that much time."

Tapping her foot in unspoken reprimand, Elizabeth continued, "I wish you'd stop putting yourself down."

"I'm calling a spade a spade."

"I don't know why you're still single. There are plenty of eligible young men in San Francisco. You're an attractive young woman."

"Good try, but I happen to pass a mirror every now and then. If you want classic beauty, then look at the woman in that portrait."

"A man like Shane Reynolds wouldn't be romantically interested in someone like the woman in your painting."

"I know from experience that you're wrong. You stand

the two of us together and there's no competition. No man in his right mind would choose me over…her." Carrie nearly spilled out Camille's name which would have been a mistake. During the few years that Carrie had been doing business with the Dove Gallery she'd gone to great lengths to keep her personal life separate from her professional one.

"Shane isn't like other men." Amusement danced briefly in the older woman's gaze, while the rest of her face remained expressionless.

"Ha," Carrie snorted. "When it comes to a beautiful woman, all men react the same way."

"Have I ever before suggested you meet a collector?"

Carrie hedged. Elizabeth wasn't a matchmaker. The other woman's persistence surprised her. "No," she admitted reluctantly.

"There's something about Shane Reynolds I think you'll like. He's enthralled with your work."

"Oh?"

"Besides, he's a bit of a free spirit himself."

Carrie admitted she was intrigued, but she wouldn't willingly meet any man looking the way she did now. "Another time, maybe."

"I'm having a party Friday night."

"Tomorrow?" Carrie groaned inwardly and offered the oldest excuse in the world. "I don't have a thing to wear. Besides, you know I hate those things."

"Buy something."

For one crazy instant Carrie actually considered it. This late in the month she was traditionally low on ready cash, but there were always her credit cards. She made a quick decision.

It could be that Elizabeth was right about Shane. If he was everything her friend seemed to think, Camille's portrait really *wouldn't* interest him. A free spirit who appreciated her art had to have some redeeming qualities.

Then again, if Shane Reynolds bought the portrait, Carrie would know not to bother with him. But maybe, just maybe, for once in her life she could find a man who saw beyond the deceptive beauty of her sister.

"Well?" Elizabeth pressed.

"I don't know. Let me think about it."

"Don't take too long. A man like Shane Reynolds won't be single forever."

"I'll let you know."

"Do that."

The receptionist joined the two women and smiled cordially before handing Elizabeth a business card. "Mr. Reynolds is here for his appointment."

Elizabeth held Carrie's eyes. "You're sure you won't meet him?"

"Maybe Friday."

The older woman nodded. "As you wish. And, darling, do me a favor and check into buying a new car. I fear for your life in that…contraption." Elizabeth stopped abruptly. "By the way, do you have a title for the portrait?"

Unconsciously, Carrie nibbled on her bottom lip as she quickly decided. "How about *No Competition?*"

"Perfect." Elizabeth turned, prepared to enter the gallery and greet her customer. "There aren't many women in the world who would want to compete against her."

"You're right about that," Carrie murmured.

Already Elizabeth's mouth had curved into a warm smile meant for her customer, and Carrie doubted that her friend had heard her. She jumped down from the edge of the desk and drew a steadying breath. Elizabeth had succeeded in arousing her curiosity. Shane Reynolds must be someone special to have Elizabeth singing his praises. Briefly she allowed a mental image to form in her mind. If beauty didn't impress him, it must be the result of some unattractive feature of his own. Men with imperfections were often willing to overlook the flaws in others. Perhaps he was short and balding. The thought served only to pique her curiosity. If he was inside an office all day, then he'd probably gone flabby. That sometimes happened to busy men who ate on the run and didn't take time to exercise or worry about proper nutrition.

As she prepared to leave, Carrie's hand was on the doorknob when she gave in to her niggling curiosity. If Shane Reynolds was standing in the other room, all she had to do was take a peek. No one would be the wiser.

Feeling a little like a cat burglar, she opened the door and glanced through the crack. Tiny shock waves coursed through her body as her mental image went crashing to the floor. At first all she could see was a full head of gray hair. No, not gray but a fantastic shade of silver, as burnished as a new coin. Her thought was that he was older, possibly nearing middle age. But then he turned around, and her heart tripped out a staccato beat of surprised disbelief. The silver was premature. This wasn't some old, dignified architect, but a rawly virile man in his early thirties. One who was suntanned and vigorously provocative. His sports jacket and dark pants revealed discriminating good taste and made for a distinguished impression. The top two buttons of his shirt were unfastened to display hard, tanned flesh. Carrie tried to tell herself he'd gotten that deep bronze from a tanning bed, but in her heart she knew she was wrong. This man didn't have the time for such vanity. He couldn't be termed classically handsome, but everything about him breathed overwhelming masculinity.

A curious ache grabbed her between the shoulder blades. Elizabeth was right. There was something about Shane Reynolds she liked. An awareness gripped her that was so strong her body went rigid. Rarely had the sight of a man affected her this way. It frightened her and, in the same heartbeat, exhilarated her beyond anything else in her twenty-seven years.

Attaining a grip on her emotions, Carrie turned and quietly slipped out the back door. She prayed fervently that Shane wouldn't buy the painting. If he appreciated Camille's flagrant beauty, he would be like all the others. Desperately, she hoped he wasn't. For once in her life, she wanted a man who could look beyond her glaring imperfections and discover the warm woman inside who was ready to burst out and be discovered. Her stomach churning with hope and expectation, she headed toward her minivan.

Thirty minutes later, when Carrie pulled into her driveway, her hands felt clammy. Her small, one-bedroom cottage sat on a cliff high above the rolling Pacific Ocean. The price had been outrageous. It was ironic that the one great love of her life would be a narrow strip of rocky beach and not a man. Camille collected men, while Carrie boldly etched her emotions across bare canvas, revealing the innermost secret places of her heart.

She breathed in the fresh clean scent of the ocean and experienced an unshakable freedom. Someday she would like to build a bigger home, but for now the cottage suited her perfectly.

Smiling to herself, she unlocked the front door and tossed her purse aside. She paced the living room once, then moved directly to the phone in the kitchen and punched out a number with an impatience she rarely experienced.

"Dove Gallery," came the soft voice of the receptionist.

"This is Carrie Lockett for Elizabeth Brandon," she said as calmly as she could manage, swallowing down her uncertainty. From the minute she left the gallery, she hadn't stopped thinking about Shane. Already she'd made a decision.

"Could you hold the line a minute?"

"Yes."

"Darling," Elizabeth answered a moment later. "It's that car, isn't it? You've had an accident."

"Of course not." Carrie laughed, and added without preamble, "Did he buy the painting?"

"Shane Reynolds?"

Who else did Elizabeth think she was referring to? Carrie mused with a hint of irritation. "Yes, Shane Reynolds."

"He was impressed with it. In fact, *No Competition* has been the center of interest all afternoon."

Her lashes fluttered down with distress. "But did he buy it?"

Carrie heard Elizabeth's sigh. "I'm afraid you're going to be disappointed, but he didn't. I felt sure he would. Do you need the money? I could probably—"

"No...no," she gasped, too happy to think about something as mundane as food or house payments or anything else. Her voice was remarkably even when she spoke.

"Don't worry about me. And, Elizabeth, about that party Friday night—count me in. I'd enjoy coming."

"What a pleasant surprise. Shane will be there. I'll introduce you, if you like."

"I'd like that very much." Already she felt hope stirring within her breast. It had been a lot of years since she'd experienced such a strong sense of expectation.

"I'll see you Friday at seven, then."

"At seven," Carrie repeated, and after a cordial farewell, she replaced the telephone receiver.

She shouldn't feel this excited. She was behaving like an adolescent and setting herself up for a big disappointment. She didn't care. A surge of exhilarated expectancy washed through her. Something wonderful was about to happen. She could feel it all the way to the marrow of her bones.

Although she hadn't eaten since early morning, she wasn't hungry. But past experience dictated that she fix herself some dinner or she would be out of sorts later. Warming up a can of tomato soup and popping half an English muffin in the toaster, she hummed cheerfully as she worked in the cozy kitchen.

The front door clicked open, and Carrie glanced up to see her twin sister saunter into the house.

"Hi." Camille was dressed in a pale pink sundress that showed off the ivory perfection of her bare shoulders. "Something smells good."

"Tomato soup. Do you want some?"

"No thanks. Bob's taking me to dinner later."

"You've been seeing quite a bit of him lately, haven't you?" Camille had been dating Bob for a couple of months. Perhaps she was feeling that the time had come to start thinking about marriage and a family. Naturally, Camille would marry first.

"Bob's all right." She helped herself to an apple from the basket on the kitchen table. "He's rich, you know."

"I didn't." But knowing Camille, money wouldn't necessarily enhance a man's attraction. For that matter, it didn't mean all that much to Carrie, either. The two of them were so different outwardly, but shockingly alike in other ways.

"He's in exports," Camille elaborated.

"That's interesting." For the moment, the only thing that concerned Carrie was why the toaster was taking so long to produce a crisp muffin.

"I think he might ask me to marry him." Camille said it as though the idea of marriage utterly bored her. She sat on an oak chair with webbed seating and crossed her long, shapely legs.

Caught off guard by the disinterested announcement, Carrie turned to face her sister. "Will you accept?"

"I don't know. Bob's really nice, but if I'm going to settle down, there are certain things I want in a man."

"Oh?" Carrie was surprised. She didn't think her sister had given the matter of what she wanted in a marriage partner anything more than a fleeting consideration. "What qualities are you looking for?" Carrie's own wants were specific. She wanted a husband who would be her best friend, her shock absorber and, in some ways, her compass.

Camille bit into the apple. A tiny drop of juice ran down her chin, and she lazily wiped it away. "Money isn't all that important. It's nice, I suppose, but there are so many other qualities I want more."

"Like?"

"He should want a family," Camille said thoughtfully.

"I want a husband with integrity and tenderness," Carrie offered.

"But I don't think he should want a large family."

"Why not?" Carrie couldn't understand her sister's thinking on that one.

"I only want one child," Camille explained.

The soup started to simmer, and Carrie removed it from the burner. "Why only one?"

"Babies fluster me. You're the motherly type. Not me."

Maybe that was because Carrie had taken over the role so early in life. Their mother had died unexpectedly when they were twelve, and Carrie had assumed many of the duties around the house. Their father worked a lot of overtime, and the twins were often left to their own devices. First thing after school, Carrie started the evening meal while Camille did homework. For Carrie, studying was a breeze. On the other hand, Camille had a difficult time with schoolwork. She often lamented her inability to "remember things the way Carrie does." Consequently it was Carrie who cooked, cleaned and struggled to maintain a balance for everything else in their lives.

"I took your portrait into the gallery today."

Camille didn't look surprised. "I imagine someone will buy it quickly." She said it with absolute certainty, but Carrie wasn't sure if this was a back-handed compliment to the work she'd done on the portrait or if Camille felt few could resist her beauty.

"It's already causing some stir." The exaggeration was only a slight one. Elizabeth would have it sold by the end of the week, and Camille's flawless beauty would be intriguing men for years to come. Few would give a moment's thought to the artist, and Carrie actually preferred it that way. Camille belonged in the spotlight, while she herself was strictly a background player.

"You're a good artist, Carrie."

Her twin's compliment came as a surprise. "Thank you. But usually it's the subject that causes a painting to sell."

A small smile revealed Camille's perfect white teeth. "Are you telling me the subject will help *this* painting to sell?"

"Undoubtedly."

"Good." Camille took another bite of the apple, pleased with herself.

The English muffin popped up from the toaster, and Carrie reached for it, piling tuna fish over the top and placing a sliced tomato over that. She carried her meal to the table and sat down opposite Camille.

"I'm happy to hear the portrait will sell soon."

Carrie spread a paper napkin across her lap. This was the second time her sister had alluded to money. "Is there something you needed?"

Camille straightened and cocked her head to one side. "I was wondering if you could float me a loan. You know I'll pay you back."

Carrie knew her sister would, but borrowing money to hold her over until pay day was becoming increasingly common. Camille's job as a beauty consultant for a large downtown store paid well. Unfortunately, she had never learned to budget. Things were tight this month for Carrie, as well, and she was hoping to buy a new dress for Elizabeth's party. "I suppose I could loan you some, but not much." She had been rescuing Camille from the time they'd lost their mother. Old habits died hard.

"You don't sound that eager," Camille returned. "You know how I struggle to make ends meet."

"We all do." Carrie stood and reached for her wallet, then handed Camille a fifty dollar bill, which left her with the loose change in the bottom of her purse.

"Thanks." An irresistible smile lit up Camille's baby blue eyes. "I'll talk to you later." Already she was on her way out the front door.

"Right. Later." With a grumble, Carrie returned to her soup. It happened every time. Camille asked and Carrie gave.

That night Carrie dreamed that Shane Reynolds was walking along the beach with her. The salty breeze buffeted them as their feet made deep indentations in the wet sand. He slipped a casual arm around her shoulders and smiled into her eyes with a love so strong that it would span a lifetime. In the morning, she woke feeling warm and wonderful. And a bit foolish. She wasn't a young girl to be swayed by romantic dreams, nor did she waste her time on fantasies. She was a woman with a woman's heart. And for the first time in months, she felt the longing for a man who would share her life.

Sitting up, she looped her arms around her knees and rested her chin there. She was determined to attend Elizabeth's party Friday night and meet Shane Reynolds. The first hurdle had already been passed. He'd seen Camille's sleek elegance and hadn't been lured by all that untarnished beauty. Elizabeth had claimed he wouldn't be, but experience had taught Carrie otherwise.

Her first order of the day was to shop. After spending a fruitless morning downtown, she found the perfect dress in a small boutique tucked away from the mainstream of the large downtown shopping complexes. The pale green dress was the most expensive thing she'd ever owned. The smooth silk whispered over her skin and clung in all the right places, giving an illusion of beauty. Wearing this dress and standing in the right light, she felt that someone might actually be able to detect the fact that Camille was her sister.

The color did something fantastic for her eyes. No longer did they resemble dirty swamp water. Unexpectedly, they held flashes of jade and a touch of emerald. The dress was definitely worth the price, she reasoned, signing the charge slip.

On Friday evening she arrived at Elizabeth's party feeling light-headed and a little nervous. Her stomach felt as if she'd been on a roller coaster all afternoon, pitching and heaving with every turn. She'd been extra careful with her makeup and pinned her hair away from her face. Her mother's pearls graced her slender neck and ears. Normally she avoided the mirror, but this evening she had stood in front of it so long that she was half tempted to ask it who was the fairest in the land. But she already knew the answer. Tonight she could give Camille a run for her money.

Still, her smile trembled when the maid answered the door and took her lace shawl. Her pulse soared at the sound of laughter, tinkling ice and the hum of conversation that drowned out the piano player.

Her eyes scanned the crowded room, seeking only one person and experiencing keen disappointment when she couldn't locate Shane Reynolds. It was still early, and he probably hadn't arrived yet. People were everywhere, sipping champagne and chatting easily, but she had never been good at making small talk. The roller coaster dipped, and she placed a hand on her stomach to calm it.

From across the room Elizabeth raised her hand in greeting and hurried to greet her. "Carrie, darling, you're positively stunning."

"Don't look so surprised," Carrie teased, her eyes gleaming. She knew she looked good. Her best. She wanted to make her meeting with Shane Reynolds a memorable one.

"But I *am* surprised," Elizabeth countered. "I've never seen you in a dress."

"I've been known to don one now and again."

"You should do it more often," Elizabeth chastised lightly. "You're really very lovely."

The compliment was so sincere that Carrie blinked. Her first inclination was to make excuses for the way she normally dressed. She quickly suppressed the idea, astonished at her own lack of self-confidence. Instead she said only "Thank you." She didn't mention that Camille had always been the one for dresses.

"Now come, there are several people you must meet." Elizabeth made it sound as though the entire party had been waiting for Carrie's arrival, as if she were the guest of honor.

Elizabeth led the way across the room. As Carrie followed, she let her gaze skid around the elegant space, thinking perhaps she had merely missed seeing Shane the first time.

Before she could make a thorough inspection, Elizabeth introduced her to a long list of her most intimate and dearest friends. Many had bought Carrie's paintings, and she spent the next half hour answering questions and making what she hoped was stimulating conversation. A glass of champagne was handed to her. As she raised it to her lips, she spotted a flash of silver across the room. The bubbly liquid stayed on her tongue as her eyes collided with Shane Reynolds's deep blue gaze.

A slow, sensuous grin lifted the corners of his mouth, and he slowly raised his own glass in a silent salute.

The champagne stuck halfway down Carrie's throat. Tingling bubbles tickled the back of her tongue until she gulped the liquid down, nearly choking. Because she didn't know what else to do, she looked away. It had been years since any man had interested her as much as Shane Reynolds did. Cursing herself for her inability to flirt, she quickly looked back again. His smile was brilliant and directed solely at her. The palms of her hands felt clammy. The roller coaster unexpectedly left its tracks, plummeting downwards.

"Carrie, there's someone you must meet," Elizabeth was saying, and Carrie turned her attention to another group of guests.

Even so, she felt Shane's eyes follow her. Drawn to him by a force stronger than any magnet, she sought him out again. From across the width of the room their gazes met and locked. This time he grinned boldly. She returned his smile and, feeling extraordinarily fearless, winked.

"Carrie, have you met Ashley Wallingford?"

"I don't believe I have," she returned, reluctantly pulling her gaze from Shane's. The first thing she noticed about the elderly woman was her exquisite eyes. Deep blue, shrewd, and perhaps a little calculating. This woman had lived a hard life, and it showed in the network of wrinkles across her intelligent face.

"I understand you do portraits," Mrs. Wallingford said conversationally.

"Some."

"Mrs. Wallingford was in this morning to see *No Competition*," Elizabeth added. "She was quite taken with it."

"You managed to portray an elegant, sometimes vain woman in a flattering light. I wonder if you always read your subjects so well."

Carrie sucked in her breath. "And I wonder if you're always so perceptive," she returned. Ashley Wallingford was a marvel.

"I try to be." A hint of amusement showed in those clear blue eyes.

Painting this woman would be a challenge and a treat. Already Carrie's fingers itched for a pencil.

"I would have purchased it," Mrs. Wallingford continued, "but unfortunately I was too late."

"It sold?" Carrie turned to Elizabeth.

Elizabeth's eyes brightened. "I thought you'd be pleased."

Mrs. Wallingford touched her arm. "I'd like to talk to you again, Carrie Lockett. You're an excellent artist. I'm hoping we can do business some day. Now if you'll excuse me?"

"Of course."

"Then I'll be getting in touch with you soon."

"I'll look forward to it."

As soon as the older woman had departed, Carrie turned her attention to Elizabeth.

"You're pleased about the portrait, aren't you?" the older woman asked.

"Very. I didn't expect it to go so quickly."

"I was rather shocked myself. First thing this morning. I hadn't been open five minutes when..."

Carrie knew. In one horrible minute she knew. Her eyes darted across the room to Shane. The dream died as quickly as it had been conceived. And with it something young and vital shriveled up and wept inside of her.

"Shane Reynolds came into the gallery. He said he hadn't been able to stop thinking about the portrait all night. He didn't care about the price, he wanted it."

The fragile smile curving Carrie's soft mouth cracked. "I see."

"I don't think you do." Elizabeth's soft lilting voice rose with excitement. "Not only is he crazy about the picture, he's dying to meet you."

Two

"No," Carrie stated, shaking her head.

"What do you mean, no?" Elizabeth's eyebrows shot up in surprise.

"I refuse to meet Shane Reynolds."

"But…why? Carrie, darling, are you feeling ill? You're quite pale."

"You're right, I'm not well. I shouldn't be here." She'd been an idiot to entertain the idea that someone as handsome as Shane Reynolds would ever appreciate her. She swallowed her disappointment. She'd been an idealistic, romantic fool, and worse, it hadn't been the first time.

"Carrie…" Elizabeth gently placed a hand on Carrie's forearm.

"Thank you for inviting me," she said, taking a step back with each word. "I'm sorry to leave so quickly."

"But you just got here. Perhaps if you lie down for a few minutes…?"

"No…no." Carrie bumped into someone and turned around sharply to apologize. "Please excuse me. I'm sorry, really sorry."

The man looked at her as though seeing someone drop

in from outer space. The floor pitched beneath her feet, and Carrie inhaled a calming breath. Abruptly, she headed for the front door.

Elizabeth followed, instructing the maid to bring Carrie her coat. "I'll call you tomorrow," she said, looking concerned.

"Fine." She would have agreed to any terms as long as she could escape quickly.

"I'm sure once you're feeling better you'll reconsider meeting Shane."

Carrie knew there wasn't any possibility she would change her mind, but she lacked the strength to argue. The sooner she was out of there, the better.

It seemed an eternity before the maid returned with her shawl. Carrie wrapped it around her shoulders, gripping it as if an Arctic wind were raging around her. But the cold that ripped through her had nothing to do with the temperature.

"You're sure you'll be all right?"

"Yes, yes." As soon as she left the party, she would be a thousand percent better.

"Thank you for inviting me." Hurriedly she stepped out the door and rushed down the front steps. When she reached her minivan, she looked back to see Elizabeth standing in the open doorway, studying her with a concerned frown.

Carrie gave a brief wave and unlocked her door. Her fingers trembled as she inserted the key into the ignition. Gripping the steering wheel, she pressed her forehead against the chilly plastic. Would she never learn? What masochistic streak did she possess that made her refuse to accept the simplest facts of life? There were no gallant princes riding around on white stallions ready to rescue her from her fate. From birth, she'd been doomed to stand in Camille's shadow. But she'd been compensated. She had her art. What more could she want?

She released a jagged breath and started the engine. *What more could she want?* The list was so long it would take a lifetime to write it all down.

Once she was home, she stripped off the dress and hung it in the far reaches of her closet so she wouldn't be faced with it every time she opened the door. She wanted only to forget her harebrained scheme.

By morning she felt much better. Her romantic heart had been wounded, but she had an incredible recovery rate. The Shane Reynoldses of this world weren't meant for someone like her. The universe was full of too many beautiful women—like Camille. She had accepted that long ago.

Standing at the kitchen window, she watched the sea gulls swoop down to the beach far below. She softly smiled and poured a cup of coffee, taking in the unspoiled beauty of the morning. White-capped waves crashed against the rocks and left a meandering path of foam across the virgin sand. A feeling of serenity crowded her heart.

Taking her coffee with her, she wandered down the steep trail that led to the beach. A few minutes of breathing fresh salty air would rejuvenate her.

The wind tugged at her unbound hair and whipped it across her face as she walked along the beach and found her favorite rock, where she sat sipping her coffee. There was something so comforting about being on the beach. It didn't seem to matter what was troubling her; twenty minutes of watching the tide roll in made her feel like a new person, ready to take on the world and its problems.

Time lost meaning. A hundred chores demanded her attention at the house, but nothing was more pressing than her need to sit in the sun.

The sound of her name caused her to turn around. Her breath caught in her throat at the sight of Shane Reynolds. He was walking down the path toward her.

He was the last person she would have expected to see, and she marched away from him, intent on escaping. She didn't want to see or talk to this man. He was trouble, and she knew it.

"Carrie Lockett?"

She trudged on, ignoring him.

The sound of someone running after her caused her to quicken her pace.

"Ms. Lockett?" Shane was out of breath by the time he reached her side. Maybe it was a crazy idea to have come to her like this, but he hadn't been able to resist. Something had happened last night to make her run from the party, and he wanted to know what.

"Yes?" She found it strange how immediately familiar his voice sounded. Cool and commanding, as though he expected an immediate response from her.

"You probably couldn't hear me call you."

Arms swinging at her sides, she continued walking at a furious pace. "I heard you."

He swallowed his irritation. "Then why didn't you stop?"

"Why didn't you get the message?" she demanded, struggling to present a facade of searing indifference. Now that she'd seen him up close, the illusion of virile and overpowering masculinity was all the more pronounced. No wonder he'd purchased the portrait of Camille: he was breathtaking. A man as perfect as Shane would appreciate the extraordinary beauty of her twin.

"What's wrong?" His anger died at the look of hurt in her expressive eyes.

"Nothing," she lied, nearly breathless as she maintained her killing pace.

"I want to talk to you."

"And I'd prefer it if you didn't."

"Why not? I bought your painting. You're a fantastic artist and—"

"Listen," she said, whirling around, her hands on her hips. "You bought my painting. Big deal. I don't owe you anything. Who gave you the right to charge uninvited into my morning?"

His backbone stiffened. She wasn't anything like he'd expected or hoped. "Just a minute here, aren't you the same Carrie Lockett who sashayed into Elizabeth Brandon's party last evening and gave me a wink?"

Oh heavens, she had forgotten that. "I…had something in my eye," she lied.

The robust sound of his laugh echoed around her. "You were blatantly flirting with me. You liked what you saw and said so. For that matter, I was intrigued, too."

"I wasn't flirting." She continued walking, forcing him to keep up with her.

"I want to know what made you suddenly change your opinion of me," he pressed. "All I really wanted to say was how much I appreciate your work."

"You've already told me that. Thank you, I'm grateful. Now you can leave."

He ignored that. "Elizabeth has mentioned you several times." He paused and struggled to maintain his control. He wanted to tell her that the only reason he'd attended Elizabeth's party was so he could meet her. But from her unfriendly stance, he could see that she would refuse to believe that. "I assumed you wanted to meet me," he added.

"Then you assumed wrong." How easy it would be to fall for this man. One look and she sensed danger. But if she got to know Shane, then it would only be a matter of time before he met Camille. And it would be over even before it began. Her fragile heart couldn't afford to trust this man.

"Have lunch with me." The low-pitched request was a surprise.

"No."

Ignoring her refusal, he continued, "I don't know what I've done to offend you, but I'd like to make it right. Somehow we got started on the wrong foot."

"I'm simply not interested."

"Are you always this prickly?"

"Only with insufferable, arrogant men who bulldoze their way into my mornings."

The cutting quality of his dark eyes grew sharper as she struck a raw nerve. "I've been called a lot of things in my life, but never insufferable and arrogant."

"I trust my instincts." She had nothing more to judge him by.

"Then accept my apology for intruding, Ms. Lockett." His voice dripped with sarcasm. Abruptly, he turned away and walked in the opposite direction. He didn't know what had happened, but he had too much pride to stand around and accept her insults.

Carrie paused as she watched him walk away. Her hands trembled, and she sank onto the sandy beach, her lungs heaving. The wind made a frothy confusion of her hair, and she let it blow around her face. Swallowing the tightness that gripped her throat, she turned her concentration to the angry waves that pounded the beach. She hadn't wanted to be rude and prickly. It would have felt far more natural to smile up at him and share the beauty of this unspoiled stretch of beach than to insult him. But it was better this way. Much better—yet far more difficult than anything she could remember.

Her thoughts troubled, Carrie climbed the steep path back to the small beach house. She tried to convince her sagging self-confidence that she was saving herself a whole lot of heartache. Pausing on the back porch, she unceremoniously stuffed a pile of dirty clothes into the washing machine.

The phone rang just as she was adding the laundry soap. She grabbed it automatically, then returned to her laundry, the receiver held between her ear and her shoulder. "Hello."

"Darling, you survived."

"Elizabeth." Instantly, Carrie's fingers froze on the washer dial. She regretted her panic of the night before. "I'm glad you phoned. I feel terrible about last night. I owe you an apology. My behavior was inexcusable."

"The only thing you owe me is an explanation."

"Yes, well, that could be a bit complicated."

Elizabeth wasn't about to be dissuaded. "I've got all

day. I've known you a lot of years, and I've never seen you behave like that."

"Then maybe you don't really know me."

"Carrie, if you'd rather..."

"No, I'll explain." She owed Elizabeth that much. "I have a sister. I guess you can say that you've met her."

"Who is she, darling?"

From the tone of her voice, Carrie could tell that Elizabeth was searching through her memory. "As I recall, you found her intriguing."

"The portrait?" Elizabeth was clearly surprised. "The girl in the portrait is your sister?"

"My twin sister."

"Your twin sister," Elizabeth repeated, still stunned. Her voice wobbled between two octaves as she struggled to disguise her shock.

"We're nothing alike, believe me."

"I can tell that, darling."

"Then you can also understand why I don't want to meet Shane Reynolds."

A short silence followed. "No, I can't say that I can."

"Elizabeth, think about it. Anyone who appreciates Camille's beauty isn't going to be interested in me. Good grief, people wouldn't even guess we came from the same family. Camille is everything I'm not."

"I thought I explained that Shane Reynolds isn't the type of man to be impressed with beauty."

"Right. That's why he bought the painting."

"He purchased that portrait because you painted it and for no other reason."

"I doubt it, Elizabeth. I sincerely doubt it."

Their conversation ended five minutes later, and with

flint-hard resolve Carrie returned to her Saturday morning chores and refused to waste another second thinking about Shane Reynolds. But as the day wasted away, she *did* think about him. She hadn't wanted to be rude. She hadn't wanted to push him away when everything in her yearned to reach out to him. Maybe Elizabeth was right and he *was* different. But she doubted it. She was certain that once he met Camille it would all be over.

Carrie's thoughts were still confused when the doorbell chimed the following afternoon. She was washing her hands, wondering what she should eat for lunch. All morning she'd been sitting with paper and charcoal, sketching faces. Every one of them was Shane. Even the women and children had a strong resemblance to the silver fox who dominated her thoughts. Her floor was littered with the evidence of her frustration. Drying her hands on a towel, she hurried toward the door. Camille never bothered to knock, so it couldn't be her sister.

On the other side of the door, Shane shifted his weight from one foot to the other. He hadn't stopped thinking about the feisty artist all night. She intrigued him. Outwardly she was as prickly as a cactus, but her work revealed a warm, loving soul. There was obviously something about him she didn't like. Fine, he would find out what it was and take it from there.

Smiling, Carrie unlatched the lock and opened the door. "Hello." The welcome faded from her eyes as her gaze met Shane's. Her heart throbbed at the unexpectedness of seeing him a second time, and she glanced guiltily over her shoulder, as if the charcoal sketches might materialize before her eyes—and his. He'd come back, and, after her rudeness on the beach the day before, she couldn't imagine why.

"Hello." His gaze softened.

Gathering her resolve, she opened her mouth to tell him to leave, but the command in his eyes stopped her.

"Listen, I don't know what was wrong before, but I'd like to talk this out."

"I—"

"Before you argue with me, let me assure you that I'm really a nice guy. And if you'll listen, I'd like to make a confession."

"What kind of confession?"

"I knew who you were long before Elizabeth's party."

"But how…?"

"You were at the gallery about a month ago, and I saw you leave. Elizabeth pointed you out to me." Remembering the woman he'd seen that afternoon told him something was wrong. That woman and the one on the beach weren't the same person.

Carrie remembered the day. It was one of those rare San Francisco days when the sun was shining, and everything in and about the world was perfect.

"I followed you to Fisherman's Wharf," he continued. "And watched you buy a bright red balloon."

"I didn't get it for me." That was only a small white lie.

"I know. I saw you give it to the little girl, but not until after you'd carried it with you for several blocks."

"I was looking for a *special* little girl." One like herself, plain and unassuming, someone who didn't command the attention of others. A child who walked in the shadow of an attractive brother or sister.

"Then you caught the cable car and—"

"You were spying on me."

"Actually, I was trying to come up with an original way of introducing myself," he admitted with a chagrined smile. "I'd just figured out that the straightforward approach would be best when you jumped on the cable car. I didn't make it."

"Oh." How incredibly inane that sounded.

"Now that I've bared my soul, I'm hoping that you'll share a picnic lunch with me." Surprise showed in her eyes, and Shane knew that half the battle had been won. At least she hadn't told him to leave again.

Carrie had to put a stop to the way her heart reacted to this man. "It looks like rain." Any excuse would do.

"There isn't a cloud in sight," Shane said, contradicting her.

"I don't have anything to pack for lunch."

"I do," he said. "I figured if you wouldn't go out to lunch with me, then I'd bring lunch to you."

"You're very sure of yourself." Her resolve managed one last rally.

"I'm very sure of what I want," he responded with a breathtaking smile that was meant to melt her defenses. He succeeded.

"And what exactly do you want?"

"To get to know you."

"Why?" she asked, lacing her fingers together. He really was something.

"That's the part that confuses me." A frown marred the urbane perfection of his features. He was unsure of his feelings. He didn't usually get much resistance from women. He was successful, wealthy, and reasonably attractive. Women gravitated toward him. After their minor confrontation on the beach, Shane had thought his own attraction to Carrie could be attributed to the challenge she represented. Today he was willing to admit differently. He'd wanted to meet her for weeks. There was a reason she'd responded to him the way she had. And he was determined to find out why.

"I...don't know." Carrie hesitated, knowing that she'd already lost the inner battle.

"Come on, Carrie, I'm not really all that bad."

With a growing sense of anticipation, she smiled and, with a nod, asked, "Can we haul it down to the beach?"

"I was hoping you'd suggest that."

She followed him out to his car, where he retrieved a small wicker basket and blanket. She still couldn't believe that he'd come back after she'd been so rude and unreasonable. She realized she shouldn't be so glad, but she was. A warning light went off in her head like a traffic light gone berserk, but she chose to ignore it, cursing her foolish heart for wanting this so badly.

Leading the way down the well-worn path to the beach, she commented, "It's a beautiful day, isn't it?"

Shane's warm gaze held hers. "Yes, it is."

A mere smile from this man could charm snakes. He obviously possessed more enchantment than her meager defenses could easily fend off. Her stomach knotted in a tight ball of nerves as she determined that she wouldn't let one picnic with him influence her feelings. No matter how difficult it was, she would remain coolly detached. She had to.

Her smile was wavering by the time they reached the sand.

"This is perfect," he commented when she paused to

spread out a blanket. Behind his lazy regard, Carrie felt that he was watching her every move. She struggled to remain unaffected.

"We don't often see bright sunshine so early in the summer," she finally said, then wondered why she was talking to him as though he were a tourist. Anyone who lived in San Francisco knew what the weather was like.

He didn't comment, almost seeming to enjoy her obvious discomfort. "The weather's generally pleasant this time of year."

Silently, she wished he wasn't so damned logical. Surely he could recognize that she was making an effort to be polite. She owed him that much. No doubt few women ignored a man like Shane Reynolds. Unfortunately, the knowledge served only to heighten her awareness of him and his many charms.

"Maybe we should eat now," he suggested.

"Sure," she agreed, eager to change the subject.

Shane handed her napkins and pried the top from a bucket of chicken. They ate in silence.

By the time they'd finished, Carrie was wondering why she'd ever agreed to this.

Stretching his long legs out in front of him, he crossed them at the ankles and rested his weight on the palms of his hands. "Do you feel like talking now?"

"I suppose." She made busy work, picking up the litter. Her gaze avoided his.

"What happened the other morning?" Once he passed that hurdle, he could venture on to Elizabeth's party.

"When you said you wanted to talk, I assumed you meant about the painting."

"Not particularly." His blue eyes smoldered as they studied her.

"Then why'd you come here?"

"I wanted to get to know you."

"I don't understand why." Carrie was embarrassed that her voice trembled.

"Elizabeth told me what a rare talent you are." Shane suspected she would feel more comfortable discussing her art.

"You don't look like the type of man who goes around forcing himself on artists."

"You're right, I'm not. Something happened the night of the party that made you run away almost immediately after I arrived. I want to know what."

"You're imagining things." If she'd known this was going to turn into an interrogation, she never would have agreed to this picnic.

"Maybe I was imagining something at the party," he reasoned. "But Saturday morning you were rude and abrupt."

"Why did you come back, then?"

"I felt that, given time, you'd change your mind about me."

His confidence grated on Carrie. "You've got a big ego."

"Agreed, but in the past it's worked to my advantage."

"Okay, you've met me. Now what?" She wasn't up to playing verbal games with him. The sooner she discovered why he was so curious about her, the sooner she could deal with her emotions.

"I'm intrigued."

"Don't be. What you see is what you get." She pushed

back a thick strand of rusty-colored hair and batted her long lashes at him.

His deep husky laugh floated with the wind. "But I like what I see."

"Then you need bifocals." He wouldn't have bought the painting of Camille if he appreciated someone like her. "Why did you buy the portrait?" she asked bluntly, needing to know.

He smiled lazily, and his handsome features looked years younger. He wondered what it was about that painting that disturbed her, and he weighed his words carefully, not wanting to reveal the true reason just yet. "If you want the truth, I needed something for my office. I was hoping a few of the unwelcome matchmakers I know would view the woman as my current love interest."

"*No Competition* should do the trick." This was even worse than she'd realized. A feeling of disappointment burned through her.

"Who is she?"

It took Carrie a moment to realize Shane was asking about Camille. "A beautiful woman." Her answer was clipped and cool.

"Yes, she's that, but the portrait isn't the first piece of yours that I've seen."

"Oh?" She pretended ignorance, even though Elizabeth had already told her Shane had purchased other paintings of hers.

"I have one of your seascapes and a couple of your earlier watercolors."

"Oh." Her vocabulary had unexpectedly been reduced to words of one syllable.

"You're very good."

"Thanks."

"It's to the point where Elizabeth contacts me the moment you bring in something new."

"I'm flattered."

"The problem is that lately I haven't been able to separate the paintings from the artist."

Startled green eyes met intense blue ones, and Carrie caught her breath before it jammed her throat. If he saw her personality in her work, then he must glimpse her insecurities and all her glaring faults.

"I feel like I already know you, Miss Carrie Lockett."

Her heart was threatening to pound right out of her chest.

"I look at your painting of spring flowers blowing free in the wind, and I sense your love of nature and generosity of spirit. You love with an intensity that few seldom see or experience."

Tight-lipped, she lowered her gaze. Every word he said was distinctly unsettling. He'd blown her up in his mind to be something she wasn't. "I'm not Mother Theresa."

"The seascape taught me that. There's depth to you. You're an anchor while others are sails. I also sense rebellion, and, with this recent portrait, perhaps a hint of jealousy."

Shane Reynolds unnerved her, and Carrie struggled to cover her confusion by responding sharply. "Who wouldn't be jealous? You bought the painting, so you obviously appreciate beauty."

Her own words echoed around her like a taunt, and she closed her eyes to a lifetime of being second best.

"Is that why you called it *No Competition?*" he asked quietly.

"Of course," she came back flippantly.

"But there's no comparison between you and the woman in the painting."

"Exactly." She rose awkwardly and brushed the grains of sand from the backs of her legs. She hoped to hide her confusion by taking a walk along the beach.

He followed. "Do you always walk away when the conversation doesn't suit you?"

"Always." The tension she struggled so hard to disguise threaded its way through her nerves. "Listen, I appreciate the compliment. Any artist would. But you've met me, and now you can see that I'm nothing like you imagined."

"But you are," he interrupted. "And a whole lot more."

"Sorry, wrong girl."

"Correction, right woman." He slipped his hands into his pants pockets. "I want the chance to know you better."

"I'm all out of résumés. Check with Elizabeth."

"I don't want to read about you. Let me take you to dinner."

"No." She hated this, and silently pleaded with him to leave things as they were.

"Why not?"

"Do I have to spell it out for you, Mr. Reynolds? Thanks, but no thanks. I'm simply not interested."

"I don't believe that."

"Have you got such a colossal ego that you believe no woman can turn you down?"

"Maybe so. I'm not giving up on you, Carrie."

"Please." Her voice softened, and her green eyes pleaded with him. "I hate being so rude. I'm simply not interested."

"Give it some thought," he coaxed gently.

"There's nothing to think about." She wanted to cry.

"Believe me, I'm flattered, but the answer is no. Plain and simple. N-O. No."

He struggled not to argue with her. He would have to come up with some other way to reach her. "You can't blame a guy for trying."

"No, I don't blame you." She looked out to the sea to avoid his smoldering gaze. "Thank you for the lunch." And everything else, she mused, wondering what it would mean to her life to send him away.

He didn't argue her curt dismissal, only cocked his head slightly and, without a word, turned and walked out of her life.

Shane was the type of man of whom dreams were made, and she was turning him away. But it was more than the fact that he'd bought Camille's picture that had prompted her to dismiss him. Shane frightened her in a way that was completely unfamiliar to her.

Monday afternoon, curiosity got the best of her, so Carrie contacted Elizabeth Brandon at the gallery.

"Carrie, darling, it's good to hear from you."

Carrie drew in a deep breath. "Why didn't you tell me about Shane Reynolds?"

"But, darling, I did."

"All this time he's been buying my paintings."

"I already mentioned that."

"I know, but you claimed lots of customers ask for my work."

"You're becoming appreciated."

"But Shane Reynolds is different."

"How's that?" The soft lilt of Elizabeth's voice indicated that she was enjoying their conversation.

"He's the kind of man women follow around, drooling."

Elizabeth gave a tiny laugh. "A customer's physical attributes have little to do with his appreciation of the arts."

"That's not what I meant." The problem was, Carrie didn't actually know what she *had* meant.

"Listen, darling, I'm glad you phoned. I was about to contact you. The president of Little & Little called this morning, hoping I could get in touch with you about doing his portrait."

Smiling, Carrie decided she was wasting so much time worrying about Shane Reynolds that she was neglecting her business. In fact, if she didn't get another commission soon she would go crazy. Today even the seascape she was painting had the shades of Shane Reynolds's eyes in it. "I'm interested."

"I thought you might be. He wants you to come to his home for the initial interview. Have you got a pen?"

"Yes." Carrie pulled out a piece of paper. "Go ahead."

Elizabeth gave her an address in the Nob Hill area. "Can you make it soon?"

"Whenever he likes."

"Is tomorrow evening convenient?"

There wasn't any reason why she couldn't make it. It wasn't like she had a busy social calendar. Tomorrow would be like any other night of the week. She would microwave a frozen dinner and immerse herself in a good book. "Sure, I can make it."

"Wonderful. I'll send over the usual contract."

The following evening, at the appointed time, Carrie pulled up across from the address Elizabeth had given her. She tucked her sketch pad under her arm and swung her purse strap over her shoulder as she looked both ways before crossing the street.

The bell chimed once, and she prepared a ready smile. These early interviews could be the most important. The smile died, however, when Shane Reynolds opened the door.

A grin slashed his handsome features. "I hoped you would be on time."

Three

"You?" Carrie cried, managing to keep her anger at a low simmer. Shane had tricked her and used Elizabeth in his schemes. She was so furious she could hardly speak.

"Good to see you, too." His smile was warm enough to melt a glacial ice cap as he casually leaned against the door jamb and crossed his arms.

She refused to be trapped in his sensuous web and fumed at the amused curl of his mouth. "You think you're clever, don't you?"

"I try to be." To tell the truth, he wasn't all that pleased with the underhanded methods he'd used to get Carrie to his home. Once again he'd spent a sleepless night wondering why her reactions to him were so cold. After their meeting on the beach, she'd represented a challenge. Now it was more than that. She was a spirited, intriguing woman, and those wide green eyes spitting fire at him melted his determination to forget her.

Stepping inside the house, Carrie discovered a wide entryway tiled in opulent marble. A winding staircase veered off to the left, and to her immediate right double doors opened into a large, old-fashioned parlor. At any other time she would have appreciated the character and personality of the house, but in the present circumstances, she couldn't see beyond Shane's deception.

"I suppose I owe you another apology," he began, but she quickly cut him off.

"Do you always go to such drastic measures when a woman refuses you?" Her voice was hard and flat. She pressed the sketch book so tightly against her chest that her fingers lost feeling. "I don't appreciate this."

"I didn't imagine you would. But I wanted to talk to you."

"We talked yesterday." Carrie couldn't take her eyes off him. His sports jacket was unbuttoned, held open by a hand thrust in his pocket. Her pounding pulse told her that she was flattered that he'd gone to all this trouble to see her again, but her head insisted the only reason was that so few women turned Shane Reynolds down, his over-size ego was on the line.

"We may have talked. But I didn't get to say all the things I wanted to," he countered. Although he struck a casual pose, she was aware that he was every bit as on edge as she was.

"If I sit down and listen, will you promise to leave me alone?"

He mulled over her words. "I don't know if I can verbalize everything."

"Then the deal's off." She spun sharply and marched out the door. No footsteps sounded behind her as she crossed the street to her car. Her emotions were in an upheaval. She was running like a frightened child from the things she wanted most in life. She *was* scared. The attraction she felt toward Shane was so strong, she had to fight against it with every breath. Things would be so much easier if he hadn't bought the painting of Camille. She might have been able to rationalize the situation then.

A turn of the ignition key resulted in a grinding sound. She stared at the gauges in disbelief, hoping they could tell her something. Her minivan might be old, but it had always been faithful. Again she tried to start the engine. This time the grinding sound was lower and sicker.

Tossing a curious glance out her side window, she noted Shane standing on his front porch, watching her. He was smiling as though he had the world by the tail. She returned his taunting grin, thinking he was the most infuriating man she'd ever known.

She climbed out of the car and walked around the front to open the hood, chancing a look in Shane's direction. He'd come down the steps and was standing under a lovely maple tree on the other side of the street.

She felt her hateful freckles flashing like neon lights, she was so flustered. Not knowing what to do, she touched a couple of gadgets as though she were a faith healer. Then, feeling like a complete idiot, she closed the hood, climbed in the front seat again and turned the key.

Nothing.

"Did I ever tell you I'm a whiz with mechanical things?" Shane called, enjoying this unexpected turn of events.

"No," she grumbled under her breath. The least he could do was offer to help, but he didn't volunteer, and she refused to ask.

"I'm quite good," he continued. "From the time I was a child, there wasn't anything I couldn't take apart and put back together again. Including a car engine."

"How interesting," she returned sarcastically, getting out of the car again.

"I'm certain we could come up with a small compromise." He advanced a step.

"Exactly what kind of compromise?" She glared at him, her hands on her hips.

"Dinner in exchange for the magical touch of these mechanically tuned fingers." He held up his right hand and flexed his fingers.

"I was thinking more along the lines of contacting Triple A." She held her shoulders stiff.

"Carrie, Carrie, Carrie," he said mockingly. "Am I such an ogre? Is the thought of dinner with me so unappealing?"

She longed to shout that any meal shared with him would be divine. It wasn't him she didn't trust but herself. It would be far too easy to fall for this man.

"If you want my word that I won't touch you," he added, "then you have it." But he gave it grudgingly.

"That's not it," she murmured miserably.

"Then what *is* it?"

She hunched her shoulders, and tears brimmed in the murky depths of her eyes. "What—what do you want with someone like me? I'm not the least bit attractive and you're...well, you're one of the beautiful people of this world. I'm so ordinary."

Shane's smiling expression was gone. Vanished. He couldn't believe what he was hearing. Not attractive. Good heavens, where had she gotten that impression? She was magnificent. Spirited. Talented. Intelligent. He crossed the street in giant strides and paused to stand in front of her. His brow creased in thick lines as his frown deepened.

"Not attractive? Who told you that? You're perfectly wonderful, and I defy anyone to say otherwise."

"Oh stop!" she cried, and wiped the moisture from her face, more furious with herself than with him. Tears were the last thing she'd expected. She would have believed him, if he hadn't bought Camille's portrait.

He began to lightly trace her face, starting at the base of her throat, stroking the triangle formed by the hollow there. The thick pad of his thumb sensuously brushed her collarbone, the feel of his finger slightly abrasive against her soft, clean skin. Carrie swallowed convulsively as the muscles in her throat contracted. She couldn't breathe properly. His touch was warm and gentle, reminding her of velvet. His words were just as smooth, and she knew she couldn't trust either one.

"I don't know you," she told him, her voice choked to a low, husky level. Her senses were whirling.

"And I feel like I've known you all my life."

"What do you want from me?"

"Time. When you get to know me better, you'll realize I don't give up easily. If I want something, I simply go after it."

"And for now you want me. But why?" Her knees shook under the intensity of his gaze. She fought off the sensation of weakness.

His hands cupping her shoulders, he tried to figure out how to put his feelings into words. When he looked at her paintings, he lost sight of the artwork, caught instead by the artist. "I'll never hurt you, Carrie. I promise you that."

Somehow she believed that he wouldn't intentionally hurt her. But already he had her senses spinning. He could easily pull her into his orbit, and then she would be lost.

"If I have dinner with you, then will you help me with my car?"

"I'd help you even if you don't stay," he said with a roguish grin. "But I'd like it if you would."

"I... I am a little hungry."

The smile that lit up his eyes came all the way from his heart. "I was hoping you'd agree." He reached for her hand, curling his fingers around hers. "I'm an excellent cook."

Her guard slipped. It was so much easier to give in and smile at him than to struggle against the pull of her heart. "You cook, too, huh? I doubt that there's much you don't do."

He laughed, and the vibrant sound echoed around her. "You do have a lot to learn about me, Carrie Lockett." He led her back inside the house and into the plush dining room. The table was set with long, tapered candles at each end, and a floral centerpiece dominated the middle.

"Do you eat like this all the time?" She had assumed he was wealthy, but he didn't seem the type who would bother with formality at mealtime every night.

He looked almost boyish when his amused gaze met hers. "I wanted to impress you."

"You succeeded."

"Good."

But that wasn't the only thing he'd succeeded in doing. Against every inner battle she'd waged, Carrie lost. He held out the shieldback chair for her, and once she was seated, he proceeded to bring out their meal.

As he'd claimed, Shane was an excellent gourmet cook. With her defenses down, she chatted easily with him throughout the meal, telling him about art school, and how she'd met Elizabeth and come to work with her.

"Ask me anything you want," he told her over dessert, pleased with how well their meal had gone. "As far as you're concerned, my life is an open book."

Carrie took him at his word. "How old are you?"

He frowned slightly and touched the neatly trimmed hair, briefly worried that his premature gray disturbed her. "Younger than I appear—thirty-three."

"I think your hair makes you look distinguished." She didn't add "devilishly handsome" to the list. His ego was big enough already.

He smiled crookedly. "It's a family trait. My father was completely gray by age thirty. By the time I was in high school I already had a few gray strands. I beat dad by two years."

Carrie found it amazing that he would be self-conscious of a trait that made him look so dignified and attractive.

"What about your tan? You didn't get that here." Not in San Francisco in June. She was sure of that.

"I recently took a business trip to Tahiti."

"It's dirty work, but someone has to do it. Right?" she teased.

"Right. Now, is there anything else that curious mind of yours wants to know?"

No need hedging around the subject. She longed to ask it, and she suspected he was waiting. "Have you ever been married?"

"No."

"Why not?"

"A variety of reasons."

She lowered her gaze to her strawberry torte. "Don't try to tell me there haven't been women."

"A few." He touched the corner of his mouth with his napkin. "During my college days I was too busy with my studies to be involved in a relationship. Later it was my career."

"And now?"

"And now," he repeated, looking directly at her, "it's time."

He said it so softly that she felt like a popcorn ball had stuck in her throat. "Oh."

"Okay," he murmured. "My turn."

Her eyes met his. "What do you mean?"

"It's my turn to ask the questions."

"All right." But she wasn't eager.

"Married?"

"No." She said it with a small laugh.

"Why is that question so funny?"

She couldn't very well tell him that she could hardly be a married woman and feel the things she did sitting across the table from him. "No reason."

"How long have you been painting?"

She grinned, warming to the subject of her art. "Almost from the time I could remember. As a little girl I gave the letters of the alphabet faces and personalities. It took me the first three years of grade school to learn to write without adding ears and mouths to each letter. Numbers were even more difficult."

"Numbers?" He frowned. "Why those?"

"It's hard to explain."

"Try me."

Somehow she believed that he would understand where

others had failed, including her own father. "To me, each number has a color and a feeling. The number one is white and pure and lonely. Two is pink and healthy. Seven is red and vibrant. Nine is black and foreboding."

"Why?"

She shrugged one delicate shoulder. "I don't know. I've always thought of them that way. I gave up trying to figure it out." For that matter, so had her teachers.

"What about family?"

"I have one sister. What about you?" she asked, quickly steering the subject away from Camille.

"Three married sisters, and a passel of nieces and nephews." His gaze shone with a curious light, and it was impossible to look away.

Gazing at Shane, his eyes warm and electric, Carrie yearned to pick up her pen and pad. He intrigued her. He would make an excellent model; the planes and grooves of his face were just short of craggy, and yet he was incredibly good looking. She longed to capture him on canvas with exactly the look he was giving her at that moment. Every facet of his features suggested strength of character and an elusive inner spirit.

"I'd like to paint you," she announced, unable to tear her gaze from his. "I don't know if you were serious when you contacted Elizabeth."

"I *was* serious." But only because having Carrie paint him would give him an excuse to be with her.

"Then you should know what you're letting yourself in for. I require ten sittings of a half-hour to an hour each."

"Fine. When can we start?"

Shane might have readily agreed to her stipulations, but she realized that sitting still was contrary to this man's personality. He was a doer, a go-getter, a human bulldozer. It wouldn't be easy for him to sit quietly for any length of time. He would be a challenge, but already she felt that a painting of Shane Reynolds could well be her best work. "I'd like to make a few preliminary sketches tonight."

"Fine."

As it turned out, Shane worked on her car while she sat on the grass and tried to capture his likeness. "You're not making this easy," she complained. He was leaning over the engine of her outdated minivan, so the only clear view she had of him was from the rear. Quickly she penciled that. Laughing, she flipped the page and drew him in oily coveralls and a heavy beard.

"What's so amusing?" His voice echoed from under the hood.

"Nothing," she replied absently as her hands flew deftly over the page. "But I don't think I dare show you what I'm drawing."

"Instead of picking on me," he instructed, "draw yourself."

She did, depicting herself as a giraffe with long, wobbly legs and knobby knees. Thick, sooty lashes framed round eyes, and her hair fell in an unruly mass of tight curls around her face. Her freckles became the giraffe's spots. "Here, for your collection," she said and tore off the sheet, handing it to him.

Amused, he wiped his hands clean with a clean rag before taking the page. But the smile in his eyes quickly disappeared as he viewed her self-image. "You see yourself like this?"

"Of course." Her own good humor vanished. The eyes

that had been so warm and gentle hardened as he glared at her, intimidating her with an anger barely held in check.

"You can't argue with the hair," she added hurriedly. To prove her point, she webbed her fingers through the glorious length, holding it out from her head. "The freckles are also beyond debate. You can't overlook them. And the knees, well, you've only seen me in a dress once, so..."

She didn't finish as Shane crumpled the portrait in a tight ball, destroying it. "Don't poke fun at yourself, Carrie. There's no reason."

"It...was only a little joke."

"At your own expense. I don't like it."

"Well tough toast, buddy." She didn't like the emotions he was bringing out in her. She wasn't Camille, and she'd been compared to her sister all her life—always coming in a poor second. Camille was the beauty and *she*... Well, she had her art.

His eyes seemed to burn straight through her. Carrie shuffled her feet uneasily. "The car's fixed?"

"You shouldn't have any problem with it now." Already he regretted his heated response to her sketch.

"I hate to eat and run, but I'd better think about heading home."

He didn't argue, and she awkwardly moved to the driver's side of the minivan. "Thank you for your help. I truly appreciate it. And the dinner was excellent. You're right about being a good cook. No wonder you never married." Realizing how sexist that sounded, she gulped and added, "That's not to say that you'd marry someone just because she was a good cook. You're not that kind of man." Wanting to make a hasty retreat, she opened the door and slid inside. "Nor would you marry a woman because she had money," she babbled on, furious with herself for not stopping. "Since you're wealthy yourself and all. What I mean…" She felt her freckles flash on like fluorescent light bulbs. "You just aren't the type of man to do that sort of thing."

Resisting the urge to laugh, Shane closed her door, his hands resting on the roof of the van. "You seem to have marriage on your mind. Is this a proposal?"

Carrie nearly swallowed her tongue. "Good grief no. It's just that…" Before she said anything more to regret, she busied herself with her keys, wanting only to escape further humiliation.

"Carrie." He said her name so softly that she jerked her head around.

He slid a finger under her chin and closed her gaping mouth. Her sensitive nerve endings vibrated with the contact. Slowly, he bent his head toward hers, his warm breath stirring the wispy hairs at her temple. Tripping wildly, her heart pounded against her ribs as she realized he was going to kiss her.

With unhurried ease, Shane claimed her mouth, his lips playing softly over hers, tasting, caressing, nibbling. When he'd finished and straightened, she gazed at him wide-eyed. Speaking, breathing—even blinking—was impossible.

"I'm serious about the portrait," he murmured, stepping away from the minivan.

Mutely, Carrie nodded, feeling lost and utterly confused. Fumbling with her key, she started the car and prepared to shift into Drive.

"Carrie?"

She turned to him.

"You're not a giraffe. You're a graceful, delicate swan who thinks of herself as an ugly duckling."

It was all she could manage just to pull away from the curb. The heat from her blush descended all the way down her neck. Like a fool, she'd babbled on, trying to cover one faux pas but instead creating another and another, until she'd made a complete fool of herself.

By the time she arrived at the beach house, she was convinced she could never face Shane Reynolds again.

"Where were you the other night?" Camille asked, her lithe body folded over in the white wicker chair while Carrie painted.

Carrie did her utmost to concentrate on her current project, a still life. "With a client. How did your dinner date go with Bob?" She preferred to stay away from the subject of Shane. Her sister was perceptive enough to recognize that Carrie's feelings toward him weren't ordinary. From past experience, Carrie knew better than to discuss any male friends with her sibling. More times than she cared to count, Camille had stolen away her boyfriends. The amazing part was that Camille hadn't even been trying. Men naturally preferred her to Carrie. Who wouldn't? Camille was beautiful.

If Camille did happen to learn about Shane, it could well be that her twin would find him as appealing as she did. Few men were strong enough to resist Camille's charms.

"Bob fancies himself in love with me." Camille's dark head dipped as she ran a nail file down the length of her long nail.

"That's not unusual."

"No, I do seem to collect admirers, don't I?"

She said it with such a complete lack of interest that Carrie had to fight to hide a smile.

"I don't know, though," Camille continued, paying an inordinate amount of attention to her nail.

"Know what?"

"About Bob."

"What's there to know? Either you love him or you don't." Almost immediately Carrie realized how uncaring that sounded. Camille had come to her with a dilemma, and she was being curt. "I didn't mean that the way it sounded."

"That's all right. Bob is my problem."

"But I'm your sister."

Camille offered her a weak smile. "There are lots of other fish in the sea. What I think I need is a break from Bob so I can do a little exploring."

"Maybe that's what we both need, to explore." But Carrie wasn't silly enough to let her sister know about Shane.

"You always could love better than me," Camille admitted with a half frown that only slightly marred her stunning good looks. "And yet the men always flocked to me, even though I'm the cold fish."

"Camille, you aren't." Her sister might have a few faults—who didn't? But Camille also possessed a wonderful capacity to love. She just hadn't found the right man yet.

Camille arched two perfectly shaped brows as she gave the matter some consideration. "You'll laugh if I tell you that I think I may be half in love with Bob."

"I wouldn't laugh. In fact, I think it's wonderful."

"Is it?"

"I think so."

"He's got his faults."

"Camille," Carrie said, and laughed aloud. "Everyone does."

Camille hesitated and concentrated on her fingernail. "I suppose. Now tell me about your new client. You're hiding something from me."

Returning her attention to the canvas, Carrie did her best to disguise her feelings. "What's there to tell? He wants his portrait done, that's all."

"Come on, Carrie." Camille laughed, sounding like a kitten purring. "You're holding out on me."

"There's a sketch of him over there if you're interested." She pointed to the pad on the tabletop.

Camille reached for the drawing Carrie had done of Shane as a bearded man in coveralls. "He doesn't look like he can afford to have you paint his portrait."

"You're probably right," she hedged.

With her head cocked to one side, Camille continued to study the drawing. "He does have an interesting face, though."

"If you like that type."

"I think I could get used to him. Did he give you the name of the garage where he works? My car's been acting up lately. I might have him look at it."

Carrie pinched her lips together in an effort to disguise her anxiety. For her to show the least amount of interest in Shane would be to invite Camille's curiosity. "He didn't say." Taking a gamble, she added, "But I have his address if you want it."

Tucking her nail file inside her purse, Camille shook her head. "Another time, perhaps."

The tension between Carrie's shoulder blades relaxed. "Whatever you say."

"I've got to go. Bob's meeting me later, and I want to look good."

Camille couldn't do anything more to improve her already flawless appearance. It was difficult to polish perfection.

As soon as Camille was gone, Carrie reached for the phone. She'd delayed calling Shane all afternoon. Every time she thought of the things she'd said, the embarrassment went all the way to her bones.

"Hello." His greeting was brusque.

"This is Carrie Lockett. Is this a bad time?"

"Carrie." Her name was delivered with a rush of pleasure.

In her mind's eye, she could picture him relaxing and leaning back to smile into the receiver. Her own pulse reacted madly, and she pulled herself up straight. "I'm calling to set a schedule for your sittings. I'd like to begin tomorrow afternoon, if possible." She felt the need to elaborate. "The first few sittings can be done anywhere. I can come to your house or your office, whichever you choose. Later it would be more convenient if you could come here."

"Either is fine. Let me check my schedule."

In the background, she could hear him flipping pages. "How does four o'clock tomorrow sound?"

"That'll be fine."

"Would you mind coming to my office?"

"Give me the address, and I'll be happy to."

"My, my don't we sound formal. Has the car given you any more trouble?"

"No...but I haven't been out today."

"The next time you're at the service station, have the attendant check the carburetor."

"All right." She hesitated, not wanting the conversation to end. "I want you to know how much I appreciate your fixing it."

"And I'm grateful that you stayed and shared dinner with me," he added softly. "I'd be willing to do a complete engine overhaul if it meant you'd come again. Maybe tonight?" The warmth in his tone was disturbing. But then, everything about Shane Reynolds disturbed her.

"No thanks, perhaps another time."

"I'll hold you to that."

"I'm taking a class tonight," she said, then wondered why she felt compelled to explain.

"I'm pleased to know it isn't because you're seeing another man—or are you?"

"No." She didn't feel like admitting that he was the only man she'd dated in a month. Her "dates" were more getting together with friends than the result of any romantic interest.

"Good. What I know won't set me to wondering."

Carrie found it highly amusing that someone as handsome as Shane would feel threatened by anyone she'd dated.

"I'll see you at four tomorrow," she told him.

"I'm looking forward to it."

Unfortunately, so was she. Far, far more than she should.

Wednesday afternoon, Carrie entered Shane's building at a few minutes to four. She'd dressed in a blue linen jumpsuit, and tied her hair at the base of her neck with a silk scarf. She'd spent a good portion of the early afternoon preparing for this meeting, but not in the way that she usually readied herself for a sitting. Instead, she sorted through her closets, and spent extra time on her hair and makeup, all the while berating herself for the time and trouble she was taking.

"I'm Carrie Lockett," she told the receptionist. "I have a four o'clock appointment with Mr. Reynolds."

The attractive woman in her early twenties smiled at Carrie. "Mr. Reynolds mentioned you'd be coming. If you take a seat, he'll be with you in a moment." She punched a button on the phone line and spoke into her headset. "Ms. Lockett is here for her appointment."

Carrie took a seat and chose a magazine, since she knew she would probably have to wait a few minutes. After idly flipping through the crisp pages, she had just settled on an article when the door opened and Shane appeared. "I'm sorry to keep you waiting."

Slowly she stood. "I've only been here a couple of minutes." They gazed at each other in a way that felt far too meaningful for what was supposed to be a business meeting of sorts.

"Come in, won't you?"

She would have willingly walked over hot coals to get to him. *You've got it bad, girl,* she mocked herself. "Thank you." She hoped her voice sounded cool and professional but knew she'd failed miserably.

"That'll be all for today, Carol," Shane told his secretary.

Carrie stepped inside his office and stopped cold. Camille's portrait hung on the wall opposite his desk in bold splendor, her dark-haired beauty dominating the room.

Shane had told her the portrait would hang in his office, but she'd forgotten. Abruptly she looked away, fighting the tightness in her heart. Every day Shane sat in this room and stared at the compelling beauty of her sister. Each time he picked up the phone his gaze would rest naturally on Camille. As much as Carrie had tried to forget it, the fact remained that Shane found Camille beautiful. And if he stared at the creamy smooth perfection of her sister long enough, he couldn't help notice the flaws that stood out like giant fault lines in Carrie.

He motioned for her to take a seat. "Elizabeth sent over the contract," he said, holding out the paper to her.

"I hope you haven't signed it," she said in a low, tight voice. "Because I don't think this is going to work. I've given the matter some thought and decided that I wouldn't be the best one for this job. I'm sorry, Shane. Really sorry." She turned and fled from his office.

Four

"Carrie—" Shane raced after her, ignoring the startled look of his receptionist, who was gathering her things. He didn't know what was troubling Carrie, but he wasn't about to let her run away from him a second time. He caught up with her outside the elevator. "What is the matter with you all of a sudden?"

"Nothing." She swallowed down another lie. "Really. I…just realized that I'm overextended timewise and… doing another portrait now would be too much for me." She couldn't tell him that it was impossible for her to work with him, knowing that he spent his days staring at Camille's perfect features. She would undoubtedly be placed in the position of having to respond to his curiosity about the woman in the portrait. No one could look at Camille and not want to know her.

"I've got a contract, an agreement made in good faith," he reminded her, placing his hand on her shoulder in an effort to get her to face him. "We've agreed on the terms, and I expect you to hold up your end of the bargain."

"Shane… I can't."

Curious bystanders were beginning to gather around them, and Carrie was feeling more miserable by the minute.

"Let's get out of here," he mumbled, reaching for her limp hand. Instead of waiting for the elevator, he led her toward the stairwell. They hadn't gone more than a few steps when he turned to face her. "What is it with you? You have got to be the most unreasonable woman I've ever known. You're hot, then cold. First the portrait's on, then it's off. You can't seem to make up your mind about anything."

"I'm sorry."

"Don't tell me that again."

"All right." From the way she behaved around him, Carrie considered it a wonder that he wanted anything to do with her. "If we mutually agree to tear up the contract—"

"No." His voice was both hard and flat. "I hired you to do my portrait." He wouldn't let her slip through his fingers that easily.

"But surely you understand that I can't."

"Why not?" he shot right back.

"Because…"

"Carrie, come on." He paused and pushed his fingers through his well-groomed hair. "Let's get out of here. It's obvious we need to talk."

While they marched down the stairs, her mind frantically sought a feasible explanation and quickly came back blank. Nothing would satisfy Shane except the truth, and she wasn't willing to reveal that.

Once outside, he escorted her across the busy intersection into a nearby hotel. Carrie was grateful for the semi-darkness that shrouded the room as he led her to a table in the cocktail lounge. Her face felt hot with angry embarrassment. She was angry with herself and embarrassed that Shane wouldn't accept her feeble excuses.

They were no sooner seated than the waitress approached. Absently Shane ordered two glasses of wine, then paid when they arrived.

"All right, I'm listening," he coaxed. "Why do you want out of the contract?"

The smile that curved her lips felt as brittle as scorched parchment. Twirling the stem of the wineglass between her palms helped occupy her hands. "It isn't that I don't want to do your portrait."

"You could have fooled me," he muttered sarcastically.

"I think I'd do a good job."

"I *know* you would."

His confidence in her abilities produced a spark of genuine pleasure. "I...like you, Shane."

"I haven't made any secret about the way I feel about you. But you're like a giant puzzle to me...."

"And some of the pieces are missing," she finished for him.

He chuckled and relaxed, leaning back in his chair. His smile was slightly off center—and devastating. "Exactly."

Carrie took a sip of her wine and felt the coiled tension drain from her arms and legs. She'd been looking forward to this meeting all day. Seeing Camille's portrait hanging in Shane's office had nearly ruined everything.

"Is there anything else you wanted to say?" he inquired, studying her.

"Yes." She paused and cleared her throat. She was anxious, yet aware of a tingling excitement deep inside her. It happened every time she was around Shane. He was the most special man she'd ever known. But she was afraid that once Camille learned about him, it would be all over. Since he found Camille's portrait so intriguing, she doubted that he would find the real woman any less so.

"Can we start again?" she asked, her voice slightly strained.

"I think we'd better." He stood and glanced around the room. His large hands folded over the back of the chair as he nodded in her direction. "I hope I haven't kept you waiting." He spoke as though he'd only just arrived.

Carrie chuckled and glanced at her wristwatch, playing his game. "Only a few minutes."

"I see you've ordered the wine." He sat and reached for his glass, tasting it. "My favorite. How did you know?"

"Lucky guess."

She resembled a frightened fawn, and Shane couldn't understand it. "Now, about the portrait," he said conversationally.

She stiffened. She couldn't help herself. "Which portrait?"

He didn't understand why there would be a question. "The one you've agreed to paint of me."

Visibly, she relaxed. "Ah, yes, that one."

"Shall we do the first sitting today?"

"Today?" She had everything with her. There wasn't any reason not to start with the preliminary sketches. "If you like."

"Of course." He stood and placed a generous tip on the table. "Are you ready?"

It took a minute for her to realize that he wanted to return to his office. "You mean now?" She groped for a plausible reason not to go back there. Her mind was befuddled. Her wits deserted her. "Today?"

"Yes." His arched brows formed an inquisitive frown. "Is that a problem?"

"Well, actually, I'm in a bit of a rush. I was thinking that since we're here...and your office is over there..." She pointed in the general direction of the street. "It seems a waste of time to travel all the way over there when we're..."

"Here."

"Right."

"Do you have something against my office?"

"Your office?" She swallowed uncomfortably. "Don't be silly. I've only been there once." As she spoke she reached for her sketchbook. "What could I possibly have against your office?"

"I don't even want to try guessing the answer to that one," he grumbled, downing the last of his wine.

Taking her thick-leaded pencil from her purse, Carrie angled the pad of paper in front of her and began sketching his bold features. Her fingers worked quickly, transmitting the image from her eye to the sheet. As soon as she completed one angle, she flipped the page and started on another, seeking the best possible way to catch the man and his personality.

She worked intently, unaware of the curious stares cast in their direction.

"When do I get to look?"

"Soon." The one word was clipped, a mark of her intense concentration.

"Do you want me to hold my head a certain way?"

"What I want is for you to keep your mouth closed."

He snapped it shut, but she noted the way his lips quivered as he struggled to hold back a lopsided grin.

Finally, when she couldn't stand it another minute, she rested the pad against the edge of the round table. "All right, what's so blasted amusing?"

"You."

"Me? Why?"

"Explaining would be impossible. But I'll have you know that I'm revealing my strength of character here."

"How's that?"

"I doubt that few men would demonstrate so much restraint."

Restraint. The man was speaking in riddles. "How's that?"

"Kissing you seems to be my natural inclination."

Shock paralyzed her. Her hand sagged against the paper, and the pencil slipped from her fingers and dropped unceremoniously to the floor. Quickly she retrieved it, her cheeks flaming with hot color.

Smiling boldly, Shane captured her gaze. "You heard me right."

"But the room's full of people."

"It's dark in here," he countered, giving her a grin best described as Cheshire-cat smug. "As I was saying, I'm showing a lot of self-restraint."

"Should I tell you how grateful I am?"

"It would help."

She finished the last sketch and handed the pad to him. "Then thank you, Mr. Reynolds."

His eyes studied the likeness she'd drawn of him. "Nice."

"Is there one you prefer more than the others?"

"No. You decide." He wasn't especially interested in her doing his portrait. It was all a ruse, an excuse to get to

know her better and learn what he could about this complicated woman.

"I will, then."

"How about dinner?"

His invitation cut into her thoughts. She was trying
to decide the best angle to capture the force of his personality.

"Pardon?"

"You know—dinner—the meal that's eaten at the end
of the day, usually after a long afternoon at the office. And
most often after the time when a man has had a chance to
relax with a glass of fine wine."

"Oh, you mean *dinner*."

"Right." He gave her an odd look. "How about it?"

"Yes, I usually eat that meal."

He chuckled. "Since it seems to be that time of day,
and we've already relaxed with a glass of excellent wine,
how about sharing dinner?"

He offered the invitation with such charm that Carrie
doubted if she could have refused him. He had to be the
most patient man in the world. Anyone else would have
considered her a prime candidate for the loony bin.

"What kind of dinner?" The shop that employed Camille wasn't more than a mile from Shane's office, and
if they chose a restaurant close by, there was the possibility that they would run into Camille. Although they
didn't look the least bit alike, the way the two of them
shared thoughts was sometimes uncanny. Only last month
they'd celebrated their father's birthday and discovered
that they'd each purchased him the identical golf shirt and
birthday card. At other times, Carrie would be thinking

about Camille and go to call her, only to have Camille ring first, claiming Carrie had been on her mind.

"What kind of dinner?" Shane repeated the question with a perplexed look that was becoming all too familiar. "I was considering food."

"A popular choice. However, I was thinking more along ethnic lines. You know... Italian, Mexican, Chinese."

"You decide."

She didn't hesitate. "Chinese." Camille had never been especially fond of Chinese food. She leaned more toward a variety of expensive seafood dishes. For that matter, Carrie was fond of those herself.

"Fine," Shane said, though he didn't seem enthusiastic.

"You don't seem thrilled with my choice." Which didn't seem fair, given that he was the one who'd suggested that she choose.

He shrugged. "I was in Chinatown for lunch today."

"It doesn't matter to me," she lied. "You decide." Her fingers trembled slightly as she sipped the last of her wine.

"Do you like seafood?"

She released an inward groan. She should have known he would suggest that. "Seafood?" Her voice echoed his.

He shot her a brief, mocking glance. "Yes. You know, fish, lobster, crab. That sort of thing. I've heard Billy's on the Wharf is excellent."

"I suppose that's fine." She dropped her gaze to the table, not wanting him to know how distressed she was. Camille had often raved about the food at Billy's.

"Mexican?" he offered next.

Instantly she brightened. "Great choice." Camille usually said Mexican food was too fattening.

He mumbled something under his breath and shook his

head. Then he stood up and said, "Let's get out of here before you change your mind."

She found it amazing that he still wanted to have dinner with her after going through all that. She reached for her pad and purse. "I'm not going to change my mind."

A smile twitched at the corners of his mouth. "I won't believe it until I see it."

Shane held the door open for her, and they stepped outside into the bright sunshine. Side by side they walked along the crowded sidewalk. Rush hour traffic filled the streets. His hand came up to rest on her back just above her waist. Its guiding pressure was light, but enough for her to be aware of the contact and be unnerved by it. But then, everything about this man seemed to affect her.

They were halfway down the block when she caught a glimpse of a teal-blue convertible that resembled the model Camille drove. Rather than take a chance of being seen with Shane, she made a sharp right hand turn and headed into the nearest store.

She had disappeared before Shane realized it. She was there one minute and gone the next. Stunned, he did a complete three hundred and sixty degree turn. He was utterly perplexed.

"Carrie?" Shane whirled around again, attempting to locate her.

The car passed without incident. Carrie was so busy hiding that she didn't notice if it was Camille's car or not. Quickly she moved back outside. "Sorry, I...saw something on sale that I've been wanting." She flicked her wrist toward the black leather bedroom outfit, complete with handcuffs and chains, displayed prominently in the window. Then her shocked eyes went from the display window to the name of the establishment, which made it abundantly clear as to their specialty.

Sucking in a horrified breath, she instantly turned fifteen shades of red. "Then, of course, I realized that I was in the wrong store. It was...some...other store."

"Naturally."

They caught a taxi at the next corner, and Shane gave the man the name of a restaurant not far from Billy's on Fisherman's Wharf. After what had happened earlier, she wasn't about to try to get him to choose another place, even though this restaurant was too close for comfort to the one Camille frequented.

Their meal was delicious. Or it would have been if Carrie had taken more than a token taste. Her appetite had vanished with the toll of her minor subterfuge.

After dinner they took a short stroll, stopping in a few shops along the way. The whole time Carrie was conscious that it would be just her luck to run into Camille. They caught a taxi at the waterfront, and Shane escorted Carrie back to her minivan.

"Thank you for dinner." She stood with her back to the driver's door. Her hands gripped the handle from behind.

"You're very welcome." Shadows darkened his face. The streetlight illuminated the area, creating a soft romantic atmosphere.

Carrie wished the lights were dimmer. She wanted Shane to kiss her and doubted that he would in such a well-lit spot.

She could feel him watching her as she spoke. "I had a nice time."

"Good. Maybe we can do it again soon."

She shrugged in an effort to disguise how pleased she

was that he asked. "Sure. There are lots of good restaurants in Daly City."

"Daly City! What's the matter with downtown?" The things she said were so ridiculous they should be documented.

"Nothing."

His throaty chuckle did little to ease her discomfort. For the entire evening, she'd made one outrageous statement after another. This wasn't going to work. As badly as she wanted to be with Shane, trying to keep Camille a secret was far too complicated. She wasn't talented enough to pull off another night like this one.

His hand rested on the slope of her shoulder as his gaze caressed her. "Carrie, I want you to answer a question."

Danger alarms rang in her ears. Her instincts told her to avoid this at any cost, but she couldn't. Nor would she continue to lie. "A question? Sure."

"Not a difficult one." His hand slid from the curve of her shoulder up to her neck in a gentle caress. "Are you married?"

She relaxed and boldly smiled up at him while gently shaking her head. "No."

"You're sure?"

"Positive."

The only thing that could justify her behavior was if she had a husband or jealous boyfriend. His mind was afloat with questions. "Have you ever been married?"

"Never." So he assumed she was hiding from a man. She was so relieved she almost forgot herself and kissed him.

His hand molded itself to the gentle incline of her neck,

his long fingers sliding into the silky length of her hair. "I want you to know how pleased I am to know that."

"At the moment, I'm rather pleased about it myself." But not for the reasons he assumed.

"I want to kiss you."

"I know." She wanted it, too.

His mouth made an unhurried descent to her waiting lips. It seemed a lifetime before his lips covered hers, his touch firm and blessedly warm. The moment their mouths met, her tension of anticipation eased away, and she responded by raising her arms and wrapping them around his strong neck.

The pressure of the kiss ended, but he didn't raise his mouth more than a hair's breadth. "I've wanted to do that from the moment I saw you this afternoon."

"You did?" All she could remember was him staring at the portrait of Camille.

He kissed her again. "After the wild goose chase you've led me on, you can't doubt it." His hands moved up and down her spine, arching her closer to his male length. "I'll see you soon?"

"Dinner?"

"If you like, but I was thinking more about the portrait."

She couldn't believe how quickly her memory had deserted her the minute she was in his arms. "Naturally. I think I'd prefer it if we met at your house…or you can come to mine." Though the latter was dangerous, on the off chance Camille showed up, which she often did. "Your place, I think."

"Fine."

"Friday?"

She blinked, trying to remember what day this was. "Okay."

He kissed her again, and the pressure at the back of her neck lifted her on her tiptoes. Her hands explored his jaw and the column of his throat, her fingers finally settling on his shoulders.

"Friday, then," he said as he breathed into her hair. Reluctantly, he broke contact. "Will you be all right driving back out to your place?"

"Of course."

"I could follow you, if you'd like."

And probably not plan to leave until morning, judging by the way he was looking at her. "I'll be fine," she insisted. "Thanks anyway."

His hand covered his eyes. Blurting out the wrong thing must be contagious. "I didn't mean that the way it sounded. It's just that I usually escort my dates home. It doesn't feel right to let go of you here."

For once Carrie felt in control. She received immense pleasure at the look of consternation that tightened his face. "Are you saying you don't find me attractive?"

"You've got to know otherwise." Keeping his mouth shut seemed to be the best thing. He reached for her again, but she easily sidestepped his arms.

"You get an A for effort." Unable to resist, she tucked a strand of silver hair behind his ear and lightly pressed her lips over his. "I'll see you Friday. Seven?"

"Fine." He opened her door for her and stepped back as she climbed inside.

She offered him a tremulous smile. Her mouth still held the throbbing heat of his kisses.

The drive home was completed almost mechanically.

Briefly, she wondered if Camille had seen her with Shane and what her sister would say if she had. Carrie knew she wouldn't be able to hide him forever. Perhaps if she subtly approached the subject of Shane, it might work.

It wasn't until the following Thursday that Carrie had the opportunity to do exactly that. Camille stopped at the beach house to repay the loan, tucking the fifty dollar bill under the salt shaker on the kitchen table.

Carrie washed her hands and made busy work in the kitchen, trying to come up with a tactful way of addressing the delicate subject.

She didn't get the chance before Camille brought it up on her own. "I thought I saw you the other day."

"Oh?" Carrie froze.

"You didn't happen to have dinner near Fisherman's Wharf this week, did you?"

Pretending to be distracted by slicing a lemon for the tall glasses of iced tea she'd prepared, Carrie shook her head. "I can't say it wasn't me." She hoped the double negative would confuse her twin into dropping the subject.

No such luck. "Were you alone?" Camille pressed.

"I went with a friend."

"Male or female?"

"Honestly, Camille, what is this? The Inquisition?"

"I'm just trying to keep tabs on you. You're my only sister, for heaven's sake."

"What were you doing there?" The best way to handle this, Carrie felt, was to raise a few questions of her own.

"Bob and I went to Billy's."

Carrie delivered the ice-filled glasses to the table. "The last time you were here, you said something about being half in love with Bob. Have you come to any conclusions since then?" Oh dear, she was going to make a mess of this.

"So you *were* with a man!" Camille cried with obvious delight. "I knew it. And obviously one you're wild about. All right, Carrie, give."

"You answer me first."

"You mean about falling for Bob? I wish I knew. I like being with him. He's fun. My whole life wouldn't depend on seeing him again, but then I think how much I'd miss him. As you can tell, I'm a little bit confused."

"Do you think about him?" Carrie's thoughts had been dominated by Shane almost from the moment she'd taken that peek at him in the gallery.

Camille shook her perfectly styled soft brunette curls. "I wish it were that easy. Whole days go by when I don't think about him. Well, he isn't completely out of mind. I don't know how to explain it." She studied her sister. "Are you in love?"

Carrie snickered. She couldn't help it. "With whom? It isn't like I've got scores of admirers just waiting for me to fall into their arms. Who would be interested in me when you're around?"

"It's not like I try to steal your male friends away. Half the time I don't even date them."

Camille had stated the problem in a nutshell. She wasn't attracted to them, but they sure were attracted to her. Shane would be, too, once he met her.

"Come on Carrie, tell me about him."

"There's no one," she insisted, taking a long swallow of her iced tea.

Camille cocked her head to one side as though viewing her sister for the first time. "You know I'd confide in you."

Carrie turned around. There had been plenty of times over the years when she'd resented her twin. Camille had it all, and for everyone to see. Few cared that Carrie had a sharp brain and a God-given artistic ability. Men in particular didn't see past the exterior.

The phone rang, and Carrie stared at it as if it were a burglar alarm blaring out of control.

"Aren't you going to answer it?" Camille asked.

"Yes." She made a show of drying her hands before reaching for the receiver. "Hello."

Her worst fears were realized the instant Shane spoke. "Hello, Carrie."

She didn't dare say his name. "Hello," she said stiffly, holding her back rigid.

He hesitated, apparently sensitive to the reserved tone of her voice. "Am I catching you at a bad time?"

Ever since their evening together, she'd been hoping to hear from him. "Sort of," she admitted with some reluctance.

"Shall I call back a little later?"

"I could phone you." Her eyes looked everywhere except at Camille.

"I'm at the office. Do you have that number?" he asked.

"Yes. I'll call you there." She would find some way to get rid of her sister. For once she was going to hold on to a man, and she didn't care what tactics she was forced to use. Shane was the best thing that had happened to her in years.

"I suppose that was your handsome mechanic," Camille said when Carrie hung up.

"My what?" Carrie was genuinely baffled until she remembered how Camille had assumed that Shane worked on cars.

"Remember, you showed me your drawing of him the other day? You aren't going to be able to keep me from meeting him much longer," Camille insisted. "Don't you think I know what you're doing? You've never been able to keep anything from me for long. Good grief, every time you lie, your freckles become fluorescent."

Carrie's hand flew to her nose. "That's not true." Even as she spoke, she knew it was.

"And right now your nose alone could light up the entire Golden Gate Bridge."

"Oh, stop it, Camille. There is no one special in my life at the moment."

"And the Pope isn't Catholic."

"Camille…"

"All right, all right. I'll meet him sooner or later. You won't be able to hide him from me forever."

The words were like an unwelcome bell tolling in Carrie's mind.

"No doubt you're dying for me to leave so you can phone your mysterious 'friend.' Well, I won't delay you any longer." Camille deposited her empty glass in the sink. "I just wish you were a little more open about him."

"Why?" Carrie asked with a trace of bitterness. "So you can steal him away from me?"

"So there *is* someone." The delicate laugh that followed produced a shiver that ran up and down Carrie's backbone. "I don't think you have anything to worry about. Our tastes in men have never meshed."

That was true. Silently, Carrie watched as Camille

waved and sauntered out the door. As far as men were concerned, beauty outdid talent and brains any day of the week. And Carrie was still afraid to believe that Shane might be the exception.

Playing it safe, she waited an extra ten minutes after Camille left before anxiously reaching for the phone.

Carrie fussed all day Friday, more nervous about this one sitting than a hundred others. This was Shane she was going to meet. Shane, the man who had withstood her rebuffs, her craziness and her complete lack of self-confidence, and liked her anyway. As she dabbed expensive French perfume behind her ears and at the pulse points of her wrists, she visualized how calm and collected she would be when they met. An eager smile curved the edges of her mouth. Shane wouldn't know her. Every time they'd been together, her behavior had been highly questionable. The man was a priceless wonder to have stuck things out with her. This evening she would shock the socks right off him with her calm, cool behavior. Tonight she had nothing to hide and no secrets to keep. She was there to sketch him, and he had insisted she stay for dinner afterward.

Grabbing a bottle of an excellent California Chardonnay, Carrie was on her way. She'd looked forward to this night. Everything was going to be perfect.

The drive went smoothly, and she was right on time when she pulled up in front of his elegant home.

Shane answered the door with a welcoming smile and rewarded her taste in wine with a light kiss across her surprised mouth.

"I thought we'd work in here tonight, if you don't mind." He led the way into the library.

"Sure," Carrie agreed, following him. It wasn't until she was inside the room that she noticed the portrait.

He had moved it. No longer was Camille's image hanging from the walls of his office. Shane had brought it home.

Five

Shane watched the expression of shock work its way across Carrie's pale features. She stood in front of the portrait and studied it as though seeing it for the first time and finding herself astonished. He wished he could read her thoughts. It was obvious to him now that the painting distressed her, yet he couldn't imagine why.

"You brought it here," she said in a tone that was so low he had to strain to hear her. "Why?"

"Is there a reason why I shouldn't have?" He moved around the desk and claimed the chair, hoping that his actions seemed nonchalant.

Carrie's attention drifted from Camille's flirtatious smile back to Shane. Taking his cue, she sat in a comfortable leather chair and set her briefcase on the Oriental carpet.

"She's lovely," Shane said, his gaze resting on the painting.

Carrie ignored him as she took out the supplies she would be using for this session.

"Don't you agree?" he pressed.

Her stomach bunched into a painful knot as she answered him with an abrupt shake of her head. The tingling numbness that had attacked her throat soon spread to her arms and legs, leaving them feeling useless.

"There aren't many women that lovely," he went on.

She clenched her jaw so tightly her molars ached. From the beginning she'd known how difficult it would be to stand in Camille's shadow. She'd so desperately wanted Shane to be different that she'd purposely ignored all the signs.

Holding her head high and proud, she boldly met his gaze. "She's probably one of the loveliest women you'll ever meet."

"I take it you know her personally?"

Her fingers curled around the chair arm, her long nails denting the soft leather. "Yes, I know her."

His eyes surveyed the portrait with what she could only describe as tenderness. "She's fantastic."

"Yes." Feeling a frantic need to be done with this assignment as quickly as possible, she began the preliminary sketch.

"She's—"

"Don't talk," Carrie barked. Her hands flew over the page, slightly softening the blunt lines of his craggy features as she worked.

Silent now, Shane relaxed against the back of the chair, crossing his legs and planting his hands on top of his bent knee. His gaze drifted from the portrait to Carrie, then back again. Slowly an amused grin appeared. Carrie had thought to fool him, but he had figured it out. She'd done an excellent job on the portrait, but he'd seen through the guise. *No Competition* had to be a portrait of the artist.

Viewing it now, he understood why the portrait intimidated her, and he wished he could change that. He was an architect, and his profession had taught him long ago that the outside was only a facade. Often alluring and appealing to the eye, but useless as anything more than a front. It was the inside that mattered. Carrie Lockett was a woman of grit. He realized that old-fashioned word didn't fit the image of this modern woman, but it was how he thought of her. In his mind's eye, Shane envisioned Carrie as she might have lived a hundred years ago. She was the pioneer type. One who would set out to tame a wild land. A woman of substance who could settle the farmlands and build the heart of a new country.

Had she lived in those times, she probably wouldn't have been given the opportunity to paint as she did now. Her artistic talent would have been utilized in different ways. Perhaps in a craft, such as quilting. His thoughts drifted to his own grandmother and mother, and he wished that they were alive so they could meet Carrie. Both of them would have loved her.

Fifteen minutes passed without a word being spoken. Carrie's concentration centered on her work. She'd captured Shane's likeness perfectly yet she'd failed to capture the way she saw him. A photographer would do as well and cost far less. Furious that she cared so much, she viciously jerked the huge sheet off the pad and wadded it into a tight ball.

"Carrie…"

Rising, she angrily met his gaze. "Do you want to meet her?"

"Who?"

"Who else?" She waved her hand at the portrait, determined to get this over with as quickly and painlessly as possible. Once he met Camille, he could have the woman he really wanted. Camille claimed that their tastes in men didn't mesh. This time her sister was dead wrong. Shane was definitely Camille's type. Handsome, secure, talented. Everything her sister wanted and a whole lot more. Of course, Camille wouldn't recognize his gentleness, his intelligence or his quick wit. But none of that mattered now. Shane wanted Camille and had from the very first. The adoring looks he'd been giving the portrait from the minute Carrie had entered the library proved as much. Shane would be enthralled to meet her twin.

"Meet her?" Once again she'd managed to perplex him. "What are you talking about?"

Rarely had a man been more obtuse. "The woman in the portrait will be at my house tomorrow evening at seven. Be there."

A long moment passed before Shane responded. "If you insist."

The soft sound of his chuckle infuriated her, and she glared at him with a lifetime of resentment burning in her green eyes. "It's what you want, isn't it? What you've wanted from the beginning? The artist was only the means of meeting the model. Fine. I just wish you had been up-front with me from the beginning."

Before he could move around the desk, she'd picked up her supplies and was marching out the den and toward the front door. "Carrie, would you just stop and listen to me?"

"No. Just be there."

He chuckled again. "I wouldn't miss it for the world."

"I didn't think you would."

He followed her down the front steps. "Do you want to schedule the next session now?"

"No."

"But I want you to continue the portrait."

She hesitated. "I doubt you'll feel that way after tomorrow."

"Don't count on it, Carrie."

Holding the handle of her briefcase as though it were a lifeline to sanity, she sadly shook her head. "We can wait until tomorrow night and discuss it then."

She had that hurt look about her again, and Shane yearned to reach out and hold her, but from experience he knew she wouldn't let him, not when she was in this mood. Some day she would come to trust him enough, but until then he had to learn to be patient.

"I'm not going to change my mind about the portrait or about you," he told her.

"Time will tell." One look at Camille, and Shane would willingly forget her *and* the portrait he'd hired her to paint. As she had a hundred times in the past, Carrie would drift into the background while Camille took the stage. Only this time it would hurt more than it ever had before.

Shane escorted Carrie to her parked car. He patted the hood and absently ran his hand over the faded paint of her outdated minivan. He lingered while she climbed inside and inserted the key into the ignition.

"Have you had a mechanic look at it yet?" he asked.

"No. The man at the gas station told me to bring it in next week." She shifted into Reverse and waited for him to step back.

He did so grudgingly. He didn't want her to go but couldn't think of an excuse for her to stay. It wasn't until she pulled onto the street that he remembered their dinner warming in the oven.

* * *

Carrie's heart was so heavy that she felt as though a ton of bricks were pressing against her body, her mind and her soul. She shouldn't blame Camille for her beauty, but this time she did. And even though the last person she wanted to speak to at the minute was Camille, she knew she had to call her sister and be done with it as quickly as possible.

Once back at the beach house, Carrie didn't feel the comfort and welcome she usually did. Shadows lurked in the corners. Even the ocean below looked gray and depressing.

She didn't bother to turn on the lights and fumbled around in the dark, dropping her equipment as she came through the front door. She curled up on the sofa, wrapping her arms around her knees and tucking her chin into her collarbone.

There was no help for this. It had to be done. Gathering her resolve, she moved into the kitchen and lifted the phone. She hesitated an instant before punching out the number that was as familiar as her own.

"Hello." Camille's soft voice was fuzzy, as though she'd been sleeping.

"Camille, it's Carrie. Is this a bad time?"

A short, surprised silence followed. Carrie seldom contacted her sister. Camille was the one who came to her with a multitude of problems and questions. Carrie was the mother, Camille the child. This time, though, their roles were reversed. Camille would solve the problem that was burning through Carrie like a slow fire.

"Carrie, what are you doing phoning me? Is anything wrong?"

"No...not really."

"You don't sound right."

Carrie didn't doubt that. She felt terrible—on the verge of being physically ill. "I know," she said and her voice dropped almost to a whisper. "Can you stop by tomorrow night, say around seven?"

"Why?"

Carrie backed against the kitchen counter and lifted the heavy hair off her forehead as her eyes dropped closed. "There's someone I want you to meet. Someone who wants to meet you."

"I don't suppose it's a man?" Camille was joking, seeming to enjoy this and noting none of the pain that had crept into Carrie's voice.

"Yes, a man, a special one I know you'll like."

"So you've decided to unveil your mechanic friend." The statement was followed by a low, knowing laugh.

"He isn't a mechanic. Shane's an architect. He's the man in the sketches you saw."

Camille hesitated. "He did have an interesting face."

"Yes." That was all Carrie would admit.

"Aren't you afraid I'll try to steal him away?"

Carrie bit unmercifully into her bottom lip. That wouldn't be necessary. Shane had never been hers in the first place. Their whole relationship had been built around the woman in the portrait. And that was Camille.

"I wouldn't, you know," her twin added, more serious now.

"He's yours if you want him," Carrie said with as little emotion as possible. "He's interested in you already."

"That's amazing, since I've never met him."

Carrie felt she might as well let the bomb drop now as tomorrow night. "He's the one who bought your painting."

"Really." A small excited sound came over the wire. "How extraordinary. And now he wants to meet me? I'm flattered."

"I knew you would be." A muscle leaped in her tightly clenched jaw as she uttered the statement in a faintly sarcastic tone.

"He must be wealthy, if he could afford one of your paintings."

"I thought money didn't interest you?" Jealousy seethed through her veins. She'd fought the battle so often and conquered it so readily that the ferocity with which it raged now shocked her. "I'm sorry to cut this short, but we'll have time to talk tomorrow night."

"You can count on it." Camille sounded like a schoolgirl who'd been promised a trip to the circus. She hesitated for an instant. "You're sure you don't mind? You know, if Shane and I go out? You seemed quite taken with him the other day."

"Mind?" Carrie forced a laugh. "Why should I mind?" Why indeed? she repeated as she severed the phone connection. Why indeed?

The following day Carrie refused to answer her cell phone. There wasn't a single person she felt like talking to, and anyone important would leave a message. By lunchtime she counted six calls. Playing back her voice mail, she discovered that Shane had phoned four times. The first time he told her that he was sorry to miss her and that he would check back with her later. The second call revealed a hint of impatience. Again he claimed he would catch her later. On the third call, he said that he knew she was purposely ignoring his calls, and that if he didn't have to attend an important meeting he would drive out and confront her. The last call was to apologize for his anger on the third call and tell her that he looked forward to seeing her that evening, when they would get this mess straightened out once and for all.

Carrie listened to each message with an increasing sense of impatience. She didn't know why Shane thought there was a mess. For the first time since she'd learned he'd bought *No Competition*, everything was crystal clear.

At six she showered and dressed, choosing her best linen pants and a pale silk blouse. No doubt Camille would arrive resembling a fashion queen. Carrie had no desire to further emphasize the contrast between them by trying to compete.

Using oyster shell combs, she pulled her thick hair away from her oval face and applied a fresh layer of makeup. The doorbell chimed just as she'd finished spreading lipstick across her bottom lip. She smoothed out the color on her way to the front door. Knowing Camille, she would be so eager to meet the man who had purchased her painting that she'd probably decided to arrive early.

She forced herself to appear welcoming as she pulled open the door.

"Hi," Shane said. "I know I'm early, but I couldn't wait any longer."

The shock of seeing him momentarily robbed her of her ability to talk.

"Did you get my phone messages?" He came into the cottage and paced the area in front of her sofa.

She clasped her hands together and shook her head. "I got them."

"But you didn't bother to return my calls."

Personally, she couldn't see any reason she should have. Seeing him again was difficult enough. "No."

"This has gone on long enough."

"What has?" He was clearly angry, but it seemed to be pointed inward, as though he was furious with himself.

"This whole business with the portrait."

She squared her shoulders. "I couldn't agree with you more."

"I know." He reached out and gently laid his hands on the ivory slope of her shoulders.

"What do you know?" Now she was the one in the dark.

"About the painting."

"Would you kindly stop talking in riddles?"

"I admit to being fooled in the beginning. The coloring was tricky, and the changes in the features were subtle."

She stared at him in wide-eyed expectation. "What are you saying?"

"I'm on to you," he said with a small laugh. "*No Competition* is a self-portrait."

Carrie was too stunned to respond.

"You took all the beauty stored inside that warm, loving heart of yours and painted it on the outside. Only—" He paused to position his thumb against her trembling chin. "Only you did yourself an injustice. Your beauty far surpasses the loveliness of the woman in the painting. Your brand of attractiveness is much more captivating than any surface beauty."

"Shane..." Shimmering tears filled her eyes. She couldn't believe what he was saying. No one had ever thought she was attractive. And certainly never lovely. Not when compared to Camille.

"If you recall, I didn't buy the painting that first day. To tell the truth, I was somehow...disappointed in it."

"But—"

The pressure of his finger against her chin stopped her. "The portrait was too perfect, almost disturbingly so, until I realized what you'd done. Then I remembered how I'd followed you to Fisherman's Wharf that day and witnessed for myself the real Carrie Lockett. And that was when I realized what you'd done and knew I had to buy your portrait. But the truth is, I don't need anything more than you, Carrie. Exactly as you are this moment."

"Oh, Shane." She blinked in an effort to restrain the ever-ready flow of emotion. "Don't say things like that to me. I'm not used to it. I don't know how to react."

"I was drawn to you the first time I saw you, and your appeal grows stronger every time we meet."

She stared at him in disbelief mingled with awe, unable to tell him how much his words meant to her flagging self-esteem.

"I don't need the beautiful woman in the portrait," he told her gently. "Not when the real flesh-and-blood woman is right here."

"You mean that, don't you?"

"With everything that's in me."

The realization that Camille—the real woman in the portrait—was about to descend on them at any second vaulted Carrie into action. "In that case, I'll let you take me to dinner."

"I was hoping you'd say that." He didn't seem to hear the urgency in her voice and walked around the coffee table to take a seat on the sofa.

Not wanting to reveal her reason for why it was important that they leave right away, Carrie reached for a light jacket and draped it over her shoulders.

"Shall we go to Billy's?" she asked, edging toward the front door.

"How about a glass of wine first?"

"I took my last bottle to you the other night." Panic-stricken, she searched her mind for an excuse to leave. "I really am starved." She made a show of glancing at her wristwatch. "In fact, I think I forgot to eat lunch."

"Then let's take care of that right now." With the agility of a true sportsman, Shane got to his feet.

She sighed in relief. Now all they had to do was get away before Camille arrived. Later she would come up with some wild excuse to give her twin. No doubt Camille would be furious, and with just cause. But Carrie was confident she could come up with some plausible explanation later.

Shane helped her into his BMW, then walked around the front of the car. She smiled at him shyly as he joined her and snapped his seat belt into place.

"You look good enough to kiss."

Quickly, she looked out the side window. She desperately wanted him to kiss her—but not now. And not here, with Camille within moments of discovering them.

"Carrie..." He touched the side of her face.

Feigning enthusiasm, she patted her abdomen. "My stomach is about to go on strike for lack of nourishment."

"Are you saying you'd rather eat than make love?" He frowned slightly.

"Feed me and you'll see how grateful I can be." She was flirting outrageously, and she knew it.

"Is that a promise?"

"We'll see."

Shane chuckled as he started the car and pulled onto the road. They weren't more than a hundred yards from the beach house when Camille's convertible came into view. Pretending to have found a piece of fuzz on her pant leg, Carrie took extreme care in removing it, lowering her head. She prayed that her sister hadn't seen her.

By the time they reached the San Francisco waterfront, Carrie's mood had become buoyant. When Shane parked the car, he paused and his eyes smiled into hers. Even as he grinned, a slow frown formed.

"What's wrong?"

"Wrong?" He shook his head, clearing his thoughts. "Nothing's wrong. I was just thinking that I've never seen you glow like this. Your whole face has lit up. You're lovely."

Her fluttering lashes concealed her reaction. "No one has ever called me lovely before."

"I can't believe that."

"It's true."

He shifted in his seat, turning sideways. "You are, you know. Gorgeous."

"Oh, Shane, I wish I knew how to react when men pay me compliments." Her heart felt ready to burst. He'd given her a priceless gift for which she would always be grateful.

"You could kiss me," he suggested, only half-joking.

"Here?" Lights shone all around them, and the sound of moving traffic drifted from the crowded street.

Sensing her shyness, he lifted a lock of her hair and let the silky smoothness slide through his fingers. "There isn't anything I don't like about you," he admitted softly, his voice low and filled with wonder. "I like the way your smile lights up your whole face." He traced the corner of her eyes with his fingertip. His mouth followed his hand, gently kissing each side of her face. "Your eyes are so expressive. No one could ever doubt when you're angry." With a tenderness she wouldn't have associated with a man, Shane leaned forward and brushed his lips over hers. He paused, then kissed her a second time and then a third. With each kiss, her mouth welcomed his, parting a little more as the kiss gained in intensity.

He paused then, his mouth hovering a mere inch above hers. "Feel good?"

For a heartbeat she didn't move, didn't blink, didn't even breathe. Answering him with words was impossible, so she gently nodded. Each kiss had wrapped her in a blanket of warmth and security. She felt cherished and appreciated. Feminine and attractive. Seductress and seducer all in one.

"Oh, my sweet Carrie." His breath felt hot against her flushed cheeks. "All I wanted was to hold you, but kissing you leaves me yearning for more." He moved his mouth to her throat, where his lips caressed her warm flesh.

She heard him draw a deep breath, as though he needed to regain control of his emotions, then he continued, "This isn't the best place to be thinking what I'm thinking. Let's go have dinner."

Her hand against the back of his neck stopped him. "I'm not hungry."

"Minutes ago you were famished."

"That was before." She tangled her fingers in his thick hair. "I…like it when you kiss me."

"I like it, too. That's the problem. And if we don't stop now, it'll be a lot more than a few innocent kisses."

The stark reality of their vulnerability to the world hit her as a truck passed, blaring its horn. The unexpected blast of sound brought her up short. She blinked and broke free, pressing her hands over her face. She couldn't believe they'd been kissing in broad daylight, with half the city looking on.

Noting her look of astonishment, Shane swallowed his growing need to laugh. Carrie never ceased to surprise him. She was a businesswoman who supported herself with her art and at the same time possessed a paradoxically sophisticated innocence.

"Are you ready now?" He was looking in the direction of the seafood restaurant they'd agreed on.

"I think so."

"Good." He got out of the car and came around for her. "By the way…" he hedged, instinctively knowing how dull his invitation would be. "There's an award banquet coming up at the end of next week. Would you be interested in attending with me?" He tried to make light of it, but it was the high point of his career so far to receive the Frank Lloyd Wright Award. Wonderful for him, but deadly dull for anyone else.

"As a matter of fact, I read about the award you'll be receiving."

He looked almost boyish. "Then you'll go?"

"I'd consider it an honor."

"My great-aunt will be there, as well. You won't mind meeting her, will you?"

How could she? Already she was falling in love with Shane. It would be only right to sit with his family when he was presented with such a prestigious award. "I'll look forward to it."

"She's anxious to see you again."

His casual announcement shocked Carrie. *Again?*

"You made quite an impression on my Aunt Ashley."

Instantly the picture of the astute older woman from Elizabeth Brandon's cocktail party flitted into Carrie's memory. "Ashley Wallingford is your aunt?"

"Does that bother you?"

"No. I'm just surprised." She lightly shook her head. "I must have gone so long without food that my brain lacks the proper nutrients to think straight."

"Then I don't think we should delay any longer." Shane slipped his arm around her trim waist and led her toward Camille's favorite seafood restaurant.

"Where were you?" Camille demanded for the tenth time in as many minutes.

Carrie continued painting, doing her best to ignore her sister's anger. "Out to dinner. I'm sorry, Camille, really sorry."

"I thought you said he wanted to meet me?"

"He does—someday."

"Then why…?"

"It was a mistake. I've apologized, so can we please drop it."

Camille didn't look pleased. "I waited forty-five minutes for you." She crossed and uncrossed her arms, unable to disguise her indignation. "God only knows what could have happened to you. I had visions…" She left the rest unsaid.

Carrie felt terribly guilty. She set the brush aside and dropped her hand. "I realize it was a stupid thing to do."

"Where'd you go?" Camille asked.

"Billy's."

"Billy's! You know how I love the food there." Her voice was low and accusing, as though it should have been her and not Carrie who went. "I wouldn't see this mechanic...architect again, if I were you," she warned.

"Why not?"

"He sounds fickle to me. You don't need that."

Carrie felt obliged to defend Shane. "He isn't, not really. He thought... He did want to meet you, but..."

"But?"

"But he decided that it was really me he was interested in."

"How nice," Camille grumbled.

"You have Bob."

"You can have him," Camille tossed back flippantly.

"Who? Bob or Shane?"

"Don't be silly. Bob's mine. I could care less about your friend who doesn't seem to be able to make up his mind. He sounds like bad news to me."

A secret smile touched the edges of Carrie's mouth. If Camille only knew, her song would be a whole lot different.

Six

Carrie went out with Shane three nights in a row. Each time they got together she breathed in happiness and confidence and exhaled skepticism and uncertainty. Eventually the time would come when he would have to meet Camille, but she decided that there was no need to rush it. Nor did it matter that he believed she was the woman in the portrait.

Their first night out, he took her fishing in San Francisco Bay. Although neither one of them got a single bite, it didn't matter. The evening following the fishing expedition, they attended a concert in Golden Gate Park. Lying on a carpet of lush green grass, her head nestled in his lap, they listened to the sounds of Mozart. The next night they ate pizza on the beach and talked until well past midnight. Shane held and kissed her with a gentleness that never failed to stir her.

Between dates, Carrie painted his portrait. She'd been right to believe this one painting would be a challenge beyond any other. She captured his likeness as she saw him: proud, intelligent, virile, vigorous and overwhelmingly masculine. With every stroke of her brush she revealed her growing respect and love. Loving him had been inevitable. She'd known that from the first moment she'd peeked at him at the Dove Gallery the afternoon she'd delivered *No Competition*.

Camille complained about Carrie's absence early Thursday afternoon. "You're never home anymore. I hardly ever get to see you." Her bottom lip pushed out into a clever pout. It amazed Carrie how nothing seemed to mar her sister's good looks. Not even a frown.

"You're seeing me now," Carrie announced as she delivered a small plate of Oreo cookies and two glasses of iced tea to the coffee table. She sat back and reached for a cookie.

"It's not the same."

"What do you mean?" Camille often came to Carrie with problems, but as far as Carrie could remember, she'd always been there for her sister. "Is something wrong between you and Bob?"

"What could be wrong? Everything's dandy."

Carrie realized that her sister was doing a poor job of acting. Camille's words were meant to disarm her, but they failed. Carrie had watched her sister's relationship with Bob with interest. Her sister really did seem to be falling in love. For the first time in her life, Camille was on unsteady footing, unsure of herself. Carrie could almost witness the small war going on inside her twin.

"I don't know about you," Carrie admitted on the tail end of a drawn-out yawn, "but I'm exhausted." The tiredness wasn't faked. Staying out with Shane until all hours of the morning was beginning to demand its toll.

A long pause followed, and Carrie could feel her sister reassessing her. "I think Bob may want to cool things a bit," she admitted without looking at Carrie. "Naturally that choice is his. Either way is fine with me. There are plenty of other fish in the sea."

It sounded to Carrie as if Camille cared very much and was struggling valiantly to disguise her emotions. "What makes you think that?"

Carrie appeared distracted, fiddling with the long spoon in her glass of iced tea.

"He hasn't said anything really, but a woman senses these things."

"He must have said *something*." Idly Carrie reached for another cookie. Her bare foot was braced against the edge of the sofa.

"Not…really," Camille said, still not admitting anything.

"But you're convinced he wants to cool the relationship?" Carrie asked. She was well aware that Camille was leaving out all the necessary details. Even so, she had to admit that this latest development didn't sound good.

Camille paused to take a sip of tea. Carrie noted that her twin hadn't nibbled on a single cookie. Oreos had long been their favorite. Camille ignoring the treat was a sure sign of her distress. "He's still crazy about me, you know."

They all were. "I don't doubt it."

As though reading her sister's mind, Camille leaned forward and reached for an Oreo, holding it in front of her open mouth. "But maybe it's time I started going out with other men."

"Are you sure this is what you want?" She remembered how willing Camille had been to meet Shane and rethought her earlier opinion that Camille was falling in love at last. If she was truly in love with Bob, it wouldn't have mattered how many men showed an interest in her. Giving herself a hard mental shake, Carrie decided that she couldn't let herself be drawn too deeply into her sister's love life when keeping track of her own demanded so much energy.

Camille bit into the Oreo. "By the way, when am I going to meet this new…friend of yours?"

"Shane?" Carrie swallowed, immediately reluctant to reveal anything about him.

"If that's his name."

Camille stared straight through her. "You still answered my question."

"I…don't know when you'll meet." Her tone was raised and slightly defensive. "Soon."

"You're not hiding him from me, are you?"

"Don't be silly." Carrie lowered her foot to the carpet and brushed off imaginary cookie crumbs from her lap. "You're not making any sense. I've always introduced you to my male friends." *And lived to regret it,* her mind tossed back.

"This one seems important."

Carrie shrugged. "Maybe. I'm like you when it comes to Bob. Shane's all right." Talk about an understatement! But she didn't dare let her sister know how involved her heart was. Some days Carrie felt that her feelings for Shane must glow from every part of her. Even Elizabeth had commented how *healthy* she looked lately. But, thankfully, Camille was so wrapped up in her topsy-turvy relationship with Bob that she failed to notice.

"Well, you certainly seem to be seeing a lot of him."

"I'm doing his portrait." That made everything sound so much more innocent.

"But you're together far more than necessary."

Carrie got to her feet and lifted her glass from the tray. "Why all the interest?"

"No reason."

"Then let's drop it, okay?"

Camille gave her an odd look. "Okay."

Her sister lingered around the beach house for another twenty minutes, asking questions occasionally. Camille had never been any good at disguising her curiosity. Carrie knew the time was soon approaching when she would be forced to introduce her twin to Shane. Dreading the thought, she quickly forced it to the back of her mind.

When Camille decided to leave, Carrie walked her out to her convertible. She felt wretched. Since their mother's death, she'd been the strong twin. Lately she'd been behaving like a fool. Love must do that to people, she decided. To her way of thinking, it was imperative to keep Camille away from Shane for as long as possible. Unreasonable? Probably. Selfish? All right, she admitted it. Scared? Darn right.

Camille pulled onto the highway, and as Carrie watched her sister leave, her discontent grew. Their conversation repeated itself in her troubled mind. She'd made her relationship with Shane sound as boring as possible. Yet, in reality, she thought about him constantly. Not an hour passed that she didn't recall his quiet strength and his lazy, warm smile. She remembered the laughter they shared and how even small disagreements often became witty exchanges. They seemed to challenge each other's thoughts.

She loved his fathomless eyes which seemed to be able to look straight through her and know what she was thinking even before she voiced the thought.

Slowing, she moved back into the house. Just thinking about Shane made her giddy with love. Somewhere, somehow, a long time ago, she had done something right to deserve a man like Shane Reynolds. Now if she could only hold on to him once he met Camille.

On the night of the award banquet honoring Shane, Carrie smoothed a thick curl of auburn hair away from her face. Her eyeliner smeared, and she groaned, reaching for a tissue, wiping it away to start once more. Again a thick curl of hair hung over her left eye. Irritably, she brushed it aside to guide the tip of the eyeliner wand across the bottom of her lid. A sense of panic filled her as she glanced at her gold watch for the tenth time in as many minutes. Oh no, this was the most important night of Shane's life, and she was a half hour behind schedule.

Frantically waving her hand in front of her eye in an effort to dry her makeup, Carrie hobbled into her bedroom with one high heel on and the other lost somewhere under her bed...she hoped. Quickly she sorted through her closet for the lovely green dress she'd worn to Elizabeth's party. Shane had already seen her in it, but that couldn't be helped. The dress was the most flattering thing she owned, and she desperately wanted to make him proud tonight.

Of all the afternoons for Camille to show up unexpectedly, it would have to be this one all-important day. At three-thirty her twin had descended on her doorstep, eyes red and puffy from tears. Sniffling, Camille had announced that she and Bob had broken up and it was for the best and she really didn't care anyway. With that she'd promptly burst into huge sobs.

Carrie had no choice but to comfort her distraught sister. Camille needed her, and Carrie couldn't kick her out the door just because she had an important date. Still, she'd been running late ever since her twin had left.

Carefully laying the silk dress across the top of the bed, she prepared to slip it over her head. The dress was halfway down her torso when it stuck. No amount of maneuvering would get it to proceed farther. Blindly walking around the room and hopping up and down didn't seem to help. It took her several costly moments to realize that the rollers in her hair were causing the hang-up.

Muttering grimly, she pulled off the dress, in the process turning it inside out. Trotting back into the bathroom, she ripped the hot rollers from her hair. By chance she happened to catch her reflection in the bathroom mirror and noticed that not only had the eyeliner on her left eye smeared—again—her right eye was bare. The job had only been half completed.

The sound of the doorbell shot through her like an electrical current. "Please, don't let that be Shane," she pleaded heavenward, reaching for her old faded blue robe.

Naturally, it was him.

He stepped into the house looking so strikingly handsome in his tuxedo that just seeing him robbed her lungs of oxygen. She felt ready to burst with pride just looking at him. He was dashing. Stalwart. Devastating. She couldn't come up with another word to describe him. He was a man people would expect to see with a beautiful woman. A Camille. Not a Carrie.

Dragging air into her constricting lungs, she froze, springy curls hanging around her head.

Shane's stunned gaze collided with hers before dropping to the hastily donned terry cloth robe, left gaping open in the middle, revealing a peach colored teddy. His gaze rose to her stringy curls and quickly shot down to her feet. One foot was bare and the other was wearing a high-heeled sandal.

"Is it that time already?" she asked, her voice shaking as she strove for a light air.

"What happened?"

She tightened the sash of the robe. "I'm running a bit late."

"I can see that."

Tears of frustration burned for release at the backs of her eyes, but she refused to vent them. She'd wanted everything to be so perfect for Shane tonight.

"Listen, Shane, maybe it would be best if you went without me." She kept her hands at her sides, hoping to appear lukewarm about the whole banquet. "As you can see, I'm a long way from being ready."

He didn't so much as pause to consider her suggestion. "I want you there."

"Look at me!" she cried, holding out her arms. She was a mess, and all out of magic wands. Her fairy godmother had recently retired. She was Cinderella long after midnight, when the magic had worn off.

A crooked grin lifted one side of his sensuous mouth. "I will admit that I'd prefer it if you wore a dress, but that's up to you."

"Don't joke," she said. "This is too serious." She sniffled loudly. "There's no way I can go now. Would you please be serious?"

"I've never been more so in my life." He pointed toward her bedroom. "Go do what's necessary, and I'll phone

Aunt Ashley and tell her we're running a few minutes behind schedule."

"Shane! It's going to take me six months to get everything in order."

"Take as long as you want." He pulled out his cell phone and claimed the sofa, sitting indolently and crossing his long legs. He propped both elbows against the back, looking as though he had all the time in the world. "I'm not in any hurry. As it is, these dinners are always stuffy affairs."

"But you're the guest of honor!"

"It's fashionable to be late."

"Oh, stop." She sank onto the sofa beside him. "I can't go."

Up until this point, Shane had found the whole proceeding humorous. But the tears shimmering in Carrie's soft eyes clearly revealed how upset she was.

"Honey, look at me." His hand captured her chin and turned her face to him.

She resisted at first, not wanting him to see the tears that refused to be held at bay.

Lovingly, his finger traced the elegant curve of her jawline. "The reason this night is so important is because you can share it with me. I couldn't care less what you wear."

"I refuse to embarrass you."

"You could never do that." The distress written in her eyes tore at his heart. Over the past few weeks he'd witnessed a myriad of emotions in her expressive eyes. She'd teased him, riled him. She'd given him an impudent sideways glance and stolen his heart several times over. He was so hopelessly in love with her that he didn't think his life would ever be the same without her now. He loved her wit and her intelligence, and the way she could spar

with him over one issue before turning around and agreeing with him, and then stubbornly defy him over another.
But this time he was determined to win. She was going to
this awards banquet with him if he had to drag her every
step of the way.

"Shane, don't make me. Please."

Gently his hand smoothed away the tumbling curls
from her forehead. "I want you with me."

"But..."

"Please." He said the word so tenderly that Carrie had
no option.

Numbly she nodded and stood. She brushed the tears
from her eyes. "I'll do the best I can."

Demanding that her frantic heart be still, Carrie worked
with forced patience. Her eyeliner slid on smoothly and
dried without smearing. With the hot rollers out of her
hair, the dress glided over her head and whispered against
her creamy skin. She wished she had more of a tan, wished
her freckles would fade away, wished she was a ravish-
ing beauty who would make him proud. A puzzled smile
touched her lips as she reached for the brush to see what
she could do with her hair. Shane should have a beautiful
woman on his arm tonight. With everything that was in
her, she wanted to be that woman. But could she?

Thirty minutes later, she tentatively stepped into the
living room. Shane was idly leafing through a woman's
magazine.

"I think we can go now," she murmured, feeling a little
like a fish out of water. For better or worse, she'd done
everything she could.

Shane deposited the magazine on the coffee table and
glanced up. What he saw caused the breath to jam in his

throat. Surprise exploded through his entire body. It wasn't the red-haired innocent who was more comfortable in faded jeans than a dress who stood before him but a provocatively beautiful woman. He couldn't take his eyes from her. The transformation was little short of amazing. Her thick, luxuriant hair spilled over her shoulders. The silk clung to her slender hips and swayed gracefully as she walked toward him.

"Shane?"

"Good heavens, you're lovely." He'd forgotten. The night of Elizabeth Brandon's party, he'd been struck by how beautiful she was. But that night he'd seen her from across the room. Now she stood directly in front of him, and he felt as though he'd been hit with a hand grenade.

"Will I do?"

He could only nod.

"Well, don't you think we should be leaving? We're already thirty minutes late."

"Right." He fumbled in the silk-lined pocket of his trousers for the car keys. "I phoned Aunt Ashley. To save time, she insisted on taking a taxi and meeting us there."

"Remind me to thank her." Carrie shared a warm smile with him.

"I will." He offered her his elbow and turned to her. It took everything within him not to bend down and kiss her sweet mouth. What a surprise she was. A marvel. Just knowing her had enriched his life. Now all he needed to do was find some way to keep her at his side for a lifetime.

"Mrs. Wallingford?" Carrie's apologetic eyes met the older woman's. "I hope you'll forgive me for this delay. It was inexcusable."

The low conversational hum of the party surrounded them. Shane had gone for drinks after seeing Carrie and his great-aunt seated at the round, linen-covered table closest to the dais.

"Call me Ashley, my dear, and no apology is necessary. I've had days like that myself."

Carrie's gaze followed Shane as he progressed across the crowded room. He didn't seem to be able to go more than a foot or two before he was stopped and congratulated.

Good-naturedly, Shane paused to talk with his colleagues, but his own gaze kept drifting back to Carrie and his aunt. He could hardly take his eyes from her, half afraid someone would walk away with her. She was breathtaking in that dress. A siren the gods had sent to tempt him. Well, it had worked. He'd never wanted a woman more than he did Carrie. It astonished him that he'd only known her a month.

"You're in love with my nephew, aren't you?" Ashley Wallingford asked bluntly.

Carrie's gaze jerked away from Shane, and she was aware that her heart must be boldly shining from her eyes. "Pardon?"

Ashley chuckled. "It's obvious."

Carrie twisted the gold link handle of her purse around her index finger. "I'd hoped it wasn't."

"I don't think Shane has guessed," the older woman reassured her. "He tells me you've been painting his portrait."

"Yes." Her eyes fell to the beaded purse resting in her lap. "He's an excellent subject."

"I can well imagine. The boy possesses a great deal

of character. For a while there I didn't see much hope for him, though."

Carrie studied Shane's great-aunt, not sure she could believe what she was hearing. "Shane?"

"All he seemed to do was study. There wasn't any fun in his life." The older woman chuckled softly. "He took everything so seriously. Responsibility weighed heavily on him. He's the only boy, you realize. After his father died, Shane did what he could to hold the family together. His mother was a frail little thing."

From conversations with him, Carrie knew that Shane's father had died the year Shane was a high school junior. His mother had followed a year later. His whole world had been ripped out from under him within the space of two years.

"He came to live with me after that."

"He thinks the world of you." Carrie told her with pride.

Ashley Wallingford lightly shook her head. "It seems unfair that a boy should be faced with such unhappiness. His sisters are all married now." Abruptly changing the subject, she continued, "There was a girl he loved, you know."

Carrie didn't. "He...hasn't mentioned anyone."

"She was a pretty thing. They met in college. To be honest, I thought they'd marry. But whatever happened, he didn't tell me. He didn't date for a long time afterward. For a while I assumed he'd given up on women. Until now. It's time." The older woman's keen eyes assessed Carrie. "Her name was similar to your own. Connie, Candy...no, Camille. Her name was Camille."

Carrie thought her heart would pound right out of her chest. Could it have been her sister? Camille left a slew of battered hearts in her wake wherever she went. It was possible that Shane could be one. But...that didn't make sense. He wouldn't have purchased the portrait if it were Camille, would he?

"Carrie?" Ashley Wallingford placed her hand over Carrie's. "You're looking pale. Was I wrong to have said something?"

"No, of course not," she assured the kind woman hurriedly. "It would be highly unlikely that Shane could reach this age without ever falling in love. I can't be jealous of anyone who helped make him the man he is."

"You're very wise."

"Not really." Only wise enough to know that she couldn't look for problems in the past when the future already held so many.

"Here we are," Shane said as he set down a round of drinks. "This place is a madhouse."

"I noticed," Carrie said with a small laugh.

"Everything should be starting any minute." He took the chair between his aunt and Carrie, and reached for Carrie's hand. "I told you we'd arrive in plenty of time."

"The entire room sighed with relief the minute you walked in the door."

"You're exaggerating," he said.

"I'm very proud of you, Shane. Proud to know you, and even prouder to be with you tonight." Emotion made Carrie's voice husky. "When I think back to all the things I said to you when we first met..."

"You mean like, 'get lost'? You certainly kept me running to keep up with you. Literally."

Carrie felt her heart swell with laughter. "You're speaking as though the chase is over."

Shane tossed back his head and laughed heartily.

A tall, distinguished-looking man approached the podium, and the room grew quiet.

From its poor beginning, the evening took a turn for the better. The dinner was probably one of the best catered meals Carrie had ever eaten.

Following dinner, the award was presented and Shane rose to give his acceptance speech. Carrie barely heard a word of what he said. Instead her eyes scanned the huge audience that filled the ballroom. She saw for herself the admiration and respect on the faces of his peers. Even his aunt looked as proud as a peacock, her ample bosom seemingly puffed up as though to announce to the world that this man was her nephew. Poignant tears of happiness welled in the older woman's eyes. Carrie pretended not to notice as Ashley pressed a delicate linen handkerchief to the corner of her sharp blue eyes.

As he spoke, a series of cameras flashed and several television crews jockeyed for position in the already cramped room.

After the banquet, he was delayed by several people from the news media who stopped to ask him questions.

The entire time, he kept his arm securely around Carrie's shoulders. His great-aunt, meanwhile, found an old friend and the two of them stood head to head, deep in conversation.

Once the interviews were over, Shane insisted they have a nightcap in the cocktail lounge off the hotel lobby. A small three-piece band played music from the forties. The dance floor was crowded, and it was apparent that this was a popular night club spot.

"Shall we?" Shane questioned his aunt and Carrie.

"You know I've always been an admirer of Glen Miller," Ashley murmured.

"Carrie?"

"I'm game." The whole evening had been even more wonderful than she'd dared hope. As it was, she was far too keyed up to go home and sleep.

Shane found them a table and ordered their drinks when the cocktail waitress approached.

"Aunt Ashley, would you excuse us a moment?"

"Of course."

He slid back his chair and reached for Carrie's hand. "I never could resist the opportunity to dance."

Carrie hesitated only slightly. Admittedly, she wasn't exactly light on her feet. Dancing was another in a long list of items that Camille accomplished so much more proficiently than she did. "I hope you don't mind if I step on your toes."

"I don't."

"Brave soul," she said under her breath as she got to her feet.

"It wasn't my soul you warned me about," he returned, leading her onto the dance floor.

The music was a slow, sensuous ballad, and he reached for her, holding her lightly against him. She wound her arms around his neck, lifting her head to smile into his warm eyes.

"What was it you and my aunt were discussing so intently earlier?"

"She was letting me in on a few family secrets."

"Uh-oh. And just which of my many indiscretions did she tell you about?"

She bit the bullet and asked, "Does the name Camille mean anything to you?"

The laughter quickly faded from his eyes. "She was a long time ago. I was a kid."

"Should I be worried about her?"

"No way. I think every guy has to lose his heart once before he learns what it is to be a man."

"My only concern would be if she's still carrying it around with her."

"No." His laugh was dry. "She tossed it back at me."

She smoothed the silver strands of hair along the side of his ear. Her heart filled with tenderness for the man who had given his love so completely, only to lose it all. "Should I admit how pleased I am to know that?"

"I don't know, should you?" His hands pressed against the small of her back, bringing her intimately closer to him. His lips nuzzled her neck, pressing tiny kisses to the delicate slope of her throat.

Carrie melted against him, aware with every fiber of her being that she loved this man. His arms around her gave her the most secure feeling she'd ever known. Camille might flit from one relationship to another, but she herself was utterly content with one man—this man.

"Shane?" she murmured a moment later.

"Hmm?"

"The music's stopped." The other couples on the dance floor were gradually returning to their tables.

"No, it hasn't," he countered. "I can still hear it loud and clear." He reached for her hand and pressed it over his heart. "Listen to what being near you does to me."

"Oh, Shane." She pressed her forehead to his shoulder, loving him all the more. "I hear wonderful music too."

"You do?" His eyes drifted open to stare into hers.

"I have from the moment you told me my freckles were beautiful."

"Everything about you is exceptional. Freckles." He paused to kiss her nose. "Eyes." His lips brushed over the corner of her eye. "But your sweet mouth takes the prize."

Artfully, Carrie managed to avoid his searching lips. She didn't know how to take him in this mood. He was serious, and yet she could feel the laughter rumbling in his chest. She became painfully conscious that they were the only couple left on the floor. "Shane...people are looking at us."

"Let them look." His grip around her waist tightened.

"Your aunt..."

"Right," he murmured, dropping his arms, and led her back to the table.

She was just about to sit when an all-too-familiar voice spoke from behind her. "Carrie, imagine seeing you here."

Dread settled like a lead balloon in the pit of Carrie's stomach. Slowly, she turned to face her twin.

Seven

"Hello, Camille." Carrie felt as though her fragile world had suddenly been stricken by global disaster. The feeling was strangely melancholy. Pensive and sad. Her numb mind refused to function properly, to question what her sister was doing here dancing when only hours before she'd been weeping uncontrollably. It took several painful seconds for her to remember how quickly Camille always rebounded from a broken heart. Bob was apparently forgotten, and once again Camille was on the prowl.

"So this is the man you've been keeping all to yourself." Smiling demurely, Camille moved forward, placing her hand on the rounded curve of her satin-clad hip as she studied Shane. She started with his handsome silver head, her eye roving downward with obvious interest. "Now I understand why." Fleetingly, her gaze returned to Carrie. "Aren't you going to introduce us?"

"Yes…of course." She couldn't look at Shane, couldn't bear to see the admiration in his gaze as he recognized the face in the portrait. "Camille, this is Shane Reynolds and his great-aunt, Ashley Wallingford. Shane and Ashley, my twin sister, Camille."

"How do you do, Camille." Shane's voice revealed little of his thoughts. "Would you care to join us?"

So polite, so formal. Carrie didn't know him like this. "I'd love it."

Sure she would, Carrie thought. Why not? Camille had been without a man since early afternoon and there was little doubt in Carrie's mind that Shane appeared overwhelmingly attractive. He was just what the doctor ordered for a slightly wounded heart. Carrie had thought he'd looked devastating only hours before. She'd watched with a heart full of pride as he accepted a prestigious award. Later, feeling blissfully content, she'd danced in his arms. Now she was being forced to stand by and watch her sister steal him away.

Like the gentleman he was, he pulled out Carrie's chair, but before she could reclaim her seat, Camille took it. The action was so typical of her twin's behavior that Carrie had to swallow down an angry cry.

Without hesitating, Shane pulled an empty chair from another table and placed it next to his own. Carrie sat, her fists balled in her lap. She could feel Ashley studying her and did her utmost to appear poised.

"You must be the man who bought my portrait," Camille began, her voice animated. "I was thrilled to hear that you liked it so much."

"Yes, I did buy it." Shane placed his arm along the back of Carrie's chair, but she received little comfort from the action. Camille had only started to pour on the charm. Once she gained momentum, no man could resist her. Carrie didn't dare believe Shane would be the exception.

Leaning closer to him, Camille murmured, "I don't suppose Carrie's told you much about me."

"No, I can't say that she has."

Carrie refused to look in his direction.

"Carrie, dear," Ashley Wallingford whispered close to her ear. "Are you feeling all right?"

"I'm fine." Even her voice sounded strained and low. "Will you excuse me a moment?" she asked, rising. This could be the most important battle of her life, and she wanted to check her war paint.

"Naturally." Camille answered for the entire group. "That will give me a chance to talk to these wonderful people."

The words were enough to give Carrie second thoughts, but she couldn't very well sit down again and suddenly announce she wasn't going.

Refusing to run like a frightened rabbit, she crossed the room with her head held high, her steps measured and sure. She located the powder room without a problem and released a pent-up sigh the instant the door closed behind her. Her thoughts were in turmoil. She should have told Shane the truth about the portrait long before now. She admitted that much. But if he cared half as much about her as she hoped, it shouldn't matter. At least that was what she told herself while she repaired the damage to her makeup. Her reflection showed wide, apprehensive eyes and a mouth set with flint-hard resolve. For the first time in her life she was in love, and she would move heaven and earth not to lose Shane. Even if it meant fighting her own twin sister.

As Carrie approached the table, she noted that Ashley Wallingford was there alone. Carrie's heart plummeted with defeat as her troubled gaze scanned the dance floor. The self-confidence she'd worked so hard to instill in the powder room vanished when she saw Camille's arms draped around Shane's neck. They were making only a pretense of dancing.

As much as possible, she tried to ignore them, reclaiming her chair next to Shane's great-aunt.

"Do you feel better?" Ashley inquired.

"I did until a minute ago." Involuntarily, her gaze darted back to the dance floor.

"I wouldn't have guessed you two were twins."

"Not many do," Carrie admitted. "Believe me, our appearance isn't the only difference."

"I can see that."

The music ended, and Camille returned to the small table, her face flushed and happy. She was laughing at something Shane had said, but she sobered as she joined the other two women.

"I like your friend, Carrie," she admitted boldly, smiling up at Shane. "You should have introduced us weeks ago. Isn't that right, Shane?"

His response barely penetrated through the wave of pain that assaulted Carrie. Clearly he was already Camille's, and in record time. Her twin had once bragged that most men succumbed in less than a week, but this...! She had never seen Camille work so fast. She was out to capture Shane in one evening.

"I've always adored men with silver hair," Camille continued, sharing a secret smile with Shane.

"It's a family trait," Ashley Wallingford stated blandly. "All the Reynolds men gray prematurely."

"How interesting." Camille barely glanced in the older woman's direction as she spoke. "I still can't get over sweet Carrie dating such a handsome man."

"Thank you," Shane returned politely. "And I'd say that beauty runs in the family."

Camille's incredulous gaze flew to Carrie in disbelief. "Yes, yes, it does, although almost everyone believes I received more than my fair share in that department. But Carrie's so talented that no one seems to notice her...little flaws."

Carrie was stunned. She'd never seen Camille be so cruel before.

Shane was angry. Angry with this clinging twin of Carrie's who possessed all the sensitivity of a corn husk, and angry with Carrie. He loved her and had for weeks. It was a shock to learn she hadn't been completely honest with him, and a disappointment, as well. He wouldn't have believed she was capable of such deception. He wanted to shake her and in the same breath reassure her. He did neither.

"But then, you've seen lots of me already," Camille continued undaunted. "After all, you did buy my portrait."

"He thought it was me." Carrie realized the instant she opened her mouth that she never should have spoken.

"You've got to be kidding." Camille's features were frozen with disbelief. "Why, that's absurd. We look nothing alike."

"We *are* twins."

"But not *identical* twins," Camille countered.

"There are similarities," Shane inserted. "But now that I see the two of you together, I realize how wrong I was to have made the comparison. Carrie's nothing like the portrait."

Carrie paled, and a rock settled where her heart had once been. With virtually no effort, Camille had managed to wrap Shane around her little finger. She had hoped for better from him. But she wasn't about to give up. This was only round one, and she hadn't even put on her gloves yet. She loved this man, and she intended to fight for him. She'd allowed her sister to snatch other men from her grasp when she hadn't even been trying. This time Camille was going for broke, but Carrie wasn't going to sit back and watch, because in the past, no one had mattered as much as Shane.

"It's been a long tiring evening. It's time we got you home, Aunt Ashley," Shane said, pushing back his chair.

"I do feel a bit drained," the older woman responded. "But it's been most enjoyable. All of it."

Carrie stood, too. Her evening bag was clenched so tightly in her hand that her fingers had grown numb. "Yes, it has been great," she agreed. "Most of the time," she added under her breath.

If Camille could dish it out, she should learn to take it as well. Although from the look that Shane was giving her, Carrie realized she would have done well to keep her mouth shut. Too late she remembered the protective reaction Camille often evoked in men.

"I know you'll want to get in touch with me," Camille said, and smiled boldly up at Shane. "I'm sure Carrie will be happy to give you my number. Of course, you don't actually need to ask. I'm in the book."

"It was nice to meet you."

"A pleasure," Ashley Wallingford murmured.

Wordlessly, the three of them left the hotel. The valet brought Shane's vehicle around, and soon they were driving through the well-lit city streets. The silence inside the car was thicker than any fog San Francisco had ever seen. Shane drove to his aunt's home in Nob Hill first. He refused an invitation for them to go inside for another nightcap. Carrie couldn't have agreed more, though she enjoyed his Aunt Ashley and knew that this perceptive lady was well aware of Camille's game. Carrie only hoped that Shane was just as intuitive.

Shane saw his aunt safely to her door and returned a couple of minutes later.

"Well?" he said once he'd climbed back inside the car.

"Well what?"

"Aren't you going to explain?"

"About the portrait? No." She couldn't see confusing the issue at this late date. Everything seemed obvious. "However, if you're seeking an apology, you have it. I should have been honest about the painting. In light of what's happened this evening, my regrets have doubled."

He thought about her answer for a moment before asking, "You feel insecure next to your sister, don't you?"

"Insecure?" She tried to laugh off the truth. "Heavens, why should I?"

"You tell me."

He wouldn't be fooled easily, and she quickly abandoned her guise. "All right. I'm insecure. I have good reason. Camille's stolen away more men than I care to count. Most of them without even trying. I'd hoped..." She hesitated, unsure of the wisdom of revealing her feelings.

"You hoped what?"

"Simply that you'd show a lot more character than the others. Apparently I was wrong."

"Just what do you mean by that?"

"You're behaving like a besotted fool. Enthralled by her beauty. Drinking in her every word. Don't you think

I already know that I'm a poor second next to Camille?" She was lashing out now, angry. "You told me I was lovely, and I was fool enough to believe you."

"You are."

"But Camille's perfect, and I noticed you certainly didn't waste any time enjoying her abundant charms. I would have thought that—"

She wasn't allowed to finish. "Just what on earth do you mean by that?" Every second of this conversation was irritating him more. He wasn't particularly fond of Carrie's twin sister, and he didn't like the sound of these accusations, either.

"I saw the way the two of you were dancing. Good heavens, you looked like you were glued together. It was disgusting."

"Was it so disgusting when I was dancing with you?"

"No," she answered honestly. "But then, you've known me longer than thirty seconds." The last thing she wanted was to argue with him, but her outrage grew and grew until she had no choice but to vent it. "Maybe you've always yearned for a Camille. That was the name of your first love, after all. Well, now you've found her again, in a way. Not exactly her, but another woman who should fit the bill nicely."

"Would you kindly shut up!"

"No. Perhaps you think I'm jealous. All right, I'll admit it. I am. But I thought so much more of you than this. If it's Camille you want, then fine. You're welcome to her. It's lucky you met her when you did. She's between men at the moment, and you'll suffice nicely. But when you've had your fun, don't come back to me. I never have appreciated Camille's rejects."

Shane's eyes narrowed to points of steel. He looked as though he didn't trust himself to speak. Instead, he started the car and pulled onto the street. His hand compressed around the steering wheel so hard that his knuckles turned white.

They didn't exchange another word during the thirty minute drive to the beach house. With every mile, her contrition mounted. She regretted each impulsive word. Only a few minutes before she'd been determined to fight for Shane, and now she was practically throwing him into Camille's arms.

He didn't shut off the engine when he reached her house. His hands remained on the steering wheel, and he stared straight ahead.

Carrie grasped the door handle, prepared to depart. Shane was angry, angrier than she'd ever known him to be. She'd been hurt by his thoughtless actions, and in her pain, she'd lashed out at him. She drew a tortured breath.

"Good night, Shane," she murmured in a small, distracted voice. "I'm very sorry that I ruined your special night. But I want you to know how proud I am of your accomplishments, and I'm so pleased you took me to the ceremony with you. I'll... I'll always remember that." Sick with defeat, the taste of failure and disillusionment coating her mouth, she slipped from the car and hurried into the cottage.

For ten minutes Shane didn't move. His instincts told him to drive away and not look back. He was tired and emotionally drained. But the sound of Carrie's tormented voice echoed around the interior of the car to haunt him. He couldn't leave her like this. He loved her. But she'd lied to him, deceived him. He needed time to sort out his reaction to that.

Angrily, he shifted the car into Reverse and roared back onto the highway. They both needed space to bandage their injured pride.

Sitting inside the house, Carrie tensed when she heard Shane's car leave the driveway. For a few minutes she'd thought he might not go. But that hope died when he revved his engine and pulled away. She knew they both regretted their harsh words. If only he hadn't been so willing to dance with Camille—though what they'd been doing could hardly be termed dancing. Her anger mounted with the memory. Unable to contain it, she paced the narrow living room, more furious now than before.

If Shane wanted Camille, then she would let him go without a backward glance. She would wash her hands of him without remorse. Cast him aside and be grateful she'd learned what she had before she was completely in love with him.

It's too late, her heart taunted. *Far too late.*

Sleeping was impossible. Her mind spun out of control with questions demanding answers that she didn't have. The bedroom walls seemed to press in around her. An hour after going to bed, she abandoned the effort of even pretending she could sleep.

As she often did when her thoughts were too heavy to escape, she walked down to her private beach with a steaming mug of spiced tea.

Moonlight splashed against the sandy shore, its silver rays illuminating the night. There was a solace here that she could find nowhere else. For a long time she had thought the one great love of her life would be this beach.

Now she knew how wrong she'd been. The only love of her life was Shane Reynolds, and she couldn't let herself just hand him over to Camille. If she wasn't careful, she was going to lose him. It might be too late already.

Sitting on the thick bed of sand, she pulled her legs up against her chest and wrapped her arms around her knees. The night was cloudless, the stars brilliant, like rare glittering jewels on a background of dark velvet.

"I thought I'd find you here."

Startled, she gasped at the sound of the unexpected intruder. The moonlight revealed Shane standing beside her. He'd discarded his tie, and the top three buttons of his starched tuxedo shirt were unfastened, revealing curling silver chest hair.

"Do you mind if I join you?"

"Please do." Her heart was singing, and she had trouble finding her voice.

He lowered himself to the sand next to her. "You couldn't sleep?" He made the statement a question.

"No. You either?"

"I didn't try. I parked a couple of miles down the road and stopped to think."

At least they were speaking to each other, even if their conversation was more like that of polite strangers.

"I tried," she admitted.

"I would have thought you'd paint."

"No." Slowly she shook her head. "Contrary to popular myth, art demands too much concentration. According to Camille, I work twelve-hour days but only make as much money as if I worked a nine-to-five job." She instantly regretted mentioning her twin's name. Shane's expression tightened, and she glimpsed a bit of his frustrated anger.

Gathering her resolve, she gripped her arms more securely around her bent legs. "I honestly am sorry for not telling you about Camille."

"I wish you had, but having met your sister explains a great deal." His eyes captured hers, demanding that she return his gaze. "I suppose seeing her portrait in my office is why you bolted that day."

Her wry grin was lopsided. She nodded, all the more ashamed now. "Camille's always been the beauty in the family. You were right when you said—"

"I can't believe you." Hands buried deep in his pockets, he stood and paced the area in front of her, kicking up sand. "If you'd only told me."

"I know."

"All this time, I thought…"

"I said I was sorry." She felt worse than before he'd come. He had every reason to be angry. But he didn't understand what having a twin sister like Camille had meant in her life. However, now, when he was upset with her deception, wasn't the time to enlighten him. Given time, he would see the truth.

She tried again, wanting to set things right between them. "I didn't mean the things I said earlier."

"I know."

"I was…jealous when I saw you dancing with Camille." Carrie doubted he knew what it had cost her to admit that.

"She was the one who invited me to dance. A gentleman doesn't refuse a lady."

Somehow she had suspected that, but it seemed as if Shane could have found a way to extricate himself. He hadn't, and that seemed to prove that he wasn't as immune to Camille as he would like her to believe.

With her head drooping, she waited as the seconds ticked by. She yearned for Shane to take her in his arms and erase the hurts and anxieties of the evening. Finally she raised her eyes to him. "Shane," she whispered achingly, "would you please hold me?"

He reached down and brought her to her feet, then slipped an arm around her shoulders, catching the side of her chin with his index finger, lifting her mouth to receive his kiss.

Carrie twined her arms around his neck and pressed herself against him. She yearned to wipe the thought of Camille from his mind and replace it instead with the warmth of her love. With a smothered moan, she met his mouth in a hungry kiss, glorying in the feel of his lips over hers.

Her body molded to the hard contours of his chest. His hand pressed possessively against her back, sliding up and down her spine as he gathered her pliable form closer to his.

"Let's never fight again," she pleaded, breathlessly.

"Are you kidding? When we can make up like this?"

Without exactly knowing how it happened, she discovered that she was sitting on his lap, her arms draped around his neck. "I was hoping we could do this frequently without needing the incentive of an argument first."

"Agreed." His mouth brushed hers.

"Carrie," he whispered. "Don't you know that you're beautiful?"

Unbidden tears moistened the corners of her eyes. "I'm not." She wanted to believe him, but too many painful lessons over the years had proven otherwise. No one who saw her next to her twin could say she was beautiful. No one.

* * *

"Carrie." Camille slid into the opposite side of the booth where Carrie was waiting. "This is a surprise. It isn't every day that my sister calls and invites me to lunch."

Carrie's smile was forced. "We should do it more often."

"Especially if you're buying," Camille joked. She picked up the menu and scanned the contents, quickly making her choice. "I had a great time with Shane the other night."

"Oh?"

"He's so good-looking. Where'd you meet him?"

"He bought a painting."

"Of course," Camille giggled. "Mine."

With forced patience, Carrie set the menu aside. Her stomach was in turmoil, but she would order and make the pretense of eating. The time was long overdue for a heart-to-heart talk with her only sibling.

The waitress came and took their order. Not surprisingly, they both asked for the same thing: spinach salad with the dressing on the side. They were alike just as much as they were different, although they always seemed surprised when they discovered it.

The waitress left after filling their coffee cups.

"I always enjoy a good spinach salad," Carrie felt obligated to defend her choice.

"Me, too."

"It...seems that there's another thing we share."

"What's that?" Camille spread the linen napkin across her lap and glanced up expectantly.

"I'm going to be honest with you, Camille. I love Shane Reynolds."

Camille blinked but otherwise revealed none of her feelings. "Congratulations. Is he in love with you?"

"I think so."

"How nice."

"Camille, I didn't ask you to lunch to discuss the weather. I want to talk about Shane."

Her twin's look was only slightly smug. "I suppose you want to ask my advice."

"Yes." Carrie felt like shouting. "But first I want to give you some. For the first time in my life, I'm honestly in love. Please have the common courtesy to keep your hands off." So much for tact and subtlety. Any attempt at diplomacy was wiped out. All morning she had rehearsed what she wanted to say. Yet the minute Camille ordered the spinach salad, Carrie knew she was in trouble. They both liked the same things, and now apparently they also liked the same man. Already Carrie could see the long lonely years stretched out before her. The one romance of her life foiled by a spinach salad.

To make matters worse, she discovered that she was shaking from the inside out. She dared not reach for her coffee. The hot liquid would slosh over the edges of the cup.

"I can't help it if he's attracted to me," Camille countered.

"You practically threw yourself at him."

"Oh, honestly, Carrie, I wouldn't do that. He was your date."

"Do you notice the way you put that in past tense? The minute you appeared, anyone would have been hard pressed to say whose date he was. You were all over him on the dance floor."

Camille looked dumbfounded. "You're overreacting."

"No." Her hand closed around the fork as she dropped her gaze to the table top. "All right, maybe I am. But for the first time in my life, I'm head over heels in love, and I don't want to lose him."

"Carrie." Camille looked shocked. "Do you think I'm going to try to steal Shane away from you?"

"I don't know."

"I wouldn't. Honest. He's cute and everything, but if he's that important to you, then I'll forget him. He's history."

Carrie was so relieved that she felt like crying. "I'm sorry about you and Bob."

"Don't be. He was getting too serious." Quickly Camille changed the subject, lowering her eyes. "So you're in love. That's great."

"I think so. Shane hasn't said anything—yet. But I think he will. I mean...well, I feel that he loves me, too."

Camille laughed lightly. "It's such a surprise, you know."

"What is?"

"You falling in love first. I always thought it would be me." She raised her coffee cup and poised it in front of her mouth. "But this does create one problem."

"What's that?"

"Shane phoned me earlier and invited me to his house this evening. I suppose you'd prefer it if I didn't go now, wouldn't you?"

Eight

"Shane phoned you?" Carrie repeated numbly, trying to assimilate the news and its meaning.

"First thing this morning." Camille nodded for emphasis. "I was really surprised. Do you mind if I go?"

"He didn't say what it was about?"

"No."

Their salads arrived, and Camille smiled her appreciation to the young waitress who delivered their order. Then she reached for the dressing and ladled it over the top of the crisp spinach leaves topped with fried bacon and slivers of hard-boiled egg.

Carrie couldn't have taken a bite if her life depended on it. Her thoughts were in chaos. There could be no logical explanation for Shane contacting her sister. Especially knowing the way Carrie would react. If he'd been looking for a way to hurt her, then he'd gone straight for the jugular. He knew her feelings. That night on the beach, she'd bared her soul to him. She'd told him of her insecurities. He knew how she felt about Camille's beauty. And his response was to contact her twin. She'd been fooled. Shane Reynolds wasn't the man she'd thought him to be.

"Well, what should I do?" Camille asked between bites. "I don't want to upset you, but on the other hand, I don't want to be rude to Shane, either."

"Go." At Camille's dubious glance, Carrie added, "I mean it. There are no commitments between Shane and me. If he wants to see you, then fine. Great. Terrific. Make the most of it. I would."

"Carrie." Camille said her sister's name softly. "I've seen you use that tone of voice before, and it usually means trouble."

"What tone of voice?" Pride demanded that she reach for her fork and plow into her spinach salad with the gusto of a starving woman. On the inside she was dying, but a smile lit up her face so no one would ever know. Not her sister, and definitely not Shane.

Camille chatted easily over their lunch, discussing her job and a pale blue summer dress she'd picked up on sale. She commented that she would probably wear the new dress when she went to Shane's that evening. She paused, her cheeks turning a light shade of pink when she realized she was distressing her sister. Quickly, she changed the subject.

The rest of their lunch passed in silence. Camille finally spoke after the waitress brought the bill to the table. "Maybe it isn't such a good idea for me to visit Shane, after all."

"I think you should. Otherwise, you'll always wonder," Carrie told her. It was the most honest thing she'd said since her sister had dropped her little bomb. Somehow she'd managed to finish her lunch, but the effort had been Herculean, and her stomach would ache afterward.

They parted outside the restaurant. On the drive back

to the beach house, Carrie noted the thick clouds swollen with rain.

Once home, she moved directly into her studio and sat in front of the canvas that revealed Shane's serious eyes and strong facial features. She was proud of this portrait. She'd outdone herself. Her love had shone through every stroke of the brush as she'd painted the face of the man she cared so much for. Loved, yes. Trusted—she didn't know.

She checked her answering machine for messages before starting to work. The phone rang three times while she painted, but she didn't stop, preferring to work uninterrupted. She was close to being done with this portrait, and she felt it was imperative to finish it soon. Although it was her best work to date, she wished she'd never agreed to paint it. Having those lovingly familiar eyes follow her every time she moved was almost more than she could bear.

She worked straight through dinner and well into the evening, until the portrait was done. She was exhausted... mentally and physically. While she cleaned her brushes, she listened to her voice mail. "Carrie, it's Shane. I'm just calling to see if you're free for dinner tomorrow. If I don't hear back from you, I'll assume that we're on for seven. I'll pick you up."

She snorted. She wasn't about to call him. He could show up at seven, but she wouldn't be here. She could say one thing for him, he sure made the rounds—Camille tonight and her tomorrow. Between the two of them, his social calendar could be filled for the next six months.

The second message was from Camille. "Carrie, it's me. I've thought about it all afternoon. I'm not going to meet Shane. You love the guy. He's yours. I don't want to do anything to upset your hopes with him. You're my sister, and I'm not going to take him away."

The third message was Camille again. "Listen, don't be mad. Oh, this is Camille, you know I hate these stupid machines. I wish you'd answer the phone like everyone else. Anyway, I've changed my mind. I *am* going to meet Shane. I thought it over and well…there could be a very innocent motive behind this invitation."

"Sure," Carrie murmured under her breath.

"Anyway", Camille continued, "I'll call you first thing in the morning and let you know how everything went."

Yawning on her way into the bedroom, Carrie peeled her T-shirt over her head and reached for her Captain America pajamas. Heavens, she was tired. A glance at the clock radio on her nightstand told her it was 3:00 a.m. She stared at it in disbelief. She'd worked that long? Amazing. But the portrait was done, and that was what mattered. Her commitment to Shane was complete.

The phone rang early the next morning, disturbing her sleep, but Carrie was still exhausted and didn't bother to answer it.

She woke around ten. Bright sunshine crept into the bedroom, its golden light making further sleep impossible. Grumbling, she stumbled out of bed, yawning as she lazily walked into the kitchen.

Her dreams had been so delicious that she hated to get up and face the chill of reality. Her heart was heavy as she pressed the button on the answering machine.

"It's me. Sorry I'm calling so early, but I'm on my way to work and I wanted to tell you how everything went last night with Shane. You're right, Carrie, he really is a wonderful man. I think—"

Viciously, Carrie cut off the message mid-sentence. She didn't want to hear it. Not any of it.

Because she'd gotten off to a late start, the day was half gone by the time she showered and dressed. Lackadaisically, she scrambled a couple of eggs. She was about to pour those into the pan when a loud knock sounded against her front door.

For a moment she toyed with the idea of ignoring it and hoping whoever was there would simply go away. She wasn't in the mood to sign anyone's petition, nor did she feel up to entertaining company.

Another knock followed, and, groaning, she walked across the carpet intent on sending away whoever was there as quickly as possible.

"Yes," she said in her stiffest, most unfriendly voice. The man standing in front of her was vaguely familiar. She was sure she'd met him before, but she couldn't remember when or where. He looked terrible. His clothes were badly wrinkled, and he was also in definite need of a shave.

"I'm sorry to bother you. I probably shouldn't have come." He buried his hands in his pockets and glanced at the sky. "You don't even remember who I am, do you?"

"No," she admitted honestly.

"Bob Langston. We met briefly a couple of months ago."

"Oh, sure," Carrie said, and relaxed. "You're Camille's Bob."

"Not anymore, I'm afraid."

"Would you like to come in for a cup of coffee?"

"If you're sure it's no problem."

"I wouldn't have asked you in otherwise." She un-latched the screen door and held it open for him. "In fact, I was just about to fix some breakfast." Bob looked as if he could use a decent meal as well, she thought.

"Please don't let me stop you."

"If you don't mind, we can talk as I cook."

"Sure."

He followed her into the kitchen and took a chair. She poured a cup of coffee and brought it to him. "Cream? Sugar?"

"No, this is fine. Thanks."

He looked so dejected and unhappy that she felt sorry for him. She had met him months ago, but his appearance was drastically altered from that first meeting. Well, she probably didn't resemble a beauty queen this morning herself. If he was looking for someone to commiserate with, she was certainly available.

Without asking, she added a couple of extra eggs to the bowl and whipped them with a fork until the mixture was frothy. "I suppose you want to talk about Camille."

His shoulders sagged as his large hands cupped the cof-fee cup. "She broke it off. I still can't believe it."

"Did she give you any reason?" She'd been so teary that day, that Carrie never had gotten the story straight.

"Tons, but none of them made sense."

A small smile lifted one side of Carrie's mouth. "I know what you mean."

"To make matters worse, she's already seeing another man. Some rich guy on Nob Hill. She went to his house last night."

"You...followed her?" If he was about to reveal the details of Camille's meeting with Shane, then Carrie didn't want to hear about it.

Bob was decent enough to look ashamed of his actions. "Yes. That has to rank right up there with the most unforgivably stupid things I've ever done."

Carrie couldn't recall much of Camille's explanation about why she and Bob had split. From what she did remember, she thought Camille had said that Bob was the one who had decided to call things off.

"Maybe you'd better start at the beginning." She added a slice of butter to the pan and heated it up, and, when it had melted, she poured in the eggs.

"There's not really much to tell. We'd been seeing quite a bit of each other. I was beginning to think that maybe we should think about getting married. We even talked about it a couple of times. Then, out of the blue, Camille says that she feels we need to see less of each other. I was furious. Good grief, I was carrying around a diamond ring in my pocket, looking for a romantic minute to slip it on her finger, and she says something crazy like that. I came unglued."

"That's funny, because it seems to me that she said *you* called it off."

"Me?" Bob's face was a study in incredulity. "That's insane. I *love* Camille. I have for months, but she took me on a wild-goose chase almost from day one."

"And last night, when you followed her, she was going to Shane Reynolds's house. Shane and I have been seeing a lot of each other."

"So it was all innocent." His relief was evident.

As best she could, Carrie swallowed down her pain. "I… I don't know."

"What do you mean?"

With her back to him, she stirred the eggs. "I did a portrait of Camille a while back, and Shane bought it."

"I wish I'd known about it. I would have loved to own it." His voice was thick with regret. "I still want to marry her, you know. I've waited a long time to settle down. I just never believed that the woman I love would walk away from me like this." He shook his head as though to clear his thoughts. "Sorry. Go on."

"There's not much to tell. Shane bought the painting. He says he did it because…well, he thought it was me." She felt a little crazy to even suggest something like that now, when the differences between the two sisters were so prominent.

"I can understand that," Bob murmured. "You *are* sisters. The coloring's a bit different, but you two resemble each other quite a bit. In subtle ways."

"Really?" Even though Shane had told her the same thing, she had trouble believing it.

"Sure."

"Anyway, I… I never corrected his impression. Then we happened to bump into Camille, and he learned the truth."

"So now you assume that he's more interested in *her?*"

"What else can I think? He invited her over."

"And she went? Knowing how you feel about Shane?" His brown eyes hardened.

Carrie nodded. "I told her I didn't mind."

"That sister of yours needs to be taught a lesson."

"As far as I'm concerned, it's Shane who should learn a thing or two." The room filled with an electric silence.

She dished up the scrambled eggs and brought them to the table. But neither of them ate.

"Well, what are we going to do about it?" Bob asked.

"I don't know."

"Shane and Camille have no business being together."

"It could all be innocent," she felt obliged to say the words, although she could offer no plausible reason for why Shane would contact Camille. "Like us being together now." The instant the words left her mouth, an idea shot into her mind. "You know, I may be on to something here."

"What?" Bob leaned forward expectantly.

"We know *our* meeting is strictly innocent, but Shane and Camille don't."

"What's that got to do with anything?"

"They could see us together and wonder. In fact, it would probably do them both good."

"I couldn't agree with you more." Bob's eyes shone with a delighted twinkle. "I think I could come to like you as a sister-in-law," he said, reaching for his fork.

Breakfast took on more appeal for Carrie, as well. "Here's what I think we should do."

When Bob returned several hours later, he'd shaved, and his hair was neatly trimmed and combed back, revealing strong features. Carrie could understand why her sister had found him so attractive.

"You're sure Camille will be at Billy's?" Carrie asked.

"Positive." He chuckled under his breath. "You know, I'm almost looking forward to this."

"Me, too."

"Where to first?"

"Shane's. I want to deliver this portrait."

His gaze met hers. "I know the way."

He waited while she locked her front door. Then he carefully secured Shane's portrait in the trunk of his car and helped her into the front seat.

During the drive into the city, they talked and joked like old friends. She found it easy to talk with him, and was furious with her sister for having led such a good man down a rocky road.

As Bob had claimed, he was well acquainted with the route to Shane's home on Nob Hill.

When he pulled up in front, he turned to her. "Do you want me to go with you?"

"No, I'd prefer to do this on my own."

"Okay, but if you need me, just say the word."

"Don't worry, I will."

Once again, he helped her with the large canvas. As soon as she was at the door, he returned to the car, leaning against the bumper.

Smiling, Carrie rang the bell and waited.

Shane appeared almost immediately. "Carrie, this is a surprise."

Her answer was a wry grin. "I only have a minute. I wanted to drop off your portrait."

"I would have picked it up myself if I'd known you were finished."

She noted the way his gaze darted past her to Bob. He picked up the canvas and studied it, his approval showing in his eyes. "This is marvelous."

"Thank you."

"Come in," he offered, "I didn't mean to keep you standing out here."

"I can't, thanks. I've got a dinner date."

"I thought *we* were going out tonight?" Again his eyes shot past her to Bob, waiting in the driveway. "I assumed—"

"I'm sorry, Shane, but I'd already made plans."

By the way his mouth compressed into an angry line, she could tell that he was striving to keep his temper. His eyes raked over her, then back past her to Bob.

"I felt we had an understanding, Carrie."

"To be honest, so did I," she said, for the first time revealing some of her own pain. "I... I've never felt closer to anyone than to you that night on the beach."

"What happened to change that?"

"That's more a question for you than me." To her horror, her voice cracked. "Really," she said and took a step backward, "I've got to be going."

"Carrie." Shane set the portrait aside and followed her onto the steps. "I don't understand."

"I don't know how you can say that. You're the one who's confused things. It's you who can't seem to make up your mind which twin interests you."

Shane was certain Carrie was referring to his meeting with Camille and was slightly annoyed. If she would stop playing the rejected lover, this would soon be resolved. "Carrie, I can explain, if you'd like to listen."

Backing away from him, she winced at the blaze of love and tenderness that shone from his handsome features. She tried to ignore it and concentrate on the anguish she'd suffered. "I heard that Camille was here the other night—at your invitation."

"I said I could explain that."

"I shared my deepest insecurities with you, and they meant nothing." She knew that dredging up everything now was unfair, but she couldn't help herself. Camille was so pretty that she couldn't blame Shane if he fell in love with her. But he didn't have to do it so soon.

"Everything you shared with me that night meant a great deal. I—"

"I imagine that once you met Camille, you were able to distinguish the differences between us more readily. She really is a beauty, isn't she? And you must admit, there's no competition between the two of us."

"Carrie, I'm trying hard to control my temper, but you're making this difficult." He realized that she was deeply hurt, and he blamed himself. He'd assumed—wrongly, it seemed—that Camille would have explained everything by now.

As she backed down the stairs, Carrie caught sight of Bob checking his wristwatch. "I don't have the time to talk now."

"I'll contact you later, then," Shane said in that calm, reasonable tone she wanted to hate. "When you've had a chance to think things through."

"Fine." For her part, she had expected to feel triumph and satisfaction for pulling off this minor charade for Shane's benefit. Turning away from him, she felt neither.

Ever the gentleman, Bob opened her car door for her and closed it once she was safely inside. She noted that Shane remained at the top of the steps even after they'd pulled out into traffic. Long after they were out of the sight of his house, she could still feel his eyes searing straight through her.

"Well, how did it go?" Bob asked, his voice keen with curiosity. "Did you bring him up short and surprise him?"

"I'm sure I did."

"Are you sorry we're doing this?"

"I don't know," she told him truthfully. "But I have the feeling it's going to work far better on Camille than Shane."

"I hope so," he grumbled, then stopped abruptly. "I didn't mean that the way it sounded. I'm anxious to get this settled with Camille. Thirty isn't that far away, and I'd like to start a family."

"That may frighten her," Carrie commented, recalling her own discussion with her sister on the subject of children.

"I'm not talking about a baseball team here. Just one child, maybe two. Camille wouldn't even have to work outside the home if she didn't want to. I make a good living."

By the time Bob had finished talking about his future with Camille, they'd pulled into the parking lot of Billy's restaurant. "You're sure you want to go through with this?" Carrie asked one last time.

"Positive. I don't want her to think I've been crying in my soup since she's been gone." He paused and chuckled, "Actually, I was weeping in my scrambled eggs, as I recall."

Billy's was divided into two distinct areas. The restaurant took up a good portion of the floor space and overlooked San Francisco Bay with its large fleet of fishing boats. The cocktail lounge engaged top-class entertainment and included a small dance floor.

"She hasn't wasted any time, has she?" Bob whispered close to Carrie's ear, and nodded toward a table directly across the room from them. Almost instantly, she spotted her twin sister.

Now that she'd had the last few days to analyze Camille's behavior, she realized that it wasn't like her sister
to jump quite so freely from one relationship to another.
Camille was carefree, but not to this extent. Carrie more
easily understood her sister's behavior the night of the
awards dinner. Camille's search for happiness had been
almost desperate that evening, and Carrie herself had been
trapped in a web of insecurities or else she would have
noticed it earlier. If Camille danced with Shane and held
him too tight, it must have been because she was pretending to be in Bob's arms. If her smile was overly bright,
then it was to hide the pain of having lost Bob.

Tonight, Carrie noted that her twin was with another
man, seeking to erase the hurt.

"Bob, will you excuse me a minute?"

"Sure," he murmured, and she wondered if he'd even
heard her. He couldn't take his eyes from Camille. Those
two were so much in love that she couldn't allow this charade to continue. Nor was she willing to cause her only
sister any additional pain.

Without telling Bob what she was doing, she left
him standing by the reservation desk and wove her way
through the tables.

"Hello, Camille," she said, reaching her sister's side.
Camille's date stood and shook Carrie's hand, introducing himself. She didn't catch the name.

"This is my sister," Camille said stiffly in explanation.

"I'm pleased to meet you, Carrie. Would you care to
join us?"

"Carrie appears to have her own date." Camille's voice
dipped softly, but she couldn't disguise her surprise at seeing her sister with Bob.

"Could I talk to you a minute?" Carrie asked.

"Alone?" Camille's eyes met her date's.

"Why don't I go see what's keeping our drinks?" Mr. Nameless said, rising from his seat.

The moment the man was gone, Carrie took the empty chair. "How did it go with Shane last night?"

"Fine. What are you doing here with Bob?" Camille leaned forward slightly, then, straightening, folded her hands in her lap like a polite schoolgirl.

"He loves you."

Camille's short laugh bordered on hysterical. "You've got to be kidding. I tested him, and he failed. If he honestly loved me—"

"He had a diamond ring in his pocket the night you said you thought that you should cool things down a bit."

"A diamond?" Camille's gaze softened as it flew across the restaurant to Bob, who remained standing in the reception area. "He was going to ask me to marry him?" She jerked her head back to study Carrie as though searching for any signs of dishonesty. "Then why didn't he simply tell me so?"

"Pride. The same kind of pride that prevented me from listening to your telephone message this morning. But I want to know now. I need to know."

"Know what?"

"Why did Shane contact you?"

"Oh, he gave me the painting. He said that…you should probably ask him why." Ever so slightly, as though being pulled by a powerful magnet, Camille's eyes returned to Bob. "Are you sure Bob's telling you the truth?"

"I'm sure." Carrie felt like the world's biggest fool. Naturally Shane wouldn't want the portrait any longer. Not when he knew the painting was of Camille and not her. She'd forgotten that completely. But she didn't have time to deal with her own foolishness now. Camille's happiness was at stake. "Bob came to me today, completely miserable because he'd lost you. He loves you."

Carrie was convinced her sister hardly heard her. "I thought I'd cry when he agreed to my crazy scheme," Camille murmured. "Then he suggested we ought to make this cooling off period permanent, and I wanted to die. For weeks I'd been thinking about being a wife, and you know what?" She didn't wait for a response. "I know I'm going to like it. I've even given some thought to having children. I wouldn't mind being a mother if I could have Bob's babies."

"If you went to him, I think you two could solve this misunderstanding."

"Maybe?" The shield of pride was quickly erected.

"Maybe!" Carrie echoed. "Don't be a fool. The man you love is waiting on the other side of this room for you. If you've got so much pride that you can't go to him, then I think you deserve to lose him." Standing, she said, "I can't do anything more for either of you. In fact, I've got my own bridges to mend." She smiled gently at her sister. "It seems we've discovered love together. Let's not be stupid and throw away something so precious."

Camille's hand around her wrist stopped her. "You're going to Shane?"

"Yes, and not a minute too soon."

They exchanged encouraging looks. "Good luck."

"You too."

As Carrie sauntered past Bob, she winked and tilted

her head toward Camille. "Everything's settled. I know you'll be a fantastic brother-in-law."

Instantly Bob's countenance brightened, and his eyes softened with love as his gaze locked with Camille's. Carrie didn't stay to watch the lovers' reunion.

A taxi was idling outside the restaurant, and she climbed in the back seat and gave the driver Shane's address. She only hoped that she wasn't too late and that he was still home.

The taxi ride seemed to take an eternity. All the way there, she rehearsed what she planned to say. There was always the humorous approach. She would tell him that dating Bob was all a joke—which it was, in a way. Then there was the "pretend nothing was wrong" angle. But she didn't know how successful that would be. Honesty would work best, but admitting what a fool she'd been wouldn't be easy.

The cab stopped in front of Shane's house. The light shining from his living room window was encouraging. At least he was home. She had visions of working up her courage and coming this far only to have the house empty.

She paid the driver, and the sound of the cab driving away echoed in her ears as she stood outside Shane's front door.

A full five minutes passed before she had courage enough to ring the doorbell. Another minute came and went until he finally appeared.

Finding Carrie standing there was a shock. All evening he'd been planning what he wanted to say to her. It was apparent that they had a terrible communication problem.

"Hello, Shane." Her smile was falsely cheerful.

He looked past her. "Are you alone this time?" His tone was gruffer than he'd intended.

"Yes. I guess I should apologize for that. I saw Camille, and she explained about the painting...well, you know."

"Yes, I do know."

"May I come in?" This was even worse than she'd imagined.

"If you'd like." He stepped aside and followed her into his home, indicating that she should go to the sitting room on her right.

She saw that he'd already hung the portrait she'd delivered that evening. Seeing it caught her by surprise. "It looks nice."

"I'll tell the artist." His features softened perceptibly.

"I want to apologize for my atrocious behavior earlier."

"I figured as much," he said, and rubbed his hand along the back of his neck. "You're needlessly insecure."

"You certainly didn't do anything to help me overcome that," she flung back, angry with him for making this so difficult. "One day I bare my soul, and the next thing I know you're dating my sister."

"Meeting her is a far cry from dating her."

"Not in my book. Surely you must have known she'd tell me. What would it have cost you to let me know your plans?" She knew she sounded like an unreasonable shrew, but she was embarrassed and angry. She'd expected that this meeting wouldn't be easy, but she hadn't thought he would make it *this* unpleasant.

"I expected you to trust me."

"From past experience with men, I find that difficult."

"What do I have to do to help you to trust me?" He threw the words at her like a challenge.

His raised voice caused her to grimace. "Well, trust is something special. It's not like we're engaged or anything."

"Engaged? You mean we have to be married before I'm entitled to your trust? Is that what you mean?"

"I…"

"This sounds a lot like a marriage proposal. Is that what you're suggesting?"

At the end of her patience, Carrie tossed her hands in the air. "I don't know. No. Yes."

"Fine, then."

Nine

"Fine what?" Carrie stared at him blankly.

"We'll get married."

She was astonished that she'd answered such an outrageous question so flippantly. Stunned that Shane treated the subject so lightly. And furious with them both.

"You don't seem very happy," he commented, his look dark and intense.

Her face was flushed, her eyes wide with shock. "When?" The feeble voice hardly sounded like her own. Still, he'd handed her an answer to her insecurities, and she jumped on it.

"Three months."

This isn't right, her conscience accused. Marriage was sacred. A blending of hearts and souls. A linking of two lives, intertwining personalities, goals, ambitions, destinies. Good heavens, this wasn't some silly game. It was their very lives they were treating so offhandedly. She should never have agreed...but yet she loved Shane. It shouldn't matter that she'd been the one to offhandedly approach the subject. He'd agreed of his own free will.

He wanted this, too. Now wasn't the time to question his motives.

"Well?" he asked. "Does three months give you enough time?"

"Yes." Once again she replied in a low, shaking tone. She couldn't quite believe this was real. She felt as if she were intoxicated. Her head spun, and a queasy sensation attacked her stomach. "I'll be a good wife to you, Shane."

"What about children?"

"Children? I haven't given the subject much thought."

"Well, if we're going to be married it's something we need to discuss sooner or later."

"I agree."

"I know your art is important to you. I want you to realize that if we have children, you won't have to give up the things you love."

From his response, she realized that he thought she didn't want a family. "I love children and… I'll love having yours." The words stumbled over each other in her eagerness to assure him. "It's just that I'm having trouble accepting that all this is happening."

"Believe it."

"Do you feel we should start a family right away?"

Shane chuckled, bringing her into his arms. His look was faintly amused. "I think we'd better hold off until after the wedding, don't you?"

"All right." She hardly realized what she was agreeing to.

His arms tightened around her waist, bringing her even closer. "In case you didn't know it, I want you, Carrie Lockett. Desperately." His voice was as smooth as satin. Husky. Sexy. Romantic.

Carrie's eyes drifted closed. This was too good to be true. She was sure she would wake up any minute and discover it had all been a delicious dream. But when his warm mouth found hers, the sensations that flooded her were far too real to be imaginary. His touch left her dazed and uncoordinated. Shell-shocked. She was drunk with love!

"We should tell someone," he whispered against her neck, continuing to spread tiny, biting kisses down the slope of her throat.

"Who?"

"My great-aunt."

"And Elizabeth Brandon," Carrie suggested. After all, it was Elizabeth who was responsible for getting them together. "And Camille."

"Should I talk to your father?"

"Dad? Why?"

"Isn't that the way these things are usually done?"

"I...don't know." This wedding idea was becoming unexpectedly complicated. "I'm sure Dad would like to meet you."

"No doubt."

"He lives in Sacramento."

"Should we phone him?"

"He's probably already in bed. He goes to sleep early."

Shane growled close to her ear. "Don't mention the word bed to me. It's going to be difficult enough keeping my hands off you for the next three months."

"That long?" she murmured.

"All right, two months."

Suddenly Carrie worried about agreeing to such a long wait. Shane could change his mind. He could call everything off at the last minute. He could want out, and she wouldn't blame him.

"Could we hurry things along?" she murmured.

"Brilliant idea. When?"

"Two weeks!"

He chuckled. "What about tomorrow?"

For an instant she honestly considered it, until she realized he had to be teasing. "Two weeks."

"If you insist." He curved a hand around the back of her neck and leaned over to kiss her again. "You have the sweetest mouth."

"Thank you."

"You know what I think?" He spoke even as he kissed the corner of her lips.

"What?"

"If we're planning to go through with this in two weeks' time, we need to talk to our families soon."

"Right."

"I'm going to phone Aunt Ashley." The conversation was momentarily interrupted by a lengthy kiss.

"Now?" Carrie asked once she'd surfaced.

"Right now." He reached behind her for the phone on his desk, punching out the number as he continued kissing her.

She could hear the ringing as the call went through. When his aunt answered, he abruptly broke off the kiss, but he continued to hold Carrie in his arms, his eyes smiling into hers.

"It's Shane," he said into the receiver.

Faintly, Carrie could hear his aunt's voice coming over the wire. "Is something wrong?"

"Something's very right. Carrie and I are going to be married."

"That's wonderful news. When?"

Carrie grinned at the delight the older woman's voice revealed. "Soon. Two weeks, I think."

"Two weeks! Why, that's impossible," Ashley continued. "Your sisters will never forgive you if they aren't invited."

"Of course they're invited," Shane countered.

"But they can't drop everything on such short notice. Caroline's youngest is only a year old."

"Yes, yes, I know," Shane grumbled.

"Tell her we'll schedule the wedding later if it's more convenient," Carrie whispered in his ear, distracting him.

"Aunt Ash, hold on. Carrie's saying something." He covered the telephone receiver with his hand and kissed her on the bridge of her nose. "Have I told you that I love your freckles?"

She felt the heat seep into her cheeks and knew that those freckles would soon switch to their glowing stage.

"According to Aunt Ashley, two weeks is out of the question. We would offend half my family if we don't give them proper notice. It looks like we may be in for a longer wait than we'd originally planned."

"How long?"

"It might be best if we go back to what we first thought— three months."

"That'll be fine." If Shane called off the wedding between then and now, so be it.

He uncovered the mouthpiece and placed the receiver back against his ear. "How's three months?"

"Much better. Can I talk to Carrie?"

Shane handed her the phone. "My aunt wants to talk to you."

She accepted the phone and paused to clear her throat. "Hello."

"Carrie, dear," Ashley Wallingford said warmly. "This is fantastic news. Welcome to the family."

"Thank you. I'm very pleased." Shane was making coherent conversation nearly impossible. While she was speaking, he was kissing the side of her neck, his lips nibbling upward toward her earlobe. Delicious shivers shot up and down her spine. She thought her knees would give out from under her.

"I realize you and Shane have a lot to discuss. We can talk tomorrow. I just wanted you to know that I'm willing to help any way I can."

"Thank you. I'll remember that." Shane had located the tiny pearl buttons to her blouse and begun unfastening them one by one.

"We'll talk soon, then."

"Soon," Carrie repeated.

"Good night, dear, and tell that rascal of a nephew of mine that I'm exceptionally pleased with his choice."

"I will."

The line disconnected. Carrie gasped for breath as they kissed again.

"I love you," she murmured, tightening her arms around his neck. "I love you so much." She couldn't get enough of him. Couldn't press herself close enough to satisfy the longings of her heart.

"I'd better take you home while I've still got the strength."

As they drove to the beach house, he hummed along with the music playing on the radio. His mood was glorious. Hers was weighted down, wondering if they were basing the most important decision of their lives on over-excited hormones.

Once they reached the cottage, Shane leaned over and kissed her lightly. He kept the car engine running while he walked her to the front door. When she asked him why, he explained, "That's my insurance." His kiss was reverent. "This way I won't be tempted to haul you into that house and cart you off to the bedroom."

He lowered his head, bringing his face inches from hers, and gave her a feather-light kiss. "Night, love."

"Night." He straightened and took a step back.

Long after he had left, she stood on the porch. Her mind was fuzzy. She didn't know what to do. They'd treated the idea of marriage so flippantly, so casually, as if to prove something to each other. This wasn't a healthy scenario.

She would sleep on it, she decided, holding back a yawn. In the morning everything would be clear and she would know what she should do.

Painting was impossible. All morning Carrie tried to occupy her mind with her art, but to no avail. At noon, she gave up the effort. As she cleaned her equipment, she sorted through her thoughts. She felt the need to talk to someone. She toyed with the idea of contacting Elizabeth Brandon, but decided against it. The one person who readily came to mind was Camille, but she wasn't entirely convinced she could trust her twin sister. Sad, but true. They were so different. Camille was water, shimmering and changing. Carrie was the earth, stable and secure. Together, they made mud.

Undecided, she changed from her faded jeans into a pale pink dress. If she was going to talk to anyone, it would have to be Camille. They might not be alike, but Camille always came to Carrie with her worries and anxieties, and now the roles were going to be reversed.

After a brief telephone conversation to verify when and where to meet, Carrie left the house, determined to tell her sister everything. She would start at the beginning, when Elizabeth Brandon mentioned Shane, and explain how attracted she'd been to him that first day. She would be forthright, she decided. She would tell Camille how she'd fought the attraction, knowing that if Shane bought *No Competition* he would probably be drawn more to Camille than to her. But those problems had been solved, others had cropped up faster than she could handle. Now she was engaged to the man, yet she wasn't entirely convinced he loved her.

Camille was waiting for her in a seafood restaurant close to her office.

"Hi. You look awful."

Carrie took the chair across from her sister. Camille had decided to disperse with tact. "Thanks, I needed that."

Camille seemed genuinely contrite. "I didn't mean anything."

Carrie waved the apology aside with a flick of her wrist. "Don't worry about it. How did things go with Bob last night?"

Camille's happy smile said it all. "Wonderful. We've decided to get married." She held out her left hand so Carrie could admire the beautiful solitaire diamond.

"It's lovely. Congratulations."

"What about you and Shane?"

"We're engaged, too." She didn't need to be told that

she revealed none of the happiness that was so obvious in her sister.

"Congratulations," Camille said, but her eyes narrowed and her perfectly shaped mouth thinned slightly.

Knowing her sister, Carrie recognized the expression as one of doubt. "What's wrong?" She decided to meet the question head on.

Camille shook her head. "You don't look pleased."

The waitress came. Carrie hadn't bothered to glance at the menu. There was no reason to. Her sister would probably order what she would have chosen anyway. Camille gave the waitress her selection of French onion soup and a fresh green salad, and Carrie seconded it.

"We've been doing that a lot lately. Have you noticed?"

Carrie nodded.

"I can't understand it," Camille continued. A tiny frown marred the smooth perfection of her face. "We fought like cats and dogs the whole time we were growing up. Sometimes you were so perfect that I thought I hated you."

"Hated *me?* For being *perfect?*" It was so close to her own feelings that Carrie was too stunned to respond. For years she'd felt totally lacking compared to Camille. Her sister was the angelic ideal. "*I* wasn't the gorgeous one." She revealed only a hint of the bitterness she'd held on to all these years.

Slowly Camille shook her head, her lovely dark curls brushing the tops of her shoulders. "I can't believe I'm hearing this. I had to play up what little beauty I had to make up for the fact that you were 'the gifted one.' And you were more than just smart. You had this incredible artistic talent. All my life, the only thing I had to compensate with was my face."

Carrie remained speechless for a full minute. "You were jealous because I did well in school?"

"Uncontrollably."

"But all my life I've envied you your beauty."

"Good looks are superficial. No one knows that better than me. I'm a beauty consultant, remember?"

A loud clap of thunder or a surging bolt of lightning couldn't have had more impact. Her gorgeous twin sister had been jealous of her! Carrie was floored.

"All these years, we've been competing against each other?"

From her startled look, this discovery had jarred Camille, as well. "It seems so."

"I can't believe this. Camille, you're warm, loving, generous and a lot of fun."

"I agree," her twin concurred with no lack of modesty. "But I didn't make the honor roll once."

"No, you were the homecoming queen when I had to scrounge the bottom of the barrel for a date." Carrie swallowed a laugh. Two days before the big dance, she'd been asked by the least popular boy in the entire school. Camille had been dating the quarterback of the football team.

"Didn't you go to the prom with Tom Schrieder?"

"Right. His athletic prowess was on the golf course as I recall." In other words, he wasn't a muscle-bound, popular quarterback.

They broke into simultaneous giggles. Carrie felt like crying and laughing at the same time. It was as if she'd been informed, out of the blue, that she had another twin sister. As if they'd been separated at birth and hadn't been given the opportunity to meet each other until now, as adults.

"I think you're wonderful, Carrie."

"I feel the same way about you."

"Then why are we always at odds with each other?"

Carrie shook her head with the wonder of it. They'd wasted a lot of years. "Not anymore," she vowed. "There'll be no competition between us. Agreed?"

"Agreed." Camille took a long drink of her iced tea. "Now that we're both engaged, what do you think of a double wedding?"

"And let you steal the show?" Carrie joked, but the humor was as artificial as her smile. Her lips trembled with the effort. Soon she was biting the corner of her mouth to control her unhappiness.

"Carrie, what is it?" Her sister took her hand and squeezed her fingers. "I don't think I've ever seen you cry."

"I do, you know. A lot lately."

"But why?"

"Shane."

"You're engaged. You love him, don't you?"

"Yes," she admitted forcefully. "I love him so much I could die from it."

"I don't believe you need to go to those lengths to prove it."

"Don't joke, Camille. This is serious."

"Sorry." She was instantly contrite. "Now tell me, what's wrong?"

Carrie bowed her head, her fingers shredding her paper napkin into a hundred infinitesimal strips. "I can't. It's too embarrassing."

"I'm your sister!"

It wasn't fair that their newfound understanding had

to be tested so quickly. "We may be engaged, but I don't know if he loves me. In fact, I proposed first."

"So? Shane didn't argue, did he?" Camille didn't seem to notice anything out of the ordinary. "He couldn't have been opposed to the idea."

"I don't really think he is, but we'd be getting married for all the wrong reasons."

"You love him. What's wrong with that?"

Spilling out the story of her various insecurities wouldn't do either of them any good, so Carrie just kept quiet and refused to meet her sister's eyes.

"If you have doubts," Camille suggested softly, "then talk to Shane. He loves you."

Carrie thought it best to avoid the subject of Shane for the moment. "Have you and Bob set a date for your wedding?"

"He's seeing what he can do to arrange things quickly. I want you to be my maid of honor."

"I'd love that. And when I get married, you can return the favor." Although at the moment she wasn't sure of her future. "However, I don't doubt that you'll get more attention than the bride."

"You could always carry a small, tasteful watercolor instead of the traditional bridal bouquet," Camille teased. "Once people saw how talented you are, they wouldn't bother to look at me."

They both laughed, feeling free to tease each other for the first time.

From the restaurant, Camille returned to work and Carrie did some shopping, killing time, avoiding the inevitable confrontation with Shane.

She'd hoped to sort out her thoughts while the afternoon passed, but she didn't have any success.

Close to Shane's quitting time, she called his office from her cell phone as she stood on the sidewalk just outside his building. His secretary put her directly through.

"Carrie, love." Shane's greeting was happy, animated. "Where are you?"

"Downstairs."

"Great. Come up. Now that we're engaged, there are several people you should meet."

She hesitated, not knowing a gracious way to turn down the invitation. "Can I do it another time? I look a mess."

"If you like."

"Have you got a moment to talk?" She braced her hand against her forehead and closed her eyes.

"All the time in the world. Hang on and I'll be right down."

"No—no thanks. I want to talk now."

"Over the phone?"

"It'll be easier this way."

"Carrie, what's wrong?" His voice grew heavy and serious.

"Nothing…everything."

"Where are you? I'll be right there."

"No!" she cried. "Please don't do that. I'm not up to seeing you."

"Why not?"

"I told you, I look dreadful."

"Not possible," he said, his tone sincere.

"I must be crazy. I'm head over heels in love with you."

"There's nothing wrong with that, especially since I feel the same way about you."

"Oh, Shane, do you really?"

He didn't know what was going on in her mind, but he didn't want to leave any room for doubt. Not about this. "I adore you."

"That's going to make what I have to say all the more difficult."

He didn't like the sound of that. Not one bit. This woman was unlike anyone he'd ever known. He supposed that was part of what had drawn him to her so fiercely.

"I've been thinking about what happened last night."

"Or what didn't happen?" he teased lovingly. Half the night had been gone before he slept. Leaving her alone at her door had been unbelievably difficult. Now he wondered if he'd done the right thing.

"Shane, listen to me, because what I have to say is important."

"What is it, love?"

She didn't pause, blurting out the words in one giant breath before she lost her nerve. "I think it's best if we call off the wedding."

Ten

"What?" Shane exploded. "Where are you? I'm coming down right now, and we're going to talk about this."

"Shane, listen to me. I apologize. I really do, but I can't go through with it. Goodbye."

"Goodbye! What do you mean by that?"

His question was angrily hurled at her. Carrie heard it loud and clear as she clicked her cell shut. Her whole body was trembling, but she couldn't see how shouting at each other over the phone—or in person, for that matter—would do either of them any good. There didn't seem any point in explaining her reasoning. She couldn't, not when it remained unclear in her own mind. She needed time to think.

The five o'clock throng of people heading home clogged the sidewalk as Carrie walked away from Shane's office building. She made a sharp left, and wove her way in and out of the mass of homeward-bound humanity.

She paused at the busy intersection closest to his office to wait for the traffic signal to change. Shane had claimed to love her. That was a perk she hadn't anticipated, but then, any man who had put up with her craziness as he had these last weeks, must hold strong feelings for her.

The light changed, and she stepped off the curb. It was then that she heard someone shout her name. She glanced over her shoulder to see that Shane had somehow managed to catch up with her.

She moved back onto the sidewalk to wait for him. The last thing she wanted was a chase scene reminiscent of some melodramatic movie.

By the time he reached her, he was panting, his shoulders heaving with exertion.

His expression was stern. He was furious, angrier than he could remember being in his life. He couldn't understand this woman. While he regained his breath, he leaned against a lamppost and shook his head. "Come on," he grumbled. "Let's talk."

"I don't think—"

"For once, Carrie, don't argue with me. I'm not in the mood for it."

He didn't say a word as they trudged the short distance back to his building. The strained silence in the elevator was even worse, if that was possible.

The door to his office was wide open in testimony to the urgency of his rush to locate her.

"Sit," he demanded, pointing to a chair.

She did as he asked, but only because she didn't have the energy to defy him.

"All right, talk," he said once he was seated across from her. His desk was the only thing that separated them.

"What do you want me to say?"

"What made you come up with that lunatic decision about calling off the wedding?"

"Insulting me isn't going to help, Shane."

"All right, I apologize. I simply want to know what led to this most recent announcement." He wasn't going to let Carrie walk out. He loved her, needed her, and in the same instant he wanted to shout at the top of his lungs at her for the anxiety she'd caused him. When he was done with that, he wanted to hold her for an eternity. If she was mixed up, he was doubly so.

Meanwhile she just stared at the items on the top of his desk. Anything that prevented her from looking at him fascinated her.

"Just explain what happened between last night and this afternoon that caused you to change your mind."

"I... I don't know where to start."

"Might I suggest the beginning?" he offered somewhat flippantly.

She shot to her feet. "This is exactly what I mean. This...casualness. We were making the most important decision of our lives based on a stupid joke."

As he'd feared, he couldn't follow her reasoning. "What do you mean?"

"You...you asked me what you could do to help me to trust you, and I blurted out what seemed like a marriage proposal."

"Didn't you mean it?"

"I... I'm not sure. Yes. But that shouldn't matter."

"I agreed, didn't I?"

She was angry all over again. "That's the crux of the problem. It wasn't right."

"Why not?"

"Because you were treating the whole thing like some big joke and it isn't. Marriage is precious."

"I realize that." He was beginning to get the gist of her problem. "And I love you. I very seriously and not jokingly love you."

"Well, thank you very much. I love you back," she said as she got up and whirled around, presenting him with a clear view of her back as she strode over to look out the window at the city below. She folded her arms around her waist and swallowed down the hysteria that threatened to choke her. If the subject weren't so serious, she could almost have laughed at what was happening. They might love each other, but a sea of murky water still lay between them.

"Okay, now that we've got that matter cleared up, let's get married."

"No!"

He couldn't believe he'd heard her correctly. "*Now* what's the problem?"

"First you were being flippant. Now you're angry."

"I don't understand you."

"Are you sure you want to be married to a woman you don't understand?"

"Carrie, please..."

"Are you raising your voice at me?"

Shane snapped his mouth shut and clenched his teeth so tightly, his jaw ached. She was so serious that he was momentarily speechless. He forced himself to be calm, relaxing the tense muscles of his shoulders. Standing, he joined her at the huge window that overlooked the downtown area. But he had no time for the skyscrapers that brushed the edges of the heavens.

"I remember the first time I saw your art," he said, his sober tone rounding off the sharp edges of his anger. "It was a seascape. The sky was the pewter color of pre-dawn, and the sun was just breaking over the horizon, golden and filled with the promise of a new day. I stared at that painting for ten minutes. I couldn't take my eyes off it. Something about it touched me as no painting ever has."

Carrie knew exactly which seascape he was referring to. She'd worked on it for weeks, searching for the proper way to express her feelings. It had been a period of disillusionment in her life. Her father had moved to Sacramento. She and her sister had been drifting apart, and she had felt like a loner, a recluse. As an artist, she didn't work with others, and her contact with the outside world had seemed to be narrowing as she found fewer and fewer interests to share with family and friends.

"I knew then," he continued, "that the person who'd painted that seascape had reached deep within herself and triumphed over disenchantment." His smile was a bit crooked. "When I learned that the painting had already been sold, I was disappointed. That was when I asked Elizabeth to call me if something else came in by the same artist."

"I remember the painting," she murmured, not knowing what else to say.

"When Elizabeth contacted me to say there was another seascape of yours available, I told her to consider it sold without even seeing it."

"You did?"

His eyes were unnaturally bright as he nodded sharply. "I wasn't disappointed."

She bowed her head.

"I think I may even have started loving you way back

then. A whole year before I followed you on Fisherman's Wharf."

"Shane…"

"No, let me finish. I couldn't understand why you were such a prickly thing. After buying all those paintings of yours, I suppose I felt you owed me something. After all, I thought I knew you so well. It was a shock to have you behave so differently from the way I expected. I don't think I fully understood you until I met Camille."

"We talked today… Camille and I. Really talked. I'm hoping a lot of our problems are over. We aren't competing against each other anymore. There'll be no competition between us again."

"I'm glad."

A short silence followed.

"I guess what I'm trying to say," Shane said, speaking first, "is that I've had an unfair advantage in this relationship. I love you, Carrie. I've loved you for months. It's true that I've probably gone about everything the wrong way, but I was impatient. I rushed you when I shouldn't have. It isn't any wonder you're filled with questions. I nearly blew this whole thing."

"You didn't do anything wrong," she said softly. "I did."

Tenderly he brushed the hair from her temple, then paused, dropping his hand as though he didn't trust himself to touch her. "When you said yes to getting married, I thought, great, wonderful. It was what I'd hoped would happen all along."

"I was outraged with myself for treating the subject so lightly. Then I was furious with you for answering me."

"If you didn't honestly mean it, why didn't you say something at the time?"

Now it was her turn to swallow her pride. "I *did* mean it. I wanted to be your wife so badly that I was afraid if I didn't follow through with the marriage now, I might not get another chance."

"Oh, my sweet, confused Carrie."

"And then you started talking about children, and I wanted to have your babies so much I was willing to overlook just about anything. I think any children we have will be marvelous."

"Yet you were willing to walk away from all this happiness when it's here waiting for you?"

"I couldn't help it!" she cried. "What else was I to think? I couldn't really believe you loved me. All these weeks I've walked around in fear that once you met Camille, I would be history. You did buy her portrait. And worse, every time you looked at her, it was like you were worshiping some love goddess."

"I thought the portrait was you."

"I know. But that only made things worse."

"How?" Once again, he had problems following her reasoning.

"Because it only made me feel more guilty about deceiving you." She recalled the relief mixed with guilt that she'd suffered during those frantic days before he found out about Camille.

He turned sideways then, fitting his hands on her shoulders. His long fingers closed over her upper arms. "I've made my own mistakes. Ones I want to undo right now. To simply say 'I love you' doesn't cover what I feel for you, Carrie Lockett. I love everything about you, from that turned-up freckled nose to that yard-wide streak of stubbornness."

The words washed over her like a cooling rain in the driest part of summer. "I think you must honestly love me to put up with me. And I do trust you—with all my heart."

"You think we should consider marriage, then?"

"Yes."

"But I'll do the asking this time." His hands dropped from her arms to circle her waist. His eyes grew warm and vital. "I've been waiting a lifetime for you, Carrie. Would you do me the very great honor of being my wife?"

She blinked back the tears that sprang readily to the surface and burned for release. Words were impossible.

"Well?" he prompted.

Her response was to nod wildly and sniffle.

"That better mean yes."

"It does. Now will you stop being such a gentleman and kiss me?"

Shane was only too happy to comply.

* * * * *

ALL THINGS CONSIDERED

One

Lanni Matthiessen dropped a quarter into the machine and waited for the thick black coffee to pour into the wax-coated cup. It would be another late night at John L. Benton Realty and the coffee would have to hold her until she had time to squeeze in dinner. A frown compressed her brow. This would be the third evening this week that she wouldn't be eating with Jenny, her four-year-old daughter.

Carrying the steaming cup of coffee back to her desk, she sat and reached for her phone, punching out the number with practiced ease.

Her sister answered on the second ring. "Jade here."

"Lanni here." She smiled absently. Her sister was of-tentimes as fun-loving as her four-year-old daughter. Jade picked up Jenny from the day-care center and then stayed with her until Lanni arrived home.

"Don't tell me you're going to be late again," Jade groaned.

Lanni's frustration echoed her younger sister's. "I just got a call from the Baileys. They want to come in and put down earnest money on the Rudicelli house."

"But, Lanni, this is the third night this week that you've been working late."

"I know. I'm sorry."

"If this gets any worse I might as well move in with you."

"You know I'd like it if you did." If Jade were there, the nights wouldn't be so lonely and she wouldn't have to listen to her own thoughts rummaging around in her troubled mind.

"No way, José," Jade argued. "This girl is on her own. I like my freedom."

Looping the thick swatch of honey-colored hair around the back of her ear, Lanni released a tired sigh. "I shouldn't be too late. An hour, maybe two. Tell Jenny I'll read her favorite bedtime story to her when I get home."

"Do you want to talk to her? She's swinging in the backyard."

"No," Lanni shook her head as she spoke. "Let her play. But be sure to tell her how much I love her."

"I will. Just don't be too late. If you leave me around here long, I'll start daydreaming about food and before I know what's come over me, I'll be eating."

Lanni's sister continually struggled with her excess weight. She claimed there wasn't a diet around that she hadn't tried. Lanni had watched her sister count calories, carbohydrates, grams and chocolate chips all to no avail. She wished she could lose those extra fifteen pounds for Jade. Her problem was just the opposite—too many missed meals and too little appetite left her as slender as a reed. She preferred to think of herself as svelte, but even Lanni admitted that she'd look better carrying a few extra pounds. When Judd had lived with them, she'd had plenty of reason to cook decent meals....

Momentarily she closed her eyes as the rush of remembered pain washed over her. Two years had passed and she still couldn't think of Judd without reliving the hurt and regrets of his departure. With no more reason than he felt it was time to move on, Judd had expected her to uproot their lives and follow him to only God knew where. Even Judd didn't know where he was headed. Lanni had refused—one of them had to behave like an adult. She wouldn't leave her family and everything she held dear to traipse around the world with Judd as though life were some wild adventure and the whole world lay waiting to be explored. Judd had responsibilities, too, although he refused to own up to them.

In the end he'd given her no option but to file for a divorce and yet when she did, he hadn't bothered to sign the papers. Lanni hadn't pursued the issue, which only went to prove that the emotional bond that linked her to Judd was as strong as when he'd left. She recognized deep within her heart that her marriage was dead, only she hadn't fully accepted their failure. She had no intention of remarrying. Some people fit nicely into married life, Lanni just wasn't one of them. Marriage to another man was out of the question. The thought of suffering through that kind of emotional warfare again was beyond consideration. She'd been married once and it was enough to cure her for a lifetime. She had Jenny, and her daughter was the most important person in her life.

The intercom on her desk buzzed and the receptionist's voice announced, "The Baileys are here."

"Thank you, Joan. Could you send them in?"

Lanni took the first sip of her coffee and her long, curling lashes brushed her cheek as she attempted to push the memories to the back of her mind. She wished she could hate Judd and cast him from her thoughts as effectively as he'd walked out on her and Jenny. But part of him remained with her every day as a constant reminder of her life's one colossal failure...her marriage.

Setting aside the cup, she stood and forced a smile as she prepared to meet her clients.

By the time Lanni pulled into her driveway in Burien, a suburb of south Seattle, it was after seven. Everything had gone smoothly with the Baileys and Lanni experienced a sensation of pride and accomplishment. The Bailey family had specific needs in a new home and Lanni had worked with them for several weeks in an effort to find the house that would fulfill their unusual requirements.

Now she prepared herself to meet Jenny's needs. A four-year-old had the right to expect her mother's undivided attention at the end of the day. Unfortunately Lanni wanted to do nothing more than relax and take a nice hot soak in the bathtub. She would, but not until after she'd read to Jenny as she'd promised and tucked her daughter in for the night.

A note on the kitchen counter informed her that Jade had taken the little girl for a walk. No sooner had Lanni finished reading the message when the screen door swung open and her young daughter came roaring into the kitchen. Chocolate ice cream was smeared across her face and Jenny broke into an eager grin as she hurried toward her mother.

"How's my girl?" Lanni asked, lifting the child into

her arms and having trouble finding a place on the plump cheek that wasn't smudged with chocolate.

"Auntie Jade took me out for an ice-cream cone."

"So I see."

Jade followed on her heels, her face red from the exertion of chasing after a lively four-year-old. "I thought the exercise would do me good. Unfortunately some internal homing device led me to a Baskin & Robbins."

"Jade!"

"I couldn't help it," she pleaded, her hazel-green eyes rounding. "After eating tofu on a rye crisp for dinner, I felt I deserved a reward."

In spite of her effort not to, Lanni laughed. "The ice cream isn't going to help your diet."

"Sure it is. Jenny and I walked a good mile. According to my calculations, I could have had a double-decker for the energy expended in the walk."

"You *did* eat a double-decker, Aunt Jade."

Placing her hand on her hip, Jade looked at the little girl and shook her head. "Tattletale."

"Oops." Jenny placed her small hand over her chocolate-covered mouth. "I wasn't supposed to tell, was I?"

"I'll forgive you this time," Jade said seriously, but her eyes sparkled with laughter.

Taking out a fresh cloth, Lanni wet it under warm water from the kitchen faucet and proceeded to wipe off Jenny's face. She squirmed uncomfortably until Lanni completed the task. "Isn't it time for your bath, young lady?"

Lanni found it a little unusual that Jade lingered through Jenny's bath and story time, but was grateful for the company and didn't comment. She found her sister in the kitchen after Jenny was in bed.

"Did you have a chance to eat?" Jade asked, staring into the open refrigerator.

"Not yet. I'll scramble some eggs later."

"Sure you will." Jade closed the refrigerator and took a seat at the kitchen table, reaching for a soda cracker. She stared at the intricate holes, then set the cracker aside.

"You know," Lanni commented, hiding a smile. "It suddenly dawned on me. For all your dieting, you should be thin enough to dangle from a charm bracelet."

"Should be," Jade grumbled. As if to make up for lost time, she popped the soda cracker in to her mouth.

Lanni laughed outright, and reached for the box, tucking it back inside the cupboard to remove temptation. Without bothering to ask, she poured her sister a cup of spiced tea and delivered it to the table.

"Jenny asked about Judd again," her sister stated with little preamble.

"Again?" Lanni felt her stomach tighten with dread.

"She talks about him all the time. Surely you've noticed."

Lanni had. She'd answered her daughter's questions with saintly patience, hoping to satisfy her curiosity. In the beginning Jenny's questions had been innocent enough. She wanted to know her father's name and where he lived. Lanni had shown the little girl a map of the world and pointed to both the state of Alaska and lush oil fields of the Middle East. The last she'd heard, Judd was somewhere over there. No doubt he'd collected his own harem of adoring females by now. Lanni winced, angry with herself that the thought of Judd with another woman still had the power to hurt so painfully.

The following week Jenny had wanted a picture of

Judd to keep on her nightstand. Reluctantly Lanni gave her daughter a small five-by-seven photograph. The image captured was of Lanni and Judd standing on the front lawn near the blooming flowerbeds. Jenny was only a few months old at the time the picture was taken, and Judd held her, smiling proudly into the camera. It nipped at Lanni's heart every time she looked at the photo with their smiling, innocent faces. Their happiness had been short-lived at best.

For a time the picture had satisfied Jenny's inquisitiveness, but apparently it wasn't enough. Jenny wanted more, and Lanni doubted that she could give it to her.

She hadn't really known Judd. It wasn't until after they'd married that Lanni realized that she was head-over-heels in love with a stranger. The details of his past were sketchy. She knew little of his life other than the few tidbits he let drop now and then. His mother had died when he was young and he'd been raised on a ranch in Montana. His father had never remarried....

"Her teacher told me Jenny's been bragging to the other children that Judd's an astronaut."

"Oh no." With all the pressure of being a single parent weighing heavily upon her shoulders, Lanni claimed the seat opposite her sister and slumped forward, holding up her forehead with the heel of her hand. "She knows that's not true."

"Of course she does. The poor kid sees her friends' fathers pick them up every night. It's only natural she'd make up an excuse why her own doesn't."

"Lying isn't natural." Depressed, Lanni released a heartfelt sigh. "I'll have another talk with her in the morning."

"What are you going to tell her?"

"I don't know."

Jade's brows drew together in a frown. "The truth?"

"No." She couldn't. The naked facts would hurt too much. She was a mature adult, but the day Judd left them had devastated her. She refused to inflict that kind of pain on her own daughter.

The real problem was that Lanni didn't know how to explain the events that had led up to the separation. Judd found Seattle stifling and claimed it didn't offer him the challenges he needed. He'd built his reputation as a pipe-fitter in Alaska and the Middle East and he wanted to return there. When she wouldn't go with him, Judd left on his own, emotionally deserting Lanni and Jenny.

Lanni couldn't tell Jenny that her father had walked out on them. For a long time after Judd had gone, Lanni wanted to hate him—but she couldn't. Not when she continued to love him.

"Do you know what the truth is anymore, Lanni? There are two sides to everything."

Lanni was shocked. Next to Judd, Jade was probably the only other person who knew everything that had happened in her marriage. Even her parents weren't aware of all the details. Now her sister seemed to be implying that there was something more. "Of course I do." Her eyes fell to the round table. But sometimes the truth had a way of coming back to haunt a person, she reflected. It was times like these—when Lanni learned that her daughter had lied about Judd—that she wondered if she'd made the right decision. Her thoughts spun ahead and returned filled with self-recriminations. Judd had loved her, Lanni couldn't doubt that. For months after he'd left, he'd written her;

each letter filled with enthusiasm for Alaska, requesting her to bring Jenny and join him. His declarations of love for her and their daughter had ripped at Lanni's heart.

Her decision had been made, she wasn't leaving Seattle and no matter what she said or did, Judd refused to accept the fact. After a while Lanni couldn't bear to read his letters anymore and had returned them unopened.

Standing, Jade brought her untouched tea to the counter. "I can see you've got lots to think about. I'll see you tomorrow, but call me if you need anything."

Joining her sister, Lanni gave her a small hug. "I will. Thanks, Jade." She followed her sister to the front room. "Anytime."

The door made a clicking sound as it closed after Jade. Both her sister and her daughter had brought Judd to the forefront of her thoughts. She stood alone in the middle of the darkened living room as a numb sensation worked its way down her arms, stopping at her fingertips. The tingling produced a chill that cut all the way through her bones.

She wasn't going to think about Judd. She refused to remember his exquisite touch and the velvet-smooth sensations he wrapped around her every time they made love. She could have died from the ecstasy she discovered in his arms, but the price had been far too precious. He demanded her pride and everything she held dear. She couldn't leave her family and friends and everything that was comfortable and familiar.

The pain was as fresh that moment as it had been the day he walked out. Trapped in the memory, Lanni swallowed convulsively. Tightening her hands into small fists, she breathed out slowly, turned and moved into the cozy bathroom to fill the tub with steaming hot water. She'd soak Judd out of her system, erase his indelible mark from her skin and do her best to forget.

Only it didn't work that way. She eased her lithe frame into the bubbly hot water and scooted down into its inviting warmth. Leaning her head against the back of the tub, Lanni closed her eyes. Almost immediately depression swamped her.

Unbidden, the memories returned. In vivid detail Lanni remembered the day Jenny was born and the tears that had filled Judd's eyes when the nurse placed his newborn daughter in his arms. Judd had looked down upon the wrinkled pink face with such tenderness that she hadn't been able to take her eyes from the awe expressed in his face. Later, after she'd been wheeled into her hospital room, Judd had joined her.

To this day Lanni remembered the look of intense pride as he pulled out the chair and reached for her hand.

"You're sure you're all right?"

She'd smiled tenderly. "I feel wonderful. Oh, Judd, she's so beautiful."

Love and tenderness glowed from his warm, brown eyes. "I don't think I've seen anything so small."

"She'll grow," Lanni promised.

"I don't mind telling you that for a few minutes there I was terrified." His gaze darkened with remembered doubts so uncharacteristic of the man who buried his feelings. "It seemed like a miracle when the nurse handed her to me." His smile was warm. Once again, he appeared shaken by the enormity of the emotion that shook him. "But, Lanni, I'll never make you suffer like that again. I love you too much."

She'd endured hours of hard labor and had been absorbed so deeply in her own pain that she hadn't considered what torment Judd had endured. "Darling, every woman goes through this in childbirth. It's a natural part of life. I didn't mind."

Standing, he leaned over her and very gently kissed her brow. "I love you, Lanni."

"I know." The moment was poignant, but Lanni couldn't stifle a yawn. She felt wonderful, but exhausted. Despite her efforts to stay awake and talk to her husband, her eyelids felt as though they had weights tugging them closed. "I'm sorry, Judd..." she paused to yawn again, covering her mouth with the back of her hand "...but I can't seem to stay awake."

"Sleep, little mother," he whispered close to her ear. "Sleep."

Lanni did, for hours and hours. When she stirred, the first thing she noticed was Judd sprawled in the chair by the window. He had slouched down in what appeared to be an unlikely position for anyone to sleep comfortably. His head lolled to one side and a thick latch of dark hair fell across his wide brow. His arm hung loosely at his side; his knuckles brushed the floor.

Lanni smiled at the long form draped so haphazardly in the visitor's chair. His strong features were softened now in sleep. Lovingly, she watched the man who had come to be her world and was astonished at the swell of emotion that went through her at the memory of the new life their love had created.

Lanni blinked back her own tears. "Judd," she whispered, afraid if he slept in that position much longer he'd get a crick in his neck.

Dazed, Judd looked up and straightened. Their eyes met and as long as she lived, Lanni would remember the love that radiated from his warm, dark eyes.

The lukewarm bathwater lapped at her skin and Lanni pulled herself from thoughts of the past and into the reality that was her life now. How sad it was that a love so beautiful and pure should ever have gone so wrong.

Lanni rose from the water and reached for the thick terry-cloth towel. Judd had been gone two years—and in reality longer than that. The last months before their final separation, he had been home infrequently. He started traveling to help pay the mounting medical expenses following Jenny's birth. The money in Alaska was good and there were even better wages, Judd claimed, in the Middle East. Lanni had been forced to admit that they had enough pressing bills to warrant his taking a job elsewhere.

Dressing in her shimmery housecoat and fuzzy slippers, she crept quietly into Jenny's bedroom. The little girl was sound asleep, curled on her side with her doll, Betsy, tucked under her arm. Gently, Lanni brushed the thin wisps of hair from her angelic face. Jenny was everything that had ever been good between her and Judd. She would always be grateful that she had this child. She couldn't have Judd, but Jenny was all hers.

The phone pealed impatiently in the distance and Lanni rushed from the room, not wanting the loud ring to wake her daughter.

"Hello," she said, somewhat breathlessly.

"Hi there. It's Steve. I heard you sold the Rudicelli house." His low voice revealed his pride in her accomplishment.

Steve Delaney was an agent in the same office as Lanni. They'd worked together for the last year and had become good friends, often teaming up for Broker Opens and Open Houses. Lanni wasn't interested in becoming emotionally involved with any of her co-workers, and she'd avoided any formal dates with Steve. They'd gone on picnics, to a baseball game when the office handed out free tickets, and even a couple of lunches at a restaurant close to the office. Steve knew Lanni was still married, but after he'd questioned her about Judd, the Realtor seemed satisfied that the marriage was over in every way but legally.

They'd continued to see each other over the last three months and though Lanni enjoyed Steve's companionship, she wasn't interested in a deeper relationship.

Recently, however, Steve had been urging Lanni to do what she could to get the divorce business settled. He felt that she would never be able to face the future until she settled the past. Although he hadn't told her he was falling in love with her, Lanni could see it in his eyes. He wanted her marriage to Judd over so he could pursue her himself.

"I took the earnest money this afternoon," Lanni said.

"Great. It looks like I may have a buyer for the Bailey place," he said, then added thoughtfully, "Have you noticed what a good team we make?"

Lanni decided the best answer was to pretend she hadn't heard the question.

"The Baileys will be pleased." They'd made their offer on the Rudicelli house contingent on the sale of their own two-storey Colonial. Now it looked like everything was going to work out perfectly.

"I think we should celebrate."

Lanni hesitated. Lately he found more and more excuses for them to be together, so not only did they share the same office during the day, but they were seeing each other in the evenings as well. He was patient with Jenny and the two appeared to get along well.

"Don't you think it's a bit premature to celebrate?" she asked. Steve knew it was common for house deals to fall through for any number of reasons.

"Maybe, but we deserve it; just you and me, Lanni." His voice dipped slightly. "I'll cook dinner for you at my place."

Still she hesitated. She liked Steve, but she wasn't ready for an emotional commitment and an intimate dinner together could cause problems. "Let me think on it."

"Come on, Lanni, loosen up a bit. Enjoy life."

Steve was a fun guy; she hated to disappoint him. "I don't know—we've been seeing a lot of each other recently."

Lanni could feel him weigh his words. "I haven't made any secret of how I feel about you. I'm not going to rush you into anything you don't want. I'm a patient man; you've been hurt and the last thing in the world I want to do is cause you any more pain. I enjoy your company, and I promise I'm not going to put any pressure on you. Let me pamper you the way you deserve; champagne, a candlelight dinner, music."

"Oh, Steve, I don't know." Lanni understood what made him the top salesperson for the firm. He was smooth and sincere and persuasive. And frankly, she was tempted.

"Jade could watch Jenny for one night," he coaxed. "What if I promise to have you home before midnight?"

"I'm not Cinderella."

"To me you are."

His voice was so warm and enticing that for a moment Lanni wavered. Everything she'd avoided in the last two years was facing her, demanding that she make a decision. She couldn't spend the rest of her life cooped up, afraid to trust and love again. She worked hard being the best mother and Realtor possible that it seemed her life was void of any real fun and laughter.

"Come on, Lanni," he cajoled.

Lanni squeezed her eyes shut. She thought of Jenny making up stories about her father to impress the other children. The girl needed male influence. Lanni's father was wonderful with the child, but Jenny seemed to require someone more than a grandfather.

"Do this for yourself," Steve prodded gently.

"I'll check with my sister and see if she can babysit," Lanni murmured, succumbing.

"That's my girl," Steve murmured, obviously pleased.

They spoke for only a few minutes longer, but by the time Lanni replaced the receiver she was convinced she'd done the wrong thing to accept Steve's invitation. The problem with Jenny lying at the preschool had made Lanni vulnerable.

The following day, Lanni regretted her impulsive acceptance, but not to the point that she was willing to cancel the date. It put everything between her and Steve in a new light. It frightened Lanni, but at the same time she realized she couldn't torture herself with thoughts of Judd forever.

But if Lanni was amazed at herself for her willingness to trudge ahead in her relationship with Steve, she was shocked by Jade's reaction.

"Are you sure this is what you want?" Jade asked that evening when Lanni mentioned the dinner with Steve.

"I think so." Lanni was nothing if not honest.

"Why now after two long years?"

Lanni was confused herself. "Because it's time." She had come a long way this week in sorting through her feelings for Steve and she wasn't about to step back because her sister disapproved. It was true that Steve didn't inspire passion within her, but she'd had that once and now she considered it highly overrated.

Jade made a rueful sound.

"What was that all about?"

"Nothing," Jade answered with a distracted look.

Lanni's green eyes darkened. "You don't like Steve, do you?"

"He's all right." For emphasis, Jade shrugged one shoulder. "I'm just wondering what Judd would say if he knew you were romantically interested in another man."

Lanni's mouth went dry. "He probably wouldn't care. I haven't heard a word from Judd in well over a year."

"That doesn't mean he's stopped caring. He's got his pride, too. How long did you expect him to continue reaching out to you only to have you reject every attempt?"

Color blossomed in Lanni's cheeks. "He should never have left us the way he did. Believe me, I'm well aware of what Judd thinks and feels."

"How can you be so sure?"

"I just am." In an effort to disguise her dismay, Lanni stood and walked to the sliding glass door that opened onto the patio and small yard. Jenny was in her sandbox playing contentedly with her toys. "I sometimes wonder if he even thinks about Jenny and me."

"Oh, Lanni, I'm sure he does."

Folding her arms around her waist, Lanni shook her head absently. "I somehow doubt it."

"But he sends you support every month—"

"Money!" The word escaped on the tail end of a long sigh. "I'll admit he's been generous. He always was—to a fault."

"Lanni, listen." Jade nodded annoyingly and joined her sister. "I'm convinced you're wrong. Judd thinks about you all the time. He must."

"He doesn't." She dropped her hands and moved away. "It's been two years, Jade. Two years. Time says it all. I'm having dinner with Steve; I deserve an evening out. If you won't stay with Jenny then I'll find someone else who will."

Jade's shoulders sagged in defeat. "Of course I'll sit with her."

Almost immediately, Lanni felt guilty for having snapped at her younger sister. Since Judd had left, Jade had been a godsend; Lanni would never be able to work as many hours as she did without her sister's help. "I didn't mean to be so sharp with you."

Jade's smile was instantaneous. "I only want what's best for you and Jenny." Making an effort to lighten the mood, Jade reached for a sack with a prominent department store's name boldly written across the side. "Hey, did I tell you I signed up for an aerobics class?"

"Not again." Lanni wasn't surprised at her sister's latest effort to lose weight. The last time Jade had signed up for a dance class, she'd convinced Lanni to join her. When her eyebrows started to sweat, Lanni knew it was time to quit.

"Get this," Jade added, laughing. "The lady on the phone told me to wear loose clothes. Good heavens, if I had any loose clothes I wouldn't be taking the class in the first place!"

"So what's in the sack?"

"Bodysuit, leotards, leg warmers, and a disgustingly expensive nylon jacket. The whole bit. I figure that since I spent my monthly food allowance on this outfit, everything will be loose by the time I take the first class."

"Honestly, Jade..."

Jade stopped her by holding up the palm of her hand. "This time I mean it."

Lanni had heard it all before, but nodded as seriously as possible, somehow managing not to laugh. "I know you can do it."

"Of course I can. Exercise is the answer. I'm going to stop worrying about what I eat and concentrate on the basic elements of burning calories and expending the proper amount of energy in relation to the amount of food consumed. Sounds good. Right?"

"Right."

"You don't believe me?" Jade challenged.

"I already told you I know you can do it."

"So says the woman who can live three weeks on a compliment."

"You're exaggerating."

"All right, two weeks."

"Now don't insult me by saying that if I caught a chest cold there wouldn't be any place to put it."

"In addition to no boobs, you're much too thin."

Lanni couldn't argue. "I'm working on it."

"You know what I think?"

Lanni was beginning to doubt the wisdom of asking. "What?"

"I think you and Judd should get back together. When you were pregnant with Jenny, you looked wonderful. I've never seen you happier."

The instant sorrow that engulfed her was so strong that for a moment Lanni couldn't breathe. What Jade said was true, but that happiness had been so fleeting, so fragile that it had lasted only a few months. She dropped her gaze and sadly shook her head. "It wouldn't work again. There's been too much water under the bridge, as they say. Judd's not coming back. After all this time, we'd be strangers." Probably even more so now.

"How can you be so sure?" Jade questioned softly.

"Listen," she mumbled, "do you mind if we don't talk about Judd anymore?"

"But it could help you—"

"Jade, I mean it. Enough. With Jenny bringing up his name every day and you hounding me with questions about him—it's just too much. I'm about to go crazy. We were married and we failed. I've got a fantastic little girl to remember him by, but my husband is gone. It's over and I've got a life to live."

Jade became strangely quiet and left soon after the conversation ended.

As the days progressed, Lanni's conscience didn't ease about the dinner date with Steve. A couple of times it was on the tip of her tongue to cancel, but whenever she approached him, Steve would smile and tell her how much he was looking forward to their evening together. His eyes grew tender and Lanni refused to give in to her doubts.

Perhaps if she hadn't made such a big issue of it with Jade, she might have found a way to gracefully extract herself.

Thursday evening, the night of their arranged dinner, Lanni felt as nervous as a teenager on prom night. Her heart pounded with a hundred questions. By the time she was dressed, half her closet had been draped over the top of her bed. Clothes said so much and the silk dress was meant to tell Steve that she was not optimistic about this dinner and their relationship.

"What do you think?" she asked her sister, feeling painfully inadequate.

"Hey, you look great," Jade murmured, stepping back to examine Lanni.

"This isn't a time to tease. I feel terrible. A hornet's nest has taken up residence in my stomach. I can't do a thing with my hair." For years she'd worn it in the same style, parted in the middle in a smooth even line. Her honey-gold hair hung loosely, framing her oval face, and tucked in naturally just above the line of her shoulder. Judd had once told her that her hair color resembled moonbeams on a starlit night. What a terrible time to remember something like that.

"What's wrong?" Jade gave her an odd look. "You've gone pale."

Gripping the back of the kitchen chair, Lanni offered her sister a feeble smile. "I don't know that I'm doing the right thing."

"It's not too late to call it off."

The doorbell chimed.

"It's too late," Lanni said evenly. Almost two years too late.

"I'll get it." Jenny rushed past Lanni toward the front door.

Lanni cast a panicked glance in that direction. "My makeup isn't on too heavy, is it?" Her eyes begged Jade to tell her that everything was perfect.

Jade, however, appeared more interested in adding sunflower seeds to her yogurt and stirring in fresh fruit.

"Jade?" she pleaded again.

"I already told you, you look great."

"Yes, but you didn't say it with any real conviction."

Dramatically Jade placed her hand over her heart. "You look absolutely marvelous, darling."

"Mommy, Mommy—" Jenny came racing back into the kitchen. "There's a man at the door who says he's my daddy."

Two

Jenny's words hit Lanni with all the force of a wrecking ball slamming against the side of a brick building. Frantically her gaze flew to her sister as though asking Jade to tell her it wasn't true. Jade's expression was as shocked as Lanni's.

"Is he, Mommy? Is he really my daddy?" Jenny began to jump up and down all over the small kitchen. She grabbed Lanni's hand and literally dragged her into the living room.

No time was allowed for Lanni to compose herself, or collect her thoughts. Her lungs felt void of oxygen, her eyes were wide with shock. Distraught, she could find nothing to say.

"Hello, Lanni." Judd stood just inside the door, more compelling than she dared remember.

"Judd." He hadn't changed. The range of emotions that seared through her were the same as the first time she'd seen him. He was tall, and as lean as an Arctic fox. His shoulders were wide and his hips narrow. Every inch of him almost shouted of strength, stamina, and experience.

There wasn't a place he hadn't been or an experience he'd bypassed along the way—including marriage.

Long hours in the sun had bronzed the angular planes of his face, creasing permanent lines on his forehead. His eyes were dark and bold, glinting with a touch of irony that told her he wouldn't be easily fooled. He knew the effect he had on her and would use it to his advantage.

Judd Matthiessen was strong-willed and had complete confidence in himself and his abilities.

In those brief seconds, Lanni knew nothing had changed about him. Nothing. He was the most devastating male she'd ever known and every prayer she'd uttered over the last two years had been for naught. She didn't want to love this man who had ripped her heart from her breast. But she had no option—she would always love him.

Only she couldn't allow him back into her life. He'd leave again and she refused to let him drag her and Jenny with him. She wasn't a camp follower. Seattle was their home; it was where they belonged—all three of them.

"Why are you here?" she demanded, her voice tight with shock.

"My father's dying."

Lanni felt her legs go weak. From what Judd had told her, the father and son had never been close. By the time Judd was eighteen he was on his own, supporting himself.

Lanni had met Judd's father when she was only a few months' pregnant with Jenny. Stuart had come to dinner at their home in Seattle. The meeting had been strained and uncomfortable; the older Matthiessen had left early. The entire evening had been spent listening to Stuart tell Judd that the time to make something of his life was now—when he had a wife and a family. He offered to support them if Judd decided to go to college. Instead of being grateful for his father's generous offer, Judd looked furious. He'd gone pale and quietly asked Stuart if he'd ever learn to accept him as he was.

After they'd separated, Lanni had written Judd's father and received a brief note in return, stating his disappointment that the marriage had failed. Conscientiously, Lanni had sent him birthday pictures of Jenny, but had never heard back from the elder Matthiessen. As far as Jenny knew, her only grandfather was Lanni's father.

"I—I'm sorry to hear about Stuart," Lanni murmured, saddened.

"I didn't think you knew him well enough to feel any sadness," Judd retorted.

Lanni stared at him, biting back angry words. For his own part, Judd's returning stare contained no emotion. He revealed no sympathy at Stuart's illness nor did he appear to feel any great sense of loss.

"Your father's illness doesn't explain why you're here," she said again, her voice gaining strength and conviction.

"Dad's never seen Jennifer."

Automatically, Lanni's arm closed around the little girl's shoulders, pressing the child closer to her side. "What has that got to do with anything? I—I've sent him pictures."

Judd's mouth thinned. "He wants to see her."

"I suppose he can come—"

"I told you he's dying. I'm taking Jennifer to him."

"No." The word wobbled out on a note of disbelief. She wouldn't let Judd take her daughter halfway across the country. Both Judd and his father were strangers to the child.

Before either of them could say anything more, the doorbell chimed again.

Jenny shot free of Lanni's grip and hurried across the room to open the front door. Steve, holding a small bouquet of pink rosebuds, stepped inside. His broad smile quickly faded as he spied the small group standing there awkwardly. Everyone's attention focused on Steve.

"Hello," he greeted cordially, and shot Lanni a questioning glance.

"Judd Matthiessen," Judd announced, stepping forward and extending his hand. "I'm Lanni's husband. Who are you?"

From the way Steve's jaw clenched, Lanni could tell that he was experiencing the same shock she'd suffered earlier. In an effort to rescue them all from further embarrassment, she accepted his flowers and smiled appreciatively. "Steve's a good friend."

"How good?" he demanded. Judd's gaze painfully pinned her to the wall, accusing her with his eyes until Lanni felt the anger swell up inside.

"That's none of your business," Lanni shot back hotly.

"Lanni and Steve were going out to dinner," Jade inserted quickly, placing a calming arm around her sister's shoulders.

"*Were* going out," Judd commented, placing heavy emphasis on the past tense. "We need to talk."

"Maybe it would be better if we arranged our dinner another night," Steve said thoughtfully. The understanding look he shared with Lanni lent her confidence. She was furious with Judd.

"Steve and I are going out," she stated with a determination few would question. "I'm ready, as you can see.

Judd stopped by unannounced, so there's no reason for us to cancel our evening."

"Let me help you put the flowers in water," Steve suggested, nodding toward the kitchen.

Lanni looked blankly at the flowers in her hand, then caught a glimpse of the direction of his gaze.

"She doesn't need any help," Judd announced.

"As a matter of fact, I do," Lanni countered quietly. Steve's hand at her elbow guided her into the kitchen.

"Steve, I'm so sorry," Lanni murmured, embarrassed and miserable.

"Don't be. It isn't your fault." Steve shot a look over his shoulder before he cupped her shoulder with his hands. His dark eyes delved into hers and without a word spoken, his gaze revealed the depth of his affection. "If the truth be known, I'm glad he's here."

"But how could you when…"

"I know it's a strain on you," he said softly, encouragingly, "but now you can get those divorce papers signed and go about your life."

"I…should, shouldn't I?" Divorce was such an ugly word—Lanni hated it, but the action was necessary. She would never be emotionally free of Judd until their marriage had been legally dissolved.

"Yes, you most definitely should." He paused to kiss her forehead. "I'll leave and we can talk in the morning."

"You're a wonderful friend," Lanni told him.

Disappointment flared briefly in his eyes, but he quickly disguised it. "I want to be a whole lot more than your friend, Lanni."

"I know." She dropped her gaze, uncertain about everything at the moment.

When they returned to the living room, Judd's look was angry enough to sear a hole through them both. Steve made his excuses and left. It took all of Lanni's restraint not to whirl on Judd and ask him to leave, but that would solve nothing.

The screen door closed with hardly a sound and Jade moved into the center of the room, rubbing the palms of her hands together. "Since I'm not needed here, I'll head on over to my aerobics class."

"It was good to see you again, Jade," Judd said casually. "You're looking good."

Jade's soft chuckle filled the stark silence that enveloped the small room. "You always were my favorite brother-in-law."

"Jade!" Lanni was horrified by her own sister's lack of tact.

For the first time since his arrival Judd grinned. Lanni couldn't term it a real smile. Only one corner of his mouth edged upward, as though smiling went against his nature and he didn't do it often.

"I'm off," Jade said, walking toward the door. "I'll give you a call tomorrow."

"Goodbye, Aunt Jade." Jenny ran to the living room window and waved eagerly to her aunt.

Judd's gaze rested on the child and softened perceptively. "You've done a good job with her."

"Thank you." Her gaze flew to Jenny and she experienced anew the fierce tug of the maternal bond between mother and child.

Seeming to feel her parents' eyes, Jenny turned around. "Are you really my daddy? Mommy never said."

"I'm your daddy."

"I've been waiting to meet you."

Judd went down on one knee in front of the little girl. "And I've been waiting to see you, too."

"You don't look like your picture."

Suddenly, Lanni realized she still had the flowers in her hand. Shaking her head, she carried them into the kitchen and haphazardly placed them in a vase. After filling it with water, she set it in the middle of the kitchen table and returned to the living room.

Jenny was sitting in her father's lap and rubbing her small hands over the five o'clock shadow that covered Judd's face.

"What's this?"

"Whiskers."

"How come I don't have any?"

Judd gave another of his almost smiles. "Girls don't. Your skin will be as soft as your mother's."

"Do you have a daddy, too?"

Leave it to her astute daughter to have picked up on their earlier conversation.

"Yes." As always, whenever Judd mentioned his father, it was done briefly. For a moment Lanni thought she recognized something in those hard, dark eyes. Perhaps regret, or maybe even doubt, but she quickly dismissed the notion.

"Is your daddy sick?"

"He's dying."

Lanni wished Judd had been a bit more subtle.

"I had a goldfish who died once. We prayed over him and Mommy flushed him down the toilet."

Momentarily, Judd's gaze met Lanni's. She smiled

weakly and gestured with her hand, letting him know she hadn't known what else to do.

"If your daddy dies will you get a new one, like I got a new goldfish?" Jenny's eyes, so like her father's, stared intently at Judd's.

"No, I'm afraid not. I only have one father and you only have one father."

"You."

"That's right, Jennifer."

Lanni took a step in their direction. "I call her Jenny." Judd had no right to step into their lives like this and make demands. She regretted that Stuart was dying, but it was unreasonable for Judd to believe that she would just hand over her daughter.

"I like it when he calls me Jennifer," Jenny said, contradicting her mother.

"Right." Lanni sat on the armrest of the sofa, glaring at Judd. She was the one who was raising their child. He had a lot of nerve to waltz in without notice and start changing the way she did things.

"What took you so long to get here?" Jenny asked.

Judd's gaze fell to his daughter and softened. Although Lanni was confused by the question, Judd appeared to understand. "I was working far, far away."

"Mommy showed me on a map." She scooted off Judd's lap and raced across the room and down the hallway to her tiny bedroom. Returning a minute later, Jenny fell to her knees on the worn carpet and flipped through the pages of the atlas until she found the pages Lanni had tabbed. The little girl glanced up proudly. "Here." She pointed to the Middle Eastern country Lanni had outlined in red.

"No, I was in Mexico."

Lanni felt a wave of fresh pain. The last letter she'd received had a foreign postmark showing Saudi Arabia. "You might have let me know." She couldn't swallow down the note of bitterness that cut deep into her words.

"And have you return my letter unopened?" He hurled the angry words at her with all the force of his dominating personality. "Besides, Jade knew."

"Jade?"

"You may not have had the decency to read my letters, but Jade kept in contact with me so I knew what was happening with you and Jenny."

"You... Jade?" Lanni was stunned, utterly and completely shocked.

"You and I didn't exactly part on the best of terms," Judd murmured, his tone grim. "And you didn't seem willing to work toward a reconciliation."

"I wasn't willing to drag my daughter to some hovel while you chased rainbows. If that makes me unreasonable, then fine, I accept it—I'm unreasonable."

He recognized the hurt in her eyes and knew that nothing had changed. Several times over the last two years he'd exchanged letters with Jade, hungry for word of his wife and daughter. He couldn't be what Lanni wanted, or Stuart either, for that matter, but it didn't mean he'd stopped caring about them. Without a moment's hesitation he would have come had he been needed. Stuart wanted him now and he was on his way to his father.

Judd watched Lanni as she nervously paced around the room. Jade had sent him long letters every four months or so, but Lanni's sister had never mentioned this Steve character so Judd assumed the relationship was fairly recent.

Equal doses of betrayal and outrage burned through Lanni. Her own sister, whom she adored, had turned on her. Lanni couldn't believe that Jade would do anything so underhanded.

Lanni watched Jenny sitting on her father's lap and her heart constricted. He wanted his daughter with him now, but he hadn't been around when the child needed him most. From birth, Jenny had been a sickly infant. She suffered from ear infections and frequent bouts of asthmatic bronchitis. Lanni spent more nights in Jenny's bedroom than her own.

Soon Judd was traveling, coming home sporadically. The space between his visits lengthened and the time spent with his family become shorter and shorter.

Finally Lanni couldn't take it anymore. There was plenty of work in Seattle for a skilled pipefitter. Judd didn't need to travel—they could find a way to meet expenses as long as he was home and they were together.

The next time Judd came home, waving the exorbitant paycheck he'd received for working in the Middle East, Lanni was waiting for him. She decided to put everything on the line—their love, their marriage, and their daughter. In her anger and frustration, she'd hurled accusations at him. Lanni burned with humiliation every time she remembered the terrible things she'd said to him. A thousand times since, she'd wished she could have swallowed back every word.

On that one horrible night, Lanni forced Judd to choose. Either he stay in Seattle with them, or everything was over. Judd had walked to the door, turned and asked her to come with him. He wanted her to travel with him—

he felt suffocated in Seattle. She had no choice but to refuse. Judd left, and ten days later, Lanni filed for divorce.

"Where's Mexico?" Jenny asked, unaware of the undercurrents flowing through the room.

Judd flipped through the pages and turned the atlas upside-down in an effort to find what he wanted.

"Here." He knelt beside her and turned to the appropriate page.

"Can I go there someday, too?"

"If you want."

"What about Mommy?"

Briefly Judd's eyes sought Lanni's. "She'd love the sun and the beach. You would, too, sweetheart."

"I want to go. Can we, Mommy?"

Still numb from his announcement that Jade had been involved in any subterfuge, Lanni didn't hear the question.

"Can we go, Mommy? Can we?"

The childishly eager voice forced Lanni into the present. "Go where, darling?"

"To Mexico with Daddy."

"No," she cried, flashing Judd a look that threatened bodily harm. If he was going to use Jenny against her, she'd throw him out the door. Her eyes told him as much. "There wouldn't be any place for us to stay." Silently she dared Judd to contradict her.

"Is that still your excuse, Lanni?" The words were issued in a low hiss that was barely audible.

"What's yours, Judd?" she flared. "You're the one who walked out on us. Remember? How have you salved your conscience?" She hadn't meant to accuse him and hated herself for resorting to angry words. It always turned out like this. They couldn't be civil to each other for more than a few minutes before the bitterness erupted like an open, festering wound.

He stood, moving close to her. The anger drained from him and he lifted a thick strand of golden hair from the side of her face. When Lanni flinched and stepped away, Judd's spirits plummeted. He'd tried so hard to reach her and had utterly failed. He had walked out, but only when there wasn't any other option. He hadn't wanted to leave, but he couldn't stay. There were plenty of things he regretted in his life, but hurting Lanni would haunt him to his grave.

It had been a mistake to have married her, he silently reflected, but he couldn't help himself. He'd wanted her so badly that nothing on earth would have stopped him. She was perfect. Lovely and delicate. Her home and family had radiated more warmth and love than anything he'd ever known.

Judd knew from the beginning that Lanni was special. With her, he could offer nothing less than marriage. He'd done so gladly, latching onto the elusive promise of happiness for the first time in his life.

He liked to think that their first year together had been ordained by God. He'd never known what it meant to be part of a family.

Lanni had flinched when Judd's hand lifted her hair. She feared his touch. Despite all the hurt and bitterness that was between them, she could vividly remember the feel of his smooth skin beneath her fingers and the way her long nails had dug into his powerful muscles when they made love. They may have had their differences, but they were never apparent in bed. Judd had always been a fantastic lover.

Dragging her eyes away from him, she turned to Jenny, lifting the small girl into her arms. Jenny was like a protective barrier against Judd.

The glint of knowledge that lurked in his smiling eyes told her that he recognized her ploy.

"I'm leaving in the morning," he told her as Jenny squirmed in her arms.

Unwilling to fight her daughter, Lanni set the child back on the carpet. "What do you mean?"

"I told you I'm taking Jenny."

"Judd, no." Her voice wobbled with regret. He couldn't come in and expect her to willingly hand over her daughter. Her eyes sparked in his direction. She'd fight him with everything she had.

"Listen." Frustrated, Judd raked his fingers through his hair. "I'll do everything possible to ensure her safety. I'm her father, for heaven's sake. Don't suffocate her the way you did me."

For a second Lanni was too shocked and hurt to speak. She refused to address his accusation. "Jenny's only a child. You can't uproot her like this—separate her from me and the only home she knows."

"Dad may not last much longer."

"Jenny's in preschool." The excuse was lame, but Lanni was desperate.

Inserting the tips of his fingers in the high pockets of his well-worn jeans, Judd strolled to the other side of the room. She wasn't fooled by his casual stance. There was a coiled alertness to every movement Judd made. "All right, we can work around those things."

"How?"

"Come with us." He turned, his gaze pinning her to the wall.

Lanni couldn't hold back an abrupt, short laugh. "I can't take time off work at a minute's notice. There are people who depend on me."

"Like Steve." He said the name as if it didn't feel right on his tongue.

"Yes...like Steve. And others, plenty of others. I've done well for myself without you. I can't—and I won't—allow you to charge into my life this way."

"Lanni, Stuart's dying. Surely you aren't going to deny him this final request."

For the first time Lanni saw the pain in Judd's eyes. He may not have gotten along with his father, but he cared. Judd honestly cared. Probably against his flint-hard will, he was concerned.

"I'm sorry, really sorry, but I can't." Tears formed, stinging the back of her eyes.

"Jenny has a right to meet her grandfather."

"I wrote... I sent pictures. What about my rights? What about Jenny's rights?"

Reaching out, he gripped both her wrists and pressed them against her breast. "You hate me, fine. I may deserve all the bitterness you've got stored up against me. But you aren't any Mother Teresa yourself and I refuse to let you punish an old dying man for my sins."

"I'm not punishing Stuart," she cried, and shook her head from side to side. "All I want is for you to leave Jenny and me alone."

Abruptly Judd dropped her hands and Lanni rubbed

them together nervously. "I won't be bullied into this. My...decision is made."

"Okay, fine but take a night and sleep on it. Once you've had time to think things through, I'm confident you'll realize we don't have any choice."

"Mommy, are you and Daddy fighting?"

"Of course not, sweetheart," Lanni said instantly.

The young face was tight with concern. "Is Daddy going away again?"

"Yes," Judd answered, then added, "but I'll be back tomorrow and we can talk again." His eyes held Lanni's. "I'll see you first thing in the morning."

It was all she could do to nod.

Judd felt Lanni's round, frightened eyes follow him as he walked out the front door. He hadn't expected her to deny him this request. He'd never asked for anything from her, not even visitation rights to his daughter. Jade had frequently mailed him pictures of the little girl. He kept them in his wallet along with the photo he carried of Lanni. But he rarely looked at them. It hurt too much. Stuart's letter had changed all that.

As Judd walked out to his car, thoughts of his father produced a heavy frown. By the time the envelope had reached him, it had three different addresses penned across the surface. In all his years of working for the big oil companies, Judd could remember only a handful of times that he'd heard from his father. This letter had caught Judd by surprise. The old man was dying and Stuart Samuel Matthiessen wanted to mend his fences. Stuart had asked to see Jenny before he died and Judd wouldn't deny him this last request.

Seeing Lanni again was difficult, Judd mused with a

sigh. He couldn't look at her and not remember. Briefly he closed his eyes as a wave of whispered desire from the past swept over him, then he climbed into the car and headed toward the motel. Lanni was as breathtakingly lovely now as the day he'd left her and Jenny. Perhaps even more so. Her beauty had ripened. One look told him the cost of her struggle to gain that maturity. He was proud of her, and in the same moment experienced an overwhelming guilt that it had been him who had brought the shadow to her eyes.

In the beginning, his intentions had been impeccable. He hadn't expected the restlessness to return. For a year it hadn't.

At first the only symptoms of his discontent had been a few sleepless nights. He'd go to bed with Lanni and after making love and holding her in his arms, Lanni would cling to him. She worried when he was late and fussed over him until he wanted to throw up his arms and ask her to give him some peace. The family he'd wanted so much to become a part of disillusioned him. Lanni's parents were wonderful people, but they wanted to control their lives, and worse, Lanni couldn't seem to get dressed in the morning without first checking with her mother. Judd felt the walls close in around him. The baby had helped give Lanni some independence, but not enough.

The day Jennifer Lydia Matthiessen was born would long be counted as the most important of his life. There was nothing in this world that could duplicate the feelings of pride and love when the nurse handed him his newborn daughter. When she became ill, Judd was sick with worry. The doctor bills destroyed their budget and he couldn't think of any option but to travel to the high-risk jobs that abounded for a man with his experience. And so he'd taken a job in the oil-rich fields of the Middle East. The money had been good, and the challenge was there. He didn't try to fool himself by thinking that he didn't miss Lanni and the baby—he did.

On the trips home, Judd could see how unhappy Lanni was, but she'd only bury her face in his shoulder and beg him not to leave her again. They never talked, at least not the way they should. They were both caught up in acting out a role, pretending there were no problems. So he'd stayed on the oil fields, coming back to Seattle less and less often, avoiding the inevitable. Lanni didn't understand the reason he'd stayed away, and Judd hadn't the heart to tell her.

Judd sighed and pulled the car into the motel parking lot. Turning off the ignition, he thought of the dark night ahead of him.

Lanni waited until Jenny was in bed, sound asleep, before she called her sister's number.

"Jade, it's Lanni."

"I'm so glad you phoned," Jade said with an eager sigh. "I'm dying to find out what happened. What did Judd say about Steve?"

"You wrote to him." The words conveyed all the feelings of betrayal Lanni had harbored over the last two hours.

Jade's voice instantly lost its vivaciousness. "Yes, I wrote, but only because you wouldn't."

At least she didn't try to lie about it. Lanni was grateful for that. "Why didn't you say anything?"

"A hundred times I tried to talk about Judd, but you wouldn't listen."

"I can't believe that."

"I did, Lanni," she cried. "Remember last weekend while we were at the mall? I asked you then if you were curious about Judd. I asked you if you had a chance to know where he was, and what he was doing, if you'd want to know. Don't you remember what you said?"

Vaguely, Lanni recalled that the conversation had taken place, but the details of it eluded her. "No."

"You told me that for all you cared Judd could be rotting in hell."

"I wasn't serious!"

"At the time it sounded very much like you were. And last Christmas, do you remember how I tried to talk you into making some effort to contact him?"

That Lanni remembered; she and Jade had exchanged heated words in that disagreement. But Christmases without Judd were always the worst. They'd met during the most festive season of the year. She'd been working part-time at the cosmetics counter of a department store and attending night school, still uncertain about what she wanted to do with her life. Then Judd had swept so unexpectedly into her existence. She'd been so naive and so easily captivated by his worldliness. They were together every day until…

"Lanni."

Jade's concerned voice broke through the fog of memories.

"Yes, yes, I'm here. I was just trying to remember…"

"Judd only wrote a handful of times. I couldn't refuse him. He loves you and Jenny, and wanted to know how you were—that's only natural. You wouldn't write to him, so I had to."

The anger dissipated. Lanni hadn't meant to be cruel when she'd returned Judd's letters. She couldn't read his words and keep her mental health at the same time. She wanted him to stop telling her that he loved her and wanted her with him. She didn't want to read about the exciting places he was living, where the sun was always shining and the white beaches sounded like paradise. He'd left her, walked out on her, and she couldn't—wouldn't—forgive him for that.

"I'm sorry, Lanni. A thousand times I wanted to tell you. Especially when Jenny started asking questions about Judd. If you'd given me a hint that you were interested in contacting him, I would have given you his address."

"No." Slowly Lanni shook her head. "You're right, I wouldn't have wanted to know. You did the right thing not to tell me."

"Then why do I feel so terrible?" Jade asked.

"Probably because I came at you like a charging bull. I apologize."

"Don't. I'm relieved that he's here. Have you decided what you're going to do about letting him take Jenny?"

"No," Lanni answered honestly. Every passing minute made the problem of Judd's dying father more complex. Judd was right to want to take Jenny. And her apprehensions about the trip were equally strong.

Lanni spoke with her sister a couple of minutes more, then replaced the telephone receiver.

That night when she climbed between the sheets, memories of their first Christmas together crowded the edges of her mind.

She'd been so much in love with Judd. He'd arrived in Seattle on his way to a job assignment in Alaska and decided to stay a few extra days in order to explore the city. Those days had quickly turned to weeks. They'd met on his second day in town, where Lanni was working in a downtown department store for the holidays.

Lanni had helped Judd pick out a gift for his boss's wife and he'd casually asked her out to dinner in appreciation for the help she'd given him. Lanni had been forced to decline, although her impulse had been to accept his invitation. She was meeting her family that evening for an annual outing of Christmas caroling. As it turned out, Judd joined her and met her family, adding his deep baritone voice with her father and uncles.

From that first meeting, other dates had followed until they spent every available minute together. Each night it became more and more difficult to send him away.

Lanni remembered. Oh, sweet heaven, she remembered the night they hadn't stopped with kissing and touching....

"Lanni, no more." Judd had pushed himself away from her, leaning back against the sofa in her apartment and inhaling deep breaths in an effort to control his desire.

In vivid detail Lanni recalled the pain she saw on his face. "I love you," she whispered urgently. "Oh, Judd, I love you so much, I could die with it."

"Lanni," he begged, "don't tell me that. Please don't tell me that."

She'd been crushed at his harsh words. She wasn't a fickle teenager who fell in and out of love at will, but a woman with a woman's heart and she was filled with desire for this man.

"Oh, my sweet Lanni, don't you know how much I love you?"

"But…"

His callused hands had cupped her face and tenderly he'd kissed her face, drawing closer and closer to her mouth. Unable to bear this any longer, she removed her sweater, peeling it over her head. Judd had looked stunned. "What are you doing?"

She'd grinned coyly and kissed the corner of his mouth. "What does it look like?"

"Lanni!" His eyes were everywhere but on her. "You can't do that."

"Sure I can."

Judd got up and stalked to the other side of the room. "This isn't right."

"We love each other," she countered. This was a night to be remembered. When he discovered that she was a virgin, he'd know how much she treasured what they shared.

"I do love you," he moaned, seemingly at odds with himself. "But I won't do this. Making love with you now isn't right."

"And it would be with another woman?"

"Yes."

Lanni supposed she should be shocked and offended, but she wasn't. "Are you saying that you won't make love to me?"

"Yes," he fairly shouted.

Smiling, Lanni eliminated the space that separated them and gently placed her hands on his shoulders. Standing on the tips of her toes, she brushed her mouth over his. Judd went rigid and groaned.

"You didn't believe me when I said I loved you. I only want to prove to you how much," she challenged softly.

"Lanni," he begged, his voice so low it was barely audible. "Not like this."

"I've been waiting for you all my life," she whispered. They had such little time. He was scheduled to fly into Anchorage the day after Christmas. "Can't you see that what we share is rare and beautiful?"

Judd tilted his head back and closed his eyes. "Oh, Lanni, you're making this difficult."

"I love you, Judd. Love you, love you, love you. I'm giving you something I've never offered another man. What do I have to do to make you accept my gift?"

He opened his eyes then and lowered his gaze to hers. Passion burned in their dark depths, consuming her with his need. "I'll take your gift on one condition," he'd said.

"Anything."

"Marry me, Lanni. Tonight. This minute. I can't wait for you any longer."

Three

"Marry you," Lanni replied softly. "But, Judd, why?"

From the way he tossed his head back, Lanni suspected he'd dislocated several vertebrae. "The proper response to the question is yes. You're not supposed to squabble with me. This isn't the great debate."

"But what about your job?"

"I'll find one in Seattle. Don't argue with me, Lanni. We're in love and people in love get married."

Lanni was enjoying this immeasurably. "People in love do other things." She cozied up to him, reveling in the feel of her torso rubbing against his firm body.

"No, they don't. At least we don't—won't—until it's right." Before she knew what was happening, he took her sweater from the sofa and pulled it over her head, leaving the knit arms dangling at her sides. "I'm not touching you again until we're married. And I don't want to hear any arguments about it, either." With all the purpose of a federal court judge, he marched to the chair and reached for his jacket. He stuffed his arms inside as though he couldn't get away from her fast enough. "Well, hurry up," he barked when he noticed she hadn't moved.

"Where…are we going?"

"To see your parents to talk to about our wedding."

"But…"

"You aren't going to argue with me, are you?"

Lanni had the distinct feeling that he wouldn't hesitate to bite her head off if she did. "No."

He waved his index finger in her direction. "You better comb your hair for heaven's sake. One look at you and your family will know what we've been doing."

A quick glance in the bathroom mirror confirmed that what he'd said was true. Her hair was mussed, her lips swollen and dewy from his kisses. Her face was flushed, but it beamed with happiness. Her eyes revealed an inner glow that came from loving Judd and being loved by him.

By the time she rejoined him, he'd taken her coat from the hall closet and held it open for her. "I'd prefer a nice quiet ceremony, but if you want the whole shebang then that's fine, too."

"I…haven't given it much thought."

"Well, the time is now. You'd better decide."

"Judd," she said, then hesitated, not knowing how to voice her thoughts. She wasn't even sure she should be saying anything. She wanted to be Judd's wife. "You… you don't seem very happy about this."

"I'm ecstatic."

"I can tell." She folded her arms across her breasts and proudly shook her head. "I told you before, we don't need to get married. I'm willing to…"

"But I'm not." His brow arched over frowning eyes. His scowling glare defied argument. "Who should I talk to first? Your father?"

"I…guess."

"Well? What are you waiting for?"

"You mean you want to talk to him now?" She checked her watch. "It's almost eleven o'clock."

"Feeling the way I do now, he'll be pleased that I've come to him instead of being here alone with you."

"Oh, Judd, am I tempting you?" She placed her hand on his shoulder and gazed lovingly into his dark eyes. "It's the most heady feeling in the world to know you want me so much."

He broke the contact and his index finger flew at her again. "I'm not in any mood for your funny business."

"Right." She swallowed down a giggle, but her gaze sobered when she noticed how serious Judd had become. "I do love you, you know."

"I don't know why, but I'm not going to question it. I want everything you have for me Lanni—a home, a family—love. I need it all."

Lanni needed it, too, although she hadn't felt it was necessary until that moment.

Together, braving the cold wind and the uncertainties that faced them, they drove to Lanni's parents' home near Tacoma.

The late-night visit with her family was little short of hilarious. Her mother brought out Christmas cake and coffee, all the while dressed in an old terry-cloth housecoat that was cinched at the waist. When Judd explained the reason for their unexpected appearance, Lanni noticed a silent tear slip from her mother's eyes.

Her father, on the other hand, sat on the sofa with his legs crossed, nodding now and again, and seemed to have been struck speechless. Eighteen-year-old Jade hid on the top stair outside her bedroom door, not wanting to come down because she had an apricot mask on her face.

After leaving her parents' place, Judd and Lanni located an all-night diner and sat drinking mugs of spiced hot cider.

"Are you sure you still want to go through with this?" she asked, half-expecting Judd to have decided otherwise.

"I want it now more than ever." His hand gripped hers as though the simple action linked them together for all time.

"Then I've made a decision."

"Okay, let's hear it."

"I want to be married on the first weekend of the new year," she stated decisively.

"I don't want a formal wedding. No bridesmaids, just Jade as my maid-of-honor and no organ music. I'm not even sure I want the long flowing gown and veil."

He nodded, agreeing with her.

"At dusk I think, just before the sun sets, when the sky is golden and the stars are outlined in the heavens."

"Sundown sounds nice."

"Our love is so unexpected and special that I don't want to be bound by the chains of tradition."

"I agree," he murmured, and smiled softly.

"I want to be married in a hundred-year-old church on Vashon Island. I'm afraid it may be closed down so we'll need to see about having it opened for the wedding." She paused to hear his reaction, but like her father only minutes before, Judd was speechless. "It's near the beach," she elaborated. "My grandmother attended services there nearly all her life. I always loved that old church. I want us to be married there."

"Anything else?" He looked skeptical.

"I don't think so."

"A hundred-year-old church that may be closed down?"

"Right."

Judd looked doubtful.

"Well, what do you think?" She knew it sounded impractical, but she was in love for the first time in her life and everything had to be perfect. She only planned to be married once.

His expression softened as he raised her fingertips to his mouth and lovingly pressed his lips against them. "All these weeks we've been seeing each other, I've wondered what it was about you that attracted me so strongly. I've known beautiful women in the past, but I've never wanted to marry any of them. Listening to your appreciation of the past and your love of beauty helps me to understand why I find you so extraordinary."

And so they were married in a tiny church close to a windswept shore as the sun set in the background. The sound of the waves slapping against the pebble beach echoed in the distance as a handful of family and friends formed a half circle around them. Outside, sea gulls soared, their calls merging with the sounds of the water. When Judd slipped the ring on Lanni's finger, their eyes met and held and Lanni knew then that she would never know a happiness greater than that moment…

A tear slipped from the corner of Lanni's eye and rolled down the side of her face, wetting her pillowcase. Somehow things had gone very wrong. Maybe she'd gotten pregnant too soon, she didn't know. Judd had changed jobs twice within the first year they were married. He seemed to become bored with routine. Then, after Jenny was born, everything had gone wrong.

She recalled the night Jenny was sick with an ear infection and cried incessantly. Helpless to know how to comfort the three-month-old baby, Lanni had walked the bedroom floor gently holding the baby against her shoulder and patting her tiny back. But nothing she did seemed to quiet her.

Judd had staggered into the room. "I can't sleep with you in here. Let me walk her while you try to sleep."

"I couldn't sleep," she said, and continued pacing. Trying to lighten the mood, she told him something her mother had recently claimed. "We should enjoy these days. It's said that they're supposed to be the best times of our lives."

Judd had chuckled. "You mean it gets worse?"

For them it had. Much, much worse.

Her pillowcase was damp before Lanni reached for a tissue from her nightstand and wiped her face. She'd assumed all her tears over Judd had been shed. The power he held to dredge up the past and hurt her was frightening. She couldn't allow that to continue. Severing the relationship was vital for her emotional well-being. Since he'd been gone, her life had been in limbo. She lived a solitary lifestyle and yet she was bound by invisible chains. Having lived with Judd those first years, she was well aware of his hearty sexual appetite. She couldn't believe that he had been faithful to her.

The instant flash of pain that shot through her was so fierce and so sudden that Lanni bolted upright. She had to get away from Judd no matter what the price.

* * *

The following morning, Jenny woke and came into Lanni's room. Her eager fingers tugged at the pillow. "Mommy, are you awake?"

One eyelid reluctantly opened. "Nope."

"I'm hungry."

It had been almost morning before Lanni had finally drifted off to sleep. When the alarm had rung, she rolled over and turned it off. Going to the office would be completely unproductive. Her head hurt and her eyes ached from hours of restless tossing.

"What time is it?" she asked Jenny, unwilling to open her eyes to read the clock.

Jenny climbed off the bed and raced into the kitchen. In an effort to escape the inevitable, Lanni buried her head under the plump pillow.

Within seconds Jenny was back. "The big hand is on the eleven and the little hand on the eight."

"Okay," Lanni mumbled. It was nearly eight. Normally Jenny would have been fed and dressed before now and ready for the day-care center. "I'll get up in a couple of minutes."

"Can I have Captain Crunch cereal?"

"Yes," she mumbled, "but I'll pour the milk."

"When will Daddy be here? He said he was coming back, didn't he?"

This time Lanni forced her eyes open. "I don't know."

"But he said…"

"Then he'll be here."

Lanni had spent a sleepless night, trapped in indecision. Judd wanted to take Jenny. She couldn't let him. The best thing to do would be to hold her ground. It was unreasonable of him to arrive unannounced and ask to take their daughter. And yet, Lanni understood. Judd's father was dying.

As the early light of dawn dappled the horizon, before Lanni slept, the questions had become more tangled, the answers more elusive and the doubts overwhelming.

Now, sitting upright in the bed, she tossed the blankets aside and stood, glancing at her daughter. "You know what I want to do?"

"What?" From the way Jenny answered her, Lanni could tell all that interested her daughter at the moment was eating her sugar-coated cereal.

"Let's go to the beach," she suggested, knowing that Jenny loved it as much as she did. "I'll call the office and tell them I'm not coming in and we'll escape for the day."

"Can I have breakfast first?"

As Lanni had expected, Jenny was more concerned with her stomach. Lanni followed her into the kitchen and poured the cold milk over her cereal. While Jenny ate, she dressed in faded jeans and a pale pink sweatshirt.

After making the necessary phone calls and sticking Jenny's breakfast dishes in the dishwasher, they packed a small lunch.

Seahurst Park on the shores of Puget Sound was only a short distance from the house. Had she felt more chipper, Lanni could have peddled her bike to the park, placing Jenny in the child's seat attached to the rear of the ten-speed. But her eyes burned from her sleepless night and she had no desire to expend unnecessary energy.

They found a parking place in the large lot and carried their lunch down to the pebble beach. The waters of the Sound were much too cold for swimming during any season of the year so they spent the first hour exploring the beach, locating small treasures.

As her father had done with her as a child, Lanni had given Jenny a love and appreciation for the sea. Barefoot, they walked along the shore. The swelling waves broke against the sand, leaving a creamy trail in their wake. Lanni paused to breathe in the fresh salt-laden air.

The four-year-old discovered a small seashell to add to her growing collection. Soon a variety of valuables were stored in the plastic bucket. A smooth, shiny rock, a dried piece of kelp and a broken sand dollar were the rare finds of the morning's outing.

"I want to show this to my daddy," Jenny told her proudly, holding a tiny seashell in her palm.

Lanni managed to disguise her distress. Jenny had a right to know and love her father, but at what price? Judd would take her for a week or two and then drift out of their lives again. Only heaven knew if he'd ever show up again.

As an adult, Lanni had trouble dealing emotionally with Judd's disappearances. If he hurt her, she could just imagine what he would do to Jenny. As Jenny's mother, she couldn't allow Judd to hurt their daughter.

When they returned from the lazy stroll, Lanni noticed a tall male figure silhouetted against the bulkhead watching them. It didn't take her long to recognize the man as Judd.

"I thought I'd find you here," he murmured, joining her. His footsteps joined hers.

"How'd you know where I'd go?"

A light but sad smile curved one corner of his mouth. "Whenever anything was wrong between us, you'd go to the beach."

"It's beautiful here. I needed time to think."

"Have you decided?"

Lanni understood his urgency, but this decision was too important to rush. They were talking about the future of their daughter's life and the memories she would store in her young mind about her father and grandfather.

"Look what I found!" Jenny's tightly clenched hand opened to reveal the small pinkish shell in her palm.

"Did you find it by yourself?"

Jenny looked up at her mother. "Mommy helped. And see what else." She lifted the yellow bucket filled with her priceless finds.

With unexpected patience Judd sorted through Jenny's small treasures, commenting on each one. The little girl beamed with pride at the words of praise and soon ran off to play on the swing set.

Wordlessly Lanni followed, sitting on a park bench within easy sight of the playground toys.

Judd claimed the seat, settling his lanky build beside her. "You look like hell."

"Thanks." Her eyes narrowed into slits and she bit back a more caustic reply. He was probably right. She hadn't bothered to do anything more than run a brush through her hair.

"When was the last time you had anything to eat?"

She shrugged and added, her tone waspish, "I had a dinner date last night, but unfortunately that was interrupted." She could feel Judd grow tense and experienced a small sense of triumph. But almost immediately she felt guilty for baiting him. They were playing the games they always did after one of his long absences.

"I didn't mean that to sound the way it did," she whispered.

"Sure you did, Lanni, but don't worry. I don't plan to stick around long enough to interfere with any more of your dates."

"I didn't imagine you would."

"All I want is my daughter, and then I'll be on my way."

She was silent for a long moment. When she spoke, her voice was soft and strained. "I didn't sleep much last night," she admitted. "Memories kept me awake, forcing me to face how I felt. I haven't wanted to do that these last couple of years."

"Lanni—"

"No, please, let me finish," she whispered. "I loved you Judd, really loved you. I don't know what went wrong. A thousand times I've gone over our marriage and…"

"Nothing went wrong."

Her teeth bit unmercifully into the skin on the inside of her cheek. "You left me and Jenny, walked out the door without so much as a backward glance. Something was very wrong. You said yesterday that I suffocated you. I didn't know that… I honestly never knew that."

"It was wrong in the beginning."

"It wasn't," she contradicted. "You can't have forgotten how good it was with us. That first year was—"

"The happiest of my life."

"Then Jenny was born and—" She stopped abruptly in midsentence, her eyes widening. "You didn't want the baby?" She'd had a miserable pregnancy, but Judd had been marvelous. He'd taken the Lamaze classes with her and had been loving and supportive the entire nine months. Maybe it was because he had been so caring and gentle with her that Lanni had been unable to recognize the root of their problems. Not once had she suspected that Jenny was the beginning of their troubles.

"I wanted children." His eyes burned into hers, defying her to deny it. "You can't doubt that."

Remembering the day Jenny was born and the emotion she'd witnessed on Judd's proud face, she realized he couldn't be lying. "Those first months after she was born weren't easy on you."

"They weren't easy on either of us," he returned gruffly. "I didn't know one baby could cry so much."

"She was colicky."

"I know. I was there."

Lanni dropped her gaze. "But only part of the time."

Jenny was less than six months old when Judd left the first time. Lanni had felt like a zombie by the time he returned. Day in and day out she was alone with the baby, cut off from the world. If it hadn't been for her parents, Lanni was convinced she would have gone crazy. She and Judd were new to the neighborhood and Lanni hadn't met any of the other mothers. The only adult contact she had during those long, miserable weeks had been her parents and Jade.

"Right," Judd echoed. "I was only there part of the time."

The silence stretched between them, heavy and oppressive. Her heart pounded wildly in her ears and she stared at him for several long seconds before she was able to continue. "All night I thought about when you left. I... I drove you away, didn't I? I never let you know what I was feeling, holding it all inside until...until..."

"Lanni, no." His hand took hers, squeezing her fingers

so hard that they ached. "Stop trying to blame yourself. It's me who was wrong. I should never have asked you to share my life. Not when I knew all along that I was all wrong for you."

"You told me once you found the walls closing in around you. You tried to tell me, but I didn't understand."

"Stop blaming yourself." Judd's response was instantaneous and sharp. "It was both of us. We were young and immature."

She held her chin at a regal angle, refusing to reveal the doubts and agonies she'd endured. "But you left anyway."

His eyes revealed the struggle he waged within himself. "I saw you hold back the tears and I hated what I was doing to you and the baby. I never wanted anything to work more than my life with you. I tried, Lanni, you know I tried."

"We've been through all this before," she whispered, hardly able to find her voice. "It doesn't do any good to drag it up again. At least for us it doesn't. The arguments have already been said."

"Mommy, Daddy, look," Jenny shouted, her shrill voice filled with glee. An older child stood behind the little girl, pushing the swing. Jenny's short legs eagerly pumped in and out. She leaned back as far as her hands would allow and pointed her toes at the sky, straining to reach higher and higher.

"Jenny," Lanni said, coming to her feet. "That's enough."

"I want to go real high."

"Jenny no…" Terror rose in her throat, strangling off her reply as the swing rose steadily until the chain buckled, swerved and tossed the little girl to the ground.

"Oh, no." For a paralyzing second Lanni couldn't move.

"Jenny." Judd's own voice revealed his silent terror.

The child lay prone on the sand, holding her stomach and kicking her stubby legs.

Judd moved first, reaching Jenny before Lanni. He bent over the child, his face devoid of color. "She's had the wind knocked out of her."

"Do something," Lanni pleaded. "She can't breathe."

"She will in a minute."

But Judd's assurances didn't ease Lanni's fear. Her fingers bit into his shoulder until Jenny sucked in a gulp of air and let out a horrifying cry. Judd picked Jenny up and handed her to Lanni. Sitting in the sand, she held the child to her shoulder and gently rocked back and forth, trying to comfort her. Lanni was trembling so hard that she felt faint for a moment.

"She'll be all right."

Judd's words barely registered above Jenny's frantic cries, which gained volume with every breath she inhaled. Gradually her cries subsided into giant hiccuping sobs.

Carefully coming to a stand, Lanni carried her over to the park bench where she'd been sitting. With the little girl in her lap, she brushed the hair from her small temple, searching for evidence of any further injuries. "Tell me where it hurts."

The child shook her head, not wanting to talk.

Standing above them, Judd's face was pinched into a tight frown.

"This is all your fault," she cried, barely recognizing how unreasonable she sounded. It didn't matter. None of it did. Jenny was her daughter. Judd was the one who left them. "Go away." Her voice was high and scratchy.

"Lanni—"

"Just go away," she cried. "I don't want you here."

Judd was as shaken as Lanni. He'd seen Jenny go toppling off the swing and his heart had stopped. Pausing, he raked his fingers through his hair. "Listen, I'll go down by the beach." She may be acting unreasonably, but he understood. Lanni had her face buried near Jenny's shoulder and refused to look at him. "I'll be on the beach," he repeated.

Still she didn't answer. Reluctantly he walked away. He wanted to slam his fist against the rock wall and welcome the release of pain.

Sand filled his shoes, but he continued walking. If Lanni claimed she'd been up half the night remembering, it didn't surprise him. He'd been up most of the night as well. That final horrible scene when he'd left two years ago had played back in his mind again and again.

Lanni had delivered her ultimatum: either he stay in Seattle or they were through. Judd recognized at the time he had no choice. He loved her, wanted her with him, and she'd refused. He'd walked out the door. He remembered the pain etched so deeply in her soft features. For nearly eighteen months she'd clung to him, begged him not to leave her again. This time she hadn't. With a calm he hardly recognized in his wife, Lanni had told him to choose. The most difficult thing he'd done in his life was walk away from her that day. The sounds of laughter filled the park as Lanni watched Judd walk away from her. Jenny's painful cries faded to a mere whimper and Lanni regained control of her fragile emotions. She continued to hold her daughter, but her gaze followed Judd's dejected figure as he meandered along the shore, his hands stuffed inside the pockets of his jeans. A brisk wind buffeted against him, plastering his shirt to his torso.

Lanni had been completely unreasonable to shout at him. It was no more his fault than hers. The frustration of the moment had gotten to her and she'd lashed out at Judd, wanting to blame him for the troubles of the world. That was the crux of the problem with their relationship. They each struck out at the other, hurting each other.

"How do you feel?" she asked Jenny.

She squirmed off her lap. "I want Daddy."

Lanni let her go and sat motionless as the small child climbed over the bulkhead and down onto the sandy beach. Her small arms swung at her sides as she rushed to join her father. Judd apparently didn't see her coming and hesitated when her hand reached for his. He went down on one knee and wrapped both arms around the child. Lanni felt the strings on her heart yanked in two different directions. Her throat muscles were so tight she felt as if she were being strangled.

Tilting her head toward the sun, she closed her eyes. She prayed for wisdom; she didn't know what to do. In all the time she'd raised Jenny, alone with only her parents and her sister for help, she'd never faced a more difficult dilemma.

When she straightened, she noticed Judd and Jenny walking toward her. Jenny's hand was linked with her father's.

"Feel better?" he asked Lanni softly.

After watching Judd with their daughter, she whispered her apology. "I'm sorry. You weren't to blame for what happened any more than I was. Accidents happen."

Judd sat down beside her. "I understand. You were angry for all the other times Jenny's been hurt and I haven't been here."

She nodded, accepting his explanation. She hadn't realized it herself.

"We need to talk about Jenny." He forced the subject that she'd been avoiding from the moment he'd discovered her at the park.

"I...know."

"Have you decided?" Pride stiffened her shoulders. He wouldn't take Jenny without her permission. Nor would he plead with her. This was the only request he'd made of her since leaving.

"I can't let you take Jenny alone."

"Then come with me." He offered the only other solution.

"I'll only do that on one condition."

"Name it."

Boldly her eyes met his. "I want you to sign the divorce papers."

Four

"What's a divorce?" Jenny wanted to know, glancing from one parent to another.

"An agreement," Judd answered patiently, his gaze lowering briefly to his daughter's before rising to pin Lanni's. He supposed he shouldn't be surprised. He'd carried the papers with him for two years. He hadn't wanted a divorce, but she'd given him no option. He supposed he should have prepared himself for the inevitable. Yet he was amazed at the fierce regret that ravaged him.

Divorce.

How final that ugly word sounded. His inclination was to agree and be done with it if that was what she sincerely wanted. But he'd seen that milquetoast agent she'd been dating and had disliked him instantly. Steve Delaney wasn't near man enough for a woman like Lanni.

"Well?" she prodded.

"Fine, I'll sign the papers."

At the sound of his words, Lanni felt almost as if a weight had settled on her shoulders. Surprised, she wondered why she was reacting so negatively. She should be glad that it was nearly over. At last she could cut herself free of the invisible bonds that tied her to Judd and make a new life for herself and Jenny.

It was apparent that if it wasn't for his father, Judd wouldn't be here now. He hadn't intended to come back. He hadn't returned because he wanted to be with her and Jenny. Basically nothing had changed between them. He hadn't given her an argument when she demanded he sign the divorce papers. He'd revealed no hesitation. From his reaction, Lanni could only assume that he wanted the divorce as much as she did.

Judd reached down and lifted Jenny into his arms. The little girl looped hers around his neck and smiled. "I'm glad you're my daddy."

"So am I, sweetheart."

"We're going on a long trip," Judd was saying to Jenny.

"To see your daddy?"

Judd's thick brows darted upward to show mild surprise.

"That's right."

"Where does your daddy live?"

"In Montana."

"Mon-tan-a," Jenny repeated carefully. "Does he have whiskers, too?"

Judd threw back his head and laughed. "Yes."

Jenny grinned. "Is Mommy coming?"

Judd responded with a sharp nod. "She'll be with us."

"Good," Jenny proclaimed, and lowered her head to Judd's shoulder. "I'm glad you're here," she murmured on the tail end of a long yawn.

"It's almost her nap time," Lanni said softly. "I'll take her home and make the necessary arrangements while she's asleep. When do you want to leave?"

"First thing tomorrow morning." His hand gently patted Jenny's back.

"I may need more time than that." Her mind scanned the calendar on her desk. Summers were the busiest time for real estate agents. Most families preferred to make a move during the vacation months of June, July and August to avoid uprooting children during the school year.

"We leave tomorrow."

Judd's words broke into her thoughts and she bristled. He must realize she had responsibilities. She couldn't just walk away from everything because he was in an all-fired rush.

Resentment simmered within Lanni. As he had all his life, Judd expected her to walk away from her responsibilities. "I said, I'll do my best to be ready by tomorrow. But I can't and won't make any promises."

"Listen, Lanni, I don't know what Stuart's condition is, but he wouldn't have written if he wasn't bad. I haven't got time to waste sitting around here while you rearrange your dating schedule."

Dating schedule. Lanni fumed as they marched to the parking lot. Judd had some perverse notion that she'd been playing the role of a swinging single since he'd been gone. Well, fine, she'd let him think exactly that. In two years the only man she'd ever dated was Steve and that had been only within the last three months.

Judd followed her to her car, slipping a droopy-eyed Jenny inside the child's protective car seat while Lanni waited silently. The little girl's head rolled to one side as she was strapped into place. If she wasn't already asleep, she would be soon. As silently as possible, Judd closed the car door.

Then, defying everything she'd told herself on the long hike to the car, Lanni turned to him, her hands braced against her hips. "I'll have you know that the only man I've dated since the minute you walked out the door is Steve Delaney and I resent your implying otherwise."

Despite the outrage flashing from her cool, dark eyes, Judd grinned. He'd always known Lanni had spunk. He hadn't meant to suggest anything and realized how offended she was. "I know. I didn't mean anything," he said, and sighed. "I'm worried about Stuart."

Lanni's indignation vanished as quickly as it came. "I'll do everything I can to be ready so we can leave on schedule."

"I'm counting on it." He hedged, needing to say something more and not sure how to do it without the words getting in the way. "I appreciate this, Lanni. I'll sign those papers you want and we can both go about our lives in peace. I'm sorry it turned out like this. I never was the right man for you."

"It was my fault," she whispered, the emotion blocking her throat. "I was the wrong type of woman for you."

"It's over, so let's quit blaming ourselves."

"All right," she agreed, her eyes burning bright with unshed tears. Part of her had hoped Judd didn't want to make their separation final and that he'd suggest they wait and give themselves another chance. She'd asked for the divorce, demanded that he sign the papers, but deep down, Lanni had held onto the belief that he loved her enough to change and make everything right between them again. What a romantic fool she was.

"I'll pick you and Jenny up around six tomorrow morning, unless I hear otherwise."

"We'll be ready," Lanni told him, climbing inside the driver's seat of the car. Judd remained standing in the parking lot. Lanni watched from her rearview mirror, his figure growing smaller and smaller.

Once home, and with Jenny securely tucked in bed for her nap, Lanni sat at the kitchen table, her hands cupping a mug of hot coffee. So it would soon be over.

Lanni knew her parents would be relieved for her sake. They liked Judd, but had been witnesses to the turmoil he had brought into all their lives. After Judd left, they'd been wonderfully supportive. Lanni was grateful, but she was concerned that her problems caused her parents to worry. As luck would have it, they were vacationing in California this month and they need never know about Lanni and Jenny leaving with Judd.

With a determined effort, Lanni forced herself to deal with the necessities of this trip. She reached for a pen and paper to make a list of people she needed to contact and appointments that would need to be rescheduled. The house was silent, almost eerie. She paused and set the pencil aside. Her heart ached. She felt as if she were dying on the inside—never had she been more lonely.

Her hand was on her phone before she could stop herself from contacting Jade.

"Mr. Boynton's office," came Jade's efficient-sounding voice.

"I need to talk to you," Lanni announced starkly, her voice tight with emotion.

"Lanni? What's wrong?"

"I'm…leaving with Judd and Jenny in the morning to visit his father."

"But that's nothing to be upset about," Jade offered

enthusiastically. "In fact, it just might be that all you two need is some time together. I've tried to stay out of it, but honestly, Lanni, I'm just not any good at biting my tongue. You love Judd, you always have—"

"We're going through with the divorce," Lanni cut in sharply, biting into the corner of her bottom lip.

"What?" For once Jade was nearly speechless.

"It's what we both want."

"It isn't what either of you want—even I can see that and I know zilch about love. Lanni, for heaven's sake don't do something you'll regret the rest of your life," she pleaded.

"Jade, please, I only phoned to let you know that I'm leaving with Judd. Jenny and I shouldn't be gone any longer than two weeks. Can you pick up my mail and water the houseplants once or twice?"

"Of course, but..." Jade hesitated, "can you hold on a minute?"

"Sure."

"Lanni," she said when she came back on the phone, "listen, I've got to go. I'll stop by on my way home from work and we can talk this out."

Almost immediately the line was disconnected. From past experience Lanni knew how much Jade's boss frowned upon his employees using the office phone for personal calls.

While Jenny slept, Lanni used the time to make the necessary arrangements for this trip with Judd. When she contacted the office, Steve was unavailable, but she left a message for him, asking that he phone her when convenient. She wasn't sure Steve would be pleased when she told him she was going with Judd. From experience, Lanni realized her fellow worker could be persuasive when he wanted to be.

The washer and dryer were both in full operation, and suitcases brought up from the basement by the time Jade arrived late that afternoon. Jenny was playing at the neighbor's.

"Hi," Jade said, entering the kitchen. "You aren't really going through with this, are you?"

Lanni glanced up from inside the refrigerator. Perishables lined the countertop. "Through with what? Traveling with Judd, or the divorce?"

"The divorce."

Lanni set a head of cabbage on the counter. "It's not open for discussion."

"It's just that I feel so strongly that you're doing the wrong thing."

"Jade," Lanni said fiercely. "I don't want to hear it. It's done. We've agreed and that's all there is to it."

Suspiciously Jade eyed the eggs, leftover spaghetti and a loaf of bread on the counter. "Fine, but either you've just recently discovered food or that's one disasterous omelette you're cooking."

"This is for you."

"Me?" Jade slapped her hand against her chest. "Hey, I know you're upset, but that isn't any reason to sabotage my diet."

"I'm not," Lanni said, smiling despite herself. "These will only spoil while we're gone, so I'm sending them home with you."

Jade reached for a pickle, munching on the end of it. "I am pleased about one thing, however. You need this time with Judd."

"It isn't exactly a vacation, you know."

"I do, but I've always thought that all you two needed…"

"Jade! Stop it! I'm going with Judd for one reason and one reason only."

"Sure you are," Jade said, batting her long lashes provocatively. "But if things happen between you two while you're away, I won't be surprised. Not me. Not one little bit."

Deciding the best thing she could do was ignore her sister's antics, Lanni set a package of luncheon meat on the counter. "Wrong again. Nothing's going to happen, because I won't let it."

Her phone rang and Lanni reached for it, hoping it was Steve. It took her a couple of minutes to inform the caller that she wasn't interested in having her carpet cleaned.

"I haven't talked to Steve," Lanni said, disconnecting.

"Don't," Jade said sharply.

"What do you mean by that?"

"It's none of his business, Lanni. He's good looking and smooth and as stable as the Rock of Gibraltar, but he isn't for you. Judd is."

"Get your head out of the clouds," Lanni barked, snapping at her sister. "My marriage was over a long time ago. Nothing's left but a thin shell." And shattered illusions, she added silently. "Judd may love me in his own way, but it isn't enough to repair the damage to our marriage. We're both adult enough to realize that."

"But…"

"There aren't any buts about it. We both want out of this farce of a marriage and as soon as possible."

"But you're leaving with him."

"Yes."

"That has to mean something," Jade argued.

"It means nothing. Nothing," she repeated, more for her own benefit than Jade's.

The following morning, at 6:00 a.m., Judd parked the midsize SUV in front of the house. He dreaded this trip, every mile of it. He didn't know what to expect once he arrived in Twin Deer. For all he knew, Stuart could already be dead. But confronting his father was the least of his worries. Little could alter the problems in that relationship. His real concern was this time with Lanni and Jenny. It wouldn't be easy being close to them. Having them constantly at his side was bound to make him yearn for the way things used to be. How easy it would be to hold Lanni in his arms again. But it wouldn't be right—she wanted this divorce. For that matter, he should have done something to give her her freedom long before now.

Judd climbed out of the vehicle and walked around the back, opening the tailgate to make room for Lanni's and Jenny's luggage. When he finished shuffling his gear, he glanced up to discover Lanni standing on the front porch, watching him.

"Are you ready?"

She nodded, seeming to feel some of the heaviness that weighted his heart.

"I brought the divorce papers with me. Do you want me to sign them now?" he asked.

Lanni hedged, then remembered the times Steve had told her that the divorce was necessary for the emotional healing to take place. More than any other time since Judd left, Lanni yearned to be whole again. "Maybe you'd better," she murmured sadly.

Judd followed her into the house. "Have you got a pen?"

"Don't you want to read it first?"

He shook his head. "I can't see the point. Whatever you want is fine."

"But…"

"I told you I'd sign them. Arguing over the finer points now isn't going to change anything."

Reluctantly Lanni handed him the ballpoint pen.

Leaning over the desk, Judd flipped the pages until he located the necessary place for his signature. He signed his name on the dotted line. "There," he said, handing her both the document and the pen. "What next?"

"I… I don't know," Lanni admitted. "I'll deal with it once we get back. Is that all right with you?"

"Whatever you want." He didn't sound concerned either way. He'd kept his part of the bargain, just as she was keeping hers.

Jenny wandered out from the hallway, her small hands fumbling with the buttons of her printed cotton coveralls. "I need help."

"I'll get them," Lanni offered, grateful for an excuse to move away from Judd and break the awkwardness of the moment.

"I already had breakfast," Jenny announced to her father. "Captain Crunch cereal is my favorite, but Mommy only lets me have that sometimes. I ate Captain Crunch today."

Judd grinned, his gaze skipping from Jenny to Lanni. "Dressed and already eaten breakfast. You always were well organized."

"I try to be," she said, striving for a light tone.

"Then let's hit the road." He lifted the two large suit-cases from the living room floor.

"I'll lock up."

By the time she'd reached the station wagon, Judd had taken Jenny's car seat from Lanni's car and positioned it in the back seat of his. Jenny had climbed aboard and was strapped into place. With the morning paper tucked under one arm, a thermos filled with coffee in the other, plus her purse and a small traveling bag, Lanni joined them.

Judd sat in the front seat, his hands on the wheel. "Ready?"

"Ready," she concurred, snapping her seatbelt into place. As ready as she would ever be.

Judd started the car and pulled onto the street. A road map rested on the seat between them. This trip wasn't going to be easy, Lanni mused. Deafening silence filled the car. Jenny played quietly with Betsy, her doll, content for the moment.

Lanni's mind flirted with some way of starting a con-versation. They couldn't discuss the past. That was filled with too many regrets. They had no future. The divorce papers were signed and as soon as they returned, she'd take the necessary steps to terminate their marriage. The only suitable topic for discussion was the present and that, too, presented problems.

"I told the office I wouldn't be gone more than a cou-ple of weeks."

"That should be more than enough time," Judd said, concentrating on the freeway stretched out in front of him. They hadn't been on the road ten minutes and al-ready Lanni was making it sound like she couldn't wait to get back. His mouth tightened with impatience. He hadn't asked her about Steve Delaney, and wondered how much her relationship with the other man had prompted her to press the issue of the divorce.

Lanni saw the way Judd's lips thinned and tried to explain. "I simply can't stay any longer. As it is I'm having another agent fill in for me, which doubles her workload. I don't like doing that and wouldn't if it wasn't necessary. I mean…" She paused, realizing she was rambling.

"It's all right, Lanni. I understand."

But she wondered if he really did.

For the first hour Jenny's excited chatter filled the silence. She asked a hundred questions, her curious mind working double time. Lanni was astonished at the patience Judd revealed. He answered each question thoroughly and in terms young Jenny could easily understand.

Lanni gleaned information as well. The trip would take the better part of three days, which meant they'd spend two nights on the road. Sleeping arrangements would need to be discussed soon. Not a thrilling subject, but one they'd face at his father's house as well. Surely Judd realized she had no intention of sharing his bed. Not for appearance's sake, convenience or any other reason. Her face grew warm at the realization that she feared her reactions to Judd should he try to make love to her. Heaven knew they'd never had any problems in bed. If anything… She shook her head sharply, causing Judd to look at her.

"Are you too warm?"

"I'm fine, thanks."

They stopped for a break on the top of Snoqualmie Pass. Jenny claimed she was hungry again and since Judd hadn't eaten breakfast, they found a restaurant. Lanni rarely ate anything in the morning, but Judd talked her into tasting something. Rather than argue, she ordered eggs, convinced it was a waste of good food. But to her surprise she was hungry and cleaned her plate.

Judd noticed and shared a warm smile with her. "Jade thinks a strong wind is going to blow you away."

"Did she suggest you fatten me up?" That sounded like something Jade would say.

"As a matter of fact, she did." One side of his mouth twitched upward. "But not with food."

Lanni's cheeks filled with hot color. She had never realized what an interfering troublemaker her younger sister could be. She still couldn't believe the gall of such a remark. "When did you two talk?" After she'd learned about Jade and Judd communications, little would surprise her.

"Last night. I took her to dinner."

A tiny pain pricked her heart. Jealous over her own sister. Ridiculous. Insane. Childish.

"She wanted to talk to me about Steve," Judd explained.

"Steve Delaney is none of your business," Lanni returned tartly, furious with Jade and even more so with Judd.

"We're married; I'd say your relationship with him concerns me."

"*Were* married," Lanni whispered fiercely. "Those divorce papers are signed."

"Signed yes, but not filed."

"They will be the minute I get back to Seattle."

"Then so be it, but until they are you'd do well to remember you're my wife and Jenny will always be my daughter."

With trembling fingers, Lanni wiped the corners of her mouth with a napkin and reached for her coffee, lowering her gaze. She'd promised herself that she would do anything to avoid arguing with Judd, yet here they were, not fifty miles from home and already going for each other's throats. "I imagine Steve wasn't the only thing my sister wanted to discuss," she said, striving for a lighter tone.

Judd hesitated, but figured Lanni knew her sister as well as he. "She thinks we should get back together again." His eyes studied her, watching for a sign, anything that would tell him her feelings. Years ago Lanni's eyes had been as readable as a first-grade primer. No longer. She'd learned to school her emotions well. He found her expression blank, and experienced a sense of regret. Her eyes weren't the only thing that had changed. The picture he'd carried in his mind did her little justice. Maturity had perfected her beauty. It astonished him that it had taken another man this long to discover her. On the tail end of that thought came another: Lanni wouldn't have encouraged a relationship. He was convinced she'd shunned male interest; Jade had confirmed that. But not because Lanni carried any great hope he'd be back, Judd realized, but because she wasn't free to do so. He believed her when she claimed Steve was the first man she'd dated in two years.

"A reconciliation isn't what either of us wants," she said slowly, raising the coffee cup to her lips.

"Right," he agreed. "It didn't work once. It won't work again." No one knew this better than Judd. But being with Lanni and Jenny was seductive. He'd spent less than half a day in their company and already his mind was devising methods of remaining close to them. He loved his daughter—she was a delight.

Just being with Jenny made him realize how much he was missing. The thought produced another: he couldn't be close to Jenny without being near Lanni. Seeing her with Steve was something he'd never be able to tolerate. Lanni deserved her freedom and the right to find happiness. When this business with Stuart was over, he'd head back to Mexico or Alaska or maybe the Middle East again. The farther away he was, the better it would be for everyone involved.

Jenny slept after breakfast, long enough not to require her usual nap. But by the middle of the afternoon, she was whiny and bored. Lanni did her best to keep the little girl occupied, reading to her and inventing games. Judd did what he could by making frequent stops, granting the child the opportunity to stretch her legs. By dinnertime all three were exhausted.

"I don't think I've ever realized what a handful one little girl could be," Judd commented, pulling into a parking spot in front of a restaurant outside of Coeur d'Alene, Idaho. It was only mid-afternoon but they were all exhausted and ready to call it a day.

"I've tried not to spoil her," Lanni said somewhat defensively.

Judd's hand compressed around the steering wheel. "I didn't mean to suggest that."

"Judd, listen—"

"Lanni—"

They spoke simultaneously, paused, then laughed thinly.

"I think we're as tired as Jenny. I've been up since before five," Lanni admitted.

"Me, too." A gentle smile tugged at his mouth. "Let's get something to eat and find a motel."

"That sounds like an excellent idea."

Lanni felt much better after a meal, although they'd made three stops previously for munchies. She took Jenny into the ladies' room while Judd paid the bill, joining him at the car.

"The cashier suggested a motel a couple of miles from here." Her eyes avoided his as he opened her car door. Doubts grew in Lanni's mind as Judd placed Jenny in her car seat, then joined her in the front of the car before starting the engine. She should say something about their sleeping arrangements, but she didn't want to seem like a prude. Nor did she wish to make an issue over the subject. Judd wasn't dense. He knew the score.

Lakeside Motel was situated on the sandy shores of Lake Coeur d'Alene and, as the cashier had said, was only a few miles from the restaurant. A paved walkway led down to the water's edge. Lanni got Jenny out of the car and walked down to the lake while Judd was in the motel office, booking their room. He joined her a few minutes later.

"I got us a room with two double beds?" He made the statement into a question.

"That'll be fine. I'll sleep with Jenny." Lanni wanted to bite back the words the minute they'd slid from her mouth. Naturally she'd sleep with Jenny. To cover her embarrassment, she stood and followed Judd back to the motel.

Instantly Jenny spied the crystal clear waters of the motel pool. "Can we go swimming?"

"We'll see," Lanni told her daughter. The comment was a mother's standby.

The room was clean and cool. Two freshly made double beds dominated the interior. Judd carried in their luggage, and Jenny automatically dug through hers, searching for her swimsuit. Lanni felt as if she had less energy than a rag doll, but she helped Jenny change clothes.

"I'll take her to the pool," Judd offered. "You look like you're about to collapse."

"We'll both go," Lanni compromised. "I can lounge on one of the chairs. All I ask is that you wear her out, otherwise no one's going to get any sleep tonight." From past experience Lanni knew that once Jenny became this hyperactive, she wouldn't fall asleep easily. All afternoon, the little girl had been acting like a coiled spring. Now she was beyond the stage of being tired.

Father and daughter splashed gleefully in the cool waters of the kidney-shaped pool. Jenny swam like a fish. She'd taken lessons since she was two years old and had no fear of water. Judd was amazed at her ability and, encouraged by his enthusiasm, Jenny outdid herself, diving from the side of the pool into his arms and swimming underwater like a miniature dolphin.

The sun was setting by the time the two finished romping in the water. The evening was glorious, the limitless pink sky was filled with the promise of another glorious day. A gentle, sweet-smelling breeze blew off the lake.

"I'll want to get an early start in the morning," Judd said, drying his face with the thick towel. Lanni purposely avoided looking at his lean, muscular body.

She nodded her agreement. "You don't need to worry about me. I'm tired enough to sleep now."

"I don't want to go to bed," Jenny said, yawning.

Judd picked her up and carried her back to their room. "You're so tired now you can barely keep your eyes open," he told her softly.

"I'm not sleepy," Jenny argued.

"But your mommy is so can you lie still and be real quiet for her?"

Reluctantly Jenny nodded.

Lanni gave Jenny a bath, and tucked her into the bed, lying beside her on top of the bedspread until she was convinced the little girl was asleep. It took only a matter of minutes. Relieved, she momentarily closed her eyes. Judd was using the bathroom. She'd have a turn when he was finished. But the next thing she knew he was shaking her gently awake, suggesting she climb under the covers.

Bolting upright, Lanni was shocked to find that it was hours later. "Why didn't you wake me?" she asked him lightly. He sat in the middle of the other bed, leaning against the headboard. His long legs were crossed at the ankles. It took her a moment to realize he wore pajama bottoms, the top half of his torso was bare. Pajamas were a concession on his part and one for which she was grateful.

"You'll note that I did wake you."

"Right." She paused to rub the sleep from her eyes. "I think I'll take a bath," she said to no one in particular.

Judd had assumed, after his shower, that he'd fall directly asleep just as Lanni and Jenny had done. He'd been quiet when he came back into the room and smiled gently at the two sleeping figures. He'd even covered Lanni with a blanket. But he hadn't slept. He couldn't. Just watching the two of them had occupied his eyes and his mind. For the first time in years, he'd experienced a craving for a cigarette. He'd quit smoking five years ago.

Lanni slept on her side, the folds of her blouse edging up and revealing a patch of her smooth stomach. The pulling buttons left a gap open in the front of her blouse so that he could see the edges of her bra. He diverted his gaze to the blank television screen. Until Jenny was born she'd worried that her breasts were too small. Then she'd nursed the baby and had been thrilled with their increased size. Judd had never been overly concerned. Her breasts were simply a part of this woman he loved. A wonderful, erotic part of her. Now he'd caught a glimpse of her bra and discovered it had the power to arouse him. It was a shock. If this was the way he was going to react, then it was a good thing she hadn't gone swimming. Heaven only knew what would happen when he caught sight of her in a bathing suit.

Expelling his breath, he bunched up the pillow and slammed his head against it. He'd ignore her and go to sleep. Instead a vision of Lanni sitting in the tub of warm water formed in his mind. His throat grew dry as he remembered how readily she responded to his touch. Judd groaned inwardly. Drums pounded in his head. He was a disciplined man. All he needed to do was find something else on which to center his thoughts. The dryness in his throat extended to his mouth and his lips.

"Judd," Lanni called softly.

He bolted upright. "Yes?"

"I can't seem to find a towel."

Five

"No towel," Judd repeated. The drums in his head pounded stronger and louder.

"It was silly of me not to have noticed." Lanni had stood for several minutes assessing her situation before saying anything, and now she was shivering with cold.

Judd paused, glancing around him. "There's probably something around here." For a panicked second, he actually considered ripping the bedspread off the bed and handing her that. Anything that would keep that scrumptious body of hers from his gaze. He was having enough trouble taming his imagination as it was. When his frantic thoughts finally jelled, he patiently searched the room and discovered a fresh supply of towels on the vanity outside the bathroom.

The door opened a crack. "Any luck?"

Judd's gaze was everywhere but on Lanni. "Here." He stretched out his arm and gave her the towel.

Gratefully, Lanni accepted it. "Thank you."

"In the future, *think*," he snapped. Being with her the next couple of weeks was going to be bad enough without her creating situations like this. He stalked into the other room and reached for his pants. He had to get out of the motel room. Already the need for a cigarette had multiplied a hundredfold. There were only so many temptations a man could be expected to handle at one time. Lanni, dressed in a nightgown, was one more than he had the strength to deal with now.

He'd just finished tucking his shirt inside his waistband when she appeared.

"Are…are you going someplace?" she asked in a small voice. She made busywork of stroking the brush through her hair, unable to disguise her surprised dismay.

"What does it look like?" Deliberately he refused to turn around and face her. "I'll be back in a while. Don't wait up for me."

Feigning a complete lack of concern, Lanni pulled back the bedspread and climbed between the clean sheets. "Don't worry, I won't," she murmured testily, furious at her inability to cloak her disheartenment. "I wouldn't dream of wasting my time on such a futile effort."

An argument was brewing. Judd could feel the static electricity in the air. The sooner he left, the better it would be for both of them. He opened the door and stalked outside. The night air felt cool against his heated face. He slipped his hands inside the pockets of his weather-worn jeans, walking purposely forward, unsure of his destination. His only thought was that he had to get away from Lanni before he did something they'd both regret.

A thin seam of sunlight poured into the room from a crack between the drapes. Wishing to avoid the light, Judd rolled onto his side, taking the sheet with him. His mouth felt like the bottom of a toxic waste dump, and his head pounded. So much for the theory that good whiskey doesn't cause hangovers. He sat up and rotated his head to work the stiffness from the muscles of his shoulders. He stopped abruptly when he noted that the double bed beside his own was empty. He was more surprised than alarmed, but hadn't the time to ponder Lanni and Jenny's absence before the little girl flew into the room.

"Morning, Daddy," she said, vaulting into his open arms.

"Hello, sweetheart." She smelled fresh and sweet and he wrapped his arms around her and hugged her close.

"I didn't think you were ever going to wake up. Mommy and me already had breakfast. I had pancakes with little yummy fruity things."

"Blueberries," Lanni inserted, entering the room carrying a Styrofoam cup. "I hope she didn't get you out of bed."

"No." Judd couldn't take his eyes from her. Today Lanni wore white shorts and a striped red T-shirt. Her blond hair was tied back at her neck with a bright ribbon the same ruby shade as the one that held Jenny's pigtails in place. Lanni looked about sixteen. A breathtaking sixteen. "She didn't wake me." He spoke only when he realized she was waiting for a response.

Lanni handed him the cup of black coffee and walked over to the bed and started fumbling with her bags. Jenny climbed onto the mattress beside her and reached for her doll. "I... I didn't know if I should get up," Lanni said. "You said something about an early start yesterday afternoon and—"

"What time is it?"

"Nine-thirty."

That late! "If it happens again, wake me."

"All right."

Judd pried the plastic lid from the coffee cup and took the first sip. "Give me ten minutes and I'll be ready."

"Fine. Jenny and I'll wait for you by the lake."

"Lanni." His voice stopped her. "Thanks."

Her nod was curt. Wordlessly she left him and led Jenny down the pathway that led to the shore of Lake Coeur d'Alene. She didn't know what had happened last night, but this morning everything was different. Judd hardly looked at her. In fact he seemed to avoid doing so. That wasn't like him. The faint scent in the room this morning had distracted her as well, and seemed to come from Judd. It took her a moment to identify it as the cloying fragrance of cheap cologne mingled with cigarette smoke.

Lanni stopped, a sudden attack of nausea clenching her stomach so violently she thought she might be ill. Locating a park bench, she quickly sat down until the pain subsided. Jenny joined her, and rhythmically swung her short legs while humming a sweet lullaby to Betsy.

The first flash of pain faded, only to be replaced by a dull ache. Lanni knew. In an instant, she knew. Judd had left her last night and found another woman. She hadn't heard him come in, but it must have been late for him to sleep until midmorning. Her lungs expanded with the need to breathe and she released a pain-filled sigh. The ink on their divorce papers wasn't even dry and already he'd found his way to another woman.

Organizing her thoughts, Lanni's heavy heart gave way to anger and simmering resentment. She shouldn't care; it shouldn't hurt this much. The fact that it did only went to prove how far she had to go to reconcile herself to the loss of this man and their marriage.

"The car's packed," Judd's rich voice came from behind her.

Instinctively Lanni stiffened. She didn't want to face him yet. She needed time to paint on a carefree facade until they could speak privately. The thought of riding beside him drained her already depleted strength and she felt incredibly weak.

"Lanni?"

"I…heard. I was just admiring the view."

"Are you ready, Cupcake?" Judd asked, effortlessly lifting Jenny into his arms.

"Do I get to see my grandpa soon?" the little girl asked eagerly.

Already Lanni could see that traveling with her daughter today was going to be difficult. Jenny had slept restlessly, tossing and turning most of the night. Being cooped up in a car with her for another eight to ten hours would be torture for them all.

"We won't see grandpa today," Judd answered, "but we should sometime tomorrow."

"Betsy wants to see Grandpa, too."

"Betsy?"

"My baby." Jenny lifted the doll for him to see.

"Right," Judd murmured and shot a quick smile in Lanni's direction, disregarding her sober look.

She ignored his smile and rose to her feet. "I don't imagine we'll get far today after this late start."

"We should do fine," Judd contradicted, eyeing her suspiciously. He didn't know what was troubling her all of a sudden, and was mystified at the unexpected change in her mood. Only a few minutes earlier she'd brought him a fresh cup of coffee and greeted him with a warm smile. Now she sat as stiff as plywood, hardly looking at him. Apparently he'd committed some ill deed to have gained her disfavor. But he hadn't an inkling of the terrible deed he'd done.

The three walked silently to the car. Within ten minutes they were back on Interstate 90, heading east. The tension in the car was so thick Judd could taste it. Even Jenny seemed affected. They hadn't gone fifteen miles before she started to whine. Judd left Lanni to deal with her. When that didn't help, Judd invented a game and involved Jenny. Her interest in that lasted a total of five uneasy minutes. Lanni sang silly songs with her daughter and that seemed to entertain her for a few minutes.

It seemed they stopped every twenty miles. Jenny wanted something to drink, Jenny was hungry. Without questioning any of his daughter's whims, Judd gave in to her. Discipline would have to come from Lanni, and again he was puzzled by his wife's surly mood. Jenny wasn't spoiled and yet Lanni seemed to give in to the child's every demand. It was a relief when Jenny finally fell asleep.

Exhausted, Lanni sighed as she tucked a blanket in the side window to keep the sun from Jenny's face. The little girl had worn herself out and was able to rest, but in the process, she'd drained Lanni of every ounce of patience. Feeling guilty, she realized Jenny's ill-temper was a reflection of her own unsettled mood. Although no cross words had been spoken, Jenny had known something was wrong between Lanni and Judd. Rather than argue with her daughter, Lanni had continually given in to her irrational demands.

Settling into her own seat beside Judd, Lanni resecured the seatbelt and leaned her head against the headrest, closing her eyes. She was a better mother than this. But she hadn't the strength to discipline Jenny. Not now. Not when her emotions were churning so violently inside her. She'd attempted to hide what she suspected, wrapping the pain around herself, struggling to deal with it alone, but it hadn't worked out that way. Jenny had been affected.

The silence was bliss and Judd relaxed, increasing the speed of the car. He wanted to make good time while he could. He attempted conversation a couple of times. Lanni's one-word replies ended that. It didn't take long for him to realize that it was far more pleasant to deal with Jenny's whining than the stony silence that hung between him and Lanni.

Determined to ignore her unreasonable, foul mood, he concentrated on driving, but his attention was drawn again and again to Lanni and the wounded look in her eyes. When he couldn't take it any longer, he asked, "All right, something's bothering you. What is it?"

"Nothing."

"Come on, Lanni, don't give me that."

She crossed her arms and stiffened. Her eyes narrowed slightly. It was a look Judd recognized well.

"I'd think you'd know."

Judd felt the internal pressure mount. It had always been like this. She'd be hurt and unhappy about something, but far be it for her to bring anything into the open. Oh no. He was supposed to pry it out of her a word at a time and be grateful when she saw fit to inform him of the grievous crime he'd committed. In two years, nothing had changed.

"Obviously I don't know, so maybe you should tell me."

Lanni glanced over her shoulder at her sleeping daughter. Jenny was stirring restlessly and Lanni wanted to avoid waking her. "Not now."

"When?" he demanded.

"When I'm good and ready," she told him between clenched teeth.

"You're angry because I left you last night," he said, his patience gone. "That's it, isn't it? You always had to know where I was and how long I'd be, as if you staked a claim to my soul. I'd thought you'd matured, but I was wrong."

"I could care less about where you go or how long you want to stay," she hissed. "The only thing I'm concerned about is who you were with."

"When?"

"Last night," she told him, despising him for this charade.

"I wasn't with anyone."

Lanni snickered, crossed her arms and glared out the side window.

"While we're on the subject of who I was with—what did you do last night? Pine away for Steve?"

"At least he's kind and sincere."

"Sure he is," Judd countered angrily. "You can lead him around by the nose. If that's the kind of man you want, he'll suit you fine."

"I prefer any man who isn't like you."

Judd's jaw knotted at her tight-lipped response. Fine. If that was the way she wanted it. He'd done what he could. She'd tell him what was really troubling her once she'd punished him enough. From experience, Judd realized it was bound to come in the form of tears or an angry tirade. And then, only then, would he discover what had caused this most recent bout of angry silence. The pattern was well set, and the separation had done nothing to change it.

Jenny slept for two hours and they stopped for something to eat when she woke. He noted that Lanni did little more than nibble at her meal. For that matter, he hadn't much of an appetite either.

Following their break they traveled another two hundred miles to Bozeman, Montana, before Judd called it quits for the day. They hadn't gotten as far as he'd hoped, but driving farther was intolerable. Jenny was fussy and unhappy; Lanni, cool and taciturn.

When Judd announced that they'd traveled enough for one day, Lanni heaved an inward sigh of relief. With every mile it became more and more impossible to hide her pain and her pride.

Time and again she recalled the look Judd had given her when he learned she'd been dating Steve. The nerve of the man was astonishing. But it hurt too much to think about it now. Tomorrow would be better. She'd have had the opportunity to speak to him without the worry of Jenny listening in on the conversation.

The motel they checked into in Bozeman was neat and clean and that was all Lanni required. A rodeo was in town and people crowded the streets. Jenny didn't eat much dinner and fell asleep watching television. Lanni gently kissed her daughter's brow and tucked the covers around her. Silently she readied for bed, determined to try to talk to Judd. But when she returned, he'd stepped out of the room. Instead of waiting up for him, she slipped into bed beside Jenny. For a long time after the light was out, Lanni lay awake. Her bed was only a few feet from Judd's, but seldom had they been separated by a greater distance. Judd had been closer to her while working in the Middle East. Infinitely closer in Alaska. For a time, far too brief, nothing had been able to come between them. The agony of the realization burned through Lanni. The pain of their failed marriage ached like a throbbing bruise.

Close to midnight, Lanni slipped into a light slumber. Before she fell asleep, she promised herself that she'd make a point of talking to Judd in the morning.

Lanni didn't know what time it was when Jenny woke crying.

"Mommy, I don't feel good," she groaned, sitting up in bed. "I think I'm going to be sick."

Waking from a drugged sleep, Lanni heard Jenny, but the words didn't penetrate the cloud of fatigue until it was too late.

Throwing back the sheets, Lanni reacted instinctively, reaching for the light. "Oh, baby," she cooed, lifting her daughter into her arms and carrying her into the bathroom.

"Is she all right? Should I get a doctor?" Concerned, Judd staggered into the bathroom after them.

"I don't feel very good," Jenny groaned again as Lanni washed her face.

Jenny's head felt cool. At least she didn't have a fever. "I think she'll be fine now. It was only a bad tummy ache."

"Is there anything I can do?" Judd felt the overwhelming urge to help. This was his child who was ill. The feeling of helplessness that he'd experienced when he'd seen her fall in Seahurst Park returned.

Lanni understood the plea in his voice. "Would you get her a fresh set of clothes?" she asked softly.

"Sure. Anything."

He was gone only a few minutes. "I called the office. They're sending someone over to clean the bed." He handed Lanni a fresh pair of pajamas, then paced the area outside the bathroom until a light knock sounded against their door.

Several minutes passed before Jenny's stomach was settled enough to leave the bathroom. For a time, Lanni held her in her lap, rocking gently to and fro while she tenderly smoothed the curls from the little girl's brow. When she returned to the room, Judd glanced up.

"How is she?"

Lanni mouthed the word *asleep.* The bed on which they'd been sleeping was stripped bare of the sheets.

"The lady from the office said it was best to air the mattress."

Lanni nodded, understanding the reasoning.

"They brought in a cot for Jenny."

Gently Lanni placed the sleeping child onto the thin mattress. Lovingly she spread the blanket over her shoulders. It wasn't until she'd straightened that she realized there was only one suitable bed in the room: Judd's.

Judd read the aggravation in her eyes.

"I didn't plan this."

"I'm not going to sleep with you." Hell would freeze over before she shared a bed with Judd Matthiessen ever again.

"What do you suggest then?"

"I don't know. But I'm not sleeping with you."

"Fine." He pulled the bedspread from the top of the bed and headed toward the bathroom.

"Where are you going?"

"Where does it look like?" he whispered furiously.

"Don't be ridiculous. You can't sleep in there." The thought of Judd trying to sleep in the bathtub was ludicrous. If anyone slept there it should be her. "I'll move in there. I'm the one..."

"This is crazy." He dragged his hand over his face, struggling for control. "I'm not going to attack you, we're married. Can't you trust me enough to believe I wouldn't do anything?"

"But..."

"Never mind. I'll get another room."

"No." Lanni swallowed her pride. With the rodeo in town, they'd been fortunate to obtain a room in this hotel. Judd was right. She was overreacting. They were married, and if he said he wouldn't touch her, then he wouldn't. She believed him. "All right."

"All right what?"

"We can sleep here."

"Thank you," he muttered sarcastically. He tossed the bedspread on top of the double bed. He didn't know what was troubling Lanni, but he couldn't remember her ever being this unreasonable. She looked confused and unsure; not unlike young Jenny. Judd longed to reassure her, comfort her. But he knew she wasn't in the mood for either.

He waited until she was settled in bed, ridiculously close to the edge, before reaching for the lamp and turning out the light. Confident there wasn't any possibility of touching her, he slipped inside the sheets and lay on his back, staring at the moon shadows playing across the ceiling. After ten minutes, he forced his eyes closed, convinced the effort to sleep wouldn't do any good.

He couldn't with Lanni like this. He'd never been able to deal with her when she was in a dark mood. Maybe if he knew what he'd done that was so terribly wrong, he could say something that would ease her doubts. He'd given up trying to understand her long ago.

Lanni lay on her back as well, holding the percale sheet over her breasts. Pain tightened her chest, making breathing difficult. She took several shallow breaths and forced her body to relax. Falling asleep the first time had been difficult, but now, with Judd at her side, it was impossible. From his breathing patterns, Lanni knew he was awake as well.

"Judd?" Her fingers gripped the sheet, twisting the material so tightly that her fingers ached. "Why'd you do it?"

"Do what?"

"Why did you go to *her* last night?" Despite her effort to sound calm and collected, Lanni's voice trembled, threatening to crack.

"Her? Who the hell are you talking about?"

"That woman."

"What woman?"

"The one you were with last night."

"Last night?" He vaulted to a sitting position. "Are you crazy? I told you once I wasn't with anyone!"

Lanni's eyes dropped closed as she struggled to maintain her composure. "Please, don't lie to me. I know differently." The pressure to give in to tears was so strong that it felt as if someone were sitting on top of Lanni's chest.

"I went to a tavern last night. Sure there were women there, but I didn't so much as look at one of them." He couldn't—not when all he could think about was Lanni. One woman had been particularly insistent, leaning over him in an effort to catch his attention, but she'd gotten the message soon enough. He wasn't interested. How could he be when his thoughts had centered around the times he'd come home late to find Lanni in bed asleep? In living Technicolor he recalled how he'd stripped off his clothes and slipped between the sheets beside her. Lanni would nestle her sleepy, warm body against him and sigh. Man and woman as God had intended them from the beginning of time.

And Lanni honestly believed he'd gone to another woman. Instead he'd been in torment, drinking in an effort to dispel the image of those days when their love had been purer and stronger than anything he'd ever experienced. Alcohol had done little to diminish the memory and he'd returned to the hotel more confused than when he'd left. A lot of things had changed over the years, but Judd doubted that their lovemaking ever could. They had been magnificent together. But anything physical between them would be wrong now. He recognized and accepted that, but the knowledge did little to eat away his desire.

"I'm not lying," he told her, shaking his head as a weariness of heart and soul settled over him. So this was the reason she'd been so taciturn all day, wreaking payment for imagined wrongs. He swung his legs off the bed and sat on the edge of the mattress. Lanni had such little faith in him. So little faith—so little trust. The pain-filled anger within him mounted with each heartbeat.

"So that's why you've been treating me like I had the plague all day. What kind of man do you think I am?" Twisting around, he gripped her shoulders and anchored her against the mattress. His eyes resembled those of a wild animal caught in a trap. Stricken. Intense. Dangerous.

"I thought—"

"I know what you thought." He glared down at her with an anger that would have panicked a lesser woman.

Startled, Lanni struggled to break free, flattening her hands against his hard chest and pushing with all her strength. The weight of his anger held her firm. He was crushed against her, his tight features above hers pinning her more effectively than the strong hold of his arms.

"Don't try and tell me you weren't with some woman last night." Her voice became a strangled whisper in an effort to keep from waking Jenny. "I smelled her perfume."

"I wasn't with anyone," he answered, just as furious. He stared down at her, silently challenging her to contradict him a second time.

Their panting breaths echoed as Lanni defiantly met the fury in his gaze.

"I know you, Judd, I know how virile you are…"

"Me?" He said it with a short, humorless laugh. "You were the one who was always so hot. How have you survived the last two years? I suppose you sought a substitute in Steve."

"That's ridiculous!"

"How far did you go with that milquetoast?"

"Judd, stop—"

"Did he kiss you?"

"Judd," she cried. "Please…"

Their gazes held for a moment longer while Judd struggled to subdue his temper. Fearing his grip would hurt her, he released her voluntarily. Moving away, he raked his fingers through his hair and stared sightlessly into the distance. "Never mind. Don't answer because I don't want to know."

"I... You wouldn't look at me this morning. Like you were guilty of something. And then I could smell cheap cologne on you."

"I'd gotten drunk. If you want the truth, there was a woman who approached me. I sent her away. I'm not proud of what I did—leaving you in the hotel while I drowned my problems. It's not the type of thing a man likes to do when his wife and daughter are with him."

"You felt bad because you had a drink?"

He nodded, unwilling to look at her.

"That's it?"

He stood and walked to the other side of the room, pushing back the drape. A wide ribbon of moonlight flooded the room. His fist bunched up the thick material as he gazed sightlessly into the night.

The numbness gradually left Lanni and she raised herself onto her elbows. Judd stood at the window, the moonlight silhouetting his profile against the opposite wall. His head drooped as if the weight of holding it upright was too much for him. His shoulders were slouched; his hand gripped the drape as though he wanted to rip it from the rod.

"I don't know what to say," she whispered, confused. She hadn't meant to unjustly accuse him. She hadn't meant for any of this to happen. He'd left her and Jenny in that hotel room the way he had always walked out on them and she hadn't been able to deal with the rejection. Not again. Not now.

Judd heard her but didn't turn around. Lanni left the

bed and started to pace the area behind him. "I was wrong to accuse you," she admitted.

He acknowledged her with a curt nod. "We all make mistakes. Don't worry about it." He forced his voice to sound light, unconcerned. "Go back to bed. At least one of us should sleep." He turned away from the window and reached for his clothes.

He was leaving her again. For two nights running, he had walked out on her. Lanni couldn't bear it.

"Don't go," she whispered desperately, holding her hand out to him. "Please, not again." She couldn't handle it. She needed him with her. Tomorrow they'd be in Twin Deer. The problems awaiting them in Judd's hometown were overwhelming. They needed to secure a peace between them and if Judd left tonight they would solve nothing.

Judd hesitated. The desperation in Lanni's voice tugged at his heart.

"Please." Her heart pounded. She had so much pride. They both did. Judd knew what it had cost her to ask him to stay—she'd sworn never to do it again.

His features were difficult to make out in the dark. Lanni didn't know what he was thinking; she no longer cared.

Judd dropped his clothes and without thought Lanni walked into his arms. His crushing grip on her made breathing difficult. She whimpered softly, holding onto him with all her strength. Judd buried his face along the curve of her neck and exhaled forcefully.

"I believe you," she whispered again. The chaos and tension inside Lanni gradually subsided. The chill left her bones. She could feel Judd's breath whisper against her hair and smell the masculine scent of his body.

"Not once in all those months was I unfaithful," he told her forcefully. "Not even once."

A huge sob slid from Lanni's throat as her heart swelled, making her giddy with relief. She didn't doubt him. Not after what she'd seen in him tonight. All these months, he'd kept their vows pure. She wasn't so naive to believe that there hadn't been temptations. She knew better. There'd been plenty of those. Lots of eager women. Months of loneliness.

Laughter blended with the tears as she gripped the side of his face and rained kisses across his brow. Her lips found his eyes, his nose, his cheek.

"Lanni." He raised his hand to stop her and discovered he couldn't. She was like a child who'd been granted an unexpected surprise. It felt too good to hold her in his arms to put an end to it so quickly.

When her mouth inadvertently brushed against the corner of his, Lanni paused and Judd softly caught his breath. Time skidded to a standstill as they stared at each other in the dark. He needed to taste her. Desperately wanted her. Unable to stop himself, Judd's mouth claimed hers, hungry with two years of pent-up need and desire. Her lips parted in welcome.

Lanni sagged against him, weak and trembling.

Hot sensation raced through him. She was like a flower. Petal soft. Silky. Lovely.

"I thought…" Lanni felt the need to explain.

"I know. I swear to you there was no one."

"I believe you." She propped her forehead against his chin. "Things will be better once we're in Twin Deer."

"Right." But he knew differently. He dropped his arms, releasing her. "I didn't mean for that to happen."

"It was my fault. I was the one—"

"Must it always be someone's fault?"

"No. Of course not."

The tender moment was over. They stepped away from each other, struggling to put their relationship back into the proper perspective.

Six

"I feel all better."

Reluctantly Lanni opened one eye to discover her daughter standing above her. Betsy, Jenny's beloved doll, was securely clenched under one arm. The plastic pacifier in the doll's mouth loomed over Lanni's face.

"I'm not sick anymore."

"I'm glad, sweetheart." Five more minutes. All she needed was a few more minutes to clear her befuddled head.

"Can I get in bed with you and Daddy?"

Jenny's request propelled Lanni into action. She climbed out of bed and headed for her suitcase. "Not now. We're going to see your grandpa today. Remember?" She took a fresh change of clothes and brought Jenny into the bathroom with her. By the time she returned, Judd was up and dressed as well. Either by design or accident, their gazes just managed to avoid meeting. They'd slept in the same bed, but had gone to lengths to keep from touching. Lanni hadn't thought she'd be able to sleep, but surprisingly, she'd drifted off easily. She didn't know about Judd.

"Morning," he said when they appeared and he offered

them a good-natured smile. He stood on the other side of the room, bright-eyed and refreshed, looking as though he'd risen with the sun after a restful night of slumber.

"I'm not sick anymore, Daddy."

"What about Betsy?" he asked, glancing at the doll.

"She's all better, too!" Jenny exclaimed proudly. "Am I really going to see my grandpa today?"

"Sometime this afternoon if everything goes well."

"I'm going to be real good," Jenny promised. "And Betsy, too."

True to her word, the four-year-old was a model traveling companion. She played quietly in the back seat of the car for a good portion of the morning. When she grew bored, she sang songs she'd learned in nursery school. Soon Lanni's voice blended with her daughter's. At familiar childhood ditties, Judd's deep baritone joined theirs. Jenny loved to hear Judd sing and clapped her small hands to show her delight.

The miles sped past. Judd was the quiet one this day, Lanni noted. But the silence wasn't a strained one. From the way his brow was creased, she knew his thoughts were dark and heavy—introspective. Lanni realized that his mind was on the approaching meeting with his father and not their disagreements.

They had a truce of sorts—more of an understanding. Their marriage was over; they both had accepted the truth of that. It had been damaged beyond repair two years before. Even longer, but Lanni had refused to acknowledge the failure before Judd left her and Jenny. Their vows had continued to bind them to each other, but it was long past the time to get on with their lives.

They stopped for lunch at a small café outside Billings.

Jenny fell asleep in the back seat of the SUV soon after. The traffic on the freeway was light and Lanni noted that for the first time Judd was driving faster than the speed limit. She found it curious that he would do so now. It was as though an urgency drove him, pushing him harder and faster as he neared the town of Twin Deer.

He hadn't told her much about Stuart's condition, other than the fact his father was dying. Lanni believed that Judd probably didn't know much more himself.

Resting her head against the headrest, Lanni allowed her lids to drift closed. She knew so little about Judd's childhood. He had mentioned his youth only in passing and usually in the briefest of terms, as if the subject were best left undisturbed. From what she had been able to glean, his younger years had been unhappy. There'd been no Christmases. No tree, no presents, no stocking by the fireplace. That much she knew. And probably no Easters or any other holidays, either.

For a time after they were first together, Lanni had suspected that Judd had married her because of her strong family ties. She was close to her parents and sister. After they'd married, Lanni's parents warmly welcomed Judd into their lives. He was accepted by her extended family of aunts, uncles and a multitude of cousins as well. It astonished her how well he blended in, as if he'd always been a part of them. It wasn't until after Jenny was born that Lanni noticed Judd withdrawing from her family. He objected when her mother and father offered solutions to their financial problems. He didn't like her dad "putting a good word in for him" with a local contractor. Nor did he appreciate the unexpected visits her parents paid them without notice.

"Another hour," Judd said. When Lanni opened her eyes and glanced at him, he realized he'd spoken aloud. He hadn't meant to.

Lanni straightened.

"Sorry," he murmured, "I didn't mean to wake you."

"You didn't. I was just resting my eyes."

Judd concentrated on the road. He'd been awake most of the night, thinking about the ranch and mentally preparing himself for this so-called homecoming. He didn't expect it to be pleasant. He'd been away from the ranch for nearly eighteen years. Not once in all that time had he looked back. When he'd left, he'd told Stuart he wouldn't return—not unless he was asked. It'd taken all these years for Stuart to send for him. And now, only because he was dying. Judd wanted to curse his father's stubborn pride, but recognized that his own was equally unreasonable.

He dragged in a breath of clean air. The scent of wildflowers brought a brief smile. Now as he neared the ranch, he realized how much he had missed Montana.

Jim Peterman, his father's foreman, had once told him that Montana was good for the soul. Funny that he'd remember that after all these years. Another quirk in his memory was that Twin Deer was only a few miles from Custer Battlefield where Lt. Col. George Custer had made his last stand against the Sioux and Cheyenne warriors. As a boy Judd had wandered over the bluffs of the battle-scarred ground. He'd even discovered a few tarnished arrowheads. At twelve he'd considered them priceless treasures, and now fleetingly wondered what had happened to them. Knowing Stuart, he'd probably tossed them in the garbage just to be ornery.

Sadness permeated Judd's spirit at the thought of his

father. The realization that the old man was dying produced a heaviness that felt like concrete blocks weighing down his heart. There was no love lost between them—never had been. Nonetheless Judd hated the thought of Stuart suffering.

"You're awfully quiet," Lanni said.

"Just thinking."

"About what?"

"The Circle M."

Lanni's brows arched. "What's that?"

"The ranch." Judd was astonished that he'd never told her the name. "It's also our brand."

"You mean they still brand cattle?"

Despite his efforts not to, Judd chuckled. "At least they did when I was last home." The word "home" seemed to echo in the close confines of the station wagon. The Circle M was home, no matter how much he tried to deny it. He was going home. Home with all its memories—with all its lures.

"Did you raise cows?"

A suggestion of a smile touched his eyes as he glanced at Lanni. "Steers."

Feeling a bit chagrined, Lanni said, "Right."

"Do you have horseys?" The eager voice from the back seat surprised them both. Lanni hadn't realized Jenny was awake.

"When I was a little boy, I had a pony."

The information was news to Lanni. "What was his name?"

"Trigger."

Lanni smiled. "You weren't very original, were you?"

"Sure I was. At the time my name was Roy Rogers."

"I'll be your Dale Evans anytime." The words came without thought. Color crept up Lanni's neck in a flush of hot pink. She didn't know what had gotten into her to make such a suggestion. "That isn't exactly what I meant to say."

"Don't worry. I know what you meant."

Lanni was pleased he did, since she hadn't the foggiest notion where the words had come from. Certainly not her head—her heart, perhaps. This time with Judd was going to be far worse than she'd imagined. Last night she'd wanted him to make love to her. Sensation after sensation had shot through her—ones Lanni had assumed long dead and conveniently buried. Thirty seconds of sexual awareness had momentarily wiped out two years of bitterness. She wouldn't allow it to happen again, and she wouldn't, Lanni vowed.

Color tinged her cheeks at the realization of what could have happened, but then Judd had always been able to do that to her. There'd never been another man she'd wanted half as much. Little had changed from the time when they'd first met all those years ago. Lanni had feared that Judd would think her brazen. At the time, her behavior had been little short of audacious. He'd been so worldly, so traveled. She'd strived to seem sophisticated, but none of it had mattered to Judd. He'd wanted her then just as he had in the motel last night and she'd nearly succumbed to his lovemaking. In the cruel light of day, Lanni thanked God that Judd had had the common sense to put an end to the kissing. All things considered, allowing their kissing to get out of hand now would be disastrous to them both.

"We're on Circle M land now," Judd announced solemnly.

"Will I get to see Grandpa soon?" Jenny's voice rang clear, light and excited.

"Real soon." The muscles of Judd's abdomen tightened with nervous anticipation. The letter from Stuart had been brief. Stark. Judd had no conception of what awaited him.

"Is that the house?" Lanni pointed ahead to the two-storey structure. The faded brown structure melted in with the surroundings so completely that they had already turned into the long driveway before she realized that the dilapidated building must be Judd's home. The house looked like something out of the nineteenth century with a wide front porch. Four pillars supported the second-storey balcony. One leaned dangerously to the side so that the upper structure tilted off-center. Shutters lined the large rectangular windows. Several were missing and the remaining few hung precariously. The house was badly in need of paint. The once white exterior had faded with weather and time to a dull shade of earthtone. Once, Lanni could tell, the house had been a source of pride and care. No longer. Like Stuart Matthiessen, the house was dying.

"That's it," Judd confirmed in a low voice.

"What about the other buildings?" Another smaller home was close to the large barn, separated by only a few hundred feet from the larger house.

"The Petermans live there."

"Neighbors?" It didn't make sense to have all this land and then allow someone to build in your own backyard.

"Dad's foreman." The shortness of Judd's response revealed how distracted he was. The house was a shock. It had never been much of a showplace, but Stuart had his pride. The house had always been kept clean and in good repair, painted white every few years. Betty Peterman had been housekeeper and Jim Peterman had been a jack of all trades. The couple had lived in the small house for as long as Judd could remember. Whenever Judd thought about the Circle M, his mind automatically included the Petermans.

Stuart's letter had briefly mentioned that the Petermans were gone, leaving Stuart to himself. Compassion filled Judd. Not only was Stuart sick, but now he was alone and friendless.

Judd followed the driveway and parked at the back of the house in the half circle that arced toward the main house. As Lanni opened the car door, she noted the gallant attempt of a rosebush as it struggled to poke its head through the underbrush that knotted what must have once been flowerbeds a long time past. One velvety red blossom stuck its head through the thick patch of weeds and aimed for the sky, valiant and determined.

Lanni's attention abruptly rotated from the brave flower to the screen door as it swung open and Stuart Matthiessen moved onto the porch. He held onto the door as though he needed the support. And from the look of him, he required something to help him remain upright.

Judd saw his father and was so shocked by the change in his appearance the words froze in his throat.

"I see you made it." Stuart spoke first.

He was dangerously underweight, to the point of being gaunt. His thinness sharpened his features to such an extent that Judd suspected Jenny would be frightened.

"You asked me to come." Judd straightened and closed the car door. Lanni climbed out and moved to the back of the car in order to help Jenny out of the car seat.

"I notice that you took your own sweet time," Stuart accused him. The intense eyes narrowed on Judd. "I suppose you thought if you waited long enough, I'd be dead."

Judd opened his mouth to deny the accusation and quickly closed it, determined not to fall victim to verbal battles with his father. Let him assume what he would; it made little difference to Judd.

"I see you don't bother to deny it. Well, I fooled you this time. You thought I'd be dead and you'd sashay in here and claim the ranch." His laugh was rusty and sharp. "I fooled you again, boy."

"I don't need a thousand acres of headaches."

"Good, because you're not getting it." The words were hurled at Judd like acid. The sight of his father and the bitter words hit Judd in the chest and for an instant, he couldn't breathe evenly. He thought he was prepared for this meeting and realized that little could have readied him for this. The man had been waiting eighteen years to have his say and wouldn't be cheated out of it now.

"I suppose you think that because you've been all over the world that the Circle M isn't good enough for you."

Judd responded with a sharp shake of his head. He had traveled thousands of miles to be insulted? He should have his head examined.

The tone of Stuart's voice paralyzed Lanni. She paused, uncertain of what to do. Her gaze skidded from Judd's father back to her husband. She marveled at Judd's control. The insults washed off his back like rainwater on an oil-slickened street. He gave no outward indication that the anger and resentment affected him in any way. But Lanni knew differently. The words to defend Judd burned on her lips. Stuart had no right to talk to her husband like this.

He'd come at Stuart's request. If there'd been any delay it had been her fault, not Judd's.

"Mommy, I want to see my grandpa," Jenny called from inside the car. "Let me out. Mommy, let me out."

Reluctantly Lanni unbuckled Jenny from the car seat. The minute Jenny was free of the confining straps, she bolted from the car and up to the porch steps where her grandfather was standing.

"Are you my grandpa?"

The transformation in Stuart's face was almost unbelievable. The thick frown softened and the tired, aged eyes brightened. "She looks like Lydia," he murmured to no one in particular. "Yes, I'm your grandpa," he said softly. "I've been waiting for you to come." Gently he took Jenny's hand to lead her into the house.

"We came a long, long ways. Daddy drove and drove and drove. I saw a cow. Daddy says he had a pony when he was a little boy. Can I have a pony?"

Left standing alone by the car, Lanni looked to Judd. "He didn't mean what he said."

Judd pretended not to hear as he retrieved the largest suitcase from the back end of the station wagon. "He meant it. Every word."

Lanni longed to erase some of the pain she knew Judd was experiencing. While she searched, Judd picked up two of the largest suitcases and headed for the house.

Carrying Jenny's doll and a few odds and ends, Lanni followed him. If the outside of the house was in disrepair it was nothing compared to the confusion that greeted her on the inside. Dirty dishes filled the huge porcelain kitchen sink. The table was littered with an open jar of peanut butter, jelly, instant coffee and a sugar bowl. The door off the kitchen led to the bathroom and a glance revealed dirty clothes in every conceivable space.

"Where are the Petermans?" Judd demanded of Stuart, setting down the suitcases.

"Gone."

"What do you mean gone?"

The anger in Judd's tone brought Lanni up short. Judd was furious and was doing a poor job of disguising it.

"They left about a month ago," Stuart elaborated briefly.

About the time he'd mailed the letter, Judd assumed. It didn't make sense to him. The Petermans had lived most of their married lives on the Circle M. They wouldn't have left without just cause. "Why would they go after all these years?"

Stuart grunted. "You'll have to ask them that."

"I plan on it."

Stuart snorted a second time and raised an arthritic finger, pointing it at Judd's chest. "I won't have you interfering in my business. You hear me?"

Judd ignored his father's words and stepped past him to the stairway, hauling the suitcases with him. Lanni claimed Jenny's small hand and followed. Two weeks. They were committed to two weeks minimum of this terrible tension. Lanni doubted that she'd last a second longer. She yearned to cover Jenny's ears.

"It doesn't look like any of the beds have been made up," Judd said apologetically, glancing in turn in the three doorways.

"That's no problem," Lanni said quickly, grateful to have something to do. "I'll get them ready."

"I didn't bring you along to do housework." The fierce intensity of his gaze pressed her to the wall.

"I don't mind. Honestly. What do you expect me to do for the next couple of weeks?"

"Not dirty dishes!"

"Can I sleep in this room?" Jenny peeked into the room located at the farthest end of the long narrow hallway. "I like it in here."

Judd's harsh countenance relaxed. "That used to be my bedroom."

"Any treasures hidden in there?" Lanni questioned, wanting to steer him away from a bad mood. She followed him to the bedroom.

Judd shrugged his shoulders. "Treasures? I don't know." It was the truth. He'd left nearly everything behind, taking only the bare essentials with him. The parting, like the reunion, had been bitter. Judd didn't know what Stuart had done with the contents of the room and was mildly surprised to find it was exactly as he'd left it. Except for the stripped bed, it didn't look as though Stuart had once come upstairs in all the years Judd had been away. His old football helmet rested on the top of the bureau, along with a picture of his mother, holding him in her arms. He'd been only a year old at the time. The narrow triangular shaped banner from his high school team remained on the wall, along with a paint-by-number picture of two horses he'd patiently painted the year he was in the sixth grade.

Lanni's eye caught the photograph of Judd and his mother first and was amazed at how accurate Stuart's statement had been. Jenny did have the same startling blue eyes as Judd's mother. Lydia was lovely. Petite. Delicate.

Refined. Lanni couldn't imagine such a gentle woman married to Stuart Matthiessen. They were as different as silk and burlap.

"There may be a few old love letters lying around," Judd teased, watching Lanni. Her gaze rested on the photo of his mother, and he wanted to distract her from the questions that burned in her eyes. They were ones he'd asked himself often enough over the years.

"Love letters? No doubt," she replied with a fair amount of feigned indignation. Purposefully she crossed her arms, boldly meeting the mischief in his eyes.

"I was known to turn a head or two in my day."

"I don't doubt that, either." He was still capable of garnering attention from the female population. After all that had passed between them, Lanni still found him devastating. She always had. Sitting beside Jenny on the bare mattress, Lanni pulled the little girl onto her lap. "Do you want to help Mommy put sheets on the bed?"

The four-year-old nodded, eager to assist.

"I told you I don't want you doing housework!"

"I've been doing it for a lot of years, Judd Matthiessen. What's different now?" Her own voice contained a sharp edge. He had to know that she didn't make enough income selling real estate to hire a live-in housekeeper. To his credit, the checks he sent every month were generous enough to afford one, but Lanni hadn't once entertained the notion of such an extravagance. A large portion of each check went into a savings account for Jenny.

"I won't let Stuart use you," Judd continued, his temper gaining momentum.

"Use me? Judd, you're overreacting."

"I won't argue about it. You take care of Jenny and I'll make up the beds."

"You're being ridiculous."

"I'm not going to stand here and argue with you, Lanni." He stalked out of the bedroom and down the narrow hallway to the first bedroom. With only a bed and dresser, this was the smallest of the three bedrooms located upstairs. The ornate four-poster bedframe had to be a hundred-year-old antique. Lanni paused in the doorway to admire the simple elegance of the piece, mildly surprised to find something of beauty in this neglected house.

"It's lovely."

"Right," Judd grumbled, pulling open the bottom dresser drawer and taking out a set of sheets. Lanni moved inside the room to help him. He ignored her as much as possible, unfolding the bottom sheet and spreading it across the bed. It lay haphazardly on the padded mattress. Lanni reached for the same corner as Judd, their hands bumping into each other's in an effort to secure the sheet.

"Lanni," he muttered.

"Yes?"

"Don't. Please."

Frustrated, she threw up her hands, releasing the smoothed edge of the cotton sheet. "All right, all right." She left the room, and immediately located the middle bedroom. This one was equally small; there was hardly room for the double bed and dresser. Again the furniture was heavy, sturdy mahogany from yesteryear. She found the sheets and blankets in the bottom drawer of the dresser. Working silently, she efficiently spread out the sheets and blanket.

"Lanni!" Judd growled from inside the doorway a couple of minutes later.

The sheer volume of his voice frightened her half out of her wits. Her hand flew to her heart. "Don't do that," she gasped in a husky whisper.

"Sorry." But he didn't look apologetic. He moved into the room, dominating what little space there was. In an effort to scoot past Lanni, his torso brushed hers grazing his chest. The contact paralyzed him for an instant. His heart began to pound almost painfully. Lanni was the sexiest, most alluring woman he'd ever known and she didn't even know it. She had yet to guess the overwhelming effect she had on him.

"Judd," she asked innocently, "what's wrong?"

"Nothing."

"Then why are you standing like that?"

"This is why," he said with a groan. He turned to her, pulling her toward him by the shoulders. The back of her knees met the side of the mattress.

Lanni's eyes widened as her gaze flew to his. It shocked her to find how good Judd's body felt pressing against her softness. Her own body reacted instinctively to his, shaping, molding, yielding to his hardness. His splayed hands spread wide across her back, arching her closer, craving the taste and scent of her softness. He moaned as her body yielded to meet his.

Sensation seared a path through Judd. Slowly, deliberately, he lowered his mouth to hers, starving for the taste of her. She was honey and wine. Champagne. Orchids. Love. Acceptance. All that had ever been good in his life. And all that had been denied.

The pressure of his hold had Lanni nearly bent in half.

When she could endure it no longer, she fell backward, taking him with her as they tumbled onto the mattress. The force of his weight over hers knocked the breath from her lungs and she gave a small cry of fright.

"What's wrong? Are you hurt?" His forearms framed her face as his wide gaze studied her.

She shook her head. Unable to resist, she raised her hand and touched the frowning lines that fanned out from the corner of his eyes. Character lines.

His torso pressed her deep within the soft mattress. His body felt incredibly good over hers. He paused, half-expecting Lanni to stop him, and when she didn't, he kissed her with a thoroughness that rocked her very being.

Lanni shut her eyes, longing to lose herself in the passion of the moment, yearning to forget all that had gone before them and savor these priceless moments of contentment.

"Lanni, Lanni," he groaned, kissing her as though he couldn't bear to let her go, even to breathe. "No. No. This is wrong. I promised you... I *promised* you..." Even as he spoke, his mouth came down on hers.

Lanni was shocked into numbness. Judd had always been extraordinarily gentle with her. This urgency was so unlike him that she didn't know how to react. At first she did nothing, letting him kiss her greedily as though she were an unwilling participant. Her lack of response lasted less than a moment. Judd's mouth gentled and Lanni was lost. Frantically she combed her fingers through his hair and pressed closer to him.

"Mommy. Daddy." Jenny's soft voice calling to them permeated the fog of passion that cloaked Judd's mind.

"Yes, sweetheart." Lanni recovered first.

"I made my bed all by myself."

Lanni pushed against Judd, wanting him to release her, but he held her fast and she doubted that he felt the pressure of her hands.

"Are you proud of me, Daddy?"

"Very proud." His voice was little more than a whisper. He rolled onto his back, freeing Lanni. His hand covered his eyes. "And very relieved." Sweat broke out across his upper lip as the shivers raced down his arms and legs. He'd come so close. Too close. He didn't know what was the matter with him. His word. He'd given Lanni his word. He'd committed his share of sins in his life, but he'd promised Lanni and himself that he wouldn't touch her. When they returned to Seattle she would be free of him.

Lanni struggled into a sitting position, her heart pounding at how dangerously close she'd been to tossing aside everything that was important for a few minutes of pleasure.

"I'm on my way, Cupcake," Lanni said, her voice incredibly weak. "Let me see your bed."

Seven

Betty Peterman's work-gnarled hands surrounded the steaming coffee mug. She looked out of place in the tiny apartment kitchen two blocks off Main Street in Twin Deer. Her husband, Jim, sat next to her and Judd was across the table from them both.

"He asked us to leave. Gave no reason," Jim stated, his eyes revealing the shock of the request. "After nearly forty years, I don't mind telling you it came as a jolt."

"But why?" Judd couldn't begin to understand what had driven his father to such drastic measures.

"He didn't give us any reason."

"Money?" Judd voiced the only plausible explanation. As far as he knew the ranch had always been financially sound. The only possible reasoning was that his father had fallen onto hard times. Judd wasn't ignorant of the problems ranchers faced—low beef prices had brought foreclosure to many of their neighbors.

"He gave us a settlement," Betty said. She smiled at him, but the effort to show any pleasure was negated by the hurt disbelief in her eyes. Judd was aware of how much the two had aged. Jim had always been tall, wiry, and bowlegged from so many years in a saddle. His hair was completely white now and his shoulders hunched forward. But his firm handshake proved that he was still as rough as a bronco and as tough as shoe leather. Twenty years had only changed the outward appearance. As few things are in life, Jim Peterman was constant.

Betty was round and motherly. More round than Judd remembered, which caused him to grin. She was the only female influence he'd had in his youth and she'd been able to give him only a minimum of attention since Stuart had claimed he didn't want Judd growing up to be a sissy. Nonetheless Betty had faced her employer's wrath on many occasions to take Judd's part. She'd been the one to urge him to leave as a young high-school graduate, although he'd seen the sheen of tears in her eyes when she told him it would be better if he left the Circle M and Stuart.

Judd had already accepted that he would never be able to get along with his father. Having Betty and Jim recognize the fact and advise him to leave had been the encouragement he'd needed to pack his bags and head out. Over the years he'd sent both the Petermans money for their birthdays and Christmas. Not once had he ever imagined them away from the ranch. They were as much a part of the Circle M as the land itself. His father must have lost something mentally to send the Petermans away so callously.

"So it isn't money?" Judd continued.

"Not from what we can see," Jim answered with a soft snort. "In fact we got the best beef prices in years."

"Then why?"

"Don't rightly know." Jim paused and took a sip from

the side of the mug, making a light slurping sound. "He had me sell off the best part of the herd. Fences are down all over, but he said he didn't want me to do any repairs. From talk in town he'd got himself a temporary ranch hand, but from what I can see, he's not doing much good."

"He hasn't been himself for months," Betty added, her gaze drifting down. "He hasn't eaten much the last few months either, although I tried to tempt him with his favorite meals."

"He's been ill, but he didn't tell me much about it," Judd told them, looking for some confirmation in their gazes. He'd come for more than one reason. He wanted to learn what the Petermans could tell him about Stuart's health. Although his father was thin and frail looking, he looked in better shape than Judd had expected.

"Is that why you've come?" Jim asked.

"He wrote and asked me to bring Jenny."

Jim and Betty's gazes shot toward each other. Forty years of marriage made words unnecessary. A small smile brought dimples into Betty's round cheeks and Jim nodded knowingly.

"Have you talked to his doctor?" Betty asked, looking concerned now.

"Not yet." But Judd had already called the small medical center in town and planned on stopping by there when he'd finished with Jim and Betty. He wanted to talk to Doc Simpson who had been the family physician for as long as Judd could remember.

"He didn't say anything to us about any medical problem, but he hasn't been himself for months," Jim said.

Judd took a drink of coffee. "How soon can you two move back?" Seeing the Circle M in such a run-down condition had affected him nearly as much as seeing his father leaning against the railing on the porch, looking fragile and sickly. "In addition to some fences, we're going to rebuild the herd."

"Hot dog!" Jim slapped his hand against his jean-clad thigh and grinned like a twenty-year-old.

"Jim doesn't hanker much for city life," Betty said, her brown eyes alight. "Can't say that I do, either."

"My wife and daughter are at the house now."

"I'll be pleased to meet them." Both of the Petermans looked as if they'd dropped ten years in the fifteen-minute visit. "I suppose the house was a disaster."

"Worse." Judd thought of the spotless kitchen Betty had always insisted upon and knew the housekeeper would have cringed at the sight of week-old dishes piled high in the sink. Knowing Lanni, she'd never be able to sit idle. He'd bet a month's wages that she'd torn into the kitchen the instant he was out the door. If there'd been any sensible way to stop her, he would have.

"You staying?"

Judd hesitated. "For now." What Stuart's doctor had to say would determine the length of his visit. For the first time in his life, Stuart needed his son. A weak voice in the back of his head urged Judd to do what he could to make his father comfortable, and then move on. But he couldn't. Judd knew in his heart that no matter how wide the rift between him and Stuart, he wouldn't desert his father now. He'd stick by Stuart until the end. Lanni would go and take Jenny with her. He couldn't hold them for any more than two weeks. Lanni had another life in Seattle now. He didn't like to think about her and Jenny leaving, but recognized that eventually he'd need to let them go. He couldn't ask anything more of Lanni than what he had already.

Humming softly as she worked, Lanni ran water into the kitchen sink. She was grateful Judd had left. He would have been furious had he seen her working so hard in the kitchen. Fine. She'd do it when he wasn't around to stop her. He didn't honestly expect her to sit down and thumb through a magazine when so much needed to be done? The house was a disaster and an unhealthy environment for a man in ill health.

A large roast was cooking in the oven and the smell of simmering meat, potatoes and onions permeated the large kitchen.

Jenny was in the living room, sitting on her grandfather's lap while he read to her from a children's book. The sight of the two of them warmed Lanni's heart. Stuart was so loving and patient with the child. The last time she'd checked on them, she'd discovered Jenny asleep, cuddled in his arms, and Stuart snoring softly.

Washing the last of the lunch dishes, Lanni paused to look around. Like everything else in the house, the kitchen was grossly outdated. The linoleum was cracked and peeling up at the corners as was the dull red countertop. The stove had a cantankerous streak and the oven was another matter entirely. Lanni had viewed the kitchen as a challenge and after working only one afternoon in it, she was ready to surrender. What she wouldn't have given for a microwave! She could deal with escrow loans, mortgage companies and feisty appraisers, but not this nineteenth-century kitchen.

The back door swung open as Judd stepped inside, giving her a knowing look. For a moment it seemed as though he wanted to argue with her, but changed his mind. He knew her well enough to realize she couldn't leave the place in such a mess.

"Hi." She smiled at him and pressed her finger to her lips, indicating that he should be quiet. She pointed in the direction of Jenny and Stuart in the other room. "They're asleep." She hoped that the need for quiet would quell his objection to her streak of domestic integrity.

If the clean kitchen hadn't been a surprise, then viewing his daughter in Stuart's arms was. His father's gaunt face was relaxed in sleep. Peaceful. Serene. Judd couldn't ever recall seeing his father so tranquil—he'd run on nervous energy most of his life, demanding more of himself than he did from others.

Judd pulled out a kitchen chair and Lanni brought him a bowl of hot tomato soup and a thick turkey sandwich she'd made earlier.

He was a little amazed at her thoughtfulness, although he realized that he shouldn't be. "I saw the Petermans."

"Good."

"They're moving back tomorrow."

"Won't your father be upset?"

"I don't see why. I'm paying their wages."

Lanni nodded and hid a grin. Over the years, Judd must have learned how to get around his father, sometimes to his own detriment. "What did the doctor have to say?"

Judd's expression changed to a dark scowl as he slowly shook his head. He lowered the sandwich to the plate. "Not much."

"What do you mean?"

"Dad's been in a couple of times with stomach ailments. But as far as Doc Simpson knows, Stuart isn't anywhere close to dying."

"He could have gone to another doctor."

"Maybe, but that's doubtful. The nearest medical facility of any worth is in Miles City, and that's more than a hundred miles. It's unlikely that Dad would go that far."

"It's obvious that he's been ill." Just looking at Stuart was proof enough. "It has to be more than stomach ailments."

"Apparently he has an ulcer."

"An ulcer?"

"Other than that, Doc claims Dad's in perfect health."

Lanni pulled out the chair across from Judd and sat. She didn't know what to think. Stuart had claimed to be dying, but from the sounds of what Judd had just learned, he was a fair distance from the grave.

"Why do you think he sent for you?"

"Not me," Judd corrected, remembering the bitterness in his father's greeting. "If you recall, he asked to see Jenny."

"He wanted you to bring her."

Judd took another bite of the turkey sandwich, chewing thoughtfully before speaking. He'd been a sentimental fool to believe Stuart wanted him home. From birth, his father had had little use for him. "I have the feeling this is all an elaborate charade."

"I can't believe that." Lanni hadn't meant to take Stuart's side, but she honestly felt that something must be terribly wrong with Judd's father for him to have sent for Judd and Jenny.

"Stuart may *believe* he's dying, but he's not," Judd murmured.

"Maybe the doctor made it sound less serious than it actually is."

Judd leaned back in the high-backed chair and shook his head. "I can't believe Doc Simpson would do that. No," he stated emphatically. "Doc said that Dad needed to watch his diet, but with the medication he gave him and a few dietary restrictions, Dad should be feeling great." He pushed the lunch plate aside. "I think the problem may be psychological. Dad hasn't been sick a day in his life. He can't tolerate it in others, let alone himself. Doc seems to believe that with his stomach causing him a fair amount of pain, Dad might believe that his number is coming up."

Lanni watched as Judd frowned thoughtfully. "What are you going to do?" The strain of being around his father was already exacting its toll on Judd. It seemed that every time Stuart opened his mouth, he made some comment about Judd's lack of ambition. Lanni disagreed— Judd had plenty of drive; she'd never known a man who worked harder than Judd. From what he'd told her, Stuart had always wanted Judd to be an attorney or a doctor. Something more than the rancher he was, and from Judd's teens, Stuart had pushed his son toward college and a professional career. It hadn't worked, and Judd had left home soon after graduating from high school. Twice since they'd arrived, Lanni had to stop herself from defending Judd to his father. She didn't like being put in that position and had remained silent. In some ways she felt Stuart was waiting for her to intervene, but she refused to get caught in the battle between father and son.

Judd stood, carrying his plate and bowl to the sink and

dumping his leftovers into the compost pile. "Don't wait dinner for me."

An icy chill shivered up her back and her hand knotted into a tight fist as dread filled her. So often when he left, Judd didn't bother to tell her where he was going or when he'd return. In light of the comment he'd made about her suffocating him, Lanni refused to ask him now. He knew her feelings and chose to ignore them.

Judd watched the anger play across her features and recognized what was troubling her. He hesitated before adding, "Jim claims there's a lot of fence down. I want to check it out."

Lanni's gaze shot to his, knowing he was making an effort. "Will you be riding a horse?"

The smile curving his lips was evidence of his poorly disguised amusement. "I'm taking the pickup; there's a lot of range out there. The Ford's parked on the other side of the barn." The Petermans' house was between the huge shed and the main house and blocked her view.

Lanni was pleased that the elderly couple were returning, but she wondered how Stuart would react to the news. It would be up to Judd to tell him, not Lanni. With other things on her mind, that was one topic she didn't want to wade into with Judd's father. As it was, their conversations were stilted and often one-sided. Lanni did the best she could to carry any dialogue, but Stuart made it nearly impossible, answering in clipped one-word sentences.

The only subject that he became animated on was Jenny. From the moment he'd seen the child, something had come over him. His harsh features had smoothed into an almost smile and his eyes had brightened. The unconcealed love he felt for Jenny transformed him into a different person.

Stuart couldn't seem to get enough of the child. He talked to her, read her stories and listened to her with all the attention of the doting grandfather he was. Lanni couldn't understand how he could be so hard on his only child and so loving to his granddaughter. Jenny's reaction to Stuart was one filled with the joy of discovery, while Stuart's love was returned a hundredfold and more. Lanni was astonished. For a man who had shown precious little patience in his life, he was a virtual saint with his granddaughter.

Their first night in the house proved to be eventful. Lanni woke around midnight when the house was peaceful and still. She rolled onto her back and pushed the hair off her forehead and stared sightlessly into the darkness. One minute she'd been asleep and the next she was wide awake. She blinked twice, and wondered at the reason for her sudden restlessness. The faint sound of the television drifted up from downstairs and, thinking Judd had returned and was unwinding with a late night talk show, Lanni threw off the covers and climbed out of bed.

She'd just finished tying the sash to her robe when she stepped off the bottom stair. She did an admirable job of disguising her disappointment when she discovered it wasn't Judd who was awake, but Stuart.

He glanced at her and then back at the television screen.

"Is Judd back yet?" she asked.

"He's home. I thought he was in bed with you." The blank face strayed momentarily from the television to Lanni.

"You know we're separated." Lanni sighed and moved into the kitchen, unwilling to discuss the subject further. Stuart flicked the television controller, stood and followed her. Doing her best to ignore him, Lanni took a carton of milk out of the refrigerator and turned, nearly colliding with the older man.

Reluctantly he stepped aside. "You'd know when Judd got home if you were sleeping with him the way a wife should. Seems to me it would solve a whole lot of problems if you two shared a bed again."

Lanni did her best to pretend she hadn't heard him.

"I bet you laid awake half the night waiting for Judd."

Purposely turning away from him, Lanni poured the milk into the glass and returned the carton to the refrigerator. "I appreciate what you're trying to do, Stuart, but it's two years too late. The marriage is over."

"I don't believe that," her father-in-law said, following her from one side of the kitchen to the next.

Lanni took a large swallow of the milk, refusing to discuss her private life with her father-in-law.

"I know Judd hasn't been a good husband to you in the past, but he'll change once he starts managing the ranch."

Lanni released a frustrated breath. "The minute we arrived, you told Judd he'd never get this land. Remember?"

Stuart chuckled. "Don't you recognize reverse psychology when you hear it, girl? Judd's been the same all his life. I say one thing and the blasted fool does just the opposite. I decided it was time I got smart. He wants the ranch now because I told him he could never have it. Only," he hesitated, studying Lanni hard, "he won't stay long unless you're here."

"I've got news for you," Lanni informed him sadly,

her throat muscles constricting with the pain of reality. "If I'm here or not will make little difference with Judd."

"I don't believe that."

Lanni carried the empty milk glass to the sink. It wouldn't do any good to argue with Judd's father. It was obvious that the old man had hoped she and Judd would resolve their differences and remain on the ranch. What a strange man Stuart Matthiessen was. He berated his son in one breath and sought to save his marriage in the other. "What's between Judd and me is none of your business."

"Maybe not, but you got a child to consider."

Lanni couldn't take any more. It was one thing to have the man treat Judd the way he did, but another for him to run interference in her life. "While we're on the subject of Judd, I want one thing understood."

Stuart's mouth snapped shut. "What?"

"Use all the reverse psychology you want, but if you utter one unkind, untruthful word about my husband in front of Jenny, the two of us will leave so fast it'll make your head spin. I mean that, Stuart. Judd is Jenny's father and I won't have you treat him disrespectfully when Jenny is around to witness it. Do you understand?"

Stuart blanched and cleared his throat. "Yes."

"Thank you for that." She brushed past him on her way out the door and marched up the stairs. When she reached the top, Lanni discovered that she was trembling. Her hands were bunched into tight fists as the anger fermented within her. She wanted to shake Judd's father for his stubborn pride. He honestly seemed to believe that if she and Jenny remained on the ranch, Judd would stay as well. Her love, their daughter, and the home she'd created hadn't been enough to hold him once. She had nothing else to offer him a second time.

"That was quite a little speech." Judd leaned against the doorjamb, his arms crossed over his bare chest, his eyes sparkling with amusement. "The next time I need a defender of truth and justice, can I call on you?"

"He infuriates me." Lanni still couldn't believe the gall of her father-in-law. He'd puzzled her the first time they'd met and even more so now.

"It's just his way, Lanni. I stopped letting him manipulate me years ago."

"I won't play his games, Judd. He wants you and me back together. He thinks you'll stay on the ranch if Jenny and I are here. But we both know differently, don't we?"

The barb struck its intended mark, nicking his heart. "I signed the divorce papers. I thought that was all you required."

"It is."

The pain in her eyes brought Judd up short and, expelling a broken sigh, he turned toward his bedroom. Regret expanded his chest, tightening his muscles until his heart and lungs ached. "Lanni." He moved toward her and paused. "I…"

"Don't." She raised both her hands and abruptly shook her head. "Don't say anything. It's better if we leave things as they are." She turned and quickly entered her room. The sound of the door closing echoed through the hallway like thunder, although she had shut it softly.

Rubbing his hand over his eyes, Judd turned back into his own room, drained both emotionally and physically.

Judd had already left the house by the time Lanni and Jenny were up and dressed. Stuart sat at the kitchen table, drinking coffee and staring absently into space with the morning newspaper propped in front of him.

"Morning." Lanni hoped to start the day on a cheerful note.

"Morning," came his gruff reply until he caught sight of Jenny, then he brightened and smiled. "Hello, Princess."

The little girl held out her arms and hugged his middle with an abundance of enthusiasm. "Hi, Grandpa. Is today the day I get to see the pony?"

"Soon," Stuart answered, looking displeased.

"What's this about a pony?" Lanni's eyes flew from one to the other.

"Oops," Jenny said and covered her mouth. "I wasn't suppose to tell, was I? It's a surprise, Mommy."

"You weren't supposed to tell me what?"

"That Grandpa's buying me a horsey."

"A horse?" Lanni exploded. "Stuart, this isn't true, is it? I told you before we only plan on being here a couple of weeks. I meant that. A horse for that amount of time would be extravagant."

He ignored her, downing the last of his coffee.

"Stuart?" Lanni demanded a second time. "What's this business about a horse?"

Jenny climbed onto the chair, clenching Betsy to her chest and looking uncomfortable. "Don't be mad, Mommy. I wasn't supposed to say anything like when Aunt Jade and I go have ice cream." Realizing that she'd done it again, the little girl looked thoroughly miserable.

"It's all right, honey, don't worry about it." Lanni decided it would be best to drop the subject for now and discuss it when Jenny was out of hearing distance.

Stuart leaned over and whispered something in the little

girl's ear and Jenny instantly dissolved into happy giggles. Lanni hadn't a notion of what schemes the two were devising, but knew given time she'd find out.

When the breakfast dishes had been cleared from the table, Stuart announced that he was taking Jenny for a walk. He didn't ask Lanni to go with them. She wanted to suggest joining them, but Judd's father looked so excited at the prospect of going outside with his granddaughter that Lanni didn't want to risk destroying his mood.

"Where was Judd off to so early this morning?" she asked instead, doing her utmost to disguise her uneasiness.

The old man's eyes narrowed as the fun and laughter drained away. "He didn't say."

"Surely he must have given you some indication of when he'd be back."

"You should know him better than that." He opened his mouth as if to add more, but at her fiery glare, he changed his mind. Lanni had no doubt her look and their midnight conversation was responsible for his change of heart. "Knowing Judd, he'll be back when he's good and ready to come back and not before. He always was like that, you know. Going away for days without a word of explanation."

A glance out the kitchen window confirmed that the pickup was gone. He was probably on the range, checking fences and whatever else he did while away from the house for hours on end. Lanni hadn't a clue.

From her view out the same rectangular window, she kept close tabs on Stuart with Jenny. He took the little girl into the barn and returned with a feed bag. Together the two fed the chickens, much to Jenny's delight.

From there they walked to the edge of the fence and

Stuart pointed to the rolling hills in the distance. Intently, Jenny stood at his side and nodded, as serious as the day was beautiful. After washing a couple of dishes, Lanni glanced outside a second time. Jenny was bending over a wild flower while Stuart smiled down on her. Bright rays of morning sun splashed the earth.

The little girl mentioned something to her grandfather and Judd's father threw back his head and laughed loudly. The sound of his mirth took Lanni by surprise. She'd never heard or seen Stuart be happy about anything. With the one exception of Jenny.

When the two ambled toward the Petermans' small home, Lanni removed her apron and followed them. She didn't want Jenny out of her sight for long.

The screen door slammed after her as she went down the sun-dried wooden steps. They creaked with age. Everywhere Lanni looked there were repairs to be made and work to be done. She imagined that with the ranch demanding so much attention, Jim Peterman had little time or energy to spare on the house. It could be, too, that Stuart didn't want anything fixed, but she couldn't imagine the reason why. He was a strange man and she understood him less than she did her own husband.

The door to the Petermans' house was left open and Lanni walked inside, amazed at how updated the home was in comparison to the main house. The kitchen was bright and cheerful, the room furnished with a dinette set and modern appliances. The white countertops gleamed.

Stuart's voice could be heard at the front of the house and Lanni went to join them.

"This will be your bedroom," Lanni heard Stuart tell

Jenny as she turned the corner from the kitchen that led to the hallway.

"Your mommy and daddy will sleep in the bedroom next door," Stuart went on to explain.

Lanni was appalled. Apparently Stuart planned to move the three of them into this small house.

"Judd's and my room?" Lanni said, stepping into the room. "How interesting."

Eight

Stuart's head came up so fast that Lanni thought he might have dislocated his neck. It was apparent that she'd heard something he didn't want her to know about.

The dark eyes met hers unsteadily. The crease lines in his face became all the more pronounced as his gaze skidded past hers.

"I've already explained that Jenny and I will be leaving next week." Lanni wanted it understood from the beginning that she wanted no part of his crazy schemes.

Stuart went pale. "But…you belong here with Judd."

Jenny's eyes revealed her confusion and Lanni desperately wanted to shake some sense into the man. He couldn't possibly believe that she'd give up her life in Seattle, abandon her parents, her home and her career because of his half-baked belief that she and Jenny would bind Judd to the Circle M.

"He'll only stay if you do."

Lanni chose to ignore Stuart's plea. She took Jenny by the hand and led her out of the house. Stuart followed in her wake, mumbling under his breath along the way.

"I had them deliver a new stove just for you," he said loud enough for her to hear.

"I already told you what I think. Can't you understand that it isn't going to work?" she asked sternly, throwing the words over her shoulder.

"But I want to talk to you about it," Stuart pressed on, undeterred.

His eyes revealed the same stubbornness that Judd so often displayed and Lanni wanted to scream at them both for their foolish pride. "There's nothing to discuss."

Outside the small house, they were greeted with bright sunlight. A soft breeze carried the scent of apple blossoms from a nearby row of trees. In other circumstances Lanni would have paused and pointed out to Jenny the source of the sweet fragrance. But her thoughts were heavy and she barely noted the beauty surrounding her as she led Jenny back into the main house. She was so irritated, she discovered her hands were trembling.

She finished the breakfast dishes and Jenny, standing at her side, dutifully helped dry them. With each dish, Lanni struggled to subdue her frustration. The Petermans were supposed to arrive anytime and she welcomed the thought of another woman at the ranch.

Lanni was filled with questions and the only one who could answer them was Betty Peterman. As much as Lanni was looking forward to meeting Betty, she didn't welcome the confrontation Stuart was bound to have with Judd over their return.

The clash came sooner than even Lanni expected. Judd came back to the house midmorning, bringing the Petermans with him. Jim and Betty walked into the kitchen where Lanni and Jenny were arranging wildflowers, using a jar as a makeshift vase.

"Hello," Betty Peterman said, smiling shyly at the pair. Her eyes were round and kind and Lanni knew immediately that she would like this woman who knew Judd so well. Her troubled gaze flew from Betty Peterman to Judd in an attempt to warn him that Stuart was sitting in the other room.

"What's wrong?" Judd knew Lanni too well not to have noticed her distress. Something had happened this morning when he'd been away. That much was obvious. Lanni looked both angry and frustrated. Heaven knew Stuart was capable of driving man or woman to either emotion, and Judd felt guilty for leaving her to deal with his cantankerous father.

"What are they doing here?" Stuart demanded from the doorway leading to the kitchen. A scowl darkened his face, twisting his mouth downward.

"I hired them back," Judd informed his father.

"You can't do that."

"I'm paying their wages."

"I'm not dead yet. The Circle M still belongs to me and what I say goes!"

Jim shuffled his feet. Betty looked equally uncomfortable. Judd saw this and was all the more angry with his father for causing their old friends this additional embarrassment.

"If they go, I go," Judd told him calmly.

Stuart glowered at his son, but closed his mouth, swallowing any argument.

Jim Peterman removed his hat and rotated the large brim between his callused hands; his eyes studied the floor between his feet. "I can see we're not wanted here. The missus and me will move on."

"And I say you stay." Judd pointed to the wiry cowhand and emphatically shook his head. Slowly, methodically, he turned his attention back to his father. "This ranch is falling apart around you. The herd is depleted. Fences are down in every section. The house is a disaster. What possible explanation could you have for not wanting the Petermans here?"

Stuart's brooding eyes clashed with Lanni's. Puzzled, Judd followed the exchange.

"Lanni," he asked, still perplexed, "do you know something I don't?"

"Your father apparently thinks you and I and Jenny will decide to live here permanently. He wanted the Petermans' house for us."

Stuart's pale face tightened as he moved into the kitchen. "The three of you belong here."

"You can't be serious?" Judd was incredulous.

"I'm afraid he is," Lanni said, coming forward so that she stood at Judd's side.

"The Petermans have lived in that house nearly as long as you've owned the Circle M," Judd countered sharply. "And they'll live there again."

For an instant it looked as if Stuart were going to argue. Stubborn insistence leapt from his eyes, challenging Judd.

Judd crossed his arms over his chest and the edges of his mouth curved up. The movement in no way resembled a smile. Wordlessly he accepted his father's challenge and tossed in one of his own. "Either the Petermans come back as employees of the Circle M or I take Lanni and Jenny home to Seattle."

Stuart looked shocked, as if this were the last argument in the world that he'd expected Judd to use against him.

"Well?" Judd pressed, staring at his father.

"Fine. They can stay," Stuart mumbled, turning. His walk was more of a shuffling of his feet; clearly it had cost him a great deal to concede the issue.

"So this is Jenny." Betty Peterman pulled out a kitchen chair and sat beside the four-year-old.

"Hi," Jenny returned, busy placing long-stemmed daisies into a jar. She gave the newcomer a bright smile, her chubby fingers bending a brittle stem. Lanni was grateful that Jenny couldn't understand all that was happening and was pleased that Betty was trying to smooth the rippling tension that filled the room.

"She resembles Lydia," Betty murmured under her breath, handing Jenny another yellow daisy to add to the vase. "It's in the eyes and the shape of her face. I suppose Stuart noticed it as well?" Betty glanced at Judd, seeking an answer. The resemblance offered a token explanation of Stuart's odd behavior.

"I'm sure he has noticed," Lanni answered for him, recalling all the pictures of Jenny she'd mailed Stuart over the years. He'd never given her any indication that he'd received the photographs.

"He loved Lydia, you know." Betty inclined her head toward the living room where Stuart sat watching a television game show with all the seriousness of a network war correspondent. "For a time after she died, Jim and I thought Stuart would never recover. He sat and stared at the walls for days."

Judd rubbed a weary hand over his face. "Sometimes I wonder if he's capable of loving anyone anymore." Judd had seen precious little evidence of his father's love. He thought he understood Stuart, but every day of this visit his father proved him wrong. They didn't know each other at all.

Jim helped himself to a cup of coffee from the stove, adding sugar to it before taking the first sip. "From what you said, I don't have time to stand around the kitchen."

"I'll go with you," Judd offered. "There's a problem with…." His voice trailed away as he went out the kitchen door with Jim. The back screen door slammed after them.

Lanni watched them leave. The two men stood in front of the pickup talking, and from the looks of it, the subject was a heavy one. Jim nodded abruptly, apparently agreeing with what Judd was saying.

"I've got a thousand things to do as well," Betty added, tacking a stray hair into the neatly coiled bun that graced the back of her head.

"Can Jenny and I help?" Lanni volunteered. She hoped to become friends with this motherly woman.

"No need." She gently patted Lanni's hand and glanced into the living room where Stuart was sitting. "I suspect he'll keep you hopping while I finish unpacking. Be patient with him. He isn't as bad as he seems."

For her part Lanni didn't want to be left alone with Stuart. "Are you sure?"

"Positive." She lightly shook her head. "He isn't normally this cantankerous. He loves Judd almost as much as he did Lydia. The problem is he has trouble showing it, just like he did with Lydia."

That had to be the understatement of the year. Before Lanni could question the housekeeper further, Betty was out the door.

At noon, Lanni cooked lunch and served it to Stuart on a television tray. He didn't comment when she delivered the meal and said nothing when she carried it back, untouched, to the kitchen. One look at his harsh features told her that Stuart was furious with both her and Judd.

Thankfully the afternoon was peaceful. Jenny took her nap in Judd's old room at the top of the stairs. While his granddaughter slept, Stuart appeared at loose ends and drifted outside. In order to kill time, Lanni cleaned out the kitchen drawers and washed cupboards. On the top shelf, she found a pre-World War II cookbook that must have belonged to Lydia. Flipping through the yellowed pages, Lanni discovered a storehouse of treasures. After a short debate, she decided to bake a cake listed as Stuart's favorite. A quick check of the shelf assured her that all the ingredients were available.

Humming as she worked, she whipped the eggs and butter together with a wire whisk. Dumping the measured flour into the frothy mix sent up a swirling cloud of the fine powder. Coughing, she tried to clear the front of her face by waving her hand.

"What are you making?" Judd asked, opening the back door that led to the kitchen. He paused, hands on his hips, surveying the tempting sight she made. An oversize apron that must have belonged to Betty was wrapped around her middle. The ties looped around her trim waist twice and were knotted in the front. Flour was smeared across her cheek and an antique cookbook was propped against the sugar canister on the countertop.

"Hi." She offered him a ready smile. "I'm baking a cake as a peace offering to Stuart. He hasn't spoken a word all afternoon."

Judd recalled how much she used to enjoy baking for him. In the first weeks after their marriage it was a miracle he hadn't gained twenty pounds. Every night she'd whipped up some special concoction for him to sample. Most of them proved to be scrumptious. Others proved less successful. It got to be that he'd rush home every night to see what confection she had planned next. Lanni had enjoyed his praise. Long ago, she claimed, her mother had told her that the way to a man's heart was through his stomach. Judd didn't bother to inform her otherwise. She'd owned his heart from their first fateful meeting.

He'd loved her then beyond anything he'd ever known and, he realized studying her now, he loved her still.

"Smells delicious." Without thought, he wrapped his arms around Lanni's waist and kissed the side of her neck. It was the most natural thing in the world to do. This was Lanni, his woman, his wife—no matter what those divorce papers said. She and she alone had filled the emptiness of his soul. Her love had helped him find peace within himself and had lessened the ache of bitterness and cynicism that had dictated his actions since he'd left the Circle M at age eighteen.

Lanni's heart leaped to her throat. Almost immediately she recognized the action as spontaneous—one Judd did without thought. For days he'd gone to lengths to avoid touching her and it felt incredibly right to have him hold her now. She wanted to comment to say something but feared any sound would shatter this spell. She yearned for his touch like a weak flower longs for the life-giving rays of the sun and the nourishment of cool water.

Heaven and earth couldn't have stopped Judd. He lowered his lips to hers, kissing her hungrily. He wondered if life could possibly be half so sweet as this moment with her.

Lanni felt his kiss throughout her body. It rocked her, leaving her yearning for more. Her heart swelled with remembered love. Her arms held him close, wanting to bind him to her for all time.

When he broke off the kiss his smile was filled with satisfaction. Lanni was velvet. Satin and silk. And he loved her. Dear sweet heaven, he loved her until there was nothing in all the world but her.

Releasing a huge sigh, he held her to him and closed his eyes. The need to hold and touch her was becoming as much a part of him as breathing. He was a man of his word, and it was increasingly difficult to keep his promise not to touch her. Already he'd broken it several times. The desire to lift her into his arms and carry her up the stairs to the bedroom was almost unbearable.

Lanni went still, savoring the welcome feel of his arms around her. She closed her eyes, wanting this moment to last, knowing it wouldn't. With everything that was in her, she battled down her weakness for Judd. There was something seductive with this ranch, this land and being with Judd. It almost made her believe there was nothing they couldn't overcome. Maybe it was Stuart, who was working so hard to fill her head with promises of a new life with Judd on the Circle M. She didn't know, but she couldn't give in to these sensations—she couldn't.

Awkwardly, Judd dropped his arms.

Still shaken by the encounter, Lanni turned back to the mixing bowl, focusing her attention on the cake once again. "Are you hungry?" The feeble sound of her own voice bounced off the empty kitchen walls.

"Starved." But Judd wasn't referring to food. He felt empty, with a physical ache that attacked with a ferocity that left him weak.

He walked over to the sink and turned on the tap.

"There's some leftovers from lunch," Lanni told him, striving to keep her voice even. On the off chance he'd be in later and hungry, Lanni had fixed a couple of extra sandwiches. She brought them to the table with a tall glass of milk and some cookies.

Drying his hands on a towel, Judd tossed it back onto the wire rack and joined her at the table. The sight of the meal produced an appreciative grin. "Is Jenny sleeping?" he asked, seeking protection in the subject of their daughter.

Seeing Lanni working in the kitchen was having a strange effect on him. It'd cost him a great deal to release her. Every male instinct demanded that he haul her into his arms and make love to her then and there. As much as possible, he ignored the powerful pull of his desire.

Lanni paused to check her wristwatch. "She'll be up anytime now." She hoped the information would cause Judd to linger a bit longer.

"Where's Stuart?"

"He left sometime after noon."

"Did he say where he was going?" Judd wolfed down another bite of the sandwich as he waited for her response.

She shook her head sadly. His plans for the Peterman house thwarted, Stuart had been uncommunicative from the moment Judd had left with the rehired foreman. Even Jenny had been unable to bring her grandfather out of his dark mood.

A worried frown knit Judd's brow as he pushed aside

his plate. His mouth thinned with irritation. "I wonder what Stuart's up to now."

"I have no idea." Lanni braced her hands against the back of the chair, studying Judd. She knew he was concerned about his father, but nonetheless Judd looked happy. More alive than she could ever remember seeing him. Content.

"I spent most of the early afternoon on the range with Jim." He paused to swallow some milk. "The herd's depleted, but with care it can be built up again." His expression relaxed as he told her about a cattle sale coming up at the beginning of next week. "Jim seems to feel that with the purchase of a few head of cattle we could be back in business again by the end of next year."

"That soon?"

Between cookies, Judd nodded. "Maybe even sooner."

"Wonderful." She could hear the excitement and anticipation in his voice. Both caught her by surprise. Judd was speaking as if he planned to be around to see the task to completion.

"It's expensive, Lanni. Damned expensive."

She nodded as if she understood everything there was to know about stocking herd for a cattle ranch. Her expertise was limited to real estate transactions, and she knew little about ranching. For the first time since she'd known him, Judd was truly serene.

He stopped and gazed out the kitchen window. "This land was made for ranching. Look at it out there—those rolling hills are full of sweet grass."

"It is beautiful," Lanni agreed. To her surprise, she found she enjoyed the peace and solitude of the Circle

M. Montana, with its wide blue sky, held an appeal that Lanni hadn't expected to feel.

"The whole state is like this." At least staring out the window helped him keep his eyes off her. He'd forgotten how beautiful she was. How enticing. How alluring. He felt good all the way to his soul. For the first time in years he was at peace with himself and the world. Working with Jim, riding side by side with the other man, had awakened in him his deep abiding love for the Circle M and Montana.

When he'd left all those years ago, Judd had closed his mind to the ranch. Now he was here and it seemed that everything was falling into place for the first time in a very long while.

Judd worked with Jim long past dinnertime. He'd told Lanni that with so much that needed to be done, she shouldn't hold up the evening meal for him. He felt guilty leaving her alone to deal with Jenny and Stuart, but the demands of the Circle M were equally urgent.

Wearily, Judd walked toward the house. The light beaming from the kitchen window gave him a comfortable feeling. He suspected Lanni would be waiting for him and the knowledge brought a sense of contentment. His body ached from the physical demand of ranching. It'd been years since he'd been on the back of a horse. His muscles protested the long hours in the saddle and as he sauntered toward the house, he rubbed the lower region of his back where a sharp pain had developed.

The kitchen was empty, and Judd was disappointed. In his mind he'd hoped to have a few tender moments alone with Lanni. He fought back the image of her asleep in bed and what would happen if he were to slip in beside her and turn her warm body into his arms. Judd groaned. The sudden physical ache of his body far surpassed any strain from riding a horse or mending fences.

The clock over the kitchen doorway told him it was far later than he'd thought. Lanni would be asleep by now and the way he was feeling tonight, it was probably for the best.

Upon further inspection, he found a plate covered with foil left warming in the oven. He smiled, grateful for her thoughtfulness, and wondered if she'd thought about him the way he'd been thinking about her all afternoon.

He ate slowly, savoring the fried-chicken dinner. When he finished, he rinsed his plate and set it aside in the sink.

The house was quiet as Judd turned off the light and headed for the stairway that led to the upstairs bedroom.

"So you're home." The voice came out of the dark. It took Judd an instant to realize that his father was sitting alone in the moonlight waiting for him.

"Did you think I'd left?"

"It wouldn't be unheard of."

The blunt response briefly angered Judd. "Well I didn't."

"So I see. I suppose I should be grateful."

"I'm not leaving. Not until I know the reason you called me home."

"You know why. I want you here; it's where you belong, where you've always belonged," Stuart's raised voice returned with a sharp edge that invited an angry response.

Judd expelled a sigh. There was always tension between him and his father. They couldn't have a civil conversation without pride interfering and old wounds festering back to life. It was on the tip of Judd's tongue to argue with Stuart, to remind him that the letter he'd sent contained a different message. The stark words had asked him to bring Jenny to the ranch. Stuart hadn't asked to see him—only Jenny.

Judd sighed. One of them had to make the first move and Judd decided it would have to be him. He claimed an overstuffed chair and sat in the dark across from his father.

"She does resemble Mother, doesn't she?" There wasn't any need for Judd to mention who he was talking about.

"Lanni sent me pictures and each year I recognized it more and more."

His mother remained only a foggy memory in Judd's mind. He wasn't sure that he remembered her at all. Betty had told him about Lydia when he was younger and Judd wondered if he confused his memory with the information Betty had given him.

"Jenny belongs with me just as Lydia did."

"Jenny belongs with her mother," Judd said softly.

"If you'd patch things up with Lanni, then you could all stay. Fix it, boy, and hurry before you lose her to that city slicker."

"City slicker?" As far as Judd knew, Lanni had never left the ranch.

"That Delaney fellow. He phoned twice before you arrived and once since." Stuart's tone lowered with displeasure. "Lanni doesn't know, and I'm not telling her. You're going to lose her unless you do something and quick. I'm not going to be able to hold this fellow off much longer. Next time he calls, Lanni could answer the phone."

Judd felt the weight of the world settle over his shoulders. "It's too late for Lanni and me."

"You can't mean that. I've seen the way you look at each other. You're still in love with her and if both of you weren't so stubborn you'd see that she loves you as well."

The urgency in the old man's voice shook Judd.

"You're the only one who can convince them to stay."

Judd couldn't do that, but telling Stuart as much was a different matter. "I'll do what I can," he said after a long minute.

The words appeared to appease Stuart. "Good."

Judd relaxed in the chair, crossing his legs. This talk wasn't much, but it was a beginning. "Jim and I were out on the back hundred this afternoon."

"That's a good place to start—been needing attention a couple of years now."

Judd welcomed the cover of darkness that cloaked the living room. So Steve had been trying to contact Lanni and he'd bet it didn't have anything to do with business matters either. Judd's fingers gripped the chair's thick arms as he concentrated on what his father was saying. "When did you stop caring about the ranch?"

Stuart snorted. "Last year sometime. I haven't the energy for it anymore."

From the run-down condition of the place, Judd knew his father was speaking the truth. "Jim and I are here now," Judd said. He knew his father expected a tirade, but for once he didn't want to argue with the old man. Tonight he yearned to pretend that they were like other fathers and sons who communicated freely about the things they loved most.

"I'm not overly pleased that you brought the Petermans back," Stuart added thoughtfully. "Now that you and Lanni are here, I don't need them anymore."

"Perhaps not, but they need you."

The truth silenced Stuart for a moment. "I wanted the house for the three of you."

"Dad," Judd said with a sigh, "listen to me. Lanni and Jenny aren't going to live here. The divorce papers are already signed. The only life Lanni knows is in the city."

"Divorce papers," he echoed, shaken. "You're divorced?"

"Not officially. Once she's back in Seattle, Lanni will need to file the papers before it's official."

"Then do something, boy. Do it now before it's too late." The desperate appeal in Stuart's voice ripped at Judd's heart. "I lost Lydia because of my pride. Don't make the same mistake I did. You'll regret it, I swear you will; all your life it'll haunt you."

Judd came to his feet. "I can't change the past for you. Lanni asked for the divorce—not me. It's what she wants."

"I'd bet the Circle M that it was that city slicker who talked Lanni into this divorce thing."

Judd's fists knotted, but he held his tongue. "I'm going to bed," Judd said.

"But not to sleep, I'd wager."

Stuart's words followed Judd to the top of the stairs. Inside the darkness of his room, he sagged onto the bed, sitting on the edge of the mattress. He was tired, weary to the bone.

His father's words echoed around the chamber, taunting him. So Steve was phoning; Judd supposed the other man must be desperate for word from Lanni. He didn't like to even think about the other man. It angered him. Infuriated him.

He needed to move—anything to still the ramblings

of his mind. Judd stood and paced the area in front of the bed. He remembered seeing Lanni in the kitchen that afternoon. The memory of their kiss caused him to groan. He gritted his teeth in an effort to drive the image from his mind. It didn't help. His reminiscences were costing him his sanity.

Jerking open a dresser drawer, he took out a fresh set of clothes. A cold shower would help. Afterward he'd leave and find a hotel in Miles City where he could spend the night. It was dangerous, too dangerous to be here with Lanni sleeping peacefully in the room across from his. If he stayed, he wouldn't be able to stop himself. He'd wake her and she'd turn into his arms and he'd make love to every inch of her until she cried for more.

As quietly as possible, Judd moved down the hall. But the cold shower did little to ease the ache in his body. He needed Lanni. But he'd promised; he'd given her his word. Within a few days she had every reason to pack her bags and walk away without a backward glance. He hadn't the right to stop her and he wouldn't. The thought of Steve Delaney holding her nearly crippled him.

The arguments echoed in his mind like demented voices flung back at him from a canyon wall. Unable to stop himself, he paused outside Lanni's bedroom door. Moonlight painted the room a soft shade of yellow. She lay on her back, her long flaxen hair splayed out on the pillow like liquid gold. Judd's chest tightened at the sight of her. She tossed her arm up and turned her head.

His breath froze in his lungs. He'd awakened her. For an instant he thought to hide, then realized the ridiculousness of such a plan. It took him another moment to note that she remained asleep.

He moved toward her, stopping at the edge of the bed. A cold sweat broke out across his upper lip. He loved her. Loved her more than anything in his life. More than the Circle M. More than anything he possessed.

His body trembled with emotion as he watched her sleep. He turned to leave and made it as far as the door. His hands braced against each side of the jamb, Judd paused. His fingers curved around the wood frame as he hung his head. His mind battled with his heart and his heart won.

He moved back into the room and stood once again beside the bed.

"Lanni," he whispered.

Lanni heard her name and knew it came from Judd. What she didn't recognize was the husky need. Her lashes fluttered open.

"Judd?" He was on the bed, kneeling over her.

"I need you," he whispered.

Nine

"Judd." Even in the dark, Lanni could see that his eyes were wild. "What is it?"

Urgently he slanted his mouth over hers, kissing her again and again as if he were dying of thirst and her lips were a clear, shimmering pool in the most arid region of the Sahara. "I need you," he repeated. "So much."

Lanni circled his neck with her arms. His weight pressed her into the mattress as the overwhelming desire to lose himself within her body dictated his actions. He needed her tonight more than at any other time because the reality of losing her was so strong. She would leave him and Steve was on the sidelines waiting.

"Judd, what is it? What's happened?"

He held her for a long minute, breathing deeply in an effort to control his desperate need. "Lanni, I can't lose you and Jenny. I want us to try again and throw away those damn divorce papers. I swear I'll never leave you. We'll build a new life together—we'll start over, here in Montana at the Circle M."

Instantly, tears began to burn the back of her eyes. It felt as if her heart was going to explode. After everything that had passed between them, the long months of heartache and loneliness, she shouldn't be this willing. But heaven help her, she didn't want the divorce any more than Judd did.

"It'll be as good as it was in the beginning," Judd coaxed, kissing her neck. "I swear, I won't let anything come between us again."

She swallowed down a sob and nodded sharply. "I love Montana." In her heart she acknowledged that she loved him. Always had. Always would. From the moment he'd shown up on her doorstep, she'd known that whatever passed between them, her love would never die. Tonight her hunger for him was as powerful as his was for her.

Again and again he kissed her, unable to get enough of her mouth. His lips sought the corners of her eyes, the high arch of her cheek, her neck—any place where her smooth skin was exposed. Then his mouth returned to hers, kissing her with raw, naked desire.

"Lanni," he whispered, breathless. "You're sure? After tonight, I'll never let you go."

She stared into his hard face, stamped with pride and love. Tenderly she brushed the dark hair from his brow, loving him more this moment than at any time in their lives.

"Lanni?" he repeated. "Are you sure?"

"I'm sure," she breathed.

He groaned. The instant his mouth claimed hers, all gentleness left him. Fierce desire commanded his movements.

Shocked by his need, Lanni clung to him, and her heady response drove some of the urgency from his mind. He must be crazy to come at her like this. A beast. A madman. But the knowledge did little to temper his actions. He was on fire and only her love would douse the flames.

"Lanni." Again and again he whispered her name, all the while kissing her. Her hands played over the velvet skin of his shoulders. Her lips felt swollen from his kisses and her body throbbed with need. She wanted to beg him to make love to her, but the words couldn't make it past the tightness that gripped her throat muscles. Nothing would stop him now, she was sure of it. In his own time, he'd claim her body. And she would welcome him, this man who was her husband.

Lanni was still trembling when Judd moved away. He lay on his side, facing her, and gathered her into his arms.

"I love you," he whispered without embellishment. Nothing more, no other words were needed.

She smiled contentedly and slid her hand over his hard ribs. Judd scooted closer, wrapping the sheets around them both. He paused to kiss the crown of her head. Secure in his love, and warm in his embrace, Lanni fell asleep almost instantly.

Sleep didn't come as easily for Judd. Although fatigue tugged at him from every direction, he found the escape elusive. He rolled onto his back, holding Lanni close to his side, and stared at the ceiling. He loved her and would thank God every day of his life that she had agreed to come back to him.

He'd meant what he'd said about them starting over. The moment they'd driven onto Circle M land, he'd felt that he was home. His traveling days were over. His heart belonged to Lanni and this thousand acres of land. His one regret was that he'd wanted their lovemaking to be slow and easy. Instead it had been a firestorm of craving and desire, but he doubted that he could have stopped to save his life.

Now that she'd agreed to be his wife again, Judd wanted to court her, give her all the assurances she needed and deserved. He vowed with everything that was in him that he'd never make her unhappy again.

Lanni woke early, feeling cozy and unbelievably warm. She pulled a blanket around her more securely and sighed contentedly. A small smile curved the corners of her mouth as she recalled the reason for her happiness. Judd had come to her in the night, loving her with such a fiery intensity that she was left trembling in its afterglow. They'd reconciled when Lanni had given up every hope of settling their differences. His traveling days were over. All Judd's bridges had been crossed and he was home and secure. And because Judd was content, she and Jenny were happy as well. Even now her skin tingled where he'd kissed and loved her.

Reaching out to touch him, her fingers encountered the sheet-covered mattress. She opened her eyes to find his side of the bed empty. The only evidence he had spent the night with her was the indentation on the pillow resting beside her own.

With a frown, Lanni sat up, tucking the sheet around her nakedness. She was disappointed. After their fierce lovemaking, she yearned to talk to Judd. Questions were churning in her mind.

She dressed quickly and hurried downstairs, hoping to find him there. As he had been the morning before, Stuart sat at the round kitchen table with the newspaper in one hand and a cup of coffee in the other.

"Morning," she greeted him. "Have you seen Judd around?"

"You look like you slept well. Judd, too, for that matter," Stuart muttered.

Lanni couldn't actually see him smile, but suspected he was. His gaze didn't waver from the newsprint.

"Then you've seen him?"

"He's in the barn."

"Thanks." Without waiting, Lanni rushed toward the back door. She saw Judd immediately. He stood beside the large chestnut horse close to Jim. She moved down a couple of stairs. "Judd," she called out and waved.

At the sound of her voice, Judd turned, his face breaking into a wide grin. He handed the reins of the horse to Jim and moved toward Lanni.

She met him halfway. "Morning."

"Morning." His gaze drank in the sight of her, and inside he felt a renewed sense of love and commitment to her and their marriage. "I didn't want to wake you."

"I wish you had."

He tugged the glove from his hand and lifted her hair from the side of her face, studying her. "You aren't sorry, are you?"

"No, but there's a lot we need to discuss."

"I know."

"Hey, Judd," Jim called out. "You going to stand there all morning saying goodbye to your missus? Kiss her and be done with it, will you? Those cattle aren't going to wait around forever, you know."

Judd tossed an irritated look over his shoulder. "Hold your horses, will you?"

"In case you haven't noticed, I'm holding yours as well

as my own," Jim grumbled and then muttered something else that Lanni didn't quite hear.

"You better do as he says," she murmured, looking up at him. "Kiss me and be done with it."

Judd slipped his arms around her waist, bringing her to him as his mouth moved over hers. The kiss was deep, and greedy, and so thorough that Lanni was left weak and trembling. "I wish I could stay in bed with you all day," Judd groaned against the side of her neck. "We have a lot of time to make up for, woman."

"I wish we were in bed right now," she murmured, having difficulty finding her voice. He was lean, hard, masculine and strong. After everything they'd shared last night, Lanni couldn't believe that her passion could be so easily aroused. "Oh Judd, I love you so much."

"You must."

"You comin' or not?" Jim growled.

With a reluctance that thrilled her, Judd released her. He paused and reached up to touch her face. His eyes grew troubled. "I'll be back as soon as I can. If it's late, will you wait up for me?"

She nodded eagerly and watched as he marched across the yard and swung his lanky frame into the saddle. For a long minute after he'd ridden out, Lanni stood there, soaking up the early morning rays of the sun and remembering the feel of Judd's arms that had so recently held her.

She moved back into the house, but was reluctant to face Stuart. Judd's father had gotten exactly what he'd wanted and was feeling very clever at the moment.

Stuart was hauling a load of his dirty clothes to the washing machine when Lanni entered the kitchen. He paused, glanced at her and chuckled gleefully. Lanni ignored him and moved up the stairs.

Jenny was still asleep so Lanni quickly made her bed. By the time she'd finished, the little girl was awake and eager for breakfast. After picking out her own clothes and dressing, Jenny hurried down the stairs.

Stuart beamed at his granddaughter when she appeared, and hugged her gently. When Lanni moved toward the refrigerator, preparing to cook their breakfast, Stuart stopped her.

"I was in town," he said.

Lanni looked at him blankly, not understanding what that could possibly mean. When he brought out a large box of Captain Crunch cereal, understanding dawned on her. "Stuart, you're going to spoil her."

He grumbled something unintelligible and placed the box on the tabletop.

The phone pealed and he raised stricken eyes toward the wall. "I'll get it," he said, pushing his way past Lanni. "I... I've been waiting for a call. Business."

The phone rang a second time and Lanni glanced at it anxiously.

"I'll take it in the other room," Stuart said, nearly throwing Lanni off balance in his rush to move into the office.

Lanni thought his actions curious, but shook her head and brought a bowl and spoon to the table for Jenny's cold cereal.

When Jenny finished, Stuart suggested the two of them feed the chickens. As hot water filled the sink, Lanni watched them leave. The few dishes they'd dirtied for breakfast were clean within minutes. It could have been her imagination, but Stuart's eyes seemed to avoid her when he'd returned to the kitchen following the phone call. She'd half-expected him to make some teasing comment about her and Judd, but he hadn't. Instead he'd taken Jenny by the hand and rushed outside, saying the chickens must be starving by now. Yet it was an hour earlier than the time he'd fed them the day before. He was a strange man.

She wiped her hands dry and decided it was time to visit Betty Peterman.

"Hi, Mommy." Jenny raced to her mother's side when Lanni came out the back door. "Where are you going?"

"To visit Mrs. Peterman."

"Grandpa and me fed all the chickens. Can I come with you?" Her gaze flew to her grandfather who granted his permission with an abrupt shake of his head.

"If you like." Lanni wasn't all that sure she wanted her daughter with her. Her mind buzzed with questions about Judd and his youth. Questions only Betty Peterman could answer. This wasn't a conversation she wanted Jenny to listen in on, but given no other choice, she took the child with her.

Betty answered Lanni's knock with a warm smile of welcome.

"I hope I'm not disturbing you."

"Of course not." The older woman stepped aside so Lanni and Jenny could enter the kitchen.

Following Lanni's gaze around the room, Betty pursed her lips together and slowly shook her head. "Imagine Stuart buying a new stove for this place. The old one worked fine. I tell you Lydia would be as angry as a wet wasp."

At Lanni's blank stare, Betty continued. "Lydia was after Stuart for years to buy her a new stove. He wouldn't do it. He claimed there was nothing wrong with the old one she had." Betty moved to the counter, took down a mug and poured some coffee for Lanni, delivering it to the table without asking. Next she opened a drawer and took out a small bag of colored dough. "Here you go, Jenny." She plopped it down on the counter with a miniature rolling pin. "You bake your little heart out."

Lanni tried to hide her surprise. She hadn't expected Betty to have anything to entertain a four-year-old.

"I've had a recipe for that play dough for years. Finally had an excuse to make it up." Betty smiled fondly at the little girl. "I still have trouble getting over how much she resembles Lydia."

At the mention of Judd's mother, Lanni straightened her outstretched arms, and cradled the steaming cup of coffee. She lowered her gaze, not wishing Betty to know how curious she was about Judd's mother. "What was she like?"

"Lydia?"

Lanni nodded.

"Gentle. Sweet. Delicate."

Those were the same qualities Lanni had seen in the photo in Judd's room. "What happened?"

Betty pulled out the chair opposite Lanni. "I don't really know. It was a shock to everyone in Miles City when Lydia married Stuart. They were as different as can be. I believe he honestly loved her and that she loved him. But she hated the isolation of the ranch. Every year I could see her wither up more. She was like a hot-house orchid out here in this desert heat. If pneumonia hadn't killed her, she would have eventually shriveled up and died from living here."

"How sad." It wasn't the first time Lanni had been

touched by the unhappy story of Lydia Matthiessen's short life.

"When she was pregnant with Judd, she moved back into the city with her parents. Judd was only a couple of weeks old when Stuart brought her back to the ranch. Things changed between them from that point on, and not for the better I fear." A bleak light entered Betty's eyes. "Stuart loved her. I'm sure he did. But things weren't right between them. I'd see her out hanging diapers on the clothesline and her eyes would be red rimmed as though she'd been crying her heart out. She lost weight and got so thin that I fretted over her. Lydia told me I worried too much."

"Why didn't he let her visit her parents if she was so unhappy?" Lanni asked. Surely if he loved her, Stuart could see what life on the Circle M was doing to his wife. It seemed only natural that he'd do whatever possible to bring some happiness into Lydia's bleak existence.

"I can't rightly say why she never went back to see her family. Too proud, I suspect. Her parents had never been keen on Stuart, said she'd married beneath herself. Pride and stubbornness were qualities they both seemed to have in equal quantities. Lydia wanted Stuart to sell the ranch and move into the city. Stuart refused. This land has been in his family for two generations. His father nearly lost the ranch in the Great Depression, but through everything—drought, famine, disease—had managed to keep the Circle M and his family together. Stuart wasn't about to leave it all because his wife wanted a more active social life. After a while Lydia's eyes began to look hollow; she was so miserably unhappy, the poor dear."

"How did Stuart react toward Judd?"

Betty sighed. "It's hard to say. He was pleased he had a son; he held and bounced him on his knee, but all Judd did was cry. The baby was the only bright spot in Lydia's life and she spoiled him terribly. Judd clung to her."

"You say she died of pneumonia?"

Betty's mouth thinned with the memory. "This is the saddest part of all. One evening in late September, when it was cool enough to add an extra blanket on the bed at night, but warm enough in the daytime to keep a window open…" She paused and seemed to wait for Lanni to nod. Lanni did. "Well, my kitchen window was open and I heard Lydia crying. She had a bag packed and was carrying Judd on her hip. She told Stuart that she'd had enough of his stupid ranch. She was sick of the Circle M. Sick of his stinginess. Sick of his precious cows. She was leaving him if she had to walk all the way to Miles City."

"What did Stuart say?"

Sadly Betty shook her head. "He told her to go. He said that he didn't need her. All she cared about was spending money." Betty paused and waved her finger. "Now that was unfair. All Lydia ever asked for was a new stove. God knows she was right, but her pleas fell on deaf ears."

"It couldn't possibly be the same one that's at the house now?" Although the monstrosity was old, it wasn't an antique.

"Oh no. Now this is the funny part. About a month after Lydia died Stuart went out and bought that stove. Now isn't that nonsense? He was so crazed with grief that he bought her what she wanted after she was dead." Betty shook her head as though even now, thirty-odd years later, the action still confused her.

"You started to tell me how she died," Lanni prompted.

"Ah, yes. Well, Lydia left all right, with all the defiance of a princess. She lifted her bag and stalked out the driveway, taking Judd with her."

"And Stuart let her go?"

"He did. He'll regret it all his life, but he let her leave and shouted 'good riddance' after her."

"But Miles City is a hundred miles from here." At least that was what she remembered Judd telling her.

"Stuart seemed to think she'd come to her senses and come back on her own, especially when it started raining."

"She didn't?"

"No. An hour later he got in the pickup and drove out looking for her. She'd gotten only a few miles, but was soaked to the skin and shivering so bad her teeth chattered."

"Judd?"

"Oh, he was fine. She'd wrapped him up nice and warm and held him to her so he didn't catch cold."

"What happened next?"

"Lydia took sick. Pneumonia. Within a week she went to the hospital, and a few days after that she died."

Lanni felt tears well at the thought of such a senseless loss of life.

"Stuart blamed himself. I suppose that's only natural with him leaving her alone all that time in the rain. He was a loner before Lydia died, but after she was gone it was like he lost heart."

"The poor man." Lanni could understand how devastated he must have been. Shell-shocked by the loss of his wife and left with a young son who yearned for his mother. "But he had Judd."

"Yes, he had Judd." Betty purposely avoided meeting

Lanni's eyes. "The problem was, Stuart felt he wasn't much of a husband to Lydia and that he was an even worse father to their child. As young as he was, Judd didn't want to have anything to do with his father. In the beginning Stuart tried everything, but he soon gave up. Perhaps if Judd had been a little bit older when Lydia died, he might have accepted his father easier. Every time he looked at his son, Stuart saw Lydia in him and the guilt nearly crippled him."

"If it was so painful then why didn't he send Judd to live with his grandparents?" Surely they would've take him no matter how they felt about Stuart.

"I wish he had, but apparently Lydia's parents blamed Stuart for her death and wanted nothing to do with Stuart. And from what I understand, his own were long dead."

"Then who took care of Judd?"

Betty smiled then for the first time. "I had him during the day, although I was a poor substitute for his mother. I took him in and gave him what love I could. Jim and I were never able to have children of our own, so having Judd here was real good for me. But each evening, Stuart came to the house to pick him up and take him to the main house with him. Every day Judd cried. It nearly broke my heart to see that baby cry. He didn't want to be with his father, but just as he did with Lydia, Stuart refused to let him go." Sharply, Betty tossed her head back, shaking free her troubled thoughts. "In a lot of ways, Judd and his father are alike. They both possess the same stubborn pride. They're both as arrogant as the sun is hot.

"From the time he was in school, Judd and his father locked horns. The two seemed to grate against each other.

If Stuart said one thing, Judd did the opposite just to rile his father. Heaven knew it worked often enough."

"They're still at it."

"I hoped things would change," Betty murmured softly. "They're both so thickheaded that I sometimes feel it will be a miracle if they ever get along. Fools, the pair of them."

Lanni couldn't agree more, but she didn't know what she could do to help either of them.

"And now Stuart's trying to persuade Judd to stay on the ranch?"

"Yes."

"Do you think he will?" Betty looked a bit uncomfortable to be asking.

Lanni smiled into her coffee, remembering Judd's promises. "Yes…it looks like we'll all be staying."

"You and Jenny, too?" Betty looked both surprised and pleased.

"Yes, Judd's content here—happy. It's beautiful country, and although there will be plenty of adjusting for Jenny and me, we're willing. I know what you're thinking," Lanni said, watching Betty. "In some ways I may be a lot like Lydia, but I'm tougher than I look."

Betty shook her head. "You're beautiful the way Lydia was, but you're no orchid—not one bit. You're the type of woman who will blossom where there's plenty of love, and trust me, girl, Judd loves you. I saw it in his eyes when he mentioned you and Jenny were with him." She paused and laughed lightly, shaking her head. "I wonder what it is about the Matthiessen men that attracts the good lookers. From the time Judd was little more than a lad, the girls were chasing him."

Propping her elbow up on the table, Lanni looked at

the older woman. "Tell me some more about his youth. Did he have girlfriends?"

Once again Betty laughed outright. "Lots of those. He was a real ladies' man in high school. It used to drive Stuart crazy the way the girls would come around here, wanting to see Judd."

"He played football?"

"Star quarterback. Jim and I attended every game. He was a real good player; the pride of his school. In those days Judd and his father argued constantly. Stuart didn't want him playing football, said he could get hurt in that crazy sport. Judd ignored him and played anyway. Crazy part is, Stuart went to every game. Arrived late, thinking Judd wouldn't know he was there. But he did. As he'd run on the field, I could see Judd looking into the stands for Stuart. The one time Stuart wasn't there, Judd played terrible."

"He left home soon after graduation?" Lanni recalled Judd telling her that once.

The sad light reentered the older woman's eyes. "Two days later. By the time Judd was eighteen, he and his father were constantly at odds. They seemed to enjoy defying each other. Stuart wanted Judd in college—he had grand plans for the boy, but Judd wanted none of it. They battled night and day about the college issue. I don't think extra schooling would have hurt the boy, but Judd was opposed to the idea of becoming some hot-shot attorney to satisfy his father's whims. After a while the fighting got to be something fierce. Jim and I sat down with Judd and pleaded with him to appease Stuart. It didn't do any good.

"Finally Jim suggested that the best thing Judd could

do was join the service. So Judd enlisted with the marines and was gone before Stuart could challenge it."

"But he kept in contact with his father."

"Stuart isn't much for letter writing, but I know that Judd wrote. Not often, I suspect, but a word now and then so Stuart would know where he was. From what I understand, Judd did take plenty of college classes, but they were the ones that interested him and not his father."

"He's been all over the world."

"I know." Betty pinched her lips together. "For the first eighteen years of his life, he was stuck on these Montana plains. When he walked out the door, he didn't look back. It's as if he needed to prove something to Stuart or to himself. I don't know which. He joined the marines and never came back to the Circle M. Not until he showed up with you and Jenny."

"Stuart came to see us once," Lanni spoke softly, remembering the miserable affair. "We'd been married less than a year."

"I remember. It was the first time either Jim or I could remember Stuart leaving the ranch for more than a few days. I suspect it was the first time he was on a plane."

"It...didn't go well."

Betty grunted. "You don't need to tell me that. It was obvious from the minute Stuart returned. He slammed around the ranch for days. There wasn't a civil word for man or beast."

"Even then Stuart wanted Judd to go back to college and become a lawyer," Lanni explained softly.

"Stuart's a strong-willed individual. He likes having his own way, especially when he believes he knows best. It's taken all this time for him to accept the fact that Judd is his own self. The last couple of years have been hard on him; he's feeling his age now.

"I don't think it's any problem figuring out why he sent for you and Jenny. He knew the time had come for him to swallow his pride. The pictures you sent him of Jenny helped. He sees Lydia in the little girl. It pained him at first, I know, but he kept her pictures by his bed stand and looked at them so often he nearly wore off the edges. He wanted Judd back, that's true enough, but he wanted you and Jenny with Judd. In his mind, I believe, Stuart longs to find some of the happiness he lost when Lydia died. It's too late for him now, but he wants it for Judd."

Judd belonged here. Within days, Lanni had witnessed an astonishing transformation in her husband. Judd was happy, truly happy here. This was his home; the one place in this world where he would be completely content.

With the insight came the realization that her place was at his side. He'd asked her to live on the Circle M and she'd agreed. Naturally there would be adjustments, major ones. But Lanni was willing to do everything within her power to be with Judd and build a good life for Jenny and any other children they might have.

When she was younger, newly married, she'd had trouble coming to terms with the thought of leaving Seattle. Judd seemed to want to travel and drag Lanni and Jenny in his wake. Lanni couldn't deal with that and longed for a reassurance Judd couldn't provide. How little they had known each other two years ago— Lanni thanked God they'd been given a second chance to make their marriage work. Now, if something were to happen and she did return to Seattle, her existence would be even more empty and alone than it had before coming to Montana.

"Grandpa's going to build us a house," Jenny announced casually. She'd rolled around bits of blue dough into perfectly shaped cookies and lined them neatly along the edge of the counter.

"What was that, honey?" Betty asked.

"Grandpa said now that you and Jim are back, he's going to build me, Mommy and Daddy a brand new house."

Lanni's and Betty's eyes met and Betty slowly shook her head. "There he goes again, taking matters into his own hands."

When Lanni left Betty's house, she discovered that the main house was empty. Stuart hadn't let her know where he was going, but he often vanished without a word to her. Lanni accepted his absences without comment. He'd lived most his life without having to let anyone know where he was going. It wasn't her right to insist he start accounting for his whereabouts now.

Jenny went in for her nap without question. Lanni tucked her into the single bed with Betsy, her doll, and the little girl soon fell asleep. Feeling at loose ends, Lanni started straightening the mess in the living room. There were plenty of projects to occupy her if she'd felt comfortable doing them, but this was Stuart's house and he would rightly object to any redecorating.

Neat stacks of magazines lined the coffee table when Stuart came into the house.

Lanni glanced up from her dusting and greeted him with a shy grin, thinking he might object to her housecleaning the same way Judd did.

Stuart stood awkwardly in the doorway leading from

the kitchen to the cozy living room. A small bag was clenched in his hand. "I was in town."

Lanni watched him expectantly, not knowing what to say.

"There's this jewelry shop there. A new place that opened up for business about five years ago."

Lanni successfully disguised a smile. A five-year-old business could hardly be considered new.

"Anyway... I saw this pretty bracelet there and I know how women are always wanting pretty things so I bought it for you." He walked across the room and gruffly shoved the sack toward her.

Lanni was too stunned to react and stared at the bag not knowing what to do.

"It's gold," he said tersely. "Take it."

"But, Stuart, why?"

Ill-at-ease, the older man set the brightly colored sack on the tallest pile of ranching magazines. He stuffed his hands in his pant pockets. "As I said, women like having pretty things."

Lanni picked up the small package and found a long, narrow box inside. She flipped open the lid and caught her breath at the sight of the intricately woven gold bracelet.

"I wish you hadn't," she said gently, closing the lid. This was no ordinary piece of jewelry, but one that must have cost a lot of money. "Stuart, this is very expensive."

"You're darn tootin' it is, but I wanted you to have the best."

"But..."

"You deserve something pretty."

"Thank you, but..."

"Judd was humming this morning and you had a sheep-ish look as well. That's good, real good." For the first time since Lanni had met Stuart Matthiessen, he smiled.

Ten

As it set, the sun bathed the rolling hills of the Circle M in the richest of hues. The sweet scent of prairie grass and apple blossoms mingled with the breeze, drifting where it would, enticing the senses. Lanni sat on the front porch swing with Jenny on her lap, reading the tales of Mother Goose to her sleepy-eyed daughter.

The scene was tranquil, gentle. Lanni's heart was equally at peace. The beauty of what she'd shared with Judd had lingered through the day and into the evening. She longed for him to arrive home so she could tell him how important she felt saving their marriage was to her.

Jenny pressed her head against Lanni's breast and closed her eyes. The gentle swaying motion of the swing had lulled the preschooler to sleep. Gradually Lanni's voice trailed to a mere whisper until she'd finished the story. She closed the book and set it aside. Her eyes searched the hills, seeking Judd. Her stomach churned at the thought of how close they had come to destroying their lives. Already she knew what her husband would say, and he was right. She had suffocated him with her fears and lack of self-confidence. When they'd gotten married, she'd been immature and unsophisticated.

He'd been right, too, about her family. She had relied heavily upon them for emotional support. More than she should. Her greatest fear had always been that she would lose Judd and yet she had done the very things that had driven him from her.

Lanni sighed and rose from the swing. She carried Jenny upstairs and put her to bed, then moved to glance out the window. Jenny had been asleep only a matter of minutes when Lanni heard voices drifting in from the yard. From her position by the upstairs bedroom window, she overheard Judd tell Jim that he'd take care of the horses. Without argument, Jim murmured his thanks and limped toward his house. It looked as if the older man had twisted his ankle and it was apparent he was in pain.

Looking tired, but otherwise fit, Judd led the two horses toward the barn.

Lanni crept down the stairs to discover Stuart asleep in front of the television. She walked out the back door and to the barn.

The light was dim in the interior of the huge structure when Lanni cracked open the massive doors. Judd threw a glance over his shoulder at the unexpected sound and slowly straightened when he recognized Lanni.

"Hello there, cowpoke," she greeted warmly.

"Hello there, wife of a cowpoke." He walked toward her, but stopped abruptly and glanced down over his mud-caked jeans. "I'm filthy."

Lanni slipped her arms around his neck and shook her head. "I could care less," she said smiling up at him. "I've been waiting all day for you and I won't be cheated out of a warm welcome."

Chuckling, Judd bent his head low to capture her mouth. Their lips clung. Judd couldn't be denied her love and warmth another minute. All day he'd thought about her waiting back at the ranch house and he'd experienced such a rush of pleasure that it had been almost painful. The minute after he was home and had a chance to shower, he was taking her to bed and making slow, leisurely love to her.

"I thought it was all a dream," Lanni whispered. "I can't believe I'm in your arms like this."

"If this is a dream, I'll kill the one who wakes me," Judd said and groaned. He kissed her then with a wildness that stirred Lanni's heart. "Oh Lanni, love, I thought I'd die before I got home to you today. No day has ever been longer. I've been a horror to work with—just ask Jim. All I wanted was to get back to you."

Their mouths fused again and hot sensation swirled through her. When he released her mouth, Judd held her to him and breathed several deep, even breaths.

"Let me take care of the horses," he whispered.

Lanni moved provocatively against him. "Take care of me first," she said, nipping at his bottom lip with her teeth.

"Lanni…" He buried his face in her neck. She was cradled against him in a way that left little doubt as to his needs. "Not here."

"Yes here."

"Now?"

"Yes, please."

Judd kissed her again, his tongue outlining her bottom lip first and then her top lip. Lanni was so weakened by the sensuous attack that she thought she might faint.

With their mouths still fused, Judd lifted her into his arms. Without thought or direction he moved into a clean stall and laid her on the fresh bed of hay. Lying half on top of her, Judd kissed her again and again.

The loud snort from one of the horses brought up Judd's head. He released a broken, frustrated sigh. "Lanni."

"Hmm?" Her arms were stretched out around his neck, her wrists crossed.

Judd looked over his shoulder and groaned.

"The horses?" she asked.

"The horses," he repeated.

"All right," she murmured and smiled leisurely. "I suppose that as the wife of an old cowhand, I best get used to playing second fiddle to a horse."

Grinning, Judd got to his feet and helped her up, gently brushing the hay from her back. "Give me fifteen minutes to shower and shave and we'll see how second fiddle you feel." He patted the stallion on the flank, moved around to unfasten the cinch from the massive beast and then lifted the heavy saddle from the animal.

"Can I help?" Lanni wanted to know.

"If you'd like." He nodded to his right. "The pitchfork's over there. Go ahead and deliver some hay to these hungry boys."

Eager to help, Lanni did as he requested. "Aren't you going to ask me about my day?"

"Sure. Did anything exciting happen?"

"You mean other than Stuart going to town and buying me a thousand-dollar gold bracelet." She didn't know what he'd paid for the piece of jewelry, but hoped to capture Judd's undivided attention.

"What!"

She had it now. "You heard me right."

"Why would he do something like that?"

"I'm not exactly sure," Lanni replied. "But from what I understand, although he was careful not to say as much, the bracelet is a gift because I've fallen so nicely into his schemes."

Judd scowled. "How'd he know?"

Lanni laughed and shook her head. "Didn't you talk to him this morning?"

"Not more than a couple of minutes. I told him where Jim and I were headed and what needed to be done. That was about it."

"Apparently that was enough."

"Enough for what?"

"Enough," Lanni said patiently, "for Stuart to know exactly what happened between us last night." To her amazement, Judd's eyes narrowed with disapproval. "You're angry?" she asked him, puzzled by his attitude.

"No," he denied, leading the horse by the reins into his stall.

"But you look furious. Is it because he gave me the bracelet?"

For a minute Judd didn't answer her. "Not exactly. However, I'm going to let my father know that if any man gives you gifts, it's going to be me." He returned to the second horse, his movements jerky, angry. So Stuart had been so confident that their little talk had reaped its rewards that he'd gone out and gotten Lanni that fancy bracelet. He was furious with the old man, and equally upset with himself for falling so readily into Stuart's schemes.

"Judd," Lanni said, placing her hand on his forearm to stop him. "Are you sorry about last night?"

"No."

"All of a sudden you're closing yourself off from me and I don't know why."

"It's nothing."

"I'm your wife," she cried, impatient now. "We were separated for two long, miserable years because we never talked to each other. I don't want to make the same mistakes we did before. For heaven's sake tell me why you're upset!"

"Stuart has no business involving himself in our affairs."

"Agreed. But you're not making sense. Why are you so mad at him—you already said it wasn't the bracelet."

Judd toyed with the thought of telling her about Steve's phone calls and rejected the idea. He couldn't risk having her suspect that pride alone had driven him to her bed. It was far from the truth and if she started to think that was his motive, she'd turn away from him. In reality, Judd had finally come to understand that if he were to lose Lanni now, life would have no meaning for him.

"I'm not angry," he said, forcing a smile. "Why don't you go fix me something to eat and I'll finish up here?"

"Judd...?" In her heart, Lanni knew something wasn't right, but this newfound peace was fragile and she didn't want to test it with something as flimsy as conjecture.

"You go into the house. I'll be there in a couple of minutes."

Bewildered, Lanni left the barn, not knowing what to

think. Something was troubling Judd, but he obviously preferred to keep it to himself.

Judd exhaled slowly, watching Lanni turn and walk away. He was going to have a heart-to-heart talk with his father, and soon.

His dinner was on the table when Judd came into the house. He ate it silently as Lanni worked around the kitchen. They were both quiet, neither speaking. When he'd finished, Judd delivered his plate to the kitchen sink. "Lanni," he said. He took a step toward her, hesitated and frowned. "Is there a possibility you could get pregnant from last night?"

He looked so serious, so concerned, that Lanni's heart melted. "I don't think so."

"I'd like another baby. Would you mind?" Gently he lifted a thick strand of her hair from her face, twisting it around his finger. His eyes softened as he studied her. Somehow. Somewhere. A long time ago, he must have done something very right to deserve a woman as good as Lanni. "I love you so much," he whispered.

"I want another baby," she answered and nodded emphatically. "Anytime you say, cowboy."

Mindless of his dirty, sweaty clothes, Judd brought her into the loving circle of his arms and kissed her hungrily. Lanni slid her arms over his chest and linked them at the back of his neck. Her soft curves molded to his hardness and Judd deepened the kiss until their mouths forged. Lanni sighed, swaying against him, weak and clinging. Reluctantly he broke off the kiss, but continued to hold her, smiling tenderly down on her. "I'm a filthy mess."

Sighing with contentment, Lanni shook her head. "It didn't bother me in the barn; it doesn't bother me now."

She looked up at him and her eyes held such a lambent glow that it took all his restraint not to kiss her again. "Where's Stuart?"

"Asleep."

"I need to talk to him."

Lanni wasn't certain what Judd wanted to say, but she thought it would be best to clear the air. "He mentioned something to Jenny that you might want to ask him about as well."

"What's that?"

"He told her that since Jim and Betty Peterman are back, he's going to build us a house."

Judd could feel the frustration build in him. "We may have a battle on our hands, keeping our lives private; I'll say something to him about that while I'm at it. Any house building will be decided by you and me—not my father."

"I agree," Lanni said, studying Judd. He looked tired. "Are you sure you don't want to save this talk until morning?"

"I'm sure." There were more than a few items he needed to discuss with his father—some were about the ranch and others about Lanni and Jenny. He could make the decisions regarding the Circle M easily enough, but he sought Stuart's input. The ranch was one area on which they were in complete agreement. They both loved the Circle M. It was as much a part of their lives as the blood that channeled through their veins. And while he was with Stuart, he would tell his father exactly what he thought of him buying Lanni gifts and filling their daughter with tales of a new house. If they were going to live on the Circle M, Stuart was going to have to learn to keep his nose out of Judd's marriage and his family.

"It's going to take a lot of commitment to get this ranch operating properly," Judd told Lanni as she finished putting the leftovers back into the refrigerator. Commitment and funds. It would nearly wipe out eighteen years of savings and be the financial gamble of Judd's life.

"This is our home now." A wealth of understanding went into Lanni's statement.

"It is home," Judd concurred. He felt it all the way through his soul. Montana. The Circle M. He loved it here. It was where he was meant to be. All these years he'd been searching for the elusive feeling that had returned the minute he'd pulled into the driveway leading to this beaten-down house.

"No more trips to Alaska?"

"Too cold!"

Lanni grinned, remembering Stuart telling her that it had registered forty below at the ranch only last winter.

"Saudi Arabia?"

"Too hot," Judd admitted with a chuckle.

Again Lanni tried to disguise a smile. Stuart had warned her that the summers could be as hot as a desert with temperatures ranging in the low hundreds.

"I'd better go have that talk with Stuart," Judd said reluctantly; he wasn't looking forward to this.

"I'll wait for you upstairs then." This evening was turning out so different than what Lanni had hoped. In her mind she'd pictured a loving husband carrying her up the stairs. Her teeth bit into the sensitive flesh of her inner cheek to hold back her disappointment. "Do you want me to wait up for you?"

Without turning to face her, Judd shook his head. "It may be a while. I'll wake you."

With a heavy heart, Lanni trudged up the stairs. Pacing the inside of her room, she felt the urge to stamp her feet in a childish display of temper. They were both trying so hard to make everything between them work that they had become their own worst enemies. Judd wanted to clear the air with his father and all Lanni wanted was her husband at her side.

She sat on the edge of the bed for what seemed like hours. Lethargy took hold and, feeling depressed, she slowly moved down the hall to shower. A half hour later, she listlessly climbed into bed.

Sleep didn't come easily. The last time she looked at the clock on the nightstand beside the bed, it was nearly midnight. Judd still hadn't come upstairs.

The next thing Lanni heard was a soft whimper. The sound activated a maternal instinct she couldn't question and she woke up.

Throwing back the covers, she climbed out of bed and hurried down the hall, not stopping for either her slippers or her bathrobe. Jenny was quietly weeping in Judd's arms.

He glanced at her and whispered, "She had a bad dream."

"Poor sweetheart," Lanni whispered, lowering herself onto the bed beside Jenny and Judd. Gently she patted the little girl's back until she'd calmed down and stopped sniffing. A few minutes later Jenny's even breathing assured Lanni her daughter had returned to sleep.

"How'd it go with Stuart?" Lanni asked.

"Not good." It was like he was eighteen all over again. Judd couldn't make his father understand that he didn't want the old man interfering again. What happened between Judd and Lanni was none of Stuart's business. Stuart had told Judd that he should thank God he'd been around that morning. Steve had phoned again and had demanded to speak to Lanni. He'd been able to put the other man off, but he doubted if he could another time.

"Did you argue?" Lanni asked next.

"Not exactly. He refused to listen to me."

"He has his pride."

"Don't I know it," Judd concurred.

Gently he placed Jenny back inside the bed and led Lanni into the hallway. "I'm surprised you heard her. She barely made a sound."

"I have mother's ears." She paused in front of her door. He looked unbearably weary. His hair was rumpled as if he'd stroked his fingers through it countless times.

Judd hesitated at her side, trying not to stare at her up-turned face. She was so incredibly lovely in the moonlight that he felt his body tense just standing beside her. "More than anything I wanted to be with you." He didn't move. His feet felt rooted to the spot and his tongue was thick and uncooperative. He wanted her to sleep with him, tonight and for the rest of their lives. They were good together, and not only in bed. There was so much they could give each other.

Lanni watched the weariness evaporate from his eyes. Now they were keen and sharp, commanding her to come to him.

Slowly, as if sleepwalking, Lanni moved to him and, without a word, her arms crept up his solid chest to encircle his neck and urge his mouth down to hers. As his head descended, she arched closer. Their lips met in a fiery union of unleashed passion. The kiss continued until

Lanni was both dizzy and weak. They broke apart panting and breathless.

Smiling, she took Judd by the hand and led him into the room. "I can't believe it took you this long," she whispered.

He brought her into his arms and nuzzled her throat. "All day I've been crazy to get home to you and it seemed like everything stood in our way." With infinite patience, he unfastened the top button of her bodice to slip the material free. Her arms stretched over her head as Judd pulled the gown free. Every part of her body throbbed with need for him. They were man and wife. Lovers. Friends.

"Judd," she pleaded.

Just when her knees were about to give out on her and she was going to collapse onto the bed, he raised his head and gently laid her down on the mattress. In seconds he was free of his clothes.

Lanni had waited all evening for him and wouldn't be denied any longer. As they made love their hearts sang out in joyful celebration. Their cries echoed each other's. The pleasure went on and on until Lanni was convinced it was endless.

Judd wrapped her in his arms, kissing the tears of joy from her face. "Oh, my love," he whispered, his voice trembling with emotion. "Was it always this good?"

"Always," she murmured, not remembering anything ever being less exciting between them. Together they were magic. During the long, lonely months of their separation, Lanni had been only half alive. She recognized that now more than ever. Her life with Jenny had been clouded with a constant sense of expectation, waiting. An unconscious part of her had been seeking a reconciliation with

Judd; without him she was incomplete—spiritually handicapped. She was destined to belong to him and only him.

"Don't leave me," she pleaded, wrapping her arms around him and burying her face in his neck.

"No," he promised. "Never again." Love for her flowed through him like floodwaters after a heavy spring rain. She was all that was important to him. The ranch could fall down at his feet tomorrow and he'd survive. He could lose all his personal possessions and never notice their loss. But he wouldn't last another minute without Lanni.

The tension fled from her limbs and Lanni relaxed, cuddling him. He reached for the sheets and covered them. Within minutes they were both asleep.

Judd woke first. Even in their sleep they'd continued to hold each other—neither seemed willing to release the other. He smiled gently and stared at the ceiling. It was later than he'd slept since arriving on the ranch. But he didn't care—Lanni was his and he was whole again.

He closed his mind to the unpleasant scene he'd faced with Stuart before climbing the stairs to bed. He didn't want to argue with his father; he'd hoped they'd come to an understanding, but apparently Judd was wrong. He'd told Stuart if Steve phoned again that he should give Lanni the phone. She would be angry when she learned they'd been hiding the calls from her, but they'd deal with that at the time.

Lanni stirred, content, satisfied. Judd's arms were securely wrapped around her. "Morning," she whispered, stretching. "What time is it?"

Judd kissed the crown of her head and moved his wrist up so he could read his watch. "Later than it should be."

"I feel wonderful," Lanni announced, turning to kiss the hollow of his throat.

"So do I," Judd answered. "It felt so good holding you that I couldn't slip out of bed. Now I'll have to face Jim's wrath for being lazy and sleeping in."

"I'm pleased you didn't leave," Lanni whispered, remembering how disappointed she'd been the day before.

"Mommy." Jenny knocked softly against the closed door, her sweet voice meek and timid.

Lanni jumped up from the bed and after pulling on her robe, she opened the door. Jenny was standing there, her doll clenched to her breast. Lanni noted that the little girl looked unnaturally pale.

"What's the matter, Cupcake? Aren't you feeling well?" Judd asked. Before Lanni had opened the door, he'd pulled on his jeans.

"I'm not sick," Jenny answered.

"Do you want breakfast?" Lanni inquired.

The little girl adamantly shook her head. "Nope."

"Aren't you hungry?" Breakfast was Jenny's favorite meal, especially when there was Captain Crunch cereal around.

"Grandpa was mean to me. He told me to go away."

Judd felt anger shoot through him. "I don't think he meant that."

"He said it real, real mean."

"Maybe Grandpa isn't feeling well today," Lanni suggested, surprised that Stuart would do or say anything to upset Jenny.

"And you know what else he said?"

"What?" Judd brushed the curls from her cheek and kissed her gently to ease the hurt feelings.

"He said I shouldn't ever answer the phone again."

"He has this thing about the phone," Lanni said, shaking her head in wonder at Judd's father's actions. "It rang yesterday and you would have thought the FBI was on the other end. He nearly wrestled me to the ground to stop me from answering. Then he raced into the other room to get it."

Judd stiffened. "I'm sure there's some explanation."

"You know what, Mommy?"

"What, honey?"

"I know who was on the phone."

"Who was that?" Lanni asked, unconcerned.

"Mr. Delaney, and he was real mad, too. He said that he wants to talk to you and that Daddy didn't have the right to keep you from talking on the phone."

Eleven

"Judd," Lanni murmured, her voice betraying her shock. "Is that true?"

"Jenny, do I hear your doll crying? Maybe you should let her take a nap." Judd turned to his daughter, ignoring Lanni's question. The last thing he needed was to deal with this Steve issue now. One look told him how furious Lanni was.

"Betsy's not crying, Daddy."

"Yes, she is," Lanni said sternly.

Jenny's lower lip began to tremble as she battled back ready tears. "Nobody wants Jenny this morning," she said, her voice wobbling. She paused and glanced from her mother to her father.

"Now look what you've done," Lanni whispered between clenched teeth, reaching for her daughter. She wrapped her arms around the four-year-old. "We're sorry, honey."

"I don't want you and Daddy to fight."

"We won't argue, will we, Mommy?" Judd challenged, raising his eyes to Lanni.

Jenny broke free of Lanni's arms. "But Mommy

looks that way when she gets mad at Aunt Jade. Her face scrunches up and her eyes get small. Like now."

"I think she has something there," Judd commented lightly.

Lanni reached for her clothes, cursing under her breath. "Now I understand why Stuart didn't want me answering the phone. How many times has Steve called?"

"I have no idea."

"I'll just bet you don't."

"Mommy."

"Not now, Jenny. This is serious business."

Jenny sighed expressively. "Business, business, business, that's all you talk about. When are you going to be a Mommy again?"

Lanni stared open-mouthed at her daughter. "That's unfair, Jennifer Lydia Matthiessen. I've always been your mother." Lanni did her best to ignore an attack of guilt for all the times Jade had picked up Jenny from the day-care center and just as many occasions that Jenny had been left with Jade or her parents because Lanni had to work late for a hundred different reasons.

"All you did was business, business, business until Daddy came. I don't want you to talk to Mr. Delaney. He sounded mad just like you and Grandpa."

"She's smarter than you give her credit," Judd tossed in and was almost seared by Lanni's scalding glower.

"I'm calling Steve to find out what's been going on around here."

Judd crossed his arms. "Be my guest." Although he strove to appear as nonchalant as possible, he was worried.

Lanni stormed out of the bedroom and got dressed in

the bathroom. Two minutes later, she raced downstairs. Judd followed her.

Stuart met him at the foot of the stairway. "You got to stop her, boy."

"Why?"

"She's going to contact that city slicker."

"Judd, do something," Lanni cried, her patience long since gone. "Your father's disconnected the phone."

"Dad. It's fine."

"Did you think to inform him that Steve could be contacting me for business reasons?" Lanni flared, her hands placed defiantly on her hips.

"No." Judd's own self-control was weakening. "You and I both know what Steve wants."

"You're jealous!"

"You're darn right I am. I don't like having that milquetoast anywhere near you."

"You tell her, son," Stuart shouted.

"Stay out of this." Judd turned to his father, pointing a finger in his direction. "This is between Lanni and me."

Chuckling, Stuart took Jenny by the hand and led her toward the kitchen. "Got to leave those young lovers to settle this themselves," he whispered gleefully to the little girl.

"Are you still mad at me, Grandpa?" Jenny wanted to know first.

Stuart looked shocked. "I was never angry with my Jenny-girl."

"Good. Betsy cried when you got cross."

"You tell Betsy how sorry your grandpa is."

"It's all right, she told me that she forgives you."

The kitchen door closed and Judd turned to Lanni. "You were saying?"

"You have a lot of nerve keeping those calls from me."

"You're absolutely right."

"If I had any sense, I'd walk out that door."

"You won't," he stated confidently. "You always were crazy about me."

"Judd," she cried. "I'm serious."

"I am, too."

"Don't try to sweet-talk me."

"Come on, Lanni, this is no snow job. I was jealous. I'll admit it if it makes you feel any better. Stuart told me about the calls the other night and I realized how serious this guy is. He isn't going to lose you without a fight and if that's what he wants, I'll give him one."

"You're being ridiculous."

"I don't think so. Apparently Delaney's been trying to reach you since we arrived. I guess I should be grateful there's no cell coverage here."

"And it never occurred to you that it could be something to do with the office?"

"Quite frankly, no. Stuart knew after talking to him only one time and he's right on target. Delaney's after one thing and that one thing happens to involve you. I recognized it the minute I met the man."

"You're imagining things."

"I wasn't seeing things when I saw him gawking at you. Don't be so naive, my sweet innocent."

"I'm not an innocent!"

"Thanks to me." One side of his mouth quirked upward.

"Stop it, Judd Matthiessen, you're only making me madder." She crossed her arms, refusing to relent to his cajoling good mood. He seemed to think this was all some big joke. "Get me the phone," she demanded.

"All right, all right; don't get testy." He went into the kitchen and returned a moment later with the telephone. He handed it to her, crossed his arms and waited.

"Well?"

"Well what?"

"I want you to leave," she hissed, "this is a private conversation."

Judd didn't budge and from the look about him, he wasn't going to. Rather than force the issue, Lanni traipsed into the small office off the living room and inserted the phone jack into place. It was doubtful that Judd would hear much of the conversation anyway.

She punched out the numbers and waited. The phone rang only once. "Steve, it's Lanni."

"Lanni, thank goodness you phoned," he said, his relief obvious in his tone. "What been going on there? I've been trying to contact you for days!"

"I didn't know. Jenny mentioned this morning that you'd phoned, but it's the first I heard of it."

"I don't know what kind of situation you're in there, but I've been tempted to contact the authorities. I think your father-in-law is off his rocker."

"He is a bit eccentric."

"Eccentric. I'd say he was closer to being stark raving mad."

"Steve, I'm sure you didn't contact me to discuss Stuart."

"You're right, I didn't. Lanni," he said her name slowly, in a hurt, self-righteous tone, "you didn't even let me know you were leaving."

"There…there wasn't time. I tried." But admittedly not very hard. She'd left a message for him at the office, but hadn't contacted his cell. Her relationship or non-relationship with her fellow worker embarrassed Lanni now that she and Judd had reconciled. It was true that their dates were innocent enough, but Lanni had seen the handwriting on the wall as far as Steve was concerned and Judd was right. Steve wanted her and was courting her with seemingly limitless patience.

"Lanni," Steve continued, his voice serious. "I'm worried about you."

"There's no need; Jenny and I are perfectly fine."

"Are you there of your own free will?"

"Of course!" The question was ludicrous. "I haven't been kidnapped, if that's what you mean."

"Your father-in-law has told me a number of times that Judd would never let you go."

"He didn't mean it like that."

"Perhaps not, but he also told me that Judd would go to great lengths to keep you married to him."

"I'm sure you're mistaken." Her fingers tightened around the receiver as she remembered the expression in Judd's eyes when he'd told her he needed her. He'd been desperate and just now he'd admitted that he'd known about Steve's phone calls a couple of nights ago.

"What made you leave Seattle with the man? Lanni, he deserted you—left you and Jenny. He's treated you like dirt. What possible reason could there be for you to trust a man like that?"

"Judd claimed that his father was seriously ill and had asked to see Jenny before he died."

"That old man sounds in perfect health to me."

"He apparently made a miraculous recovery when we arrived." Steve almost had her believing his craziness and she paused a moment to recount the details of her coming.

"Lanni," Steve said, and breathed heavily. "I want you to do something for me."

"What?"

"I'm very serious about this, Lanni, so don't scoff. I want you to try to leave and see what happens. I'm willing to bet that Judd and his father are holding you and Jenny captive and you just don't realize it yet."

"Steve, that's loony."

"It's not. Tell them something serious has come up and you have to return to Seattle."

"Steve!"

"Do it. If I haven't heard from you by the end of the day, I'm contacting the police."

Lanni lifted the hair from her forehead and closed her eyes. "I can't believe I'm hearing this."

"Tell me you'll do it."

"All right, but you're wrong. I know you're wrong."

"Prove it to me."

"I can't believe I'm agreeing to this." She shook her head in wonder, but then Steve had always been persuasive.

"You'll phone me back?"

His plan wouldn't work, Lanni realized. "What am I supposed to say after I've got my bags in the car and am ready to leave? They're going to think I've lost my senses if I suddenly announce that this is all a test to see if they'd actually let me go."

"You'll think of something," Steve said confidently.

"Great." Lanni felt none of his assurance.

"I'll be waiting to hear from you."

"I'm only doing this to prove to you once and for all that Jenny and I are perfectly safe."

"Fine. Just do it."

Lanni didn't bother with any goodbyes. She replaced the receiver and sat down, burying her face in her hands, assimilating her troubled thoughts.

"Did you tell him?" Judd asked, standing behind her.

Frightened by the unexpected sound of his voice, Lanni jumped and jerked her head around. "Tell him what?"

Judd's mouth thinned with displeasure. "That you and I are back together and that there will be no divorce."

"No, I didn't tell him."

"Why not?"

Lanni studied him, feeling the overbearing weight of newfound suspicions. Not for a minute did she believe she and Jenny were being kidnapped by Judd and his father. Steve was overreacting because he was naturally suspicious of the circumstances of her leaving Seattle. The whole idea that such a drama was taking place was so farfetched that it was inconceivable. But something else, something far more profound, had captured her attention.

"When did you learn Steve had been trying to contact me?" she asked, surprised at how steady her voice remained when her emotions were in such tumult.

Judd inserted two fingers into the small pocket near the waist of his jeans. "I already told you, Stuart mentioned it the other night."

"What night?"

Judd cursed under his breath. She knew—she'd figured it out. Explaining to Lanni wasn't going to be easy. He sat down across from her. "The night you suspect."

"Then the only reason you came to me—"

"No," he cut in sharply. "That night, for the first time in my life, I realized how right my father was. If I lost you there would be nothing left for me. Nothing. Oh, I'd stick around the ranch for a while, maybe several years, I don't know, but there would be no contentment, no peace. You give me that, Lanni, only you."

"It didn't work in Seattle. What makes you believe it will here? Aren't you asking a lot of me to abandon everything I know and love on the off chance you'll stick around here? You *think* you'll be content on the Circle M, but you don't know that."

"I do know it. I left the ranch eighteen years ago and now I'm home."

"Maybe."

"I'm home, Lanni. Home. But it doesn't mean a whole lot if you're not here to share it with me. I've loved you from the moment we met; believe me, I've fought that over the last couple of years. There are plenty of things I'd like to change about the both of us. But the underlying fact is that I refuse to give up on our marriage. It's too important to both of us."

"You were jealous of Steve?"

"You're darn right I am," he admitted freely, then added, "but you should know what that feels like."

After her experience in Coeur d'Alene when she'd believed Judd had slept with another woman, Lanni had experienced a mouthful of the green-eyed monster. Enough to make her gag on her own stupidity.

"I have to leave."

Judd shook his head to clear his thoughts. He couldn't

believe she meant what she was saying. "What do you mean leave?"

"There's a problem in Seattle—a big one and I've got to be there to handle it. There are people counting on me, and I can't let them down."

"What about letting me down?"

"This is different."

"It isn't," he said hotly. "What kind of problem could be so important that you'd so willingly walk away from me?" He battled down the overwhelming sensation that if he allowed her to drive away from the Circle M, it would be all over for them.

"A house transaction."

"That's a flimsy excuse," he said darkly. "What is Steve holding over you?"

"Nothing. Don't be ridiculous—this is strictly business."

"Obviously that's not true. You were on the phone for a good fifteen minutes. You must have discussed something other than a real estate transaction. I want to know what he said," Judd demanded.

"And I already told you. I need to return to Seattle." She pushed herself away from the desk and stood. "I have to pack my things."

"Lanni," he whispered, his hand stopping her. "Look me in the eye and tell me you're coming back."

"I'm coming back." He had yet to learn she had no intention of leaving. Not really. This was a stupid game and she was furious that she'd agreed to do this. But Steve had been so insistent, so sure she was caught in some trap. She walked past Judd and into the living room.

Her father-in-law was standing in the middle of the

room when Lanni came out of the office. His face was pale and pinched and his gaze skidded past Lanni to his son. Questions burned in his faded brown eyes.

"Lanni needs to make a quick trip to Seattle," Judd explained, doing his best to disguise his worries. "There's some problem at the office that only she can handle."

"You letting her go?"

"He has no other option," Lanni cut in sharply.

Stuart ignored her and narrowed his eyes on his son. "Are you going to let her go to that no-good city slicker? He's going to steal her away."

"I have no intention of letting Steve do any such thing," Lanni informed him stiffly. "Judd and I are married and we plan to stay that way for a very long time."

Stuart continued to pretend she wasn't there. "I let Lydia leave once and after she came back things were never the same."

"I'm not Lydia."

"Mommy's name is Lanni," Jenny informed them softly, clenching Judd's hand and staring wide eyed at the three adults.

"Go ahead and pack," Judd spoke softly, resigned. He wouldn't stop Lanni—this was her decision. Unlike his father, Judd was willing to let her go. Sorrow stabbed through him as he thought of the night the roles had been reversed—she'd let him go. But he had begged her to go with him. "I'll call the airlines and find out the time of the next flight. I'll drive you into Billings."

"Boy," Stuart shouted angrily. "What's the matter with you? If Lanni goes it will ruin everything." His hand gripped his stomach. "Don't let her go. Don't make the same mistake as me. You'll be sorry. All your life you'll regret it." His hand reached out and gripped the corner of the large overstuffed chair as he swayed.

"Dad?" Judd placed his hand on his father's shoulder. "What's wrong?"

"Pain," he said through clenched teeth. "Most of yesterday and through the night."

Judd had never seen a man more pale. "Here, let me get you into the bedroom." With his arm around his father's waist, Judd guided the older man into his bedroom and helped him onto the bed. "I'll contact Doc Simpson."

Lanni was so furious that she couldn't stand in one place. She paced the small area in front of the outdated black-and-white television set, knotting and unknotting her fists.

"He's not sick," she hissed in a low whisper the minute Judd reappeared. "This is all a ploy to keep me on the ranch."

"Why don't we let the doctor decide that?"

"Do you honestly believe this sudden attack of ill health?"

Judd's eyes bored into hers. "As a matter of fact, I do." He returned to the tiny cubicle of an office and reached for the phone. He'd experienced enough pain in his life to recognize when it was genuine.

"What wrong with Grandpa?" Jenny asked, tugging at the hem of Lanni's blouse.

"He's not feeling well, sweetheart."

"He didn't eat any Captain Crunch cereal this morning."

Lanni recalled that Stuart hadn't eaten much of anything in the last twenty-four hours.

Judd reappeared, looking toward his father's bedroom door.

"Well?" Lanni was curious to what Stuart's physician had to say.

"I repeated what Dad told me and Doc Simpson thinks it would be best if we drove into Miles City for a complete examination at the hospital."

"Miles City," Lanni cried. "That's over a hundred miles."

"It's the closest hospital."

"Judd, don't you recognize this for what it is? Stuart isn't sick. This is all part of some crazy ploy to keep me on the ranch."

"You're free to go, Lanni. Jim can drive you into Billings to catch the next flight for Seattle or you can come with me and we'll get you on a private plane to connect with the airlines in Billings."

Lanni crossed her arms over her chest and shook her head. "I can't believe this is happening."

"I don't have time to discuss the options with you now. Make up your mind."

"I'll go with you." And have the extreme pleasure of watching Judd's expression when the doctors in Miles City announce that Stuart was in perfect health.

"Can I come, too?" Jenny wanted to know.

"It would be better if you and Betsy stayed here with Betty. Can you be a good girl and help Betty?"

Jenny nodded eagerly. "I like her."

Judd had apparently already thought to leave the little girl with the housekeeper because Betty arrived a minute later. Jenny was whisked away and Lanni heard the older woman reassuring Jenny that everything was going to be just fine. A smile touched Lanni's lips when she heard Jenny respond by telling the woman that she wasn't afraid, but Betsy was just a little.

While Judd brought the SUV to the front of the house, Lanni took out some blankets and a pillow.

Judd got his father into the back seat of the car and Lanni lined his lap with blankets. For the first time Lanni noted how terribly pale the older man had become. He gritted his teeth at the pain, but offered Lanni a reassuring grin.

"You leaving for Seattle?"

"You're a wicked old man."

"Agreed," Stuart said with a faint smile. "Stay with my son, girl. Fill his life with children and happiness."

"Would you stop being so dramatic. We're going to get you to Miles City and the doctors are going to tell us you've got stomach gas so stop talking as if the back seat of this car is going to be your deathbed. You got a lot of good years left in you."

"Ha. I'll be lucky to make it there alive."

Judd climbed into the front seat and started the engine. "Ready?" he asked, trying to hide his nervousness.

"Ready, boy," Stuart said and lay back, pressing his weathered face against the feather pillow.

The ride seemed to last an eternity. With every mile Lanni came to believe that whatever was wrong with Stuart was indeed very real.

They hit a rut in the road thirty miles out of Miles City and Stuart groaned. Judd's hands tightened around the steering wheel until his knuckles were stark white. Lanni dared not look at the speedometer. The car whipped past the prairie grass at an unbelievable speed, making the scenery along the side of the road seem blurred.

The only sound in the car was that of the revved engine. Lanni's breathing was short and choppy. It wasn't until they reached the outskirts of Miles City that she realized her breathing echoed Stuart's shallow gasps. Only his were punctuated with a sigh now and again to disguise his pain.

Judd drove directly to Holy Rosary Hospital on Clark Street, running two red lights in his urgency to get his father to a medical team as quickly as possible.

After Stuart had been taken into the emergency entrance, Judd and Lanni were directed to a small reception area. The waiting, not knowing what was happening, was by far the worst.

"When did he say he started feeling so terribly ill?" Lanni asked, reaching for Judd's hand, their fingers entwined, gripping each other for reassurance.

"Apparently he hasn't been up to par all week. He saw Doc Simpson yesterday afternoon and the doctor was concerned then. Dad's ulcer is apparently peptic."

"English, please."

"It's commonly referred to as a bleeding ulcer. They're bad, Lanni, painful."

"I feel like an idiot." She hung her head, ashamed at her behavior and how she'd accused Stuart of staging the entire attack so she'd remain in Montana.

"Don't," Judd said, giving her fingers a reassuring squeeze. "Given an identical set of circumstances, I might have believed the same thing. Dad has a way about him that sometimes even I don't trust."

"Why didn't he say something earlier?"

Judd recalled the argument they'd had the night before when he'd confronted Stuart about the bracelet, building the house and fending off Steve's calls. Stuart had been quick tempered and unreasonable, and Judd had attributed it to his stubborn nature. Now he understood that Stuart had been in a great deal of pain even then.

"Judd?" Lanni coaxed.

"Sorry. What were you saying?"

"I wanted to know why Stuart didn't tell us something was wrong earlier."

Judd's smile was off center. "Pride, I suspect. Telling anyone would be admitting to a weakness. In case you haven't noticed, the Matthiessen men refuse to appear weak no matter what it cost."

"Never," Lanni confirmed, doing her best to disguise a smile. "They're not stubborn, either, and hardly ever proud."

When the doctor approached them, Judd rose quickly to his feet. Lanni stood with him, trying to read the doctor's expression and failing.

"Mr. and Mrs. Matthiessen?"

"Yes. How's my father?"

"He's resting comfortably now. We'd like to keep him overnight for observation and a few tests, but he should be able to leave the hospital tomorrow."

Judd sighed with relief. "Thank you, Doctor." The minute the physician turned away, Judd brought Lanni into his arms and buried his face in the curve of her neck.

"I don't mind telling you I was frightened," he whispered.

"I was, too. He's a crotchety old man, but I've grown fond of him."

"It's funny," Judd said with a short laugh. "I'm relieved that he's going to be fine and in the same breath I'd like to shake him silly for worrying us so much."

"I feel the same way."

Judd slid his arm around her shoulder. "Let's go see him for a minute and then we'll drive on out to the airport and see about getting you a plane to Seattle."

Twelve

"Yes, well," Lanni shifted her feet. Her mind went blank for a plausible excuse to cancel the trip. "I may have reacted hastily. I'm sure if I make a couple of phone calls I'll be able to work out the problem from this end of things."

"What do you mean?" Judd's eyes looked capable of boring holes straight through her. "Three hours ago it was imperative that you reach Seattle. You made it sound like a Biblical-style catastrophe would befall the realty if you weren't there to see to it."

"I could have exaggerated a teensy bit." Lanni swallowed uncomfortably, feeling incredibly guilty.

"Lanni?"

"All right, all right," she admitted, hating herself more by the minute. "I made the entire thing up."

"What!" Judd was furious; it showed in every feature of his chiseled masculine face. His eyes narrowed, his nostrils flared and his mouth thinned dangerously.

She couldn't very well admit that Steve had this senseless, idiotic notion that she was being held against her wishes. "Steve seemed to think I was needed in Seattle." Even to her own ears that excuse sounded lame.

"I'll just bet he wanted you back, and I'm smart enough to know the reason why even if you aren't."

"It wasn't like that," she flared.

"You had time to discuss this scheme with Steve, but not enough to tell him we'd reconciled."

"I'll tell him."

"You're darn right you will." His grip on her elbow as he led her into the hospital parking lot was just short of being painful.

"I can't believe you. You're behaving like Steve Delaney is a threat to us. Judd, I swear to you, he isn't," Lanni muttered, slipping inside the front seat of the station wagon. "I'm yours, Judd Matthiessen, and the only thing that could ever come between us again is of your own making."

"And what's that?"

Her unflinching gaze met his. "If you were to leave me again, it'd be over in a minute. Judd, I mean that. My love is strong enough to withstand just about anything, but not that."

"It isn't going to happen."

Lanni leaned her head against the headrest and closed her eyes. Judd started the car and pulled onto the street. His assurances rang shockingly familiar. It seemed every time he returned from a trip in the beginning, she'd made him promise he wouldn't leave her again. To his credit, he'd taken a job in Seattle and a month, maybe two, would pass before he'd find some excuse to be free of her and travel again.

"I'll never leave you, Lanni. I swear to it by everything I hold sacred."

"What happens when money gets tight?" In her mind

Lanni had listed the excuses Judd had conveniently used in the past.

"Simple. We'll sell off a few head of cattle and cut down expenses."

"What happens if Jenny gets sickly again?"

"We'll get her to a doctor."

Lanni shook her head and crossed her arms over her chest. "Doctors cost money." He'd used that excuse the first time. Lanni recognized that she sounded like an insecure little girl, but she refused to live in a dream world no matter how comfortable it was. Too much was at stake and she needed to know that this reconciliation with Judd was concrete.

"Montana is a bit different from Seattle. Doc Simpson's a patient man. He'll wait."

"What if…"

"I'm home, Lanni. We all are."

She squeezed her eyes shut. It would be so incredibly easy to give in to her desire to bury the unpleasantness of the last years and start fresh. She wanted it so badly, perhaps too badly.

Judd apparently had a few questions of his own. "What about your family?"

"What about them?"

"They aren't going to be pleased we're back together. Nor are they going to like the idea of you moving to Montana."

Lanni knew what he said was true. It could cause an ugly scene, but Lanni prayed that it wouldn't come to that. "They may not fully understand, but in time, they'll accept it. They'll have to."

"I know how close you are to your mother. I don't want to take you away from her."

"I realize that, and I believe she does as well, but I'm twenty-seven. It's time I left my security blanket behind, don't you think?"

"Yes," he admitted starkly. He reached for her hand, which rested on the seat between them, and brought it to his lips. "We have a lot of time to make up for, Lanni. There've been too many wasted years for us. I'm not going to kid you and say everything's going to be easy. We have some rough roads to travel yet with the ranch. The amount of work that needs to be done is overwhelming."

She nodded. She knew little about ranching, but if the run-down condition of the house was indicative of everything on the Circle M, then she could put it into perspective.

"It's going to require every penny I own to restock the herd. Jim wants me to fly down to Texas on Thursday and look over some stock he read about there. I'm going to do it and put several thousand dollars on the line. It's a gamble, but a calculated one. Are you with me, love?"

"One thousand percent."

Briefly their eyes met and it took all Judd's control not to pull the car to the side of the road, turn off the engine and haul her into his arms.

Jim was pacing the yard restlessly by the time Judd returned. As soon as Judd parked the wagon, the two men were off in the pickup for what Jim called some ranchers' meeting. Feeling better than she had in some time, Lanni moved across the yard to the Peterman's house to get Jenny.

Betty stood at the back door and opened the screen when she approached. "What did the doctors have to say about Stuart?"

"He'll be fine. They're keeping him overnight for tests and observation. Judd will pick him up in the morning."

Betty poured them each a cup of coffee, stirred hers and focused her gaze on the plain stem of the spoon. "Knowing Stuart, he's going to be a handful once he's back on the ranch, wanting to do more than he should."

"We'll manage him." But Lanni had her own doubts. Stuart Matthiessen could be as stubborn and strong-willed as his son. "It's likely I'll need your help."

"You've got it," Betty said, showing her pleasure that Lanni had asked. "The neighbor down the road, Sally Moore, phoned this morning," Betty told Lanni. "She wanted me to extend an invitation to you for the Twin Deer Women's Luncheon on Friday of this week."

"I'd enjoy that."

Betty's cheeks formed deeply grooved dimples as she grinned.

"I don't suppose you had anything to do with this invitation?"

Chuckling, Betty shook her head. "It's about time you met some of the other young wives in the community. They're anxious to get to know you."

"I'm looking forward to meeting them."

"Most of them are curious to meet the woman who tamed Judd Matthiessen," Betty teased affectionately.

"Then I'm sure to disappoint them."

"Ha!" Betty sputtered. "You've got half the town talking as it is. You're going to fit in nicely in Twin Deer." Betty added emphasis to her statement by nodding. "It does my heart good to see Judd home after all these years. It's where he belongs."

And because Judd belonged on the Circle M, Lanni and Jenny did as well. She'd make Montana their home, with the assurance that Judd would never walk away from her here.

Early on, Lanni had discovered that she loved the wide blue skies of Montana as much as Judd did. She'd always been the homey type and although it didn't look like she would be able to continue in her career as a real estate agent, she'd already picked up on the information that the local grade school needed a third grade teacher. Of course she'd need to renew her teaching certificate, but that shouldn't be so difficult.

After coffee and conversation, Lanni headed back to the house with Jenny and tucked the little girl upstairs for her afternoon nap. She delayed making the call to Steve as long as she dared. Finally she called him from the kitchen phone, leaning her hip against the wall as she spoke.

"Hello, Steve, it's Lanni."

"Thank goodness you phoned. I've been worried sick."

"I'm fine."

"Well don't keep me in suspense for heaven's sake— what happened?" He sounded agitated, his usually calm voice raised and jerky.

"Nothing much. I announced I had to get back to Seattle and it created a lot of heated discussion, but Judd agreed to take me to the airport. However, Stuart had this stomach attack and we ended up having to take him to the hospital first."

"He was playing on your sympathy. Couldn't you see

through that ploy, Lanni? With your solid gold heart, you fell for it."

Lanni was furious with her coworker for even suggesting such a thing until she realized her first reaction had been to doubt the authenticity of Stuart's ailment. "No, it was real enough, although to be honest, I had my doubts at first."

"Stuart wants you to stay on the ranch." Steve didn't sound pleased at the prospect. "You are coming home soon, aren't you?"

"Eventually, I'll be back." Lanni heard the soft gasp over the wire and experienced a nip of regret. Steve had been a good friend and she hated to hurt or disappoint him.

"You don't mean what I think you do? Please, Lanni, tell me you're not seriously considering going back to your husband and moving into that godforsaken piece of tumbleweed?"

"Actually, Steve, that's exactly what I'm going to do." Her fellow worker was silent for so long that Lanni wondered if he were still on the line. "Steve, are you there?"

"I'm here," he mumbled, his voice thick with disappointment. "I remember the first time I met you," he said softly. "You were like this emotionally wounded combat soldier, and I was intrigued. In the beginning you were just another challenge, but it soon became more than that. It took me months to gain your confidence and each and every day I made an effort to show you that I cared."

"Steve, please, don't, I—"

"Let me finish," he cut in sharply. "First you became my friend. You'll never know how excited I was when you agreed to attend that baseball game with me. Later when we went out to dinner, I felt as excited as a schoolboy. I love you, Lanni. I've loved you for months."

Lanni closed her eyes to the waves of regret that washed over her. "I thank you for being such a good friend."

"But I want to be so much more than that."

"It's impossible. You know how much I love Judd; I always have. Even if things hadn't turned out this way, you would have always gotten second best from me. You're too good a man to accept that."

"It would have been enough—with you."

"Oh Steve, please don't say that. This is hard enough. Let's part as friends and remember that what we shared was a special kind of friendship. I'll never forget you."

Another long silence followed. "Be happy, Lanni."

"You, too, partner."

"Keep in touch?" He made the statement a question.

"If you like." For her part she preferred to make a clean break of it.

Again Steve hesitated. "You're sure going back to your husband is what you want?"

"I'm sure. Very sure." Lanni had no doubts now. She had sealed her commitment to Judd the minute she'd let him into her bed.

"Goodbye then, Lanni."

"Yes, goodbye, Steve."

Lanni discovered when she replaced the receiver that her hands were trembling. She'd hurt Steve and that hadn't ever been her intention. He was a good man; a kind man who had cared a great deal for her. He'd been patient and gentle when she'd needed it most. She'd meant what she said about remembering him fondly. In the future, she wanted only the best for him.

The sound of the front screen door slamming brought her thoughts up short.

"Lanni." It was Judd.

"In here," she said somewhat breathlessly, doing her best to appear nonchalant. "What are you doing here? I thought you and Jim had gone to some ranchers' meeting?"

Judd looped his arms around her waist and lowered his voice to a husky whisper. "I came back," he said, looking at Lanni. He wanted to talk to his wife. From the time he'd gotten in the pickup with Jim, Judd had let his conversation with Lanni fill his mind. She was willing to give up everything for him. Her home. Her career. Her family. Her love had given him the most priceless gift of his life— their daughter. His heart swelled with such love that there weren't words with which to express it. His large hands circled her waist and brought her back inside his arms.

His ardent kiss caught Lanni by surprise. While his mouth continued to cover hers, his fingers worked her blouse loose from her waistband and lifted the shirttail enough to allow his hand entry. They sighed in unison when his fingers caressed her breast.

"What about work?" Lanni whispered.

"Not interested." He worked the zipper of her jeans open, kissing away any protest.

"Judd?" Between deep, soul-drugged kisses, Lanni managed to get out his name.

Judd lifted her into his arms, and headed for the stairway.

"Judd," she groaned in weak protest. "It's the middle of the day."

A crooked grin slashed his sensuous mouth. "I know."

* * *

Stuart arrived home early the following afternoon, looking chipper and exceedingly pleased with himself. Lanni brought him his dinner on a tray and set it in front of the television.

"I see you're still around," he grumbled.

"No thanks to you."

"You belong here. A city slicker isn't ever going to make you happy."

"I think you may be right." His head came up so fast that Lanni laughed outright. "I have no intention of leaving the Circle M."

Stuart's grin was the closest Lanni had ever seen to a Cheshire cat's smug expression. "This land will be good to you. Mark my words."

With time Lanni would come to appreciate this unorthodox man, she mused. She'd viewed the transformation between father and son. Judd and Stuart could talk now without arguing and that was a good beginning. The icy facade Stuart wore like a Halloween mask the first days after their arrival had all but vanished now. They were all making progress—slow, but sure. Lanni had also come to realize that once Judd accepted that he deeply cared for his father, he'd experienced a sense of release. A freedom. Stuart had lived a hard life. The only real love he'd ever known had been taken from him. Stuart had never forgiven himself for Lydia's death, Lanni believed, and had only recently come to grips with the pain of her loss. He didn't want to see his only son make the same mistakes.

Lanni was mature enough to realize that living on the Circle M in close proximity to Stuart was bound to create certain problems, but ones they could work together toward solving.

For the first time in his life, Stuart accepted Judd for who he was. It didn't matter that Judd hadn't become the attorney or doctor the way Stuart had always planned. Stuart cared about his son and together they would build a solid relationship.

Judd woke Lanni early Thursday morning. The room was still dark, cloaked in the darkest part of the night that comes just before dawn. He knelt above her, fully dressed.

"I'll be leaving in a few minutes."

"Already?" Lanni struggled up onto one elbow in a half-sitting, half-lying position.

"Jim's going to stay here in case there's any problem on the ranch."

Lanni nodded and brushed the wisps of blond hair from her face. "We'll be fine—don't worry about anything here."

Judd's hand eased around the base of her neck. "I'll miss you."

"It's only two nights." After all the weeks and months without him, she could withstand two lonesome nights.

He bent his mouth to hers and kissed her fervently. "I wished I didn't have to go."

Lanni giggled—she couldn't help it.

"What's so all-fired funny?"

"You. For years I couldn't keep you home and now I can't get you to leave. May I be so bold as to remind you that this little jaunt is an important mission for the Circle M ranch? You're going to bring back a sturdy bull to service all our female cattle so that we can have lots of little bulls and little cows and whatever else bulls and cows produce."

"You know why I find it so difficult to leave, don't you?" His hot gaze rained down on her face in the moonlight—his eyes were smoky with desire.

Lanni gave no thought to resisting him as she parted her moist lips, inviting his kiss. She moaned at the sensual pleasure he gave her and her fingers stroked his hair, holding his head to her.

He broke away from her just long enough to unhitch his pants, his gaze holding hers while his fingers worked at his belt.

"Your plane?" she whispered, welcoming him. She pulled him closer, and arched her hips wantonly against his as their mouths feasted on each other.

"The plane can wait," he moaned, sliding into her until they were united completely.

Lanni let out a deep sigh of pleasure and bit her bottom lip to keep from crying out.

"But I can't," Judd finished.

Their lovemaking was long and lusty and Judd held her, their bodies still connected long after they'd finished.

Jim honked the car horn from the yard below, and Judd pulled away reluctantly. "I don't think that I can do without you for two nights." He paused and kissed her hungrily. "Be ready for me when I arrive home."

"Aye, aye, Captain. Just bring back that famous bull."

"I'll do that, love," he told her, already on his way out the bedroom door.

Lanni nestled back against her pillow and sighed her contentment. Not even the first weeks of the marriage had been this lusty. She didn't know how long this honeymoon period would last, but she suspected it would be a very long time and she welcomed it just as she had her husband. There was little she could refuse him, her love was so great.

Although she'd made light of the nights he'd be away, Lanni realized that they would be difficult for her as well. She was becoming accustomed to being well loved. At this rate, Jenny would be a big sister within the year.

Stuart was waiting for her when Lanni came down the stairs an hour later.

"Judd get off okay?"

She nodded, pouring herself a cup of coffee. "This bull must be pretty darn special for him to travel all the way to Texas."

"Heard tell he is. Good bloodlines are important."

Lanni pulled out a chair and joined her father-in-law at the table. "You look like you slept well."

Stuart snorted, then glared at her with a twinkle in his faded eyes. "It ain't me who's got rosy cheeks this morning, girl."

Lanni blushed and reached for a section of the morning paper, doing her best to ignore Stuart's low chuckle.

As she suspected they would, the days passed at a snail's pace. The mornings and afternoons were long, but the nights were worse yet. She didn't hear from Judd, but then Lanni hadn't expected that she would. After all, he was only scheduled to be away three days and two nights.

Saturday afternoon, Stuart, Jenny, Jim and Betty all decided to take the drive into Billings to meet Judd's plane. They made an outing of it, stopping along the way at a restaurant to eat dinner. Stuart kept Jenny occupied in the car with tales of his boyhood on the range.

They arrived at the airport an hour before Judd's scheduled flight and Lanni bought a magazine to help fill the time. Betty took Jenny on a walking tour while Stuart and Jim swapped ranching stories.

When Judd's flight landed, Lanni stood and watched the plane taxi to the building and viewed the jetway fold out to meet the arriving passengers. Lanni was eager to feel her husband's arms and stepped back, surveying each face as the people disembarked.

"Where's Daddy?" Jenny wanted to know when Judd hadn't appeared.

"I don't know, sweetheart." The plane had been empty five minutes.

Jim asked one of the flight attendants to check the roster and learned Judd had never been on board the flight.

"Must have missed his connecting flight," Stuart grumbled when Jim appeared.

"You'd think he'd phone," Betty said, carefully studying Lanni.

Lanni gave the worried housekeeper a bright smile as synthetic as acrylic and murmured, "I'm sure there's a logical explanation. There's no need to fret."

"Right," Betty confirmed. "I'm sure there's no reason to worry; there's a perfectly good reason why Judd wasn't on that plane."

They waited around the airport several more hours until Jenny became fussy and overtired. What had been excited expectation on the long drive to Billings became eerie silence on the ride home.

Lanni didn't sleep that night. It seemed as if the walls

were closing in around her. The disappointed tears she was trying to hold back felt like a weight pressing against her breast.

Each time the phone rang the following day, Lanni's heart shot to her throat. They were all on edge. Stuart turned taciturn. Jenny complained continually that Betsy needed her daddy back until Lanni broke into tears and held her daughter to her, giving way to her emotion.

"I could just shake that boy," Betty announced, bringing in a freshly baked apple pie. "I take it no one's heard anything."

"Not a word."

"He checked out of his hotel room just when he was supposed to," Jim said, following his wife inside the kitchen. "I can't understand it."

"I can," Lanni said softly.

All four faces turned to her, wide eyed and curious.

"It's happening again."

"What are you talking about?" Stuart grumbled.

"He's done it before and although he promised he'd never leave me again, he has."

"I don't understand what you're saying," Jim barked.

"Judd will be back when he's good and ready to come home. He's gone."

"Gone? You're not making any sense, girl," Stuart shouted. "Of course he's gone. He went to buy that bull from the Francos."

"No, he's left us—all of us this time and not just me. But I told him and I meant it. When he leaves, I do." She lifted Jenny into her arms. "Jenny and I will be returning to Seattle the first thing in the morning."

Thirteen

"You can't leave," Stuart argued, looking lost and defeated. "Judd's coming back. I feel it in my bones."

"Oh, he'll be back," Lanni countered softly. "He always does that, usually bearing fancy gifts as though that is supposed to wipe away all the pain and worry." Jenny wiggled and Lanni placed the little girl back on the floor.

"You mean to tell me Judd's done this sort of thing before?"

"Not exactly like this," Lanni explained, her voice low and incredibly sad. "Usually when he left I realized he'd be gone a good long while. I imagine it'll take him a month to find his way home, but who knows, it could be six."

"I don't believe he'd do a thing like that," Jim said, defiantly crossing his arms over his chest. "There's too much at stake."

Silently Lanni agreed to that. Their lives together. Their reconciliation. Their marriage. Everything was on the line. Lanni had trouble believing he'd do something like this herself. Surely he could find some way to get to a phone no matter where he was. Although Jim had mentioned contacting the hotel, Lanni had already done that herself, in addition to every hospital within a fifty-mile radius of Laredo. Judd had disappeared. Oh, he'd show up again, Lanni was confident of that. In his own time and in his own way. But this time she wouldn't be waiting for him.

"Lanni, don't do something you'll regret," Betty said, patting the back of her hand.

"I won't," she concurred.

The phone pealed and everyone turned and looked at it as if it were a miracle come to save them from themselves. It rang a second time before Lanni stood and reached for it.

"Hello." She tried to hide the expectancy in her voice.

"Lanni, it's Steve."

"Could you hold the line a minute?"

"Sure." Steve hesitated. "Is something wrong?"

"No, of course not."

Lanni placed her hand over the earpiece. "It's the real estate company where I work in Seattle." There wasn't any reason to irritate Stuart with the news it was Steve. "Apparently there's a problem. I'll take it in the other room."

Disappointment darkened the three adults' faces as they turned back to their coffee. Gently Lanni set the receiver aside and hurried into Stuart's office. She waited until the other phone had been reconnected before she spoke.

"Okay, I'm here now."

"I called to let you know the deal on the Rudicelli house closed. Your commission is here if you'd like me to mail it to you."

"Yes, please do," Lanni said, forcing some enthusiasm into her lifeless voice.

"Something's wrong," Steve said with such tender concern that Lanni felt the tears sting the back of her eyes. "I can hear it in your voice. Won't you tell me, Lanni?"

"It's nothing."

"You're crying."

"Yes," she sniffled. "I can't help it."

"What's happened? If that no-good husband of yours has hurt you, I swear I'll punch him out."

The thought of Steve tangling with Judd, who was superior in both height and weight, produced such a comical picture in her mind that she swallowed a hysterical giggle.

"As soon as the check arrives, I'm leaving. I told him I would and I meant it…" She paused and reached for a tissue, blowing her nose again.

"Oh, Lanni."

"I know, I know. I'm such a bloody fool."

"You're a warm, loving tender woman. I wouldn't change a hair on your head."

"Stop it, Steve. I'm an idiot; I haven't got the good sense I was born with—all I want to do now is get back to Seattle. I swear I'll never leave home again." The longer she spoke the faster the tears came.

"Poor sweetheart."

"Do you think," she said and sniffled, striving to find some humor in the situation, "that if I closed my eyes and clicked my heels together three times the magic would work and I'd be home in a flash? Seattle's known as the Emerald City, you know."

"Problem is, Lanni—you could end up in Kansas instead."

"The way my luck's been, that's exactly what would happen and I'd end up there with a house on my head."

"Lanni, I wish I could do something for you."

"No, I'm fine, but do me a small favor, will you? Call

Jade and let her know Jenny and I are coming home as quickly as we can."

"Consider it done. What are…friends for?"

They finished speaking a couple of minutes later and feeling both mentally fatigued and physically exhausted, Lanni trudged up the stairs. It took her only a half hour to empty the chests of drawers and neatly fold their clothes inside the suitcases.

The following morning Stuart was sitting at the kitchen table when Lanni came down the stairs. She'd spent another sleepless night tossing, turning and worrying. She could scratch Judd's eyes out for doing this to all of them.

"He'll be here soon," Stuart spoke into the paper.

Lanni's fingers dug into the edge of the counter so hard, she cracked three nails. "Will you stop saying that?" she asked him. "Every morning you make this announcement like you've been given some divine insight. Well in case you haven't noticed, he isn't back yet." She knew she was being unreasonable, but she couldn't stop herself. "I've got to get out of here—I told him I'd leave. I told him." To her horror, Lanni started to cry. Scalding tears seared red paths down her cheeks. She jerked around and covered her face with her hands, not wanting Stuart to view her as an emotional wreck.

The weathered hand that patted her shoulder astonished Lanni. "Cry it out, girl; you'll feel better." It surprised her even more when she turned into Stuart's arms and briefly hugged the old man. "I don't know what any of us would do without you," she told him, drying her eyes by rubbing her index fingers across the bridge of her nose and over her cheeks.

By evening there was nothing left to occupy her time.

She'd done so much housework that the place gleamed. Dinner dishes dried on the counter and the sun was setting in a pink sky. Betty wandered outside to weed the small garden she'd planted and Lanni ventured out to help.

Dust flying up along the driveway caused both women to sit up on their knees. Few visitors came out this far. Lanni's heart went stock-still as she settled back on her haunches afraid to hope. Each day she faced a hundred discouragements.

A flashy red sedan pulled into the yard and Lanni's hope died another cruel death. As soon as the dust had settled down, the driver's side opened and Steve Delaney stepped out.

"Steve." Lanni flew to her feet, racing across the yard. She stopped in front of him, suddenly conscious of the mud-caked knees of her jeans and the fact she was without makeup and her hair was tied back in a bandanna.

"Lanni?" Steve looked stunned. "Is that peasant woman inside those rags really you?"

If she didn't realize he was teasing, she would have been offended. Steve's humor was often subtle. "I don't exactly look like a young business executive, do I?"

"Not quite the Lanni I remember."

"Well," she said, so happy to see him that she had to restrain herself from throwing her arms around him, "what are you doing here? How'd you ever find this place?"

"It's a long story to both, let me suffice by saying that I'm delivering the commission check in person and have booked three airplane seats for early tomorrow morning out of Billings. We're headed back to God's country—Seattle."

"Hello, Mr. Delaney." Jenny joined Lanni, clenching her doll to her breast.

"Could this sweet young thing be Jenny?"

"Yup," the four-year-old answered. "My daddy went away."

Steve squatted down so that they could meet eye-to-eye. "I've come to take you home, Jenny, so you won't have to worry about your daddy anymore. Are you ready?"

"Nope," Jenny announced. "I want to wait for my daddy."

"That could be a very long time, Jenny, and Mommy needs you with her." Lanni did her best to explain it to the child. She directed her attention back to Steve. "Give me five minutes to clean up. Do you want to come inside? I can get you something cool to drink while you wait."

Stuart appeared on the top step of the porch, glaring at Steve with a furious frown.

"No thanks," Steve said and ran a finger along the inside of his shirt collar for effect. "If you don't mind, I think I'll be more comfortable standing here in the setting sun."

"Stuart won't do anything," Lanni sought to reassure him.

"Nonetheless I'd rather remain here. But hurry, would you, Lanni? I don't like the looks that old man is giving me. I have a suspicion Custer's men had much the same feeling riding onto the Little Big Horn as I did pulling into this driveway."

"Nobody's going to scalp you."

"Don't be so sure."

Lanni was halfway to the porch when the sound of a truck coming into the driveway caused her to whip around. Judd. She knew it immediately. He honked several times and stuck his hand out the side window waving frantically.

He pulled to a stop and didn't appear to notice Steve or the red sedan. The door flew open and he jumped down from the cab, sending dust swirls flying in his rush to reach Lanni. Without pausing to explain, he grabbed her by the waist and kissed her with such a hunger that she was bent over his forearm by the pressure of his kiss.

Lanni was too stunned to react. For days she'd been worried half out of her mind. "You bastard," she cried, twisting her mouth free of his, then wiping her lips with the back of her hand.

"Lanni, don't be angry. I did what I could."

With both hands flat on his chest, she shoved against him with all her might until Judd freed her voluntarily. "How dare you waltz in here like a returning hero," she cried, hurling the words at him, growing more furious by the moment.

"Has she been this unreasonable the whole time I was away?" Judd directed the question to his father.

Stuart answered with a nod in the direction of Steve.

"What's he doing here?" The humor drained from Judd's gaze as reality hit him between the eyes.

"I'm leaving you, Judd Matthiessen."

"You've got to be kidding!" His happy excitement rushed out of him like air from a freed balloon.

"This is no joke." She pushed past him and into the house and took the stairs two at a time until she reached the top floor. Marching into her room, she located her luggage, and hauled all three suitcases down the stairs with her. Judd met her halfway down the stairway.

"Will you kindly tell me what's going on here?" His eyes revealed his shocked dismay.

"Two nights, remember? You were supposed to be gone two nights. Well in case you can't add, it's been considerably more time than that."

"I know."

"Your nerve galls me. You come back here without a word of explanation and expect me to fall gratefully at your feet. I'm leaving you, Judd, and this time it's for good."

"You can't do that."

"Just watch me. I told you if you ever left me again, it was over. You agreed to that."

"But there were extenuating circumstances. I—"

"Aren't there always extenuating circumstances?" Lanni cut in woodenly.

Judd sagged against the wall, and wiped a hand over his tired face. This was like a horror movie. He'd been driving for fifteen hours straight with a fifteen-thousand-dollar bull in the back of his truck and he was greeted with this?

Lanni pushed past him and out of the house, handing Steve her luggage. "He couldn't have waited fifteen minutes before showing up?" Steve grumbled as he placed the suitcases in the trunk. "Oh, no. Here comes trouble."

"Just what the hell are you doing with my wife, Delaney?"

"Hello, Matthiessen," Steve said, straightening. "I'm taking Lanni home."

"She *is* home."

"You might want to ask her that."

"You left me," Lanni shouted. "I told you that if it happened again, it was over between us."

"What is going on here?" Judd turned to Stuart, his eyes wide and perplexed.

"Where were you, boy?" Stuart asked.

"You don't know?" Now Judd looked utterly shocked. "I got arrested in Mexico."

"Arrested!" Both Lanni and Stuart shouted together.

"It's a long story. Brutus, the bull, got loose and wandered across the border. The Mexican authorities and I had a minor disagreement and I ended up in the local jail, but I paid a king's ransom for—" He stopped abruptly, his fists slowly knotting. "You weren't notified of my whereabouts?"

"No one contacted us, son."

Judd closed his eyes as the pounding waves of frustration swamped over him. "You must have been sick with worry."

"Oh no, we sat around drinking tea and nibbling on crumpets," Lanni informed him primly.

"Lanni, oh love, I thought I'd go crazy before I got home to you. Don't let this minor misunderstanding ruin our lives."

"Minor misunderstanding?" she shouted. "This is a major one, Judd Matthiessen."

"He needs you," Stuart said starkly, his eyes pleading with Lanni to reconsider.

"Then he should have thought of that before he went traipsing halfway across the country."

"Lanni," Judd pleaded.

"Be quiet," she cried, pointing her index finger at him. He was always leaving her, asking her to wait, and for the first time she was giving him a sample of his own medicine. "It's more than a matter of not knowing where you were—I don't know if I can trust you anymore."

"Lanni," he said and raised his arm to reach for her. When she stepped away to avoid his embrace, Judd dropped his hands to his sides. "I swear by everything I hold dear that I'm not going to leave you again."

"And what exactly do you consider so valuable. Me? Jenny? Your father? The Circle M?" The tears rained freely down her face.

"None of it means anything without you," he said, his voice husky with need. Overcome with emotion, Judd turned to Steve. "I'm sorry you went through all the trouble of coming here, Delaney, but Lanni won't be going back with you." He reached inside the trunk to take out her luggage.

"If you don't mind, I'll make that decision myself."

"Lanni?" Judd's eyes looked murderous. "I haven't come this far to lose you over a stupid bull. You don't trust me now, but you will in time because I'll never give you cause to doubt again. I need you," he coaxed. "We're home where we belong and I'm not going to allow you to walk away from that."

"I..." She wavered, caught in a battle that raged between her head and her heart. But the love that shone in his eyes convinced her she had no choice but to cast her fate with him. Her heart demanded as much. "For all the money you spent on him, you would do well not to insult the animal by calling him stupid." She crossed her arms over her chest; she hadn't come this far to lose Judd, either.

"You can't deprive Jenny of a family." Judd murmured, his gaze holding hers tenderly.

"On the next business trip you take, will I get to go along?" Lanni offered the compromise.

"As long as it isn't Mexico."

"Agreed."

"Does that mean she'll stay?" Stuart wanted to know, directing the question at both men, uncertain of what was happening.

"She's staying," Judd answered, wrapping his arms around her waist. "Is that right, heart of mine?"

"If you say the magic word."

"Please?"

Lanni shook her head.

"Thank you?"

"Nope." Her arms circled his neck as he lifted her off the ground so that her eyes were level with his own.

"I'm sorry?"

"Not that, either." She placed a hand on both sides of his face and kissed him square on the mouth.

"You'd better hurry and decide, love; I'm running out of vocabulary."

"How about a simple I love you."

"You know that already."

"But I like to hear it every now and then."

"I love you," Judd said tenderly and then set Lanni on her feet.

"Now that that's settled," Stuart said and stepped forward, extending his hand to Steve. "Would you like something cool to drink before you head back to Seattle?"

"Mommy, Mommy, can I hug Daddy too?"

Judd squatted down so that he could enfold Jenny in his arms. The little girl planted a juicy kiss on his cheek. "I like the bull."

"Good thing, darling, because Daddy isn't about to take him back." Judd chuckled and hugged her to his massive chest. Lanni knelt and hugged both of them.

"I have to go tell Betsy that you're home. She was worried." With that, Jenny ran into the house after her grandfather and Steve.

Still kneeling on the ground, Judd's arms circled Lanni. "No more bridges. No more wanderings. Everything I want is right here."

"Oh, Judd, I love you so."

"I know, love, I know," he said, looking out around him at the Circle M. This was their future. Here they would build their lives. Here they would raise their family. This land would heal them both. Love and trust would blossom, nourished by contentment and commitment.

Helping Lanni to her feet, Judd wrapped his arm around her and paused to glance at the pink sky. It was filled with beauty and promise.

* * * * *